SCOTT SIGLER

THE
CRYPT
SHAKEDOWN

aethonbooks.com

In memory of the 60,000-plus submariners lost in World War II.
They went where no man had gone before, never to return.

Susannah Rossi character developed with Phil Rossi.

Anne Lafferty character developed with Mur Lafferty.

Mac "Stone Balls" Cooley character developed with Paul Cooley.

Francis "Book" Sands character developed with Basil Sands.

1

Everything seemed louder. Everything seemed brighter. Everything seemed... *more*.

Boot heels echoed through the narrow, empty passageways, reverberating like rhythmic dark applause for Trav's pending demise. The two guards escorting him wore battleship-gray LASH armor. *Full* armor, inside a carrier stationed well-clear of any combat zone. Opaque helmet visors hid their faces, giving them anonymity, even though magnetic patches on their left breasts revealed their names and ranks: MASSEY, with the three chevrons of a sergeant, and ORTEGA, with the two bars of a Spec-2.

At least they weren't wearing TASH rigs. LASH rigs—*Light Assault Suit, Hermetic* were for duties inside a ship. The heavier *Tactical* version was for exterior duties. Like venting a prisoner into the void, for example.

Trav's chains jangled in time with his steps. They weighed little if he didn't count their overpowering burden of dishonor. Just as there was no need for combat armor, there was no need for the restraints. Where was he going to go? Where could he run?

It wasn't about him being a flight risk.

It wasn't about him being a danger.

It was about shaming him.

Because that's what Fleet did to cowards.

The carrier's passageways were empty. The guards escorted him past closed hatches. Maybe most of the *Chimborazo*'s crew of 5,000-plus was on liberty. Trav didn't know. He'd never been on a carrier before. At 1,000 meters long, 167 meters high amidships, and with a beam of 190 meters, there was a lot of space in the PUV *Chimborazo*.

Trav had always dreamed of serving aboard a carrier, always dreamed of captaining one, of commanding the 200-plus voidcraft housed within its hull. He'd dedicated his life to learning all he could and moving up the promotional ladder to make those dreams a reality —but those dreams were dead.

Trav might soon be dead himself. It all depended on the court's verdict.

"Here we are, Major Ellis," Massey said. "You have fifteen minutes."

Trav stood before the passageway's only open hatch. Inside, a coffin of a comm-booth where the *'Razo*'s crew could make calls to other ships, bases, or planetside when a planet was nearby. In this case, a call to married housing on Crindalon Base, to which the *Chimborazo* had docked.

Trav looked at his escorts—lifted his hands to show the restraints.

"Mind taking these off? I haven't seen my wife in six months. This might be the last..."

The thought of losing Molly was a hand on his throat, choking off the rest of his sentence—*the last time she sees me alive.*

Ortega's helmeted head turned to look at Massey. "Sarge, can we do that?"

Massey's blank visor remained centered on Trav.

"My brother was on the *Boudicca*," Massey said. "You can wear those chains with pride, Yellowbelly."

Ortega didn't seem to understand. Trav did. The *Boudicca* was gone. Massey's brother was gone. Was that Trav's fault? Maybe, maybe not. Too many variables in that battle to know either way.

At least that's what Trav had been telling himself.

Yellowbelly Ellis. It wasn't the first time he'd heard that insult since the battle. He suspected it wouldn't be the last.

"Fourteen minutes and counting," Massey said. "I suggest you get at it. *Sir.*"

Trav lowered his chained hands and stepped through the hatch. He sat on a hard seat bolted into the deck, a seat that had supported the behinds of countless thousands of crewmembers making calls to parents, siblings, friends, lovers.

In one way, at least, Trav was lucky—the *Chimborazo* happened to be stationed close enough for him to call his family.

He straightened and faced the blank screen. This unit was newer than the one he'd used on the *Schild*. Only the best for carriers—the Union's castles in space. The screen had enough reflection for a quick look to make sure his dress-whites uniform was precise, that everything was perfect. While on trial, his appearance was the only thing he could control. Even in chains, he'd managed to keep himself inspection-sharp.

That's what career-track officers did; they looked the part. They set an example for everyone.

Career-track officer. Not anymore.

Trav spoke the routing number to his home. He waited as the system connected, angry at every passing second, knowing those were seconds wasted.

The screen flashed to life.

"Hi, Molly," he said.

His pregnant wife stared back at him, eyes puffy and bloodshot. She bounced little Aven on one knee, an automatic reaction a parent did without thought. Aven had one spit-gleaming finger in her mouth. She had her mother's shiny blonde hair, not her father's black curls. She had Trav's amber eyes, though. The same shade that somehow made people think Trav was looking straight into their souls.

"Just tell me," Molly said. "I can't take this waiting."

She spoke with the same guarded voice she used during intense arguments. She knew raising her voice sometimes made Trav do the same. Raised voices led to loss of control, to saying awful things to the person she loved more than any other, led to the person she loved more than any other saying awful things to her.

"The tribunal recessed to deliberate," Trav said. "Nance made a great case. I'm sure I'll be exonerated."

In truth he wasn't sure, but that wasn't what Molly needed to hear. If he was found not guilty, he'd get his scheduled leave and be able to reunite with his wife. For ten days, at least.

A single tear ran down Molly's cheek. She snarled, slightly, as she sometimes did during an argument or during sex. In that moment, Trav wanted her desperately. What he wouldn't give for just one more chance to lay with his wife before everything was taken away.

"Trav, honey... did you cut a deal?"

He couldn't answer her. He stared at his daughter. They'd already named her sister-to-be—*Kinley*. A lovely name. Trav knew she would be a beautiful baby, just as beautiful as Aven.

"We talked about this," Molly said. "When you vid me into your talk with defense counsel. Remember?"

It had been a lecture, not a talk. Trav's counsel, Lieutenant JG Kratos Nance, wanted to throw Antoine Williams—captain of the *Schild*—under the bus. Nance wanted to make a deal with the prosecutor that might let his client get off without so much as a slap on the wrist. Trav had asked Nance not to mention that possibility to Molly. Nance had ignored the request—he and Molly tag-teamed Trav, telling him in a dozen different ways the benefits of letting Williams take the fall alone.

Trav had ignored their pleas. Now he wished he hadn't, but he'd made his choice.

"You know I wouldn't do that," Trav said. "I won't betray my captain."

"*Betray* your *captain?* Fuck your captain. Fuck your Fleet. The punishment for cowardice in combat is death, Trav. *Death*."

That possible punishment had weighed heavily on Trav's shoulders since the *Schild* returned, since he and Williams had been put into custody. Execution was the worst-case scenario. Williams might face that result, but not Trav. Williams had given the order to leave the battlefield. When Williams was injured, Trav became acting CO—he'd implemented Williams's original order. If the tribunal found Trav guilty, it was far more likely he'd be sentenced to a stint in the brig or, possibly, a dishonorable discharge.

If Fleet kicked him out, would that be so bad? His lifelong dream to command was already shattered. He could find something else, something that would let him actually spend time with his family.

A life without Fleet, though? Almost unthinkable.

Fleet was everything.

Fleet had been his way out of the small town where he'd been raised by his crazy grandmother. She'd been a hoarder, filling every inch of their one-bedroom public housing apartment with knickknacks and smelly old clothes, with moldering books, with boxes of empty food containers. She had a hundred different collections of random things, from rocks to old coins to bugs to hundreds of empty jars of the sickeningly sweet skin lotion she wore—the kind that made her stink like funeral flowers.

Acceptance to Fleet Academy got him out of there, gave him a life that was more than thrift-store clothes, crushing poverty, and an old woman who called him *Satan* because he wouldn't go to church with her. In the Academy, he'd excelled. The structure, the competition, the discipline. There, he wasn't the smelly kid with no money. He was on a level playing field where his work ethic and his toughness were all that mattered.

After graduation, he'd made the most of every opportunity. In the Second Galactic War, he'd shone as head of operations on the PUV *Ikhaka*. Then, at Williams's direct request, he'd been transferred to the PUV *Schild*. Williams had only one tour left before an inevitable promotion to Commodore. Trav was his hand-picked successor to take over the *Schild*.

Now, though, *Schild* was in the scrapyard. The CIC—combat information center—looked like Swiss cheese, if Swiss cheese were made of metal, plastic, blood, and bone. They were probably still scraping body parts out of the engineering section. Of the crew of 24 officers and 176 enlisted men, 90 had perished in battle.

Another tear trailed down Molly's cheek. A drip of snot peeked from her left nostril. She didn't seem to notice.

Massey leaned through the hatch. "Time's up, Major Ellis."

"But you told me I had fifteen minutes."

"Your verdict is in," Massey said. "Move it."

Trav looked at his wife, his partner, the love of his life, the mother of his children.

"I have to go," he said.

Her tears flowed. "Don't go." She squeezed Aven, too hard. The girl's face wrinkled in surprise and discomfort. "Honey, please don't go. *Please.*"

"I have to."

"But you can still—"

Massey reached in, grabbed Trav's chains, and yanked him out of the room. Trav caught his foot on the seat. He stumbled and fell to the deck, landing on his knee.

"Pick his ass up," Massey said.

Hands grabbed under Trav's armpits and yanked him to his feet. Those same hands stayed firm on his arms to both shove and pull him down the passageway.

"I can fucking *walk*, Sergeant," he said.

Massey let go. "Then walk."

From the booth, Trav heard his wife screaming at him to come back.

He turned, faced down the passageway, and marched toward his end.

———

It was all Trav could do to not look at his knee, at the smudge marring his otherwise-pristine dress whites. His jacket was rumpled, in a way he couldn't fix because of the goddamn restraints. A sub-par uniform was low on the list of things to worry about, but the knowledge of it poked at him, tried to draw his attention away from the situation at hand.

Vice Admiral Pamelia Bartos smashed her gavel down on a wooden block.

"The defendants will rise," she said.

Trav and Colonel Williams rose from their chairs. They stood ramrod straight: chests out, heads back, eyes forward. Nance also stood, as did William's counsel, Lieutenant Hans Meissner.

Williams looked awful. Bandages covered the left side of his face. He'd suffered third-degree burns when the *Schild*'s CIC took a hit. A piece of shrapnel had taken off half his right foot, but from the way he stood—and his mirror-bright shoes—no one would ever know. Throughout the three-day trial, he'd showed no sign of pain.

6

Williams was as tough as they came.

They were in the ready room of Squadron Eight, the carrier's long-range scouting wing. Narrow, angling down from the high rear to the low front, the room was basically an aisle with pairs of red leather seats on either side.

Trav and Nance were on the left side of that aisle, Williams and Meissner on the right. Even now, at the end, Fleet wanted Trav and Williams kept apart. They'd been separated shortly after the battle, ensuring the two accused couldn't collaborate on a story to explain their failure.

Chimborazo entered service in 2549, not quite three years before the end of the Second Galactic War. After four combat tours, she was just beginning to show her age. Red tape covered small tears on the seats. Bulkheads showed faint dings and scuffs that resisted efforts to scrub them away. And everywhere, just like in all Fleet ships, the endless, uniform gray bulkheads.

Plaques hung on the bulkheads, denoting battles fought, enemies destroyed, craft lost. One plaque had six names on it, with room for more: the names of pilots and crew lost in combat. Or in accidents—those happened more often than not.

Normally, courts martial were held in an enlisted mess, so everyone could watch what happened when someone disobeyed orders. This time, however, the brass didn't want anyone to see. Ortega, Massey, and four additional guards—also in LASH armor—were the only witnesses. The trial had been kept quiet. That didn't make it any less serious or the potential sentencing any less grave.

At a table at the front of the briefing room sat Vice Admiral Bartos, Colonel Dieter Rolvsson of BII—Bureau of Information and Intelligence, the Union's spy shop—and the prosecutor, Lieutenant Viktor Camillari. Tablets and flexipaper lay spread out on the table, displaying the records of Trav and Williams, showing data from the battle, listing evidence, and detailing sworn statements from the PUV *Schild*'s crew.

Bartos read aloud from a sheet of flexipaper.

"Regarding the incidents of July 17, 2557, standard Earth Time, summarily known as the Battle of Asteroid X7, the defendants, Colonel Antoine Williams and Major Travis Ellis, stand charged with cowardice in the face of the enemy, and gross dereliction of duty."

Trav remained silent. He'd had his chance to speak, to tell his side of the story.

"This court has reached a verdict." Bartos looked up, stared first at Williams, then at Trav. "You have both been found guilty on all counts."

Trav's heart dropped past his stomach, landed somewhere around his balls. This was it. He was screwed. He'd held out hope Bartos would understand he'd followed the orders of his commanding officer.

"In the middle of a combat action," Bartos said, "you were both personally responsible for pulling the *Schild* off the line of battle. That action likely contributed to the destruction of the destroyer *Boudicca*, and to the capture or death of the *Boudicca*'s crew of three hundred enlisted personnel and twenty-five officers."

This couldn't be happening. It *couldn't*. Trav had sat through the trial. He'd spent hours going over the case with Nance. He'd known what might come, thought he'd been ready, but now that the moment had arrived he couldn't process it.

"You are both sentenced to execution by venting," Bartos said. "Sentence to be carried out tomorrow morning at oh-eight-hundred."

Trav went numb.

Execution?

But his second child wasn't born yet. His daughter, his wife... they'd be alone.

Execution?

He knew his rights. Rather, his *lack* of rights, considering the charges he'd been found guilty of. He wouldn't get to call Molly or say goodbye to his daughter.

Trav felt Williams looking his way. Trav couldn't meet the man's one-eyed gaze, *would* not meet it. If he looked at Williams, the last of his composure would flee the line just as the *Schild* had.

Nance and Meissner remained quiet. They'd already said all there was to say. They'd worked hard to defend their clients.

"However," Bartos said, "I will offer a single, alternative sentence."

A rush of hope, of desperation. A chance to survive? Whatever it was, Trav would take it. Anything that would allow him to someday see his wife and daughter again, to see the face of his yet-to-be-born second child.

Bartos glanced down at the table, then visibly forced herself to raise her head and look each of the accused in the eyes. She swallowed audibly, straightened.

"I will stay your execution order and eliminate it, upon completion of a two-year tour aboard the PUV *James Keeling*," she said. "Colonel Williams, you will be demoted to the rank of Major and serve as the *Keeling*'s executive officer. Major Ellis, you will be demoted to the rank of Lieutenant and be assigned a role to be determined by the *Keeling*'s current captain."

The *Keeling*—also known as *the Crypt*.

It was real. The quiet whispers in Fleet's dark places, the constant debate over drinks late into the night—did it exist or not? The *Keeling* was rumored to be little more than a prison ship that flew combat missions, the most dangerous missions there were. If you fucked up bad enough, they put you on the *Keeling*, and that was it for your ass.

Trav had, apparently, fucked up bad enough.

"If you accept this assignment and complete your tour," Bartos said, "all charges will be expunged. At that point, you will be given the option to retire from Fleet or continue your careers. Major Travis Ellis, which sentence do you choose?"

She was *asking* him, not *ordering* him. He had to volunteer? That word was in quotes, with a big asterisk next to it. Several asterisks. Volunteer or find out what it was like to see the void without a vacsuit.

Two years. Then he could be with his family again. He and Molly could raise their children together. Grow old together.

As if there were any choice at all.

"Admiral," Trav said, "I will serve aboard the *Keeling*."

Bartos picked up her gavel and rapped it twice against the wooden block.

"Let the record show that Lieutenant Travis Ellis volunteered to serve a two-year tour aboard the PUV *James Keeling*," she said. "Colonel Williams, which sentence do you choose?"

Williams cleared his throat, paused, then cleared it again.

"I have faith in my lord Jesus Christ," he said. "I prefer to go to heaven, rather than serving two years in hell. I choose execution."

This time, Trav couldn't stop himself from looking at his captain, his mentor, his friend. Williams stared straight forward, jaw muscles twitching, a bead of sweat dripping down his temple to soak into his bandages.

"*Lieutenant Ellis*," Colonel Rolvsson said, "eyes forward!"

Trav snapped back to attention.

What was Williams doing? The man was a tactician, a true thinker. He had to have a plan of some kind.

"Very well," Bartos said. "Security, escort Colonel Williams to the brig, prepare him for execution tomorrow at oh-eight-hundred hours. Lieutenant Ellis, you are hereby assigned as the executive officer aboard the Planetary Union Vessel *James Keeling*. Security, arrange for Lieutenant Ellis's immediate transportation. Place him in maximum security under heavy guard, full suicide watch from now until he is delivered to the *Keeling*."

"Trav, don't do this," Williams said. "Change your plea, I beg you."

Bartos slammed the gavel down so hard it hit like a gunshot.

"*Silence*! The convicted is not permitted to speak! Security, get this coward out of my sight!"

In an instant, the armored guards were on Williams, gripping him by the arms. He let his feet go. The guards dragged him up the aisle.

"Trav, *kill yourself*," he said. "Save your soul!"

One of the guards drew a stunstick from a thigh holster and jabbed it into Williams's ribs. The former warship captain jerked and thrashed, then fell limp.

The guards hauled him away, his restraints rattling.

Trav felt hands on his arms; Ortega and Massey gripping him, only without the harsh, painful strength Massey had used before.

"Come with us, Lieutenant," Massey said.

They led him away. Trav's feet worked of their own accord, little engines that propelled him along without instruction.

He wasn't a dead man. Not yet, anyway.

But was that a good thing?

2

"Olivia, please be silent," Anne said. "I need to concentrate."

Olivia quieted down. She was a good friend like that. A good listener.

Resting on left hip and elbow, Anne chewed on her lip, hesitating. The bracelet display flickered in the air above her upturned left palm, the only illumination in the dark space. The tip of her right index finger hovered in front of the glowing *READ* icon.

If her father was disappointed in her, yet again, Anne wasn't sure if she could take it.

She poked the icon. The message flared to life.

TOP-NOTCH RESEARCH. THE BOSS IS PROUD OF YOU. INVESTMENT FUNDS SHOULD BE CLEARED BY NOON, TODAY, YOUR TIME.

Anne turned off the display. Warmth bloomed in her chest. She blinked rapidly, used a knuckle to wipe wetness from the corner of her eye.

"My dad is proud of me," she said. *"Proud... of me."*

When was the last time she'd heard that? When she was six? Maybe seven?

His approval, his love... it meant everything.

The boss is proud of you. That wasn't in code, like the other two sentences. That was from Daddy. He'd pulled strings to give her this shot, this dangerous mission, and she'd delivered.

Top-notch research meant her CO and his superiors accepted her recon report. She'd given them all the intel they needed to make a decision.

Investment funds should be cleared by noon, today, your time. An assault force was en route. Anne's orders were to cut the head off the snake before that force arrived in—she glanced at her bracelet's faint clock display—one hour and seventeen minutes.

Not much time, but she'd prepared for this eventuality.

In a way, the rushed schedule was good news. Things were starting to get smelly. Certain odors you can only hide for so long.

Her CO, Kashim Staley, that weaselly prick, had wanted to send in a three-operative team. Anne told him she wanted to work alone. Staley denied the request, even went so far as to mock her, asking if she thought she was on par with BII operatives like Mac Cooley or Babetta Lukane. Anne made a not-so-subtle suggestion that she would ask her father to examine the decision. The threat of BII Director Bart Lafferty examining Staley's decision was enough to get Anne what she wanted.

Daddy knew Anne needed to go alone. Daddy knew who she was. He'd quietly given her two prime directives: *don't disappoint me*, and *don't get caught*.

The PUV *Silverbill* had punched a hole through the surface ice of Varaha, fourth moon of Reiger 2. Anne took a coffin-sized solo pod deep into an ammonia ocean, spent a week guiding that pod to the undersea settlement of Eden. She spent the following week recording and observing from afar: determining the roles of the city's eleven domes; understanding the comings and goings of shipping; mapping the movement patterns and schedules of exterior maintenance workers.

Even before the mission, the tapping at the back of her mind had been growing. The isolation and the stress compounded that tapping, magnified the *need*.

For her base of operations, she chose Dome Eleven, which was still undergoing internal construction. Then came the nerve-wracking hours of steadily moving her pod closer, making sure she wasn't detected by sensors or seen by the Harrah work crews tending to Eden's domes and the crisscrossing tubes that connected them.

Construction within Eleven was not an all-day, every-day event. Anne timed things well, worked her way inside, and set up shop in a service duct.

In the process she met Olivia, one of Eden's true believers. The two women became fast friends. Olivia helped keep Anne's stress level manageable, which kept the tapping at bay. That was only a stop-gap measure, though—Anne's need burned, slowly, incessantly.

Olivia explained many things about Eden. In just two years, it had grown from a few hundred settlers to a community of roughly ten thousand. Big enough that the faces one saw were more likely to be strangers than acquaintances.

Anne borrowed Olivia's clothes and explored Eden, participated in religious services, and moved around the city's domes. Anne tallied up Eden's assets, key personnel, weapons—including the three hunter/killer nuclear subs owned by the church, and the squadron of mercenary Harrah fightercraft the church paid to be on-station.

The subs and the fighters were probably the reason BII was coming in hot.

Anne pinched her bracelet, which lit up in a warm, amber-white glow, partially illuminating the close-in walls and overhead pipes. Service ducts were for maintenance, not living, yet she and Olivia had made the best of things in this one for the last four days.

Anne crawled past her cache of rations, bottled water, the first aid kit, her tools, and the little atomizer toilet. She maneuvered over the bulky gear bag, past her small transceiver, and to the rehydrator shell she'd collected for use as a mirror. Time to check the details.

Because details mattered.

Her wig looked fine. Long and brown, mussed up enough to give it that *I haven't showered in two days* look. She'd left her eyes green—their natural color—but wore contacts that altered her eye iris pattern. The red scarf tied around her neck looked newer than her grubby work clothes. New-*er* but not *new*; in case she was questioned, she needed to have the appearance of someone who converted a few weeks ago, not a few hours ago.

Anne heard a groan. In the rehydrator's reflection, she saw the gear bag move slightly.

"Olivia, I told you to be quiet. If I have to ask you twice, you won't be happy."

The movement ceased, along with the noise.

"I'll be back before you know it," Anne said. "Or I might not leave at all. Maybe I'll sit here, in the dark, just like last time, waiting to see what you do when you think I'm gone."

The bag stayed very, very still.

Anne crawled to the access grate, which was at floor level. The passageway beyond looked empty. It usually was—this section of the dome had yet to be filled up with homes, stores, storage, and whatever bullshit church admin was needed next.

She loosened the clamp that held the grate in place. She crawled through, then refastened the clamp. Anne gave the grate a once-over to make sure it looked secure. It did. That was good.

Because details mattered.

———

Religions all started out the same. A bunch of losers thinking they were the victims of endless and unfair persecution at the hands of *Them*—the powers that be. Anne could never figure out how every group of chosen people believed in an all-powerful god or gods, yet those same deities couldn't protect said group. No, the group always had to run like bitches. In church terms, that was called "an exodus" and was the stuff of glory, destiny, and all that chosen-people crap.

This particular group—the *Korvak Anabaptists*—was an offshoot of the Capizzi Anabaptist movement. Naomi Korvak founded the sect. She had the charisma and drive that made people follow her, donate huge sums of money to her, and help her build Eden. Right, "Eden," set in the middle of a sub-zero ammonia ocean that wanted to kill you at the first opportunity.

She wasn't all smiles and promises, either. Korvak understood how to guide a colony's development. Probably a nation's development, for that matter, if she was left alone long enough. Like any good colony leader, she'd focused much of her early efforts on finding, mining, and refining native sources of uranium, enough to build the small nuclear reactors that partially powered Eden. Fissionable materials couldn't be transported from one world to another. Well, they *could* be transported, but the physics that powered both FTL and impulse drives stripped away extra protons or neutrons from any radioisotope, meaning your shipment of uranium went through full radioactive decay, almost instantly, and arrived at the destination as a useless lump of lead.

Korvak understood the basics and excelled motivating her people. Her power and influence were growing fast. So fast that BII wanted her shut down before her sect built up enough wealth and momentum to send out proselytizers. If the Korvak Anabaptists grew large enough, fast enough, it might never be fully eliminated.

The Union had learned that lesson the hard way, thanks to the warmongering Purists. What had once been a problematic-but-tolerated religion now controlled four planets. The Purist Nation was a theocracy hell-bent on someday conquering Earth and every other Human-controlled world.

Anne didn't feel sorry for Korvak's sect. What did they think was going to happen when they acquired warships? Well, that was religion for you—people rarely *thought* about anything.

BII higher-ups, Daddy included, worried that Korvak's strong leadership could anchor stiff resistance against any attack. Stiff resistance meant casualties on both sides. Anne's first priority had been gathering intel and reporting back to her CO. With the assault force incoming, her job was to eliminate Korvak in hopes that the Anabaptists might give up without a fight.

Thanks to Olivia, Anne knew Korvak was a creature of habit. Those habits would be the cult leader's undoing.

Planting the bomb hadn't been easy, but Anne got the job done. All she had to do now was steer clear of Eden's "security forces" and activate the timer. The security goons weren't trained soldiers. They were meat heads with guns, flush with the confidence that they were God's chosen warriors. As long as Anne avoided their attention, she'd be fine.

She passed through the open bulkhead door that led out of the construction area and into a well-lit tube connected to Dome Four.

That tube had an intersecting tube leading to Dome One, and several side-tubes leading to smaller domes.

Eden's hull material blocked RF signals. Watertight bulkhead doors were only wide enough for two people to pass through at a time —not enough room for signals to travel unimpeded. That meant Anne had to be *inside* Dome One to activate the bomb she'd planted there.

Side-connecting tubes brought more foot traffic, people cutting across the network of intersections to reach all areas of Eden. Most were believers wearing red bandanas around their necks. Some were smugglers who brought goods into the city. Others were cocksure security guards, each carrying a hip-holstered Glock-Harper 56. Solid weapons for the situation: replacement parts were cheap; the .22-caliber bullet couldn't punch through the hull material; and even a poorly trained thug could keep the firearm in working order.

Four gray-skinned Harrah fluttered in from a side-tube, their wide wingflaps propelling them along in the space between Human heads and the tube's apex, their long tails trailing gracefully behind. Some people still called the alien race *stingrays*, due to their passing resemblance to an Earth fish, but that nickname had largely faded from common usage anywhere other than on that planet.

Harrah did the bulk of exterior maintenance and a significant portion of new construction. They had no problem with the ammonia ocean outside; their hollow, gas-filled bodies withstood the low temperature and the intense pressure. Give them an air supply, they were good to go.

Anne turned down the large tube leading to Dome One. In the past few days, she'd seen only one or two meatheads at a time in this tunnel—she now saw five. They seemed to study passersby with more intensity than before. Had Eden security detected the incoming assault sub?

Should she go back? She could return to her duct, wait for the assault force to strike. She still had to deal with Olivia—it wouldn't do if someone found out Anne had been fraternizing with the enemy.

If Anne turned back now, though. Daddy would be disappointed.

She didn't have to go far into Dome One, but if she wanted to trigger the bomb, she *did* have to go in.

A guard walking in the opposite direction eyed her as they drew near. A rush of fear and excitement; had she been made? Could she take this man out before he knew what she was capable of?

As they passed, he smiled at her, a leering thing full of entitlement and lust. No, she wasn't made—she was a woman in a place where men outnumbered women five to one.

Anne felt his eyes on her back. She kept walking, getting closer to Dome One. Twenty-five minutes until midday prayers. Korvak would be donning her robes, prepping for her daily sermon.

More meatheads. Guards were stopping people, asking questions. Politely, calmly, but questions nonetheless. Security was looking for someone—Anne might be their quarry.

So close now. The bulkhead door to Dome One was just ahead.

Anne put her hands in her jacket pockets. Her left hand felt the folding ceramic tanto knife she took everywhere. Her right hand gripped the small remote control that would start the bomb's timer.

A guard at the Dome One bulkhead door scrutinized the steady stream of people entering and exiting. Anne thought he might stop her, question her, but he didn't—she walked right past.

She was in.

Food stalls and shops lined the dome's outer edge. Directly below the dome's apex lay the Holy Stage, where Korvak would soon give her sermon. Over a thousand worshipers were already packed around it, red handkerchiefs making a uniform out of mismatched and widely varied clothing.

When the bomb detonated, some of those people would die. But that wasn't Anne's problem.

Inside her pocket, she pressed the remote's button.

Twenty minutes until detonation. Anne started counting off the minutes in her head.

She bought a soft pretzel from a vendor. There was enough time, and the pretzels were *so* good. After adding mustard, she returned to the bulkhead door. It was all over but the crying. The bomb would go off one minute into Korvak's sermon—Korvak *always* started on time.

Fifteen minutes until boom-boom. Time to get clear.

She took a bite—the soft, warm pretzel tasted amazing. There was something different about the way that vendor made them. Anne would miss the delicious treats.

Out the door and into the main tube. She walked toward the inter-section leading back to Dome Eleven. When the bomb blew, she'd be safe and sound in her duct. There, she would say her goodbyes to Olivia, clean up the mess, activate the transceiver signal so the assault force could find her, then wait for retrieval.

She took another bite—her mouth froze in mid-chew. Up ahead, leaning against the opening of the tunnel to Dome Four, was the same security guard who'd eyed her up. He smiled at her. Had he been waiting for her to come back this way?

There was no point turning around and going the other direction. That would look suspicious. Besides, in less than five minutes, the tubes would be full of confused, frightened people, as well as angry, untrained, armed meatheads.

She walked and chewed.

Did the guard know who she was? Was he going to try and hurt her? Maybe he was smiling because he enjoyed causing pain. Some people were like that.

Four minutes until detonation.

She drew closer to him.

He touched his fingertips to his chin, then held the fingers a little higher. A casual salute. She met his eyes, briefly, unsure of what signal to send, then she stared straight ahead, turned down the tunnel to Dome Four, and kept walking.

Maybe he wouldn't follow.

She didn't have time for an elaborate route. She had to get back to her cover before the bomb went off.

The crowd thinned. By the time she reached Dome Eleven, it would evaporate altogether.

Two minutes until detonation.

Anne entered the construction area. She heard footsteps behind her. She hurried toward her grate and reached for the clamp but stopped short—the footsteps told her she didn't have time to get inside.

"What are you doing in this section?"

Anne turned to face her pursuer—the same meathead. He'd followed her. He was three meters away, hand on the grip of his holstered pistol. He was a lefty. He wasn't smiling anymore.

"I said, what are you doing in this section?"

Anne made a show of chewing fast so she could talk.

"Eating a pretzel," she said. "I like to eat in private, that's all."

"Eating a pretzel is more important than listening to Reverend Korvak's sermon?"

She smiled. Men liked smiles. Usually. She thought of going for her knife. Could she close the distance before—

—he drew his pistol, but kept it angled toward the floor.

"What's your name, girl?"

One minute until detonation.

Anne let herself look scared. It didn't take much acting.

"I don't understand," she said. "What did I do?"

It wasn't what she'd done, it was what she *hadn't* done. She hadn't paid attention to the details. He'd seen something she'd missed.

"Your *name*," he said.

"I'm Miriam. Miriam Webster. I was just out for a walk. No one told me I couldn't walk in this sector."

A mistake, she knew it the second she said it.

The man tilted his head toward a yellow sign on the wall: *NO UNAUTHORIZED PERSONNEL ALLOWED.*

"Maybe you don't read so good," he said. "Hands against the wall, spread your feet."

Thirty seconds. Anne had to be patient.

"But my pretzel."

"Drop the fucking pretzel already."

Anne tossed it aside and put her palms against the wall.

He came up behind her—she felt the cold chill of a knife against the left side of her neck.

Fear surged; anxiety pinched her stomach. Anne fought to control herself.

Had he holstered the pistol?

"Word is there's a Union spy in Eden," the guard said. "I have the right to search you. Stay real still."

She felt his right hand slide into her left pocket, come out with her knife.

"Well, well, well," he said. "You're armed."

"It's just for self-defense."

She'd lost count, but the moment was close.

The guard's hand slid into her right pocket, came out with the remote clicker. He held it in front of her face.

"And this? What is this?"

Despite the fear, she had to find a way to get in his head, to get him to make a mistake.

"Oh, that thing? It's a remote detonator. You know, for a bomb."

"A *bomb*, huh?" He shoved her hard, pressing her face against the wall. "That some kind of a joke?"

The floor and walls trembled, ever so slightly. An instant later, the explosion's report reached them, a low, drawn-out bass rumble amplified by Eden's long tunnels.

She felt his weight come off her back, the knife's touch lighter on her neck. He'd reacted automatically, instinctively, looking toward the sound of the explosion, taking his eyes off her.

A moment was all Anne needed.

She pushed backward as hard as she could, throwing her weight into him, catching him flat-footed. Even as she did, she reached up to grab his wrist.

But she was too late.

As he stumbled away, she felt a cold pain lace across her left shoulder and down her back.

Anne turned in time to see her assailant thud against the far wall— she closed the distance.

He reacted quickly, pushing off to come at her, but in doing so he made his second mistake—Anne had already started her down-kick when the man put all his weight on his left leg, locking it. She drove her heel into his kneecap, heard something snap. He screamed as his leg bent the wrong way.

Down he went, grabbing at his ruined knee.

She snap-kicked hard, felt her boot's toe crush his windpipe. His hands went to his throat. He made sounds like wet hiccups.

The tapping raged to the front of her thoughts—the *need* swept over her.

She picked up his dropped pistol. She checked the safety: *on*.

His knife lay on the floor just to her left.

She reached for it, but her left arm refused to move. Pain raged down her shoulder, seethed across her back.

Anne shoved the pistol into her belt. With that same hand, her right, she picked up the aggressor's knife.

Tap, tap, tap...

Maddening. *Infuriating.* She knew how to make the tapping go away. One sweet, exquisite way to be free of it.

Anne drove the blade into his thigh.

He threw his head back and screamed, or at least he tried to—only a gravelly gurgle escaped his mouth.

His pain made the tapping in her head sound like kettle drums the size of continents.

Tap, tap, TAP, TAP...

The need. The *heat.*

She wanted to spend time with this man, a lot of time, but that wasn't in the cards.

Anne pulled the blade free. She drove the point into his belly. His eyes went wide. No scream this time. Not even a gravelly gurgle. He was already on his way out thanks to the crushed windpipe, but she couldn't stop herself—the tapping wouldn't let her.

She stabbed him in the belly a second time, watched his eyes grow even wider.

Anne couldn't hear anything *but* the tapping as she dragged the knife sideways and upward within him, *sawing* with it, slicing intestines and stomach.

The look in his eyes, his expression of *what is happening, why is this happening?* enveloped her like a warm, thick blanket.

"This is for your own good," she said.

He gazed, dumbfounded, as life faded from his eyes.

Anne fell to her ass. The kettledrum tapping faded. The heat eased.

She stared at what she'd done. The man's clothes, soaked with blood. His broken knee. Stubs and curls of intestine poking out from the flap she'd cut into his belly.

The pain hit her anew, all at once, a screaming, searing bolt through her left shoulder. Her shirt and jacket felt cold and wet.

Anne heard klaxon alarms and the faint, echoing shouts of people reacting to danger.

More meatheads might come. She didn't know how long it would be until the assault force rescued her.

She had to hide.

With her right hand, she undid the clamp and set the grate aside. Her left arm was numb. She kept it close to her body, hoping she wouldn't leave a trail of blood.

Anne crawled through the opening. She pulled the grate shut and, somehow, fastened the clamp.

She sagged, suddenly dizzy. Dizzy from blood loss already? Not much time.

A muffled moan: Olivia wanted to know what was happening.

Anne couldn't manage a reply.

The assault force—Anne had to let them know where she was.

She clambered over the gear bag. She'd pre-programmed the transceiver; the push of a single button activated the encrypted homing signal.

She crawled to the first aid kit, her blood-wet hand sliding across the duct's smooth floor.

Nanocyte salve—her only chance.

Anne tried to open the kit with one hand, fumbled with it, finally popped open the lid. Inside were bandages, meds, and a sealed white jar with a pull-tab. She pinched the jar between her knees and yanked the tab free.

Dizziness almost brought her down as she dug her fingers into the jar's thick, blue goo. She slid her right hand under her shirt, reached up to her left shoulder and smeared the goo against the knife wound, grunting against the pain.

She again reached for the jar... wait... why did she want that?

What was she doing?

Why was she so cold?

Anne slumped to her side, heart racing. She just needed a minute to catch her breath.

———

She awoke to the sound of muffled whimpering, faint crying, but also to echoes of distant, heavy footsteps. Some kind of new construction activity, maybe? If so, she had to make sure the vent grate was clamped, and...

...the assault.

Union forces were here.

Anne looked to the gear bag. Her soul sank. Her father's words taunted her—*don't get caught.*

Daddy would be disappointed.

There was still time. If Anne could drag the bag deeper into the duct, it could work.

She tried to rise—dull agony tore through her. Crusted nanocyte salve cracked and crumbled. The goo had spread through her wound, stopped the bleeding, and accelerated the healing process.

Anne fought against weakness, against the pain. She crawled past the transceiver, saw that it slowly pulsed a soft white light, a signal that the assault force was trying to contact her.

They were close.

She crawled to the gear bag. The bag moved from within, as if it saw her coming, as if it knew what she was about to do and wanted to crawl away.

Anne unzipped the bag.

She looked down at the woman inside—bandage-wrapped stumps where her legs had been, bandage-wrapped stumps where her arms had been.

Olivia stared up, terrified beyond words. A bloody gag pulled her lips back in a rictus grin.

This woman had kept the tapping at bay. Anne had fantasized about the moment she'd end Olivia's satiating pain, the day Olivia's energy would quench Anne's demon-need, filling her up and letting her be *normal.*

But that tapping wasn't there. The need, the *heat*, wasn't there. The meathead's essence had made it all go away.

"Thank you, Olivia."

On one hip, Anne slid to her tools. She'd acquired them from careless workers who left them out. *A place for everything and everything in its place.* If the workers weren't punished for their mistakes, how could they learn?

The tools: a pair of vise-grips, a metal pipe-saw, and a long Phillips screwdriver.

Anne picked up the screwdriver and crawled back to her friend.

Through the gag, Olivia started to scream.

"Hush now," Anne said. "I enjoyed spending time with you. You helped me. You're a good friend. Thank you."

Olivia's head thrashed. Anne clumsily laid her left forearm against Olivia's jaw and pressed down, holding the woman in place long enough to punch the screwdriver through her temple.

Olivia spasmed.

Anne angled the handle, rotating the shank through the woman's brain.

Olivia fell limp.

The sound of a grate being ripped free and tossed on a metal floor.

"Lieutenant Lafferty, sound off!"

She knew that voice. Who was it?

Beams of light bounced around the duct, swinging, searching.

She couldn't move. It was too late.

Don't get caught.

Lights hit Anne's eyes, making her squint.

"Lieutenant! Are you all... Oh my God."

Yes, she did know that voice. Staley, her CO. He'd come for her himself.

A moment too late, Anne realized she probably should have let go of the screwdriver.

3

Maia Whittaker had a quota to fill—Admiral Epperson's quota. One did not disappoint Admiral Epperson. Not unless you wanted to wind up on the *Keeling* yourself, which Maia most certainly didn't. Not at her age. Hell, not at *any* age.

She knew the people she assigned to the PUV *James Keeling* would likely die. They had the last three times she'd fleshed out the crew, at a rate of almost eighty percent.

Eight out of ten of the people she'd sent to that ship never left it.

Other than that, she didn't know much about the *Keeling*. Few did. Details were scarce. Rumors, though, were plentiful, and had spread throughout Fleet. Rumors about the death rate, among other things, made Maia's job that much harder.

In the endless power games played among the flag ranks—vying for bigger and better assignments, battling over resources and funding, the constant maneuverings to get the best people under their commands—generals, vice admirals and admirals alike found ways to shield their chosen officers and NCOs from assignment to the *Keeling*.

The best of the best were protected. So, too, was anyone with the right connections, a powerful family, or friends in high places. Not that Grade-A personnel were completely inaccessible for the quota, not if they fucked up so badly that their patrons could not—or *would* not—protect them.

Maybe people didn't know what the ship was, but they knew they didn't want to die on it.

Today, at least, she wasn't worried about those with connections. Most Raiders didn't *have* connections. The poor bastards. If sailors on the *Keeling* had an eighty percent mortality rate, what hope was there for Raiders?

Maia liked to do the easy tasks first. Build up momentum that would sustain her motivation through the hard parts of the job. Epperson's team had brought in two hundred candidates to fill thirty-seven slots. If all went well, she'd have the new Raider platoon filled by day's end.

After the Raiders, she'd switch gears and start on the harder work. Filling the Intel Chief position would be quite a challenge, as would the *Keeling*-only rank of "xeno mate." Finding Raiders and sailors was one thing—finding candidates from the Bureau of Science & Technology who could understand the ship's unique aspects was another thing altogether. BST people were a weird bunch.

She pressed her intercom button. "Adela, send in the first prospect."

"Right away, Major."

Maia pulled the first file folder from atop a pile stacked neatly on the right side of her desk. File folders. *Paper.* It still boggled the mind.

Everything about *Keeling* was secret, down to avoiding data entry on a keyboard or flexipaper. As soon as she finished each interview, she'd shred the files. Seemed like Purist Nation spies were everywhere these days.

Nationalites—fucking primitive savages. Maia wouldn't shed a tear if all their planets and colonies got sat-bombed so thoroughly they glowed from within.

The door to her office opened. In walked a kid straight off a recruitment poster—blond high and tight, wide in the shoulders, a jaw that could take a punch, and light brown eyes burning with excitement for all things Fleet. He wore standard gray-camo utility fatigues, complete with an eight-pointed utility cap. Biceps strained the folded-up sleeves. His thick chest pulled at his jacket's hidden fastener strip, indicating he'd gained significant muscle since the jacket had been issued.

Back in Maia's day, if she'd been called to an assignment interview, she would have worn the more formal service grays. Not just her —*anyone* would have. But the Fleet wasn't what it had been eighteen years ago, now was it? Not since the brass lowered educational requirements in an effort to bolster the ranks.

The kid strode to the desk, stood straight, and snapped off a sharp salute.

"Specialist-One Jim Perry reporting as ordered, *sir!*"

Jesus, that was a lot of energy for 09:15.

Maia casually returned the salute. She could have stood to do that, but her knees hurt, and she had hundreds of interviews ahead of her.

"At ease, Spec," Maia said.

Perry spread his feet shoulder width apart and clasped his hands behind his back.

Maia flipped through his record. As she did, she understood why Epperson's people put Perry on the list. Nineteen years old, straight out of Brittmore. Expert rifleman. Psych report indicated little sense of self-preservation. And, most important of all, no surviving family.

"Sir, may I ask a question?"

For fuck's sake, this boot didn't have the good sense to keep his mouth shut?

"You may not," Maia said.

She kept reading. Perry was a combo package: half-amazing, half-idiot. He'd pegged his scores for all combat-related tests. Non-combat tasks, though? Not so much. Horrible scores in cultural sensitivity awareness, and he wasn't exactly a math whiz. That hurt him. Hurt him for advancement, anyway. For armoring up and crossing the gap, though? That helped. Some high-IQ types were good at calculating odds; the less a Raider understood the odds of survival, the better.

"Spec Perry, you're being considered for a special assignment."

Perry's smile had a wolfish quality to it.

"That's paper, right, sir? *Real* paper?"

Maia closed the folder. "Spec, did you just ask me a question when I specifically told you not to ask questions?"

"Yes sir."

"Why?"

His big body shook a little before he answered, as if he was a battery so full of charge that sparks leaked out the seams.

"Because paper is only used for secret shit. I mean secret *stuff*. Sir. That's what I mean."

The kid thought he was going to be an action hero or something, not wind up with his innards splattered across the void in frozen organ-cicles that would forever float through space.

"Spec Perry, it says here you don't have any living family. Is that correct?"

His big dumb grin widened. "I *knew* it, sir."

"You knew what?"

"That something special was coming. That's why you're asking about family, right? So you can assign me to something special? I knew it. I *felt* it."

Oh, to be this young and naive again.

"That's nice, Spec," Maia said. "Your feelings are very important to my decision-making process."

The kid nodded. Maybe he didn't get sarcasm when it came from a superior officer. Maybe he didn't get sarcasm at all. Maia didn't care.

"It says in your record that... Spec, what the *hell* are you doing?"

Perry was pulling open his jacket. "I *knew* it, sir. That's why I got this tat!"

Maia had seen a lot of shit in her day. A gung-ho jizzie opening his jacket in front of a superior officer? This was new.

"Spec Perry, you must have had your head up your ass and left your brain in there when you pulled it out. You better—"

Perry yanked his jacket open to show his broad chest, the words SCREAM AIM & FIRE tattooed in some Old English font from shoulder to shoulder, collarbone to sternum.

"Check it out, sir! Fucking sweet, am I right?"

Perry hadn't gone for a digital tat, he'd opted for old-fashioned ink. The ampersand had a little arm on top, ending in a fist with an extended middle finger.

Yep—Jim Perry was a real asset to the Fleet.

"Scream, aim, and motherfuckin' *fire*, sir! That's what it's all about! *Boo-yah*! Wherever you send me, I'll lay *waste*, sir!"

In a way, she felt better about starting this process off with Perry. Unlike many of the people she had and would assign to the *Keeling*, he had no significant charges in his record. Although, that was probably because he was young and had yet to be unleashed upon the galaxy. Given enough time, a guy like Perry would probably wind up on the *Keeling* anyway.

She stood. When she did, her knees popped. The left one sent a jolt of pain up her thigh.

"Spec Perry, you will button up your uniform, and you will do it *now*."

He refastened the seam. Oh, how she longed for the days before the war, when Fleet still had educational requirements—even for Raiders.

Perry tugged at his jacket's hem to straighten it.

"Sorry, *sir*! My enthusiasm got the better of me. I want action. I'm ready. I'm a beautiful bullet—point me in the right direction and pull the trigger."

Keeling was the best place for him, really.

"If it's action you want, Spec, it's action you'll get. Wait outside, one of my people will show you where to go. You'll depart soon."

"Depart for where, sir?"

"That's classified," Maia said.

From the look on Perry's face, one would have thought she was Santa Claus, and he was eight years old.

"Yes, *sir*!" Perry snapped off another smart salute. "Thank you, *sir*!"

He held the salute until Maia returned it.

"That is all," she said. "Dismissed."

Perry left the office.

Not bad. One down, thirty-six to go.

She pressed the intercom button. "Adela, have a runner escort Spec-One Jim Perry to the quartermaster. Send in the next candidate."

Maia used the arm rests to lower herself into her chair. Getting old was a pain in the ass. As time rolled on, her artificial knees hurt more and more. They'd never been quite right, even fifteen years ago when she first got them. Some people could have entire limbs replaced and function just fine. Not her, though. Her body, apparently, hadn't been built with spare parts in mind.

Perry would ship out that day on one of a dozen small transports allocated to Maia. The new Raider platoon and replacement crew members wouldn't travel together until the *Ishlangu* took them to the *Keeling*, wherever it was.

She slid Perry's folder into the shredder, then pulled the next folder off the stack.

The door opened. Another Raider entered, this one older. Maia frowned—she wasn't supposed to interview sergeants until after lunch.

The man stepped forward, saluted. A perfectly fine salute, but lacking Perry's unbridled energy.

"Specialist-Three John Bennett reporting as ordered, sir."

Spec-*Three*? At his age?

She lazily returned the salute. "At ease, Spec."

Maia opened the folder and looked at the man's age. *Fifty-six years old?* What the hell? Then, she saw his commendations. Six Purple Hearts. Four Raider Hammers, the award given to those who boarded an enemy ship in combat. Two Fleet Crosses. Not just one, which was rarified air, but *two*.

Maia looked up; she was staring at a war hero.

Bennett was every bit as broad and wide as Perry had been, but where the young buck was a fresh-cut steak, Bennett was a walking piece of gristle. His charcoal-colored service grays looked like they'd been dry cleaned only moments before. Not a spec of dirt on him, not a thread out of place. Spit and polish covering a killing machine.

Maia could only imagine what this man looked like in dress grays. Although, he probably looked just as stoic in the black and gray cammies Raiders wore most of the time.

There had to be a mistake. These were paper records, after all. Handwritten. People screwed up details all the time.

"Spec, maybe my information is bad. It says here you're fifty-six years old?"

"That is correct, sir."

What the flying fuck was Epperson's team doing sending this man here?

"Someone screwed up," she said. "I'm sorry. I'm reviewing personnel for a combat role."

Bennett nodded. "Yes sir. That's what I asked for. I follow orders real good, sir. I shoot straight."

She flipped through the pages. He was near the end of his *eighth* five-year stint. Thirty-eight combat missions. And... holy hell... *twenty-four* confirmed kills?

A soldier like this deserved to be on a fundraising tour, not thrown into the flesh mangler that was the *Keeling*. Maia couldn't control much, but she could control this—she wasn't going to let Bennett walk into a nightmare.

"We're done here," she said. "I will not put a fifty-six-year-old *spec* on the... well, I'm not giving you this assignment."

He stared straight ahead, not *at* her, but at some point *past* her. A certain hollowness to his green eyes. Hollowness, and honesty.

"Sir, please reconsider. I have valuable combat experience. I'm ready to fight. I passed my physical."

That didn't surprise her. Bennett was a block of granite. All the working out in the galaxy, though, couldn't hide his crow's feet or the slightly sagging skin around his bull neck. Maybe he would have looked better with cosmetic surgery, but that wasn't something one could afford on an enlisted salary.

"Spec Bennett, this assignment isn't for you. Why haven't you retired?"

"I did," he said. "After my twenty. My first twenty, I mean. I thought I'd seen enough killing. Moved back to Earth. Fort Worth, Texas. I... well I lived by myself for six months. Didn't really know what to do. There was no one telling me when to eat, when to train. I got fat. And I couldn't sleep, sir. Maybe because I could go to bed whenever, wake up whenever... I couldn't get used to it. So at night, when I couldn't sleep, I'd sit there and think. Think about all the things I did while I was deployed, when I was fighting. I never thought about those things when I was active, you know? But you take off the uniform, and some of that stuff comes back to you. You've been in combat, right?"

She couldn't stop herself from looking at her knees, then back up at his sad eyes.

"Sort of," she said. "In my first deployment, a Purist AP round punched through my crawler. Ruined my legs. I was downgraded to non-combat status. I've *technically* been in combat, but I never fired a shot."

Why had she told him that? She didn't tell anyone.

"That must have been hard, sir," he said. "Must still be hard."

He wasn't patronizing her, he was *sad* for her. She'd never tested herself in battle. To this day, she didn't know what she was really made of. She never would.

"Yeah," she said. "It is hard."

Maia brushed off the thought. This wasn't a confession booth. If she ran into Spec-3 Bennett at a bar, they could have this conversation, and also whatever came after it. But not here. She had a job to do.

She looked at his medical. He'd had leg replacement surgery. He was on his third liver, second spleen, and second heart—all cloned from his own cells, all to repair wounds suffered in battle. No artificial parts, which would have excluded him from assignment to combat vessels.

A guy like this should be a master sergeant, even a warrant officer. She read the handwritten notes listing his promotion evaluation scores —three tests, three failures. That didn't line up with her brief evaluation of this man. Maia's gut told her Bennett failed at nothing. Not unless he *wanted* to fail.

His record listed dozens of battles: boarding action in '23 against the Sklorno; ground action in the '27 Rodina Uprising; repelling League of Planets boarders in '38, just to name a few.

Bennett had done his part. She would *not* put him in Epperson's meat grinder. No way. That sanctimonious prick of an admiral didn't deserve a warrior like this.

"Spec Bennett, you're two years from your second twenty. That's one hell of an accomplishment. I know a dozen flag officers who would take you on their staffs in an instant. It's time for you to get off the line and ride into the sunset."

Did his lower lip tremble? Maybe. If it had, it returned to stone-stillness so fast Maia couldn't be sure.

"Please, sir," Bennett said. "Retirement ain't for me. Life outside Fleet ain't for me. Let me go out shooting."

Something in his voice pulled at her, told her he had an agenda.

"Specialist, do you know what assignment I'm interviewing people for?"

Bennett swallowed, as if he'd considered lying before remembering he was shit at lies.

"I believe so, sir." He leaned forward slightly. "You're assigning Raiders to the *Crypt*."

The *Crypt*—*Keeling*'s unofficial yet highly accurate nickname.

"How do you know about that, Specialist?"

Bennett straightened. "Just a rumor, sir."

Maybe he wasn't the type to lie, but no soldier made it as far as he had without knowing when to keep his trap shut.

"You're on thin ice, Bennett. I'm trying to be patient with you, but—"

"Let me die a Raider." His voice was a hoarse whisper. "Let me die shooting. Please. It's all I ever knew."

He was desperate. A big, proud, decorated Raider begging to stay in the service.

Maia's own twenty was up in seventeen months. She couldn't wait to get the hell out, to find a nice house on a lake somewhere. Get drunk when she felt like it. Sleep whenever she wanted to.

Bennett didn't desire that life. At all. And he'd earned the right to choose his own destiny. He wanted to fight? He wanted to die in his TASH armor? Well, that was something Major Maia Whittaker could make happen.

She closed his folder.

"It will be a two-year hitch," she said. "You need to know that. There's no getting out of it early, Bennett. When you're finally able to choose your path again, you'll be *fifty-eight* years old. Can you live with that?"

"Yes sir, I can."

Maia stood. Her knees popped again, but she didn't care.

"You have the assignment you wanted, Spec-Three Bennett. Wait outside. One of my people will show you where to go. You'll depart soon."

She waited for the usual *depart for where?* Bennett didn't ask.

He saluted. "Yes sir."

Maia returned the salute, returned it *properly*, not the half-assed gesture she'd given Perry.

"You're dismissed."

Bennett turned on one heel and smartly strode out of her office.

Maia was sending him to his death. A death he longed for.

She again lowered herself into her chair.

"Adela, have Spec-Three Bennett escorted to the quartermaster. Remind the quartermaster, again, that I want these Raiders spread out on as many ships as he can manage. I don't want them talking to each other in transit. And send in the next candidate."

Maia slid Bennett's file into the shredder, then pulled a folder off the stack.

Thirty-five to go.

4

Nitzan Shamdi and Arimun—no last name, just Arimun—stumbled out of the Lowlight Grille on Deck 17. They were as fucked-up as fucked-up can get before the party flies headlong into the Land of the Passed-Out.

People steered clear of them, because people were smart enough to realize that big, drunk Raiders with hell in their eyes got the right of way. Especially big, drunk Raiders who'd already had at least one bar fight, as evidenced by torn fatigues, bruises, scrapes, and bloody knuckles. Even the civilian merchant-marine toughs that liked to start shit averted their eyes; they calmly stepped aside so as not to invite trouble from the drunken pair.

Nitzan and Arimun stopped stumbling long enough for Arimun to puke up half his beef stew. They didn't clean it up. No one said a word to them. As rule of thumb, when on Zackmann Station, you didn't talk to Raiders.

"Nitzie, mate, I gotta go back to the ship," Arimun said. "I'm tanked."

"One more bar, Ari," Nitzan said. "We're going to that place I been telling you about. It's great, I promise."

Nitzan was running late. He tapped at the bracelet on his right wrist, which made his cell interface appear above his right palm. Oh-two-thirty. He also had a half-dozen texts from other Raiders, wanting to drink the night away, and one from his sergeant politely reminding him what would happen were he late to boarding drills the following morning.

"Why do you keep checking the time?" Ari asked, then bent over and vented the second half of his dinner.

Nitzan shut off his bracelet display. "Just curious to see how long we've been drinking."

"*Too* long," Arimun said. "That's how long. Come *on* man, if we run into those slack-balled sailors again, I might be too drunk to kick their asses."

"Whatever, Ari. Remember that fight you started last year? Down on Deck Four?"

Arimun laughed a long, slow, drunken laugh. "Oh yeah, that's right. At the navy officer's club? Man, there were, what, *ten* of those clams against the two of us?"

"That's because I was the only one dumb enough to go with you."

"You *always* back me up, mate." Arimun thumped Nitzan's shoulder. "You got my six."

"Always will," Nitzan said. "But I left that bar with fifteen stitches. You *owe* me. Come on, one more drink?"

Arimun blinked slowly, the liquor gumming up his gears. He thought for a moment, then nodded.

"You're a fucker to call out that marker, Nitzie. You know that?"

"Can't argue with you there."

They stumbled along the deck and took the next lift to Nineteenth —an international deck. Humans with skin in the common tones of pink, tan, brown, and the weird bleach-white of Tower natives. A few of those ugly, six-legged Ki. Floating Harrah zipping about near the ceiling. And, occasionally, Whitokians, the nastiest of all. Leekee, too, but on Zackmann the few members of that species usually kept to the waterbars frequented by Dolphins and Aqus.

Nitzan found the Nineteenth fairly empty. Carousing crews from civilian ships, sure, and the usual sailors, strikers and Raiders from the half-dozen Fleet warships docked at Zackmann, but it wasn't the passageway-filling party spot he'd expected.

"My feets don't work," Arimun said. "Give us a hand, will ya?"

He threw his arm over Nitzan's shoulder. Nitzan led him down the passageway.

"Black Beast's balls, Ari—have you gained weight?"

"Yep. New bench-press max, too. I'm fucking yoked, man."

Nitzan stopped them at a bar door. "We're here."

Arimun looked up at the flashing neon sign above the entrance: *Huygen's Hidey Hole.*

"Nitzie, this one of those red joints? I fuckin' hate Martians."

"Quit your bitching, Ari. We're going in."

Huygen's Hidey Hole didn't have much of a crowd, a fact mostly hidden by the dim lighting. Three Harrah hovered around a man seated at the bartop's left corner. Assorted working boys and girls moved from table to table, offering their goods. Men and women in crew jackets, shoulder patches showing their boat's home system— Rodina, New Earth, Neptune Net Colony, and two crews from Saturn Net Colony. A Whitokian, alone at the bar's right corner.

Three clams, sitting at a table, their white uniforms perfectly pressed, stared insolently at the two *real* fighting men who'd just walked in. Nitzan disliked sailors. Drunk as he was, he hoped they started some shit.

He helped Arimun to an empty table and sat him down.

"I gotta piss," Nitzan said. "Get us a couple of drunks."

"We *are* a couple of drunks."

"Drinks," Nitzan said. "I mean *drinks*."

"Got it."

Nitzan kept his balance, mostly, as he stumbled to the bathroom. He had to walk past the cone-shaped Whitokian to reach it.

They were utterly vile creatures. This one was male; you could tell by the slime-covered green skin. Females, with their orange skin, generated more slime, which was why they weren't allowed in most Human-run joints. The male had both pairs of spindly legs—Nitzan thought they looked a bit like lobster legs—propped up on the bar stool's rungs. Folds of flesh hanging between each pair sagged almost to the floor. In the water, Whitokians were graceful and powerful. On land, they had all the beauty of an old man's wrinkly nut sack.

Nitzan could say one thing for the nasty creature, though—the Whitokian was drinking hard. Two empty steins sat on the bar top in front of him. His spindly arms wrapped around a third like he was ready to protect it against booze thieves who might snatch it away.

For a century and a half now, Humans and Whitokians had interacted, embraced trade, shared technology and culture. That, without a doubt, was one of the many reasons the Union had gone to hell in a hand basket. Non-Humans. Disgusting.

Nitzan entered the Human bathroom. One guy at the urinal, taking a leak. A quick visual scan under the four stalls—no feet.

There, on the base of the toilet in the second stall, a bit of red electrical tape. Nitzan checked to make sure the urinal guy was still pissing, then tried the stall door. Locked. Nitzan coughed three times.

The stall's lock slid back, allowing Nitzan to push the door open and quickly step inside. He shut and locked the door behind him. A man sat on the flat toilet tank, his feet on the seat. He wore a black jacket, brown slacks, brown shoes. No jewelry. He looked like a typical messenger for any of the gaudy businessmen who packed Zackmann Station.

You are late, the man signed with his hands.

My apologies, Nitzan signed back.

Hand-language was the first thing they taught you in the Cloister. Nitzan had picked it up quickly, along with mastering dialects and accents from the Union's bigger planets. He'd learned so much in the Cloister, far more than just languages and culture. He'd learned tradecraft. He'd learned how to kill. How to act, to lose oneself in a role, to so deeply become someone else you didn't think it was someone else at all.

Five years in the Cloister. At fifteen, the bishops declared Nitzan ready to serve, had sent him away from the Purist Nation to Thomas 3 in the Planetary Union. There, he'd been placed in an orphanage. That had been an eye-opener. Little information about the Union reached the Nation. The info that did get through was mostly about sports figures, movie stars, and the ultra-rich scum that secretly ran the galaxy. In the orphanage, Nitzan saw evidence of the Union's corrupt culture: bribery, assault, extortion, pedophilia, and more.

When he turned seventeen—or at least when he turned seventeen according to the birthdate of his false identity—he was booted out of the orphanage. That was expected. Nitzan took the few dollars he had to his name, called a transport, and went straight to the Fleet recruiting office. Hours later, he started the pre-enlistment steps. He slept at the office. Fleet recruiters had signed up many a teen just like him. Recruiters were quite familiar with kids showing up who had no place else to go.

The next day, Nitzan boarded a shuttle for Brittmore Base. There, he gave his oath of loyalty to the Union, and he started boot camp to become a Raider.

It is time for your service, the man signed.

Nitzan's heart pounded a double beat. *Finally*. After three years in Fleet, his handlers had a mission for him, something other than pretending to be a Unionite, something other than fighting and killing his own Purist Nation countrymen.

I am ready, Nitzan signed.

The blasphemers have a secret warship. The James Keeling.

The *Keeling*. The *Crypt*. But that was just a story, wasn't it?

We thought it destroyed, the handler signed. *The heathens repaired it. Chatter indicates they are adding crew. We know almost nothing about the* Keeling, *but we believe it is capable of a new kind of stealth travel. If it is back in service, we need you on board. We must know more about this vessel. We will find a way to contact you there, but we do not know how to do that yet.*

I don't know how to get transferred to it, Nitzan signed.

The handler smiled. *They use discipline cases for much of the crew. Cowards, thieves, rapists, perverts... and murderers. Kill your companion. Right now. We'll handle the rest.*

Kill Ari?

I should kill one of the sailors instead, Nitzan signed. *Raiders hate sailors, it makes more sense.*

The man's eyes narrowed.

You will do as you are told. Have the heretics corrupted you?

Nitzan shook his head, shook it hard. No, he hadn't been corrupted. He *couldn't* be, that was why they'd sent him to the Cloister, why they'd invested so much time and capital into putting him in the right place at the right time.

But Ari... his friend...

Nitzan forced the doubts away. He had his orders. Nitzan Shamdi —once known as Abbas al-Kenja—knew what had to be done.

The handler reached out with his index finger and gently touched Nitzan's forehead. Softly, so softly, the handler traced the pattern of an infinity sign.

The gesture made Nitzan's heart ache with joy. It meant that after the mission, he would be fully confirmed as a Purist Church elder. When the mission was over, he could, at long last, go home.

Praise be to High One, the handler signed.

Nitzan walked out of the stall. No one at the urinals or the sink. He headed back into the noise of Huygen's Hidey Hole.

A drunken woman fell in front of him, her short skirt sliding up her bleach-white thigh. Sluts from the planet Tower—they couldn't hold their liquor. Some side effect of the gene mods that removed all color from their skin. It kept them from getting cancer or something like that.

He helped her to her feet, leaned her against a table. She gave him the eyes—she wanted him. He didn't want her. He wouldn't have wanted her even if she'd been sober. Skin like hers wasn't among the tones created by High One. Someday she'd burn in the pits of hell. Maybe Low One would give her the hard fuck she so obviously needed.

Nitzan slid past other patrons, sat down at his table. Arimun held a mag-can of lager. Another can—already opened so it would be properly chilled—was waiting for Nitzan.

"That was a load off," Nitzan said. "Had to go so bad I saw yellow. You feeling any more sober, mate?"

Ari nodded. "A little. Maybe." His *maybe* stretched out, slurred, revealing he wasn't one bit more sober. "But those fucking clams keep looking over here. Especially the big one. I think they want to brawl."

Nitzan smiled. He reached down to his right ankle and pulled out the tactical knife he kept in a holster there. He set the knife on the table. No one was supposed to carry weaponry on-station, but who the fuck was going to question a Raider carrying a little ol' folding knife with a little ol' 13-centimeter blade?

Ari looked at the knife. He smiled a drunken smile.

"You never go anywhere without that thing, Nitzie. You gonna give them clams a little mark to remember us by?"

Slowly, quietly, Nitzan unfolded the blade. He set it flat on the table, covered it with his forearm. He turned in his seat to grin at the clams.

"Hey," Nitzan called out. "Hey, you waste-pipe pieces of sailor-shit."

A hush fell over the bar.

The big sailor glowered back. He and his two dress-whites cluster-buddies must have come from a ceremony of some kind. That, or these choads thought dressing up would get them laid for free. Fucking clams, ready to have a fancy, pinkies-out tea party at the drop of a hat.

"Hey," Nitzan called out again. "You flat-backers sipping champagne over there? Does it taste like your captain's asshole, or is that flavor permanently embedded on your tongue?"

The biggest of the three sailors stood. He looked like an iron pipe someone had wrapped in white tissue.

"You should shut up now," the sailor said. "This isn't a conversation you want to have, jizzie."

Jizzie. Fleet slang for Raiders. *Clams* hid in their shells, while *jizz* got shot into space.

"Not a conversation," Nitzan said. "More like show and tell. I got something to show you."

The sailor smirked. "And what's that? Your tiny pecker?"

The big guy's buddies also stood. One man, one woman, both ready for a fight.

"Ari," Nitzan said, "before we mop the deck with their pretty white suits, I wanna tell you a secret."

"A secret?" Arimun wobbled, almost fell off his chair. "What secret?"

Nitzan leaned closer. Arimun did the same.

"I want you to know, Ari, that the Union will fall."

Nitzan thought back to his drill instructor, who'd hammered one mantra home above all others—*slow is smooth, smooth is fast, fast is final.*

In one calm, measured motion, Nitzan grabbed the knife and slid the tip into Arimun's neck, a smidgen to the right of his windpipe—the blade sank deep.

Arimun stared, blinked slowly, as if he wasn't sure if it hurt or not.

Nitzan had a moment to think about all the good times he and Arimun had together. About the times they'd been under fire together. About the times they'd lost squadmates together. About the times they *killed* together.

Then, shouts from the clams, from all across the bar brought Nitzan back to the moment.

"Ouch," Arimun said.

Nitzan ripped the knife sideways, grunting with effort to slice the edge through the carotid and jugular, through muscle, ligaments, and skin. Blood spurted from the slash, gushing on the table, on the floor, on Arimun's shoulder.

Footsteps pounding on the floor told Nitzan he had only seconds.

He made them count.

"Sorry, brother," he said to his dying friend. "Tell Low One I'll be sending more of your kind his way."

The clams slammed into Nitzan and dragged him down.

5

He's a blasphemous urine-drinker.

A tragic first impression. Susannah attempted to remain focused, but the subtle reek of Major Tom Bratchford's breath wafting across the metal desk had already weakened her resolve. Simply put, she couldn't shake the image of him gulping down a hot, steaming mug of his own pee—not the best way to picture one's new boss.

Susannah forced herself to make eye contact.

"We're pleased to have you, Lieutenant Rossi," Bratchford said. "Do you prefer to go by rank or be addressed as *Doctor*?"

He smiled, revealing yellowed teeth and receding gums. Bratchford's mouth was probably filthier than the waste treatment tank of the *Nicholas Otto*, the research vessel to which Susannah had been assigned.

"Since I'm here as a scientist, sir, *Doctor* seems more fitting."

Bratchford needed to trim his nose hair. Ear hair, too. No wonder he was such a miserable person—the hair fleeing his scalp had found other places to flourish.

Susannah glanced around the small compartment. Dents and scratches in the gunmetal gray walls. Dust tentacles fluttering from an overhead vent vibrated as stale air blew past them.

"Lieutenant, are you upset about being recalled?"

Ask how she'd like to be addressed, then ignore her preference. The man probably thought that was clever.

She fought the urge to defer to Bratchford. Defer to him simply because he was male. Over the last ten years of her life, she'd come to accept that a woman's role was to support the men who furthered the faith. Within reason, though. She'd had a run-in with a holy man who wanted things High One did not permit. Susannah took that man down.

Her instincts screamed at her to look away, to act submissive in both demeanor and voice. But the religion that taught her such behavior no longer wanted her. She'd been excommunicated. This was her life now. She would stand up for herself, or at least try.

"It's not what I wanted, Major," Susannah said. "But I assure you I won't let my feelings get in the way of doing my job."

"Honesty." Bratchford huffed a laugh. "That can have its uses. Do you intend to keep your hair that long? No place for long hair in a lab. Most of the older women who work for me cut theirs much shorter."

Older women? Susannah was two years shy of forty. Hardly *old.*

"The length is within regulations, sir."

It was, but barely. She wore her dark hair—gray strands and all— pulled back in a tight ponytail. Her hair was heavy enough that it hung straight down, without any frizz or puffiness that might get her cited for appearing unkempt.

"Regulations," Bratchford said. "Those have their uses, too."

There was something ominous about the way he said that. Was he the kind of leader who just came out and told you what he wanted or was he the type that gave little hints and then raked you over the coals for not reading his mind?

Susannah felt so far from home. But what was *home* now? The Union wanted her. She didn't want the Union. She wanted to be in the Nation. The Nation didn't want her.

"I haven't had a Purist under me before," Bratchford said. "At least not someone so... *blatant*... about their faith. I would think one facial disfigurement was enough."

Wonderful. A religious bigot for a commanding officer, one who seemed to think Susannah cared about her looks. She was *proud* of her face. The infinity tattoo on her forehead and the scar that split her right eyebrow with a flash of pink skin were both marks High One had put upon her.

"*Doctor* Rossi," Bratchford said. "Maybe I should call you *Sister* Rossi. Did you really spend ten years as a... let me see if I have this right—" he checked her record "—as a truck driver for a Purist convent?"

He wanted to get under her skin. They'd only just met. This was another test from High One, and she would pass it as she'd passed all the others he'd set before her.

"The Shrine of the Blessed Landing had a hauler donated by a benefactor," Susannah said. "Sourcing our own supplies saved money. I'm good at learning, so I learned how to fly it."

Bratchford clicked through her record.

"You earned your automatonics doctorate at twenty-one," he said. "Extremely young for such an accomplishment. I suppose you *are* quite good at learning. BST paid for that education. Then again, BST pays for a lot of things while playing catch-up with the League of Planets. And some of those paid-for doctorates—" he waved a hand dismissively "—aren't like the degrees people earned when I was younger. But I'm sure you know this."

A convoy of insults. Insinuating she hadn't earned her degree? What a jerk.

"You got your PhD, then you turned your back on Fleet," Bratchford said. "You joined the Union's bitter enemy. Why?"

He was looking at her record. Anyone with a brain could suss out why she'd left.

"I needed a change, sir. I didn't *turn my back*. I did my mandatory decade, then I cycled out. And the Purist Nation government might be an enemy, but the Purist Church is not. There are over twelve million practitioners of Purism in the Planetary Union."

How long would she be stationed on this isolated ship? Too fucking long, even if it was only a week.

"Twelve million," Bratchford said. "That makes it sound like so many people, when in fact Purism has fewer members in the Union than Sikhs or even Jews."

As if Susannah didn't know that. Purism was a fringe group in the Union, whereas it was the Nation's dominant religion. Depending on how many decimal points one wanted to count, the Nation's *only* religion.

"You can't separate Purism from the Nation," Bratchford said. "Not when the government is a theocracy. Anyway, it doesn't matter. Your country—your *real* country, not your adopted one—sounded the call, and you answered. Welcome to the *Nicholas Otto*, Lieutenant Rossi. Or as we like to call her, *Saint Nick*."

"Thank you, sir."

She didn't want to thank him. She wanted to see him punished for his blasphemy. She had to serve under *him?* Yes, she did. No choice in the matter. BST had paid for her doctorate. In exchange, Fleet required ten years of service from the day she received her PhD, and also required her to be a reservist for life. If she refused this assignment, she'd spend the rest of her life in prison.

The major's eyes flicked upward. She followed his gaze to a small security camera mounted high on the wall.

"Keep in mind, Lieutenant, that on this ship, someone is always watching." Bratchford smiled his yellow-toothed smile. "That *someone* is me. You'll find that although this is a research vessel, I enforce the strict hierarchy of a warship. You might even go so far as to say, on this ship, *I* am the High One."

Blasphemy. Right in her face. Rage swirled in her chest.

"I'll fulfill my obligation to Fleet, sir."

Susannah forced a smile. Perhaps a positive attitude would speed the conversation along. Banished from her adopted homeland, all she could do was trust in High One and wait for Him to reveal His plan.

"That's enough chitchat," Bratchford said. "Let me show you to your lab."

———

Bratchford led her down a passageway. Tarnished rivets held discolored wall panels in place. Panels like these were common on all research vessels—the flip of a "cook" switch in the command center would instantly heat the walls to 1,000 degrees, killing everything inside—microbes, animal life... and people. Vessels like the *Nicholas Otto* often housed horrors of all sizes, things that could wipe out entire planets. The discoloration indicated the cook switch had been flipped more than a few times.

That wasn't a surprise. While it was rare to obtain samples of the Prawatt species, fear trumped scarcity. No one, including Susannah, was certain how many tiny minids it might take to create a root factory, the Prawatt's form of reproduction. Better to err on the side of caution and scorch samples than to risk a root factory quietly growing somewhere in the ship.

The passageway ended at an unremarkable door panel. Bratchford placed his hand on the access plate; the door slid open. Susannah followed him in, instinctively staying one step behind, one step to the right, as Purism dictated she do. She'd have to shake that habit. She'd have to shake many habits.

The room held a single lab table topped by an assembly of dusty beakers, vials, and two gas burners—mainstays of research that had remained constant for centuries while computers and AIs steadily added to the repertoire of science.

Along one wall were the tools of Susannah's trade: incubators, centrifuges, nano-assemblers, raw material crushers, digesters, and dozens of other specialized machines only found in labs built for self-assembling materials.

In the room's far corner sat two plastic crates stacked one on top of the other, both marked with biohazard symbols. As with most classified material, the Fleet never announced its value with silly labels like "top secret" or "for authorized personnel only."

Dust covered everything. Like the rest of old *Saint Nick*, this room had a feel of age, a patina of disuse.

A buzzer sounded, indicating the door had locked.

"This does not look like a very good lab." Susannah gave the gear a cursory once-over. "I don't see a nano-bit compiler. I want to file an equipment request right away. Perhaps you could—"

"Fucking Churchie *garbage*."

She turned at the sound of Bratchford's voice, shocked by the words. It was one thing to throw veiled shade, another to directly insult someone's religion.

His eyes radiated hate. He stepped toward her. Susannah froze in place, riveted by a decade's worth of subservience training. She lowered her gaze. His fetid breath assailed her anew.

"Major Bratchford, my freedom of religion is protected by Union law. I assure you that I will live up to my obligations of—"

She saw the uppercut coming but couldn't react in time. His fist smashed into her jaw, sent her sprawling to the cold floor.

Susannah's world spun. She blinked, not entirely sure what had just happened.

Bratchford gazed down at her, seeming amused and angry all at the same time.

The last time she'd felt a blow like that...

"I haven't met many Purists," he said. "The ones I have met were primitive shitheads, praying to stars, practicing all kinds of ridiculous mysticism. To think that a scientist of your supposed caliber believes... well, it leads me to conclude you're not that smart after all."

He raised his fist and brought it down. Susannah reached up to block the strike but moved too slowly—knuckles smashed into the top of her head. Brilliant flowers of white light exploded before her eyes.

"Ouch! You goddamn *stupid cunt!*"

She felt blood trickling down her scalp, matting her hair.

You must survive.

The voice. Did she hear the voice? It had been so long, *so* long...

The room spun. The *pain* on her head—*in* her head.

"You broke my hand, you fucking pig whore!"

She leaned heavily on one elbow. Bratchford held his right hand curled up tight against his chest. His eyes flared with fury. A strand of spit dangled from his lower lip.

Maybe he was finished. Maybe it was over.

You know it's not over, my child. Let me deal with him.

The voice. It *was* the voice.

"Major, please... I... please don't hurt me."

Bratchford looked at his right hand, waggled it, looked again. He flexed it slowly.

"While I haven't met many Purists, my sister certainly has," he said. "She was on the *Blackmouth*."

Susannah's clarity of thought returned as if by the snap of magical fingers.

The *Blackmouth*. She'd heard about it. The Fleet staffer who'd processed her reservist activation had been only too happy to tell her the details about the Battle of Asteroid X7.

Blackmouth had been captured by Crusaders, the Nation's equivalent of Fleet Raiders. The Crusaders had brought *Blackmouth*'s guns to bear on the PUV *Schild*, which turned and fled rather than firing on another Fleet vessel still filled with Union crew. *Schild*'s retreat left *Boudicca* unprotected. Purist forces capitalized on that opportunity and destroyed *Boudicca*. That much of the story Susannah believed—the rest she'd dismissed as Union propaganda.

"Those animals you churchie bastards call Crusaders held *Blackmouth* for three days," Bratchford said. "By the time Raiders from the *Spurdog* recaptured it, my sister had been raped so many times she'd lost count. She... lost... *count*."

"That's not true," Susannah said. "Crusaders wouldn't rape anyone. Fleet made that up to poison—"

Bratchford kicked her in the ribs. The air inside her rushed out. He grabbed her by the collar and shoved her hard into the lab table, knocking beakers and burners askew.

Her vision filled with unfocused colors, unclear patterns, with swelling, sparkling clouds of gray.

Susannah blacked out.

———

Consciousness came back as a thousand white-hot pin pricks, mental static tickling across her brain.

Susannah became aware of a cold floor against her cheek, against the bare flesh of her legs.

Where were her pants?

She tried to move—her wrists were tied behind her back. Tied with... it felt like a leather belt?

Terror flooded her. She remembered where she was, what was happening.

She craned her head and looked around. A pair of belt-less pants and stained underwear lie crumpled on the floor. Near them, feet in black socks pulled up around otherwise bare legs.

Bratchford.

His hand gripped his erect penis.

His shirt was still on.

Her pants were nowhere to be seen.

Had he... *had he...*

"I waited for you to wake up." Bratchford's voice sounded distant, as if he was in another room. Not here with her—about to *take* her. "I'm sure my sister knew what was happening the whole time. As will you."

He was crazy. *Crazy.*

"I had nothing to do with your sister!" It hurt to speak. Susannah's jaw throbbed. "How can you not realize that story is propaganda?"

He grabbed her ponytail, yanked her head back.

"I *saw my sister in the hospital!* She told me about it, *to my face.*"

He believed what he was saying, believed with all that he was.

But could it have happened? Could Purist Nation troops have raped a woman? *Many* women, *many* times? That was a war crime.

"Hurting me won't help her," Susannah said. "Please, let me go!"

This man wants dominion over you, my child. Take the power back and I will save you.

Susannah's whiplash emotions suffered another twist, another grinding shift. The voice had returned at long last, but how could High One save her?

Take the power back. What did that mean?

Bratchford slowly stroked his cock.

"No, this won't help Janelle," he said. "I know that. But what is it you primitives say? An eye for an eye?"

Power and lust. Take away both, my child. Take them away and see who he really is.

She understood.

It seemed so obvious now.

Hands restrained behind her back, Susannah grunted against the pain, pushing herself up so her naked ass rested on the cold floor.

She looked up at the security camera.

Bratchford looked as well. He laughed.

"You superstitious twat. I told you I watch the cameras here. Only me. *Saint Nick* has a crew of thirty-five and I keep them busy all the time. Oh, and did I forget to mention they don't have clearance or access to this section of the ship? Here, I'm the law. You're going to be my slave. I will rape you again and again, like your soldiers did to my sister. Welcome to hell, *Doctor* Rossi."

She focused her thoughts. No hands, but she still had her eyes. And her mouth.

"I don't mind the rough stuff, Major."

She heard her own voice, ringing with confidence, ripe with eagerness.

Bratchford's smile faded slightly.

"To tell you the truth, I kind of get off on it," Susannah said. "But you should know better than to hit a girl in the face—don't leave marks others can see."

He took a half-step back. He'd expected a mewling victim—her assuredness seemed to surprise him.

"I'll leave any mark I like, Rossi. That, and many more."

She gave him her best lust-drenched grin, looking up at him from under her eyebrows.

"I've been in a Purist convent for a decade," she said. "Know who they let you fuck in a Purist convent? No one. They kicked me out. I'm excommunicated from the Church. I owe those fuckers nothing, but it's been ten years, Major—I owe *myself* something."

She saw confusion in his eyes. This wasn't what he wanted. Fear. That's what he wanted. Terror. Susannah hid those things from him, *withheld* them from him.

He was an ugly man. Sallow face. Disgusting nose hair. A thinning pate that looked ridiculous because his insecurity probably stopped him from shaving it down to the scalp. And that breath. And those *teeth*. She didn't know much about men, but she knew women didn't throw themselves at Tom Bratchford.

Susannah made her voice as thick and sultry as she could.

"I have nowhere to go, Major. There's no need to take something by force that I want to give freely."

Awkwardly, she shifted to her knees.

One sliding knee at a time, she moved toward him.

Bratchford took another half-step back, seemed to catch himself doing it. He stood tall, his chest puffed out like a bad actor pretending to be a great man.

Susannah reached him. Gazing up, casting out passion with her eyes, she leaned forward and kissed the inside of his right knee.

His breath hissed in fast. She kissed him there again, pressed hard. Through her lips, she felt his pounding pulse.

Susannah swirled her tongue across his skin—he tasted terrible.

Finally, a hint of his horrid grin teased the corners of his mouth.

"You want it, do you, you Purist whore? If I'd known what a slut you were I might have gone easier. For a little while, anyway." He gripped his cock, pointed it at her face. "You will *obey* me."

Susannah smiled. "Yes, master."

She leaned forward to take him into her mouth, then let her balance betray her—she fell forward, bumped against his leg, and slipped past to land clumsily on her hip and shoulder.

You're almost there, my child...

Susannah forced out a laugh. "Lost my balance." She raised her bound wrists behind her, making a grand show of how awkward it was. "I know tricks with these hands, Major—tricks I haven't used in a decade."

Could he really be stupid enough to fall for it? Was he that blinded by lust and power and ego?

Bratchford reached for her wrists. He tugged at the belt holding her tight, releasing her.

He grabbed her by the back of her neck, yanked her to her knees, pulled her head close to his cock.

"Now, Lieutenant, show your nonexistent sky daddy what you can do for me."

Yes—he *could* be that stupid.

With her left hand, Susannah grabbed his dick.

Bratchford let out a soft moan.

He liked to punch people, did he?

She slammed a payback uppercut into his naked balls.

He screamed, reached for her hands—she squeezed his dick harder, *twisted* it, and punched him in the balls a second time.

Bratchford tumbled sideways, hit the floor. He coughed, curling into a fetal ball.

He is a sinner, my child. Make him pay for his evil ways.

6

"You have brought shame upon this family. At least your mother isn't alive to see the creature you've become."

The words punched raw holes straight through Anne.

His eyes... the way he looked at her. Like she wasn't worth as much as dog shit he might scrape off his shoe.

"I'm sorry, Daddy," Anne said, her words a desperate whisper.

His fist slammed against the table, a gavel of flesh and bone that had rendered countless guilty verdicts against her all her life long.

"You're sorry, *General Lafferty.*"

Anne nodded. "I'm sorry, General Lafferty."

He wore his black BII service uniform, complete with the two stars of a general positioned above his impressive fruit salad of ribbons and medals. His black peaked cap sat on the table. His bald head gleamed. He must have shaved it within hours of coming here, and he'd trimmed his salt-and-pepper mustache.

How nice—her father wanted to look his best when visiting his daughter in the brig.

Anne couldn't hold his gaze any longer. She stared at the interrogation room's table. The guard had run her handcuffs under a scuffed restraining bar, which kept her from raising her hands more than a few centimeters.

"The report said you almost died." Disgust laced his words. "Too

54

bad you didn't. It would have put an end to this nightmare. I thought you were getting better, Lieutenant. I thought..."

His words trailed off.

Yes, she'd almost died. That's what the doc on *Silverbill* told her. Blood loss. Anne had been lucky the meathead panicked and sliced rather than stabbed. That "luck" resulted in a laceration from her trapezius to her latissimus dorsi, scraping her scapula, slicing flesh open above four ribs. She'd spent the entire three-day trip back to the *Vishvakarman* drydock in *Silverbill*'s state-of-the-art infirmary. Muscle grafts were still healing. She'd been prescribed some serious painkillers—her injuries went far beyond "pinkies," Fleet's usual cure-all—but she hadn't taken any pills that morning. This pain was *hers*, a punishment for not paying attention to the details.

She looked at her father, raised her cuffs until the chain pulled taught against the restraining bar.

"Are these necessary, General?"

He sneered, nostrils flaring wide.

"I can't get you out of them, and I can't get you out of this," he said. "Not this time. Staley took video. I saw what you did, Lieutenant. I saw what you *are*."

Alone in this tiny room, with no listening devices on—because General Bart Lafferty ordered them turned off—even then, he wouldn't call her by name. Nor would he call her *daughter*.

"I know there were... problems," Anne said. "But the mission was a success. Doesn't that matter?"

He sighed, leaned back in his chair.

"Results always matter," he said. "We captured a city of ten thousand and suffered only one death, five casualties total."

Anne knew the stats. Staley had been kind enough to give her the final mission results when he'd visited her in the infirmary.

"One death," Anne said. "It could have been dozens, if not hundreds. One death because I excelled. I did my job. I got the intel. I softened the target. Weren't you the one that taught me to get the job done by any means necessary?"

He stood, sharply and suddenly. For a moment, Anne thought he might slap her.

"What I told you was that *details... fucking... matter*! What I told you was to *not... fucking... get... caught*!"

Anne flinched away, would have backed up to the wall if her handcuffs hadn't held her in place. In an instant she was a little girl again, about to feel the wrath of her angry father for dropping an easy out in softball, for finishing second in the swim meet, for having the unmitigated audacity of saying she missed her mother.

Bart Lafferty believed in corporal punishment. And emotional punishment. Probably any kind of punishment there was, as long as he thought it would guide his daughter's growth.

But Anne knew, deep inside, that his strict, unforgiving discipline was an act of love. He'd worked tirelessly to mold her into a BII operative capable of accomplishing amazing things, of making a difference.

Bart Lafferty sat, blinking madly as he always did when he'd lost his temper and was trying to regain control.

"I can't get you out of this one," he said. "This isn't like the birds and the mice. This isn't like Boomer. Hell, Lieutenant, this isn't even like the nanny."

Anne flushed with shame. She hadn't been able to help it with the birds and the mice. And Boomer... Anne missed that dog. Missed him so much. The nanny? How could that be Anne's fault? Anne and the nanny had been close friends. The nanny had gone away.

"Staley went over my head, the miserable prick," Anne's father said. "He kept it quiet, but he told the right people. You know he's getting a goddamn promotion out of this? He'll be a colonel."

No surprise there. Staley had commanded a massively successful op. Successful because of *Anne*. The fact that her father put her on the mission would not be factored in. Technically, a parent couldn't have direct authority over his own child—that meant the credit for Anne's success rolled upward to Staley, and there it stopped.

"What you did to that woman," her father said. "It's... it's barbaric."

Barbaric? No. It had been *necessary*.

"General, I needed intel to keep our assault force safe. I made an asset of an enemy combatant, and from her, acquired mission-critical information."

Her father laughed, a hopeless sound devoid of joy or humor.

"*Enemy combatant?* Olivia Wagner was seventeen years old, a runaway from the Neptune Net Colony. She'd been in Eden for all of four months. She worked at a goddamn *pretzel stand*, Lieutenant."

Anne and her father sat in silence. Did he want her to feel bad? It had taken extreme measures to achieve mission success. Anne hadn't flinched from her duty.

Her father absently rubbed his bald head. "Staley had a full autopsy done. Pathologist said the amputations took place over the course of three or four days." He sagged in his chair. "The victim had open sores in her mouth from the constant gag. She'd screamed so much her larynx was raw and bleeding. Staley filed charges, Lieutenant. What you did is considered a war crime."

A war crime—punishable by firing squad or venting, if found guilty.

Her father sat up straight, tried to regain his composure, to be the professional soldier he'd been all of Anne's life.

"Lieutenant, do you know what you did was wrong?"

Wrong? He'd sent her on the mission. She'd executed the mission. Maybe it hadn't gone exactly according to plan, but she knew what her father wanted to hear.

"Yes, General. I know it was wrong."

The ethics of it didn't really matter anymore. No tapping in her head—the dark impulse was gone. Olivia had been the last. If Anne got out of this spot of trouble, she knew she'd never again be burdened by that urge.

"You are your own worst enemy," her father said. "You stop yourself from being great. I've seen many sailors and Raiders and operatives like you over the years. Well, not like you in *that* way, but people who can't control themselves, who can't master their demons. The difference between mediocrity and greatness is a decision, Lieutenant. You have yet to make that decision."

The door opened. Master Warrant Officer Sheila Drummond—her father's long-suffering aide-de-camp—leaned in.

"My apologies, General," she said. "There's someone here you need to speak with."

He slapped the table. "I told you to leave us be. If I have to tell you twice, you won't be hap—"

"*Now*, General Lafferty," Drummond said.

He leaned back, somewhat surprised.

Anne had spent time around Drummond. The woman was a consummate officer. She followed orders to the letter. She pushed back only when she knew doing so was for the good of her CO.

Anne's father stood and walked out with Drummond, who shut the door behind him. Anne stared at the peaked hat, which he'd left behind. Jet black, BII's primary uniform color. Silver chain-and-key embellishments on the brim. The silver cap device of the department's crest, a six-pointed cog with crossed swords behind it, ringed by the words KNOWLEDGE, DISCOVERY, PROTECTION.

Her father hated her. She *repulsed* him. It wasn't fair. Things got a little out of hand with Olivia, sure, but Anne had needed information. And besides, the tapping was gone. Anne was done with it. It had taken her most of her life to beat it, but finally, she had.

If only that meathead hadn't cut her.

If only she'd been able to move Olivia somewhere else.

If only—

The door opened. Anne's father came in, accompanied by a forty-something woman in a charcoal gray Raider service uniform.

He shut the door, no longer looking quite as angry, quite as despondent.

"Lieutenant Lafferty," he said, "this is Major Maia Whittaker, Fleet logistics."

Logistics? What was going on?

Anne shrugged. "I'm afraid I can't stand and salute you, Major Whittaker."

The woman held a sheet of flexipaper. No, wait—was that *real* paper?

"I understand, Lieutenant," Whittaker said. "Word of your successful mission reached my department. I'm here to give you your new assignment. You're being promoted to Major. You'll be intel chief on a Fleet warship."

Anne stared, dumbfounded. A promotion? A command position?

Had her father pulled strings after all? No, no way—he would have told her.

"This is... unexpected," Anne said.

Whittaker nodded. "I imagine so. There is, however, a condition."

Anne glanced at the handcuffs holding her to the table. "What condition is that, Major?"

"You must complete a two-year stint aboard a classified vessel," Whitaker said. "If you do, any and all charges against you will be dropped. If you choose not to serve aboard this ship, you will be immediately prosecuted for your actions at Eden."

Anne looked at her father. He stood there, rigid, a single tear rolling down his left cheek.

In her twenty-six years, Anne could remember Bart Lafferty crying one time, and one time only—when his wife, Anne's mother, had died of cancer.

"This is for your own good," he said. "The ship is the *Keeling*. You're volunteering—and you *will* volunteer—to serve on the *Crypt*."

7

Spec-3 John Bennett sat quietly, staring out the tram car's window at the sprawling vastness of Gofannon Station, and far beyond it, the grayish-tan behemoth of Saturn and its rings. Everything he owned he either carried on his person or was stuffed in his duffel, stashed in the rack above his seat.

Gofannon was Fleet's biggest dry dock. Fifteen ships were docked within its massive, spider-web frame, including some he'd served on: the heavy cruiser *Jakarta*; the destroyer *Tasunke-Witko*; the frigates *Vahan* and *Clipeus*. And the heavy cruiser *Toronto*, site of the worst fighting he'd ever endured.

A few sailors wore dress whites. Most wore either light gray utility coveralls or gray and black service uniforms. The Raiders on the tram were all in cammies, some with sleeves folded to show off the arms they'd worked so hard to bulk up. Three striker pilots in this car, all in dress blues. John wondered where they were going. There were dozens of civilians, too, with their clearance badges openly displayed, and a curious amount of Globals in their various green duty uniforms and fatigues. Weird to see surface-pounders here, as Saturn had neither land nor water on which to operate, and any planetary air wings were probably composed of Harrah pilots operating the spherical voidcraft unique to that race.

"Ship incoming," one of the civvy techs called out. "Starboard side, about three o'clock."

Heads turned. People who were standing and holding handrails leaned over to look out the car's windows. They wanted to catch a glimpse of one of the galaxy's most beautiful sights—a ship entering realspace. John's starboard-side window seat gave him an unobstructed view.

Roughly two klicks out, a dim, purple light began to pulse. It flashed faster and faster, brighter and brighter, grew larger and larger. Like a glove with a hand sliding into it, the light stretched, turning white. Other colors sparkled as the glowing shape took form. A destroyer? No, a heavy cruiser.

"It's the *Chicago*," said a Raider with his gear bag slung over his shoulder. RADULSKI on his fatigues. He had the blue skin of a Satirli 6 native, something you didn't see often in Fleet. "I served on her for a year. She's a beaut."

The glittering shroud tightened around the ship. John could make out the armor-thick prow, then the double-barreled forward artillery batteries—one topside, one bottomside—then the stubby directional thrusters, the rear topside battery, and, finally, the chemjet ports.

The *Chicago* sparkled like it was covered in crushed diamonds, a piece of high technology dipped in magic. That was the moment when a ship was blind from punching back into realspace, helpless to anyone that wished her harm.

"I never get tired of watching that," someone said.

The passengers murmured in agreement.

There was something divine about watching ships enter or exit punch-space. John wasn't immune to the spectacle, not even after decades of service, of seeing dozens—if not hundreds—of ships make those transitions. It wasn't just the stunning visual display, there was something *eternal* about it. Punch-space had allowed Humanity to escape the Sol system, ensuring the species could spread out and survive even if Earth itself were to be destroyed.

Punch-drives let man travel the stars—the curvine let him fight amongst them. Two aspects of the same tech, from what little John had bothered to learn. A punch-drive pinched curves of space-time together, drastically shortening the distance between planets. People said it wasn't *actually* faster-than-light travel, but that was a semantic argument for eggheads; FTL was FTL, as far as John was concerned. A curvine—shorthand for *space-time curvature turbine*—allowed a ship to travel along threads of space-time in a manner not all that different from the way the tram car he was in rode along its elevated rail.

To enter punch-space, a ship had to be in a punch-zone near the right kind of planet and had to use the curvine to accelerate at a fixed rate in a straight line for a minute or more. That made them sitting ducks for enemy fire. John had heard of two warships that had taken fire while accelerating for a punch—those ships had never been heard from again.

He watched *Chicago*'s glitter fade to nothingness, leaving only the ship behind: gray, bulky, heavy, blocky, built for war in the void.

A young Raider standing in the aisle lightly nudged John, pointed at a docked ship.

"Look at that mutha," the man said. "Ever see a ship that big?"

The Raider—a Spec-2, SHAMDI on his fatigues—was handcuffed. An MP in LASH armor stood close behind him.

"It's the *Akathaso*," John said. "Biggest carrier ever. I saw it docked at *Vishvakarman* a couple of months ago. It's Admiral Epperson's new flagship."

That was the way of Admirals—they always wanted the biggest, the best, the newest.

The young man huffed. "Epperson overcompensate much?"

The MP leaned closer to the young raider. "Do me a favor, Shamdi—don't badmouth the brass. I'd like to get out of this without having to file a statement about your behavior."

"Don't get your panties in a bunch," Shamdi said. "I'll be out of your hair soon enough."

Shamdi looked to be about twenty-four. Twenty-five, tops. Maybe the kid had missed muster, and MPs rounded him up. That happened a lot, especially after combat. John had never missed muster, not once, but he didn't judge when others did.

"I'm heading for the *Ishi* myself. I'm John Bennett."

"Nitzan Shamdi."

John nodded toward the cuffs. "Big night out or something?"

"Yeah," Shamdi said. "Something like that."

They rode on in silence, the tram whipping them along the dry dock's center ring.

John saw the frigate *Ishlangu*, the ship that would take him to his new assignment.

"*Ishi*'s a Dhal-class," he said. "I served on one of those, the *Kalkan*. Good Raider quarters. Small, but at least we weren't sleeping on the training deck. Better than the Element class before her. I spent a year aboard the *Gallium*. Was like living in a toilet. You like the *Ishi*?"

Shamdi shrugged. "I suppose I'll find out soon enough."

So much for John's guess that Shamdi was late for muster. But if that wasn't the kid's ship, why was he heading there in chains?

The tram continued to roll along Gofannon's outer ring, closing in on *Ishi*. While significantly smaller than *Chicago* or *Toronto*, *Ishi* was no lightweight. Like all Dhal-class frigates, she was 150 meters from front armor to her rear chemjet ports, 19 meters at the beam, and 23 meters high.

Ishi's main offensive power consisted of two Type24 guns, one mounted flush bottomside, the other topside on a barbette that let it shoot over the ship's single-layer superstructure and the clear, shallow dome of her bubble-deck. The 127-millimeter, 54-caliber weapons were a mainstay of Fleet frigates and destroyers. While not as insanely powerful as the bigger artillery pieces found on cruisers, assault ships and carriers, the versatile 24s packed a world of hurt.

The tram slowed to a stop at pier four's station. The arrival chime sounded. The doors slid open.

John grabbed his duffel and stepped out onto the platform's metal-grate deck. He could see down through the grate to the station's main level, and to the wide pier against which the *Ishlangu* was docked.

Up and down the tram's four cars, men and women stepped out, duffle bags slung over their shoulders. Raiders in fatigues, including the blue-skinned Radulski. Sailors in dress whites or service grays. Two men in BII black. No striker pilots or crew, which wasn't a surprise considering frigates like *Ishi* didn't carry voidcraft.

Five of those people, Shamdi included, were handcuffed and accompanied by a LASHed MP. Spec-1 Raider MAFI, so big John wondered if he could fit in standard armor. Red-haired Spec-3 medic

WATSON, whose darting eyes made John think she might be a druggie. Spec-3 Raider TAYLOR, a crawler tech's insignia on her collar. Warrant Officer BANG, a smiling, sunglasses-wearing Raider pilot so casually confident she made her handcuffs seem like a fashion choice rather than restraints.

Five people in chains. All, apparently, headed to the *Ishi*. What the hell was going on?

Everyone filtered to the updowns and dropped to the station deck, where a Raider master sergeant waited in front of a scuffed muster line painted on the pier. He wore an eight-pointed cover, bent bill set low over his eyes.

"Raiders," he said, "*fall in!*"

John recognized the voice, like steel wool for vocal cords, then the face—Francis "Book" Sands. Small universe.

"Step on the line when I call your name." Sands read from a flexi-paper. "Laior. Perry. Mafi. Sarvacharya. Bang. Bennett. Taylor. Shamdi. Oneida. Radulski. Abshire. Honored guests from the military police, kindly line up behind your charges."

As most of the tram's passengers headed down the pier, John got on the line along with ten other Raiders.

Oneida, Perry, and Abshire had the wide-eyed look of soldiers just out of boot. Laior as well, her expression all the more comical thanks to her big blue eyes and bleach-white skin.

Sands tucked his flexipaper under one arm.

"I am Master Sergeant Francis Sands. You will refer to me as *Master Sergeant Sands*. You *will not* refer to me as *Top*. For those of you who arrived in restraints, I have the right to keep you in them as long as I deem necessary. I trust that if I, in my infinite wisdom and boundless benevolence, decide to let you out of those chains, you will behave like proper Raiders and will not be stupid. Am I correct in that assumption?"

"*Yes, Master Sergeant*," the chained Raiders called out in unison.

"*Magnificent*," Sands said, stretching out the first syllable. He looked at the ranking MP. "Release these warriors on my recognizance."

The MPs undid the restraints, then headed for the updowns.

"We will board *Ishlangu* shortly," Sands said. "*Ishi* will take us to our assignment. Do not ask me or anyone else where that assignment is. Do not ask me or anyone else how long it will take to get there. You are passengers. Act accordingly. The platoon's commanding officer is Lieutenant Lindros. The platoon's exec is Warrant Officer Winter. If any of us three tell you to do something, you do it. Have I clearly educated you as to your immediate chain of command?"

"*Yes, Master Sergeant!*"

"*Magnificent,*" Sand said. "A word of caution to you formerly restrained Raiders. If you lugubrious lummoxes do not understand what *on my recognizance* means, it means everything you do reflects on me. If you pull some dumbass stunt, that reflects poorly on me. If you get out of line, that reflects poorly on me. I assure you that if you make *me* look bad, I will make *you* look bad, vis-a-vis, a prison work detail with all the trimmings. This is not something you wish to endure, for *endure* it you will, as even the smallest transgression will be met with a shitstorm of biblical proportions. Do I make myself clear?"

"*Yes, Master Sergeant!*"

Sands had come a long way from the pimply-faced string-bean John knew twenty years earlier. God, but did time fly.

"Master Sergeant," a Raider shouted, "may I ask a question?"

Maybe *shouted* wasn't the right word for it. The guy was so loud he could have been heard on the far side of the drydock's main ring.

Sands's cheek twitched. He strode down the line to John's left and stood in front of the inquisitive Raider.

"Spec-One Jim Perry, you interrupted my introduction," Sands said. "I'm sure that your question is of the utmost importance and could not possibly wait until I was finished."

John hid his smile. Perry had to be fresh out of boot to be this stupid.

"Yes, Master Sergeant," Perry shouted. "I believe that it is."

"Then by all means, for the edification of your platoon mates, ask away."

"Master Sergeant, what is a *lugubrious lummox*? I'm not sure how to... ah... process that, Master Sergeant."

Sands took a step backward. "Crawler Crew Chief Robin Taylor, do *you* have any concerns about my vocabulary?"

"No, Master Sergeant," Taylor said. "None whatsoever!"

"*Magnificent.* Spec-One Neal Abshire, are you flummoxed by my luminescent lexicon?"

Abshire snorted a laugh. Just a fast one, a choked off gunshot through the nose.

"No, Master Sergeant," he said. "I am not flummoxed."

"Color me delighted," Sands said. "On my command, all of you, except for Spec-One Perry and Spec-Three Bennett, will take your gear and follow this pier to the *Ishlangu's* second access hatch, where you will be led to your berth. If you put one toe out of line, I will see to it that said toe is cut off. Spec-One Perry, do you know what *cutting off a toe* means?"

"Yes, Master Sergeant!"

"*Magnificent,*" Sands said. "Do you know what *do pushups until I grow weary of watching your puny toothpick arms tremble in agony* means?"

"Uh... um..."

John could almost hear the gears turning in Perry's head. They were small gears.

"It means you want me to do pushups until you tell me to stop, Master Sergeant?"

"*Magnificent,*" Sands said. "Drop and start counting."

John had just enough peripheral vision to see a wide cinderblock of a Raider fall forward over his toes, back stiff as a board, to land on his palms. Perry snapped off pushups with perfect form. His arms most certainly did not look like puny toothpicks. He bellowed the number of each rep.

"Raiders, fall out," Sands said. "Double-time."

John remained at attention as eight raiders grabbed their duffels and jogged down the pier.

As Perry counted away, Sands turned on his right heel, walked until he was in front of John, stopped smart, turned on his left heel, and stepped close.

Same blue eyes, the skin at their corners more wrinkled. Same black caterpillar tangle of eyebrows, a bit thicker and a bit more tangled than before. That small, curved scar on his left cheek had faded some, softened some. Good God... Twenty years in the blink of an eye. Why did the people who survived always have to get so damn *old*?

"If it isn't John Bennett," Sands said. "I thought I knew what ugly was, then I didn't see you for two decades and I forgot. Now here you are, and you know what?"

"You remember what ugly is, Master Sergeant?"

"*Magnificent*, Bennett."

The grizzled, *I-will-kill-you-for-something-as-trivial-as-not-pass-ing-the-potatoes-quickly-enough* face broke into a smile.

"It's good to see you, John."

No one seemed to be watching, so John smiled back.

"You, too, Master Sergeant. Looks like you've done well for yourself."

"Thanks to you, I have." Sands glanced at John's rank insignia. "And you're in the same place you were when you took a wet-behind-the-ears boot under your wing and saved his ass more than once. How is it possible you haven't been promoted, John?"

"I have no idea, Master Sergeant. Perhaps the promotions board did not appreciate the artistry of the anatomically correct vaginas I drew on my exam."

Sands laughed, then cut it off quick, as if laughter wasn't allowed in his tough-guy persona.

"Forty-*five*," Perry yelled. "Forty-*six*. Forty-*seven*."

Sands glanced at the thick-bodied kid. "Can you believe how young they make them these days?"

John listened for a moment as Perry shot past fifty without slowing or breaking form. A kid his age should be out chasing tail and pounding brews with his buddies, not preparing to ship out so he could kill or be killed.

"No, Master Sergeant," John said. "I really can't."

They watched the younger man go past sixty, then seventy. Perry didn't just *do* the pushups, he *attacked* them.

"This is his first deployment," Sands said. "Of any kind. He doesn't know a bullet from his balls. From what I read, he's as gung-ho as gung-ho gets. Bennett, I'd appreciate it if you'd do for him what you did for me."

John sighed.

"I'll do whatever the Master Sergeant asks, but I would like to point out I'm fucking *old*. You don't have someone younger in the platoon who can blunder and thunder with this eager beaver?"

Sands grimaced, spoke quietly. "This isn't exactly a crack outfit. There are some bad people in this platoon, John. I can't tell you more than that. *Beaver* here is the kind of kid who could be a good Raider. You can say *no*, but I'm asking you to help him out."

The existence of time sheared, slipped away, and for an instant, John found himself looking at eighteen-year-old Spec-1 Frankie Sands, not a man twenty years older and six ranks higher.

"Sure thing, Book," John said. "I got your back."

Sands nodded once, and just like that, the memory-fed illusion of youth vanished.

"Spec-One Perry," Sands said, "get your ass up."

Perry hopped up and stood at attention. "Yes, Master Sergeant!"

Sands shook his head. "You really are an eager one, aren't you? From now on, Perry, your name is *Beaver*. Do you understand?"

Perry's face wrinkled with confusion.

"Uh, Master Sergeant, may I ask a—"

"A beaver is an aquatic mammal known for its supple fur and earnest work ethic," Sands said. "Do you hear me, Spec-One Beaver?"

"Spec-One Beaver understands loud and clear, Master Sergeant!"

"*Magnificent*," Sands said. "I have to wait here for the next batch of fuckups. Bennett, escort Spec-One Beaver to his first assignment."

John and Perry grabbed their duffels and hurried down the pier. The pier's arced, crysteel roof let them gaze out at *Ishlangu*.

"Lord almighty," Perry said. "Just look at her."

From afar, she was a beauty. Up this close, only a dozen meters away, she was a hard-edged goddess of war. Thick plates of armor—reactive atop composite atop reactive—would let her shrug off most small missile strikes and survive a direct hit or three from enemy artillery.

Running alongside the superstructure's side was a ten-meter-long, five-meter diameter EDP—*exterior deployment fortification*—an armored tube commonly known as a "trench." During close-in combat, TASH-suited Raiders took cover in trenches until it was time for them to repel boarding attempts or cross the gap and attack enemy vessels.

"I can't believe I get to jump out of *that*," Perry said. "Scream, aim, and fire, am I right?"

John had no idea what the kid was talking about.

"We have to report in," he said. "We can walk slower, give you a couple of minutes to recover."

Perry glanced at him, forehead wrinkled.

"Recover? From what?"

"You just did a hundred pushups."

Perry thought for a moment. "A hundred and three, actually."

The kid wasn't sweating. He wasn't winded in the least. Ah, youth.

"Let's get going," John said. "I like my toes attached to my feet. Oh —" he offered his hand "—John Bennett."

They shook. The kid had a grip as strong as a deck plate clamp.

"Jim Perry. Ain't you a little old to still be a spec?"

John gestured down the pier. Shoulder to shoulder, the two Raiders walked toward the access hatch.

"I prefer the term *finely aged*," John said.

Perry stared, blinked, then his face broke into a big-toothed smile.

"Oh, you mean like cheese?" He laughed a laugh almost as loud as his bellowing voice. "That's funny, man. Like *cheese!*"

John had meant *like wine*, but whatever.

"Where you from, Beaver?"

"I'm from Reiger, but I grew up on Wilson 6. I know, I know, League of Planets and all that shit, right? Fucking gene-queens. I ain't part of the cold war with them, I hate 'em just as much as you do."

"I don't hate—"

"I hope we get to fight them," Beaver yelled. "When we do, those bastards are for the sand. That's a thing people say on Wilson 6, on account of how you can bury someone in the desert there and they never rot. The bodies wind up all stiff-stiff, like a statue, and—"

John put his hand on the man's shoulder.

"Beaver, anyone ever tell you that you talk too much?"

"Yeah, I hear that a lot."

"Lesson one about being a Raider," John said. "*Don't* talk too much. One idea at a time. Got it?"

Beaver nodded.

"Good," John said. "Let's report."

They walked on, two soldiers separated by three decades of age, yet both took in every detail of the frigate like they were virgins and *Ishi* was going to show them the ways of the world.

They reached the second access hatch, where two sailors were waiting.

"This is gonna be awesome," Beaver yelled.

"Second lesson," John said. "You're not in boot anymore. You don't have to yell everything."

Beaver's brow furrowed.

"But I'm not yelling," he yelled. "What do you mean, Bennett?"

Well, wasn't this going to be fun? Sands's thanks wouldn't be enough—the bill would come due with several drinks.

"Just get inside, Beaver. And let me ask the questions."

8

Trav sat on his bunk, slowly winding his titanium stopwatch. He didn't know much about artificial gravity, but he knew it and the real thing shared one defining trait—on a planet or on a ship, shit always runs downhill.

Ishlangu's lowest deck served as an auxiliary storage area for extra cargo, rescued fleeters or regular spacers, room for additional Raider platoons, or—in this case—troop transport.

Even down here, though, the *Ishi* was nice. It had the dings and scratches expected of a warship, but all were painted over. *Everything* was clean because Captain Vesna Jakobsson wouldn't have it any other way.

In that regard, at least, she hadn't changed a bit since the Academy.

Collapsible walls separated the new *Keeling* crew members. One section for Raiders, one for enlisted sailors, one for NCOs, and one for officers. As the XO, he was *Keeling*'s highest-ranking crew member on the *Ishlangu*, which allotted him a bit of privacy. Trav had a small section to himself: a cot, a small table with an infodeck, and a folding chair.

He had yet to walk around and meet his new crewmates. He needed to do that, he knew, but his heart wasn't in it. His job on the *Keeling* would be to implement the captain's commands and complement the captain's command style. Would it be the usual role of "good cop" captain and "bad cop" XO? Or was the captain a steel-spiked prick, which made it Trav's role to play the understanding confidant? That lack of knowledge gave him all the excuse he needed to hide away, for at least a little while longer.

The stopwatch had been a first anniversary present from Molly. The thing was a real work of art. It tracked the primary time, plus two additional splits. The ideal gift for the man who might have to simultaneously track outgoing torpedoes and multiple incoming missile salvos.

On the back, she'd had engraved: *someday we'll have all the time in the world.* Typical passive-aggressive behavior from his wife. Even back then, still in the start of their lives together, she'd been annoyed by the amount of time Trav had to spend away from home.

A knock on his divider wall—a formality, when whoever was there could have simply walked through the open space that served as Trav's door.

"Enter."

A woman in BII black service kit entered. LAFFERTY. Green eyes, *hard* eyes, and a stubble of red hair on her shaved head. A major's silver circle on her collar—Trav felt a pang of jealousy even as he stood.

"XO Ellis, I'm Anne Lafferty, your intel chief."

He shook her hand. Inside a ship, salutes were reserved for the first time one met a CO, when one met an officer of command rank, or when one was reporting for an ass-chewing.

"I gathered up the highest-ranking crew member from each department," Lafferty said. "I thought you'd like to meet them as soon as possible."

A hint of rebuke in her tone, telling him he should have done this already. She wasn't wrong.

Trav nodded. "Thank you, Major. That's a good idea."

Lafferty waved four people into the small space. In front, a lieutenant with engineering insignia—KERKHOFFS—and a navigation Warrant Officer JG—ERICKSON—both in sailor service uniforms. Behind them was a pair of Raiders in fatigues. A thin, young male,

Lieutenant LINDROS, and WINTER, a thicker, older, female warrant officer.

"I'm Sascha Kerkhoffs, engineering department head."

She was tall, only a tad shorter than him. As department head, she would manage all of engineering, including punch-drives, curvine, electrical, and environmental. Her blonde hair was a little long for regulations—she'd either have to keep it in a ponytail or get it cut.

"Engineering department head of a ship you've never set foot on," Trav said. "You're in the deep end, just like me."

She nodded. A hint of a smile. Where Lafferty's eyes were hard as stone, Kerkhoffs were relaxed.

Erickson extended his hand. When he did, Trav caught Kerkhoffs giving the man an inadvertent side-eye and small sneer.

"Doug Erickson, navigation chief."

He was a good fifteen pounds over regulation weight for a man of his height. He seemed soft, if not outright doughy, both in looks and personality. Here because he was a good navigator or from some white-collar crime? Perhaps both.

"I'm told Ops is already onboard *Keeling*," Erickson said.

Ops—the operations department head, and Erickson's direct superior. At least that department would have ship-specific leadership experience.

Chief Erickson had a smarminess to him. He seemed like the kind of man who thought his charm could get him anything he wanted.

Trav nodded toward Kerkhoffs. "You two know each other?"

She sneered again, a tiny thing, but unmistakable. She wasn't good at hiding her emotions.

"We served together on the *Bismuth*," Erickson said, some of his fake charm crumbling away.

The two had a history, and not a good one. Trav would check on that later.

Trav looked at Lindros. "I take it you're the top Raider?"

"Lieutenant Gary Lindros, platoon commander. I've got my work cut out for me. We're a new unit. Thirty-seven Raiders, and eleven of them arrived in chains. *In chains.* I need to know what they did, XO."

Lafferty shot him a glare. "As I already informed you, Lieutenant, that information is classified. Need-to-know only."

Eleven Raiders in chains. Clearly, Trav wasn't the only one sent to the *Keeling* as a punishment.

"I'll need to know damn soon," Lindros sad. "Hard to lead people if you don't know the *color* of their metal, so to speak."

The color of their metal—a subtle but clear insinuation at Trav's new nickname, *Yellowbelly*. As if he could, or should, expect anything less from a soldier willing to throw himself across the gap into enemy fire. Trav would have few fans amongst the Raiders. He'd have to do something about the perception that he was a coward.

But was the nickname accurate? He didn't know anymore.

Lindros nodded toward Winter.

"This is my PXO, Katharina Winter," he said. "I met her all of an hour ago. As you can imagine, it will take a while to develop unit cohesion."

Winter's chin jutted out. The PXO—platoon executive officer—looked like the kind of person who could take a punch, be it physical *or* mental. Her broad shoulders were as wide as Lindros's, even though she was a full head shorter than him. A constellation of small scars pocked her left cheek, their color slightly darker than her light brown skin. Trav had seen marks like that before—the leftovers of molten metal burning through a TASH suit visor. Winter had seen her share of combat.

"Don't you worry, Lieutenant Ellis," she said. "Our platoon will be ready to eat iron and shit steel in no time flat."

Now *there* was the positivity Raiders were famous for. Lindros blushed. Maybe he hadn't realized how negative he sounded until his second in command spoke up.

"I didn't get a head count yet," Trav said. "How many of us newbs are down here?"

"Seventy-seven," Lafferty said. "Including thirty-seven Raiders, who are an addition to the crew."

That meant forty replacements for former crew—all to replace casualties from the last patrol? People cycled off ships all the time, but most ships didn't have a nickname like "the *Crypt*."

"So you four represent engineering, intel, ops, and Raiders," Trav said. "Anyone from weapons?"

"No department heads," Erickson said. "We have some gunner's mates, torpedo mates, and sensor operators. Weps and Guns must either be aboard or coming from somewhere else."

Weps, the weapons department head, and *Guns*, the artillery chief. Trav hoped they were, indeed, already aboard. Based on the four people present alone, there wasn't a lot of experienced *Keeling* hands to be had.

The 1MC—the primary public address channel that let personnel speak to the entire ship—let out a whistle, followed by a voice Trav knew all too well.

"Attention, *Ishlangu* guests, this is the captain speaking. I'm Colonel Vesna Jakobsson. Welcome aboard. We will ferry you to the rendezvous point, where you will transfer to your new vessel. The trip will take three days. I am not authorized to tell you where we are going, but I can tell you it's not the pleasure troughs on Casmara."

Past the collapsible walls, Trav heard laughter from the future *Keeling* crew.

"Mess schedule will be posted soon, as will availability of the training deck," Vesna said. "When not at mess or training, I expect all guests to be in your assigned berths. Kindly stay out of my crew's way. They are here to operate my ship, not to answer your questions. That is all."

Even in the Academy, Vesna had the voice of command. Her short speech, while friendly enough, left zero doubt that on this ship she was God, and transgressions against God would not go unpunished.

Another knock on the collapsible wall.

"Enter," Trav said.

The four *Keeling* crew members made room for a young ensign.

"Lieutenant Ellis, the captain requests you in her quarters."

———

"Lieutenant Ellis reporting as ordered, sir."

Vesna was in her captain's conference room, sitting in an office chair at the head of the eight-person table. A couch on one side of the table, three padded, folding chairs on the other. On the bulkhead was an oblong shield made of stretched cow hide, brown spots on white— an ishlangu, the shield of ancient Zulu warriors.

"Ensign, you're dismissed," Vesna said. "Close the door on your way out."

The ensign did as she was told.

Vesna stood. She smiled wide. "For fate's sake, give me a hug."

They embraced. It felt so good to hold her again. She still smelled the same.

"Great to see you, Vez."

"Same here, Trav. Same here."

She gave him two solid thumps on the back, then returned to her seat. She gestured to the folding chair at her left.

Trav sat. "Ciprian's got to be four now. How is he? And Lucian?"

"Lucian is getting *fat*, and I love it," Vesna said. "Ciprian just turned six."

Six. Time flew by so fast.

"How about your daughter, Trav? Aven would be... almost three now?"

Trav hadn't spoken to Vesna in at least a year, hadn't seen her in over four, yet she remembered how old his daughter was? She'd always had a mind for numbers.

"Aven is doing well," Trav said. "Molly is an amazing mother."

An amazing mother who had done it all on her own, for far too long.

"Molly has to be upset about your assignment," Vesna said.

Trav looked at the conference table. He nodded.

"She's pregnant," he said. "Six months."

Vesna winced. "Oh, Trav."

The understanding of one Fleet parent to another. Every deployment meant your family might never see you again.

"Things weren't great between Molly and I even before this happened," Trav said. "I wouldn't be surprised if she divorces me before this stint is up."

Vesna reached across the table and squeezed Trav's hand. No words were needed. The demanding life of Fleet personnel led to the end of many relationships.

She let go and sat back.

Trav stared into the eyes of his dear friend, his former lover.

"What am I getting into, Vez? What do you know about the *Keeling*?"

She stiffened, shifting from a *we should catch up over a fifth of tequila* face to an all-business demeanor.

"What little I do know, I can't tell you. I'm sorry they busted you down."

As cadets, they'd boasted to each other about who would advance the fastest, who would make XO first, who would command first. She'd won all those races. She'd been a rank above Trav even before his demotion to lieutenant. Now? Vesna had a legitimate shot at stars —one for a general, two for a vice admiral, maybe even three for a full admiral. Trav, on the other hand, would be lucky if he commanded a transport ship.

From the day they'd met as plebes, they'd competed against each other at everything and anything. Chess. Basketball. Cribbage. Who could get the highest grade, the highest vidgame score, who could eat the most chocolate pudding, who could juggle the most baseballs. They studied their asses off. They attacked every drill and assignment like it was the last thing preventing them from captaining a carrier. They fooled around whenever they could, which wasn't that often— cadet fraternization was frowned upon, to say the least.

In their final year at the Academy, they decided to end their romantic relationship. They both thought they weren't ready for a long-term commitment. Then, only a year after they'd split, Vesna found Lucian—a civilian and an *excellent* cook—and Trav found Molly.

"Trav, what happened at X7? What *really* happened? I read the after-action report. The *Blackmouth* was under enemy control. Williams should have gone after it, not ordered a retreat. When he went down, you could have countermanded his order and engaged. You didn't. That doesn't sound like the man I know."

Correction—it didn't sound like the man she *used* to know.

Trav remembered the screams, the fire, the stench of burning flesh.

"It was bad," he said. "We'd taken significant damage. Before he was incapacitated, Williams ordered us to get *Schild* out of there, to save the ship. When he went down, I implemented his orders."

Which was only partially true.

The whole truth was, in that crucial moment, Trav thought about Molly and Aven, about how he might never see them again. He thought of his unborn child.

The smoke, the blood, the screaming, the bodies...

"You should have targeted *Blackmouth*," Vesna said.

Yes, he should have. Better to finish off your own ship than let the enemy use that ship's guns against your side. Instead of doing what he knew was right, he'd followed Williams's orders, because that got the *Schild* clear, got *him* clear.

"You weren't there, Vez."

"You came off the line of battle," Vesna said. "Because of that, we lost *Boudicca*. Hiroshi was on that ship. So was Skinny. They're dead."

Trav stared. Hiroshi Maeda and "Skinny" Vinnie Payton. Academy classmates. Back in the day, the four of them were thick as thieves.

Now Hiroshi and Skinny were gone.

If he'd stayed and fought, would they still be alive?

If he'd stayed and fought, would Molly be a widow? Would Aven and Kinley grow up fatherless, just as he'd done? What if Molly went off the deep end like Trav's grandmother? What if his daughters grew up in squalor, surrounded by worthless old coins and books with covers ripped off, and dead bugs forever frozen in clear crysteel, and a huge bundles of old sticks and—

"Trav?"

He sniffed in a sharp breath. He'd lost his place in time.

"Let me guess," Vesna said. "Thinking about your grandmother?"

Vez knew. Of course she did. She'd been the first person he ever opened up to about his home life, about losing his parents at an early age and growing up in Meemaw's Stinky House of Weird. Vez knew things about Trav's childhood he still hadn't shared with his wife.

"You used to do that during finals," Vesna said. "Or when we were on the *Kippen*, and they told us we'd be kicked out of the Academy if we didn't repair the curvine in thirty minutes flat. Remember?"

How could he forget? Near Neptune, the instructor had quietly shut down *Kippen*'s main drive, demanded Trav and Vez find the problem and repair it or they'd get the boot. Trav had no idea how to fix it. Neither had Vez.

But Hiroshi had.

Such a loss.

"No," Trav said, "I didn't know they were on the *Boudicca*."

"Your ship *left* them. You were in *command*, Travis, because you're supposed to be capable of making the tough decisions."

He met her hard stare.

"You weren't *there*, Vez, all right?"

She put her hands flat on the table. She did that when she'd had enough—a tic of hers then, a tic of hers still.

"When we rendezvous with *Keeling*, make sure your crew are in the bubble," she said. "You will all want to see it."

Any fleeter would want to see their new ship. So why did her words sound so foreboding?

"I need all personal weapons collected from your crew," Vesna said. "And anything metal. I mean *anything*, Trav. No knives. No brass knuckles. Not even a souvenir spoon. Tag each item with the owner's info and where they'd like it shipped."

No metal?

"Vez, with this crew, I understand no personal weapons, but—"

"Just do it. You will be provided plastic straps to replace identification tag chains. The only metal allowed on *Keeling* are the tags themselves."

They didn't even allow *dog-tag chains* on board? What could the reason be for that?

"If anyone has banned objects on their person or in their bag when they leave *Ishi*, those items will be discarded," Vesna said. "No shipping them home at that point. When we rendezvous, make sure your crew's bags are packed and stacked. My crew will transport them to *Keeling*." She stood. "I have a lot to do, Lieutenant. If there is anything you or your people need, call Operations. Ops is instructed to assist you in any way they can."

Lieutenant, was it?

Maybe he'd changed but Vesna hadn't. She'd been happy to see him, true. She'd given him a chance to tell his side of things, to explain why he'd done what he'd done. She'd assumed—more likely had *hoped*

—that he'd provide a reason not listed in the after-action report. Something that could justify him taking a ship off the line.

He did have a reason; the reason was *cowardice*.

He'd lost his rank, his advancement track, and irreplaceable time with his family. Perhaps worst of all, though, was that he'd lost the respect of his oldest friend.

"Thank you for your time, Captain," Trav said. "Will that be all?"

To her credit, Vesna forced a smile. "That will be all."

Trav left the captain's suite and let the ensign take him back to the lower deck.

9

Nicholas Otto had a brig. A single cell, but a brig nonetheless. For three days she'd been here, measuring time by the breakfast, lunch, and dinner trays her fellow *Saint Nick* crewmates slid under the cell door. They wouldn't talk to her. They wouldn't answer questions.

They treated her like a prisoner. No lawyer. No communication.

It was enough to drive a girl crazy.

The cell had a metal cot with a crappy bedroll, metal toilet that reeked, and a metal basin with a small metal mirror. The bruise on her cheek had healed some, but still looked like a brand of shame. Someone had sutured the cut on her head before applying nanocyte salve; the wound still hurt but would be fully healed in another day or two.

All alone, she'd spent her three days of incarceration mostly talking to herself. That, and praying. Oh, how she desperately longed to hear High One's voice again.

The first time she'd heard it, it had saved her life.

She'd been crew on the PUAV *Shirley Jackson*, a BST research ship orbiting an uninhabitable planet in the Meissner 80 cluster. Jackson's crew focused on one thing—studying the Prawatt. The synthetic species had escaped Earth three centuries earlier, traveled millions of lightyears across the Milky Way, and established a multi-planetary culture. A culture that, unfortunately, would start a war on a whim.

Prawatt were utterly ruthless. If they couldn't conquer a world, they were more than happy to saturation-bomb the hell out of it. If that meant the possible extermination of a sentient race? No big deal.

Susannah had been married at the time. To Melanie. Susannah now knew she'd been confused, that it was a sin to love a woman, but back then, her heart had burned for Melanie—a brilliant biologist specializing in jellyfish. Susannah's work was so important to BST that they let Melanie study on the *Jackson* with her.

They'd reveled in the scientific freedom bought by black-budget government money to study a possible enemy of the Union, one that wouldn't bat a biomechanical eyelash at destroying all life on Earth. Not that Prawatt had eyelashes. Or eyes, for that matter.

Jackson had been a scientific playground. Anything Susannah wanted, Susannah got. The best equipment. The best people. No research topic was off-limits—if her work potentially provided insight into the biology, culture, or mind-set of an artificial collective sentient organism that liked to blow things up, then someone, somewhere, funded it.

Trouble was, there was one rather insistent objector to that research—the Prawatt themselves.

Back then, before the creation of the Ki Rebel Establishment, Meissner 80 had been within the boundaries of the Ki Empire. It was also within celestial spitting distance of Prawatt Jihad territory. The Union paid the Empire for the right to station *Jackson* in the M80 cluster, which was far enough inside Empire space that no one thought the Prawatt would, or *could*, mount a cross-border strike. Live and learn. Well, at least for Susannah, anyway.

She should have died that day. The blast ripped the *Jackson* damn near in half, throwing her against a bulkhead, splitting her scalp and giving her the long scar she carried to this day. Susannah now knew that scar was the mark of the High One.

She'd been on the deck, dazed and bleeding. She'd tried to rise until the voice—as clear as Israfil's trumpet—spoke two words: *stay down.*

Stunned, Susannah did as she'd been told. And by staying down, for just an extra second or two, she survived a shrapnel shower that killed the other four people in her lab—including Melanie.

At the time, Susannah hadn't understood what was happening, hadn't understood how she'd been saved, how she'd been *chosen*.

After the attack passed, after the Prawatt boarded the *Jackson* and removed all samples of their species, Susannah had looked down at the face of her decapitated lover. Melanie's eyes, relaxed in death. Her lips, red with her own blood. Susannah kissed those lips one last time, then stumbled to a lifeboat. She was the last one in. In her subsequent grief, Susannah came to understand that it could not be a coincidence —a higher power had knocked her down, out of harm's way, told her to *stay* down, then held the door of the lifeboat just long enough for her to reach it. She had been spared. Why? She still didn't know, but there had to be a reason.

With only two months remaining on her obligated ten years, Susannah did little work. *No* work, to be truthful. At least not for BST. She spent her final days in Fleet searching for answers to the voice. In doing so, she found Purism.

Before the Prawatt attack, if you'd claimed that Susannah—an atheist scientist—might find a sudden calling in a religion? She would have labeled you a fool. But Purism provided answers that science could not. The religion gave her solace. Only Purism could explain the High One's miraculous actions.

When Susannah cycled out, Fleet tried to convince her to re-enlist and continue her research on the Prawatt. They promised promotions. She didn't care. They threatened to activate her from reserve status. Before they could make good on that, Susannah emigrated to the Purist Nation. She spent the next ten years as Sister Susannah of the Dark Reach.

Susannah learned much during that time. The sisters taught her the ways of the Purist faith. She studied Stewart's Testament. She learned that Melanie died because Melanie was an unrepentant lesbian. Homosexuality was against High One's will. Susannah had been spared so she could rescind her evil ways and find the true path High One intended for her.

Then came the next inevitable, idiotic war. Always war. *Always*. The Third Galactic War was a doozy. The Ki emperor signed a peace treaty with the Harrah Tribal Accord, an act so infuriating to his subjects that two planets seceded. The Purist Nation supported the rebels, the Planetary Union backed the Empire, and the two old adversaries were once again at each other's throats.

The Nation's Ministry of Patriotism dug deep into the records of all citizens. Clerics had been less than thrilled at Susannah's Union military background. They excommunicated her, kicked her out of her adopted home. If she didn't leave the Nation, she would be literally stoned with stones until dead. Simple math, even for someone who did not have a doctorate in automatonics. Susannah spent the only money she had to buy a seat on a ship traveling from Solomon to Rodina, the closest Union planet.

When she arrived and went through customs, she found Fleet waiting for her. Even ten years later, she was still technically a reservist. They activated her. She gave lip-service to filing for conscientious objector status, but that hadn't lasted long. They told her that if she did, Fleet would see to it that no one in the private sector would hire her. Ever.

Susannah had nowhere to go. No family. No home. She stopped fighting and let the system take her where it may.

That system took her to the PUAV *Nicholas Otto*.

That system delivered her to a blasphemous urine-drinker.

If High One wanted to test her, he was doing a grand job of it.

The door to her cell swung open, hinges complaining like a demon with pubic lice. She expected to see one of her meal-delivering *Saint Nick* crewmates, but instead in walked a woman she'd never seen before. HeavyG, two meters tall and thick all around. Shoulders like a linebacker, big arms hidden by a perfectly cut, pitch-black BII service uniform. Master Warrant Officer insignia on her collar. No name patch.

Chain restraints dangled from her hand.

"Jewelry?" Susannah gave her fakest of smiles. "For me? Really, you shouldn't have."

"I'd appreciate your cooperation, Doctor Rossi."

"And I'd appreciate a lawyer," Susannah said. "I was *attacked*."

"It's been a long trip here, Doctor, and I'm tired." The woman raised the chains, gave them a little swing. "You're going to wear these one way or another. Let's make it easy on both of us."

The big woman's tired eyes sent a clear message that she wasn't all talk.

Susannah had been through enough violence. She offered her hands.

The woman quickly restrained Susannah's wrists and ankles, then stepped back and held the cell door. Another woman, far shorter, far smaller, entered. She wore a sailor service uniform with three stars on her collar—an admiral.

"Hello, Doctor Rossi. I'm Admiral Adrienne Bock. May I sit?"

The only place to sit was the cell bunk. Susannah nodded.

Bock sat, folded her liver-spotted hands on one knee. Her black hair had mostly gone to gray, cropped short. Her left eye, bright blue, her right, milky and mottled, the eyelid gnarled with scar tissue.

"Henrietta, leave us," Bock said. "Shut the door behind you."

The HeavyG woman stepped out of the cell and closed the door behind her. Susannah noticed it didn't lock.

"Admiral Bock, do you mind telling me what this is all about?" Susannah made a show of lifting one leg as far as the chains would permit. "My superior officer assaulted me. He tried to *rape* me. I defended myself. He should be in this cell, not me."

Bock raised an eyebrow. "*He* should be in this cell?"

Susannah fought back tears. What in the name of Low One was happening?

"That's right," she said. "Major Bratchford should be court-martialed and put away. Look at my face. This bit of color isn't rouge."

Bock tilted her head. "Doctor Rossi, what do you think happened?"

"Bratchford tried to—"

"I mean *after* he tried to rape you."

Susannah started to talk, stopped before any words came out. After? Bratchford had attacked her. Susannah had heard High One's voice. She remembered playing to Bratchford's ego. Remembered punching the bastard's testicles. Bratchford had fallen, and then... and then...

... and then waking up in this cell.

"Doctor Rossi, your country needs your help," Bock said. "With your expertise in automatonics, in particular."

Why couldn't she remember? Because Bratchford had hit her in the head?

"Admiral, the only thing I'll help *my country* with is taking millions in a lawsuit. I don't want to hear—"

"You're facing a murder charge, Doctor Rossi."

Susannah stopped breathing. *Murder?*

"Second degree murder of a superior officer, to be precise," Bock said. "That'll get you a death sentence or put you in a cell for the rest of your life. A cell not quite as spacious as this one."

Susannah couldn't stop herself from glancing around, taking in the three by four-meter space.

This nightmare should be *over*, not getting worse.

"My commanding officer tried to rape me. I want a lawyer. I didn't *murder* anyone. I defended myself."

Bock reached into her pocket, brought out a mini projector.

"Doctor, you're certain you don't remember?"

Susannah stared at the projector. A haziness hung in her mind, a blank space where the missing memories should have been. It wasn't uncommon for victims of assault to not remember what had happened, at least not all the details.

So why did the projector frighten her?

"Someone came in and got him," Susannah said, almost whispering. "They took him away."

Bock nodded, perhaps understanding, perhaps patronizing.

"The footage is disturbing," she said. "It's difficult to look at, so I can only imagine what it was like to endure it. Bratchford recorded the entire thing."

I'm the only one watching, he'd said. Something like that. It was all a bit fuzzy.

"Admiral, if you make me watch my own attempted rape, without counsel or a therapist present, you might as well hand me a blank check from Fleet so I can write in whatever amount I like—and I'm quite fond of zeroes."

Bock nodded, this time in understanding. Susannah was sure of it.

"I doubt it will come to that, Doctor. This must be extraordinarily traumatic for you. I'll cut to the part you don't seem to remember."

She set the projector on her knee and pressed a detent. A beam of light played against the cell's gray wall—Bratchford, curled into a fetal position, spit coating his lips and chin, his eyes smashed shut. Susannah standing above him, legs bare, wearing only her uniform shirt.

"Frankly, I wish you'd torn his pecker clean off," Bock said. "But that's neither here nor there. You incapacitated your assailant. Had you tried to reach the rest of the crew at that point, had you pounded on the door, had you done *anything* to try and get help, I think you'd be in the clear. Unfortunately, Doctor Rossi, that's not what you did."

Susannah shook her head. The haze was still there, but a living blackness within it clawed to break free. Something bad had happened. Something even worse than rape.

"Your claim of self-defense won't cover this," Bock said.

She pressed the detent a second time; the image burst into movement.

Susannah watched herself turn toward the lab table. When she'd slammed into it, the Bunsen burners had toppled over.

She watched herself pick one up.

Watched herself turn and step toward the downed man.

Watched herself straddle him, her crotch on his left hip.

"Turn it off," Susannah said.

"If only *you* were the Admiral. Then you could give the orders."

In the image playing against a gray brig cell wall, Lieutenant Susannah Rossi, PhD in automatonics, tilted her head this way, then that. She studied her fallen aggressor, then angled the burner toward his eye.

"This is where it gets upsetting," Bock said. "The sound is quite good, though."

Projector Susannah tilted her head again, and to Real Susannah, it looked like a bird staring at a wiggling insect.

Bratchford made a croaking sound, as if taking the shallowest of breaths wasn't easy after one's genitalia had been violently rearranged.

"Look at me, Bratchford," Projector Susannah said. "Look at me or face His wrath."

The pantsless man shuddered with fear.

Real Susannah said *turn it off*. Or tried to say it. Or maybe said it in her head. She would never really know.

On the wall, Bratchford cautiously opened his right eye.

Projector Susannah jammed the burner into that eye, plunging the metal tip into the soft tissue.

Bratchford flailed and kicked instead of trying to attack, to defend.

Projector Susannah threw her weight on the burner's base, driving it deeper.

Bock was right about one thing, at least—the sound was excellent. Real Susannah heard a definitive *crunch* when the burner tip broke through the back of Bratchford's eye socket.

He spasmed. His left hand flopped back and forth at the wrist, sickeningly, as if he was making a sarcastic mockery of waving goodbye.

Bratchford fell still.

Projector Susannah turned her head and looked up, directly into the camera. She smiled the smile of a psychopath.

Bock paused the playback.

Real Susannah closed her eyes, searched in the haze, tried to make the memories come back. They danced away, slipping out of her grasp.

She'd killed a man, yet she remembered none of it.

Bock was right. Any tribunal that saw that footage would take zero leniency. Yes, Susannah had been through a trauma. She'd been assaulted. But that didn't justify killing a helpless superior officer. Life in a military prison was the *best* she could hope for.

Susannah had spent her old life studying murderous automatons, only to become one herself.

And yet... there had to be a reason for it.

Why would High One have thrust this burden upon her unless He knew she could endure it? Endure it and fulfill His plan for her.

Whatever that plan might be.

"What is it you want from me, Admiral?"

Bock turned off the projector, slid it back into her pocket.

"It's not what *I* want, Doctor Rossi. It's what the Union wants. More accurately, what the Union *needs*. Do you know who Mathias Epperson is?"

Epperson, the war hero who became an admiral.

"I do. He commanded Sixth Group."

"Still does," Bock said. "Fleet has developed a cancer, Doctor

Rossi. A cancer of power and control. Admirals have become more like feudal lords ruling over fiefdoms than fellow commanders working together for the good of the Union. Epperson has a special warship, one he's keeping hidden. You need to find out what is going on aboard that ship, the *James Keeling*."

The *James Keeling*. A person's name, which meant the ship was either a destroyer honoring a war hero or a research vessel honoring an ancient inventor.

"I've never been on a warship, Admiral. What kind of a ship is the *Keeling*?"

"That is what you're going to tell me, Doctor." Bock's face darkened. "For now, though, that is not your concern. Your mission is to become part of the crew. When the time is right, Henrietta or one of her associates will find you and tell you what comes next. That could be a month from now. That could be a year from now." The Admiral stood. "The incident with Bratchford will have a ripple effect. Word will get out, as word always does. I'm going to give you a new identity. Henrietta, come in here."

The cell door screeched open. The HeavyG woman walked in, carrying a leather-bound portfolio which she handed to Susannah.

Susannah opened it to find real paper detailing the life of one Bethany Darkwater. An ID card showed Darkwater's personal details and Susannah's holographic face, but with two major differences—a banged bob instead of Susannah's heavy black ponytail, and a forehead missing both scar and infinity tattoo.

"You are now Ensign Bethany Darkwater," Bock said. "Xeno mate."

Susannah looked at the Admiral. "*Xeno mate? What is that?"

"In short, it means you are the lowest rung on the three-rung ladder of xenomechanical officers aboard the *Keeling*. That is all I can tell you right now."

Xenomechanics—alien technology.

"I don't know xenomechanics. My degree is in automatonics."

"Then learn," Bock said. "Quickly. I'll provide BST's first-year xenomechanics curriculum. You have three days to learn it. *All* of it, as well as memorizing the background of Bethany Darkwater. I trust someone of your I.Q. can handle that?"

Someone of *double* Susannah's I.Q. would probably struggle, but what options did she have?

"How long will I have to keep this charade up?"

"Two years. Perform this duty for me for two years or until I tell you to stop, and the Bratchford incident will go away. I will permanently release you from any obligation to Fleet. You can start fresh. If you still wish to return to the Purist Nation, I can—and will—make that happen."

The hand of the High One at work. So blatantly obvious. Susannah had thought this woman a beast, when in reality, Bock could be Susannah's ticket back to the promised land.

"You should have led with that, Admiral. You could have saved yourself some time."

Bock smiled. "When I play poker, I stack the deck in my favor. A philosophy I suggest you embrace."

If that wasn't good advice, Susannah didn't know what was.

"If the *Keeling* is Epperson's ship, how do I get assigned to it?"

"Fleet Academy takes fraud quite seriously, Bethany," Bock said. "Accepting large sums of money to take tests for other cadets? Shameful. When my people post that transgression, a logistic officer named Maia Whittaker will contact you. She will offer you a stint on Epperson's secret ship. You will accept."

Imprisonment, execution, or Susannah could pretend to be someone else and become Bock's mole. Not much of a choice.

"Yes, Admiral," Susannah said. "I accept."

"I have a cosmetic surgeon waiting on my ship," Bock said. "Your infinity tattoo will be removed, and your scar will be repaired. You *will* become Bethany Darkwater. Learn all you can about the *Keeling*. If you fuck this up, if *anyone* learns who you really are, my people will find you. You'll be dead before you know it. Do you understand?"

A glance at Henrietta was all Susannah needed to know Bock's threat was real.

"Yes, Admiral," Susannah said. "I understand."

Bock smiled.

"Good luck, Ensign Bethany Darkwater," she said. "The Union is counting on you."

10

The unmatchable, staggering beauty of space.

Civilian starships and research vessels were often built with that spectacle in mind. One couldn't make an entire ship out of crysteel, but one could install strong, durable windows and viewports.

Military vessels, on the other hand, were not built to provide breathtaking views. Even if sealed and shuttered, a viewport was a weak spot, which was why warships had none. Anywhere there could be armor, there was armor—meters thick, dense, multi-plated with both passive and reactive layers. Once you were inside a warship, that warship was your world—it was all you would see for months on end.

Some warships, however, had one exception, a place where the crew could take in the glittering black expanse of existence: the "bubble," a crysteel blister affixed to a ship's exterior.

Bubbles were inexpensive to make—by military standards at least —and could be easily replaced. When the ship engaged in battle, a bubble could be, and often was, blown clean off without impacting the armor beneath.

Dhal-class frigates like *Ishlangu* and *Schild* had topside bubbles, fifteen meters wide and twenty meters long. With main artillery batteries located port and starboard, *Ishi*'s bubble offered an unobstructed, half-sphere view of eternity. Cheap, expendable bench seats lined the interior, letting downtime crew sit and stare at the abyss to their heart's content.

Trav loved all aspects of warships. The weaponry, the armor, the punch-drives, the people, the rituals and traditions, and—until recently—the camaraderie. One aspect he loved above all others was to be in a bubble, atop armor twice as thick as he was tall, staring out at the ship's area of influence. A warship owned the void around it, as surely as the old land-based countries of Earth owned kilometers of ocean surrounding their shores. A fully stocked, fully equipped warship was a tiny nation unto itself, able to deliver violence against any threat.

As Vesna had ordered, the replacement *Keeling* crew members were topside, waiting to see their ship arrive. Trav stood dead center in *Ishi*'s bubble, limiting the amount of distance his new crewmates could have from him. He saw their glares, *felt* them as well. Most of the enlisted and Raiders tried to avoid *Yellowbelly Ellis* altogether.

He had a job to do—they'd better get used to him.

He had to get used to them as well. Those who'd reported in chains had been found guilty of one crime or another. Some who had *not* reported in chains—like him—had likely been found guilty as well. Would the criminals be bitter toward Fleet? Maybe toward the Union itself? Would that make it hard to form them into a cohesive fighting unit? Hopefully the *Keeling* captain, whoever they might be, would be experienced at such things.

Most of the replacement crew members stared out and up, twenty degrees starboard, getting a last look at the *Creeper*. The coldship accelerated away, becoming nothing more than a flickering, fading point of light lost among a million stars. *Creeper* had punched-in only two hours earlier; it would be another twenty hours before its punch-drives recharged. The ship's crew wasn't cleared to lay eyes on *Keeling*, so off it went, its curvine taking it away at flank speed.

Creeper had delivered the final two replacements: Brinson Sorro, a bone-thin electronic countermeasures operator; and Bethany Darkwater, an engineering ensign who looked like she was forty if she was a day.

Someone bumped into Trav. He stumbled forward a step, turn to see a young, wide-eyed Raider, mouth agape.

"Sir, I'm sorry. I was looking at the stars and backing up and I... I'm sorry, sir."

The baby-faced kid looked like he could go two or three days without shaving and still pass inspection, but that hadn't stopped him from growing a thin, scraggly mustache.

"Don't worry about it, Specialist—" Trav glanced at the name "—is that pronounced *Oh-need-ah* or *Oh-nai-dah?*"

"*Nai-dah*, sir."

"Don't worry about it, Specialist Oneida. Is this your first deployment?"

"How did you know, sir?"

"I'm an officer," Trav said. "We know things."

"Yessir, it's my first deployment."

"Then a word of advice, Specialist. When on a ship, look where you're going."

Oneida nodded. "Will do, sir."

He turned—without looking—and bumped into a propulsion mate —Corporal SALVATORE—who proceeded to give Oneida the same advice Trav had.

Trav stepped away, leaving the *yes sirs* and *sorry sirs* behind.

"XO Ellis, may I have a word?"

The question came from a Raider warrant officer in fatigues. Above her name—BANG—a silver winged beetle pin denoted her status as a Ochthera pilot.

"Go ahead, Warrant Bang," Trav said.

"My call sign is *Biggie*, XO. Use that if you like. I just wanted to tell you that my brother was a gunner's mate at the Battle of X7."

A sinking feeling. Yet another person to tell him they'd lost someone close, and he was to blame. Was there no end to this parade of regret?

"I'm sorry for your loss, Biggie. A lot of good people died on the *Boudicca*."

Her nose wrinkled. "He wasn't on *Boudicca*. He served with you on the *Schild*."

A face flashed in Trav's thoughts, a face that looked a lot like the woman standing before him.

"Your brother is Spec-Three Dustin Bang?"

Biggie smiled. "You know his name, man. Can't say I'm surprised, the way he raves about you."

In the battle, Dustin's turret had taken a hit. He'd lost his left arm.

"He's a good sailor," Trav said. "How is he doing?"

"As well as can be expected. I got to talk to him before I got arrested."

Ah. She, too, was here as a punishment.

"Arrested for, Warrant Bang?"

"Let's just say it's a bad idea to allegedly partake of mind-altering substances and then allegedly borrow an Oh-Six's personal shuttle for a joy ride and do a barrel roll past the flight tower."

That wasn't something a commodore was likely to brush off with a *Raiders will be Raiders* attitude.

"An *alleged* barrel roll, I presume?"

Bang sneered a smile. "Exactamundo, man. Anyway, I was surprised to see you here. I thought you'd like to know Dustin told me he's alive because of you. He said if you hadn't got *Schild* out of there, he'd have been toast. Sucks to lose an arm, but at least he's alive to use the one he's still got."

In the furor of the trial, the stress of leaving his family behind, the dread of what came next, Trav had focused on how many people died because of his decision—never once on how many lives that decision might have saved.

Did one sailor's survival outweigh the loss of 325 others? Not even close. But still, it was something.

"Thank you, Biggie."

A flash of light drew their attention—port side ninety, up high. It wasn't deep purple or the sparkling gimmer he'd expected, that *everyone* expected, because that was how punch-space worked. This flash of light seemed instantly and utterly *wrong*.

In one fixed spot, space appeared to bulge, to breathe, as if coming to life. That area filled with color—swirling ochre laced with the red and orange of inferno heat. Like a boil swelling with pus that stretched skin to transparency, the light show expanded, deforming the void itself.

The bloated boil ripped apart from within, birthing kilometers-long, puke-yellow plumes that flashed spasmodically with blasts of purple-blue lightning.

And then, a monstrosity tore through the spot, billowing brimstone trailing from its sides.

When it angled away from that gateway to hell, Trav's heart stopped. The ship didn't fire directional thrusters to change its pitch and yaw, then apply forward thrust to send it in a new direction. Instead, the ship *bent*, like an eel curving into its new course, an eel with three tails that trailed along behind it, marking its path, each tail ending in what looked like a long, curved, pointed barb.

Several people ran for the hatch that led down into the ship, as if the *Ishlangu* was under attack. Maybe it was. That abomination out there couldn't be the *Keeling*.

The *all-alert* tone sounded from the 1MC.

"This is Captain Jakobsson. *Keeling* crew, stay where you are. That is your ship. We are not in danger. I repeat, we are not in danger."

The mad exodus came to a sudden halt. Raiders and sailors pointed at the thing. Some even backed away from it, as if there was anywhere else for them to go.

That was the *Keeling*? His new home? It couldn't be.

The monster drifted closer. The three tails shortened, shrinking like a chameleon's contracting tongue, coming together in one solid mass a third the length they'd just been. The curved barbs remained, reaching back like ornamental scimitars.

"Hey, XO?" Biggie's voice was a taut monotone. "Remind me later to not steal stuff. Allegedly."

The ship now seemed as straight and inflexible as any other starship. Had he imagined the bending and curving? In the smoke and lightning, had his eyes been fooled that a solid object could move that way, like a childhood rubber pencil trick writ impossibly large?

"I ain't getting on that fucking thing," Oneida called out. "No fucking way."

"Be quiet, Spec." Lindros's voice, sounding far less authoritative than he probably meant it to be. "Not another word."

"You heard the LT!" That was Sands, the platoon sergeant, his broken-bullhorn words echoing off the bubble's crysteel. "Straighten up, Raiders! Not a word out of the lot of you!"

The last of the strange smoke or vapor or whatever it was dissipated into nothingness. Heart hammering, Trav took a deep breath, fought to calm himself, to process the visual assault of *new* and *familiar* and *strange* and *wrong*.

From the barbed tail section to the tip of the hideous bow—a bow he could not force himself to focus on, not yet—the ship looked to be about 110 meters long, roughly the length of an American football field if measured from the back of one end zone to the back of the other. *Ishlangu* was longer by a third.

Topside amidships was a superstructure that looked familiar enough—battleship-gray, roughly ten meters high, a two-deck ziggurat layout composed of the hard edges, acute angles, and flat planes common among all Union warships. A 20-millimeter point-defense gun angled up from the top deck. EDP trenches ran along the lower deck's port and starboard sides.

The hull that superstructure sat on, though, was anything but familiar.

More scrimshaw axe handle than smooth surface, the metallic hull was some twenty meters deep with a beam of perhaps ten meters. The mottled green-black material reminded Trav of a battered, tarnished, centuries-old coin his grandmother had in her many collections of antique things. A *penny*, she'd called it. The hull's curving plates and pieces melded together with a fluid precision that conjured images of abstract art rather than military might—a molten metal Rorschach sculpture, its texture random and chaotic. Not a hard angle in sight. Irregular whorls, curves, and gnarled patterns covered the surface. In some spots, though, laid out like fresh scars, sunlight gleamed from streaks and patches of bright, smooth copper.

The ziggurat's port and starboard sides continued down the hull like the fenders of a horse saddle. On each "fender" was a stubby barbette topped by a heavily armored Type24 127-millimeter, 54-caliber gun. The batteries had the lop-sided teeter-totter design of all warship artillery, with eight-meters of barrel pointing forward from the front of the armored gunhouse where the gun crew operated, and another two meters of counter-barrel pointing out the back.

A torpedo room, also gray, hung bottomside, forward of amidships. A smaller version of the same was bottomside, well aft of amidships. A 20-millimeter point-defense turret topped each unit.

The aft section—he refused to think of it as a "tail," even though that's what it looked like—was a bit less than a third of the ship's total length. The thicker amidships section took up little more than a third. The final third? Trav could avoid it no longer. Skin crawling, sweat beading, he took in the bow.

What psychotic engineer had designed such an atrocity?

Some twenty meters of gnarled, tarnished hull extended beyond the ziggurat's front edge. From there, the top and bottom of the bow continued on like the prongs of a massive tuning fork. The top prong, perhaps five meters thick, stretched out another twenty-five meters, its underside an organic-looking mishmash of long curves and stubby protrusions. The slightly thicker bottom prong was ten-odd meters longer than the top. Multiple, curving points extended up from the bottom prong, like abstract sculptures designed in a violent, drug-fueled stupor.

Trav couldn't help but wonder what his daughter would do if she saw this thing.

Aven would scream.

She would have nightmares, because she would see what her eyes showed her, not filter perception through an adult's experience and logic. Aven would see just one thing—the pincer jaws of a huge monster.

Trav didn't think of a monster, though. He remembered his grand-mother's collection of insects. Some were on pin boards. Others were simply smashed between the pages of books and left to dry. A few choice specimens were encased in clear blocks of crysteel, transparent little coffins forever trapping that which had once been alive. Aside from the spiders—especially the delicate and deadly black widow—the most frightening of all her insects had been a thick Hercules beetle. The beetle's gleaming upper horn was longer than its entire body. The lower horn was slightly shorter. Both were lined with odd, smooth barbs that ended in sharp points. Flip the top for the bottom, increase it to obscene proportions, and the Hercules beetle's horns were in the ballpark of the *Keeling's* two-pronged bow.

A tug on his sleeve—Biggie, wide-eyed, leaning close.

"XO, snap out of it," she said. "The natives are getting restless."

He instantly became aware of sailors and Raiders muttering, yelling, even threatening. The *Keeling*'s form was so different from what they knew that it shocked them, terrified some of them.

"That is *nasty*," a Raider said. "What the hell is that thing? 'Cause it sure as *fuck* ain't no ship. I want out of this chickenshit outfit."

Sands strode toward the Raider, boot soles stomping on *Ishi*'s thick armor.

"You secure that shit, Shamdi," Sands said. "Bitch one more time and I'll give you something to bitch about!"

Looking at the *Keeling*, Trav felt weak in the knees. His stomach fluttered. He couldn't blame Shamdi nor Oneida nor any of the others who'd cried out. They didn't want to get on that ship. Neither did he. No sane person would.

The 1MC's alert tone sounded.

"This is Captain Jakobsson. Attention, crew of the *James Keeling*. Your new CO is coming aboard to introduce herself. Stay in the bubble. That is all."

Trav tried to process what he saw, to understand the position he found himself in. That thing out there offered him a chance to clear his shameful record, an opportunity to save his career and deliver for his family.

Gazing at the ugly, misshapen ship, he made up his mind. He wasn't a cadet. He wasn't a lowly ensign. He was a lieutenant of the Planetary Union Fleet, the most efficient, deadliest fighting force in the history of mankind.

He would do whatever it took to fulfill his obligations.

He would serve on the *Crypt*, and he would serve well, or he would die trying.

"Everyone, compose yourselves," Trav called out. "Sailors, move to the port side. Lieutenant Lindros, assemble your Raiders to starboard."

11

The *James Keeling* sat alongside *Ishlangu*, close enough now that it filled up the bubble's starboard view. The bizarre vessel looked like it hung perfectly still in space, but like watching a shadow slowly stretch across a sidewalk, if you stared long enough, you could tell it moved slightly in relation to *Ishi*.

Anne kept an eye on the white umbilical stretching from *Ishi*'s port cargo hatch to the *Keeling*'s superstructure. Her new ship was such an odd combination—traditional, heavy, bulky Fleet tech atop something the likes of which she'd never seen. The superstructure and side artillery batteries made her think of a concrete trapper hat strapped to the long body of a legless Komodo.

"*Keeling* crew, four files, port side," XO Ellis said. "Lieutenant Kerkhoffs, Warrant Officer Erickson, Major Lafferty, up front with me."

Sands, the Raider platoon sergeant, yelled at his people to line up in ranks to starboard.

Anne moved forward, joining Ellis in the front rank near the open hatch leading deeper into *Ishlangu*.

She didn't know what to make of Ellis. While she was certain no one knew of her "crime," just as she didn't know the records of other sailors and Raiders assigned to the *Keeling*, everyone knew about Antoine Williams and Trav "Yellowbelly" Ellis. Maybe not all the details, but enough. The two cowards had pulled the damaged yet still combat-capable *Schild* out of harm's way, leading to the loss of the *Boudicca* with all hands aboard.

Some people thought Williams and Ellis had done the right thing, but that was a minority viewpoint. As for Anne's take, she didn't know what to think just yet. Daddy had trained her not to make rash judgements, to stay opinion-free until she had enough data to make an informed decision.

Ellis stood front-row, right-most rank, a meter of space between him and Lindros, who was leftmost in the Raiders' front rank. Anne lined up to Ellis's left. To Anne's left, Sascha Kerkhoffs, then Doug Erickson.

Weren't those two a pair. Before Anne had shipped off to Eden, she'd seen notes on an investigation into Hunata Industries, a civilian contractor firm that bribed Fleet officers into directing lucrative ship-supply contracts to the company. Locking out competition while over-charging for food, waste removal, repairs, maintenance, and more, Hunata defrauded Fleet out of millions. Thirty-three fleeters were indicted in relation to the scandal. That number included Kerkhoffs, Erickson, and Daniel Monstranto, the *Keeling*'s new supply chief.

Anne glanced at the Raiders. Their lines looked uneven, far from the razor-sharp ranks Raiders were known for. Some of them made a halfhearted effort to straighten up their formation, resulting in grumbling and low-throated insults when hands pushed or shoulders bumped.

"*Officer on deck,*" Ellis called out.

Where a proper unit would snap to attention as a single entity, stomping right feet in unison, this sad bunch sounded like half were on-point and half were dragging ass.

A tall woman climbed out of the hatch. She wore light gray sailor coveralls, which were unbuttoned down to her sternum, revealing a sweat-stained white t-shirt. A colonel's circle-and-bar on her tab, a trident pin signifying her status as a ship captain above the name patch: LINCOLN. A black bandana, slightly darker than her dark skin, covered her hair. This was an officer who didn't give two squirts of piss about her appearance.

A keloid scar ran from the right side of her nose almost to the corner of her mouth. From a severe burn, perhaps. Anne knew that scar, but couldn't place it...

"No fucking way," XO Ellis said, so quietly that only Anne could hear, and barely at that.

"I am Colonel Kiara Lincoln," the woman said. "I'm the captain of the PUV *James Keeling*."

No fucking way was an understatement. Kiara Lincoln, hero of Capizzi 7. Vessels under her command had been credited with the destruction of eight enemy warships—she had more kills than anyone in Fleet history. Anne hadn't heard so much as a peep about Lincoln in years. No one had.

"You will address me as *captain*," Lincoln said. "Not *cap*. Not *cappy*. Not *skipper*. Not *momma*. When I ask a question to which the answer is *yes*, you will say *aye, Captain*. When I give an order, you will repeat the order back to me and add *aye-aye, Captain*. Now, we'll test your ability to do as you're told. When I say *do you understand*, you will all reply with *aye, Captain*. Do you understand?"

"Aye, Captain," Anne said in time with most of her new crewmates. Two people, maybe three, said *aye-aye*, the extra syllable making them choke off *captain* when they realized they were the only ones still speaking.

"Dismal," Lincoln said. "You'll learn and you'll learn quickly. At ease."

Anne spread her feet slightly wider, folded her hands behind her back.

"I came to the *Ishlangu* to introduce myself, because on the *Keeling*, we don't have a big, fancy space like this," Lincoln said. "I like to describe my boat as *oh so cozy*. Those of you who think you have claustrophobia? Get over it. Fast."

Lincoln walked to her right, looking over the sailors.

"I know you all have questions about my ship," she said. "Most of those questions will go unanswered. There is classified. Beyond classified is top-secret. Beyond top-secret is *you get shot if you accidentally see it*. Beyond that, there is the *Keeling*."

Lincoln stopped, turned to her left. She looked at Anne, who focused on staring straight ahead and not making eye contact. Anne felt Lincoln's gaze, though, and felt *judgement*.

The *Keeling*'s captain strode in front of the Raider column, her eyes flicking across the soldiers.

"Literally *everything* on this ship is on a need-to-know basis," Lincoln said. "I determine who needs to know. There are two things you should get in your head right now."

She turned again, stopping in front of the aisle between the sailors and Raiders. She held up a finger.

"Item one. You are here because you fucked up or you got fucked by the luck of the draw. Either way, the key word is *fucked*, which is what you are. There is no transfer off the *Keeling*. I'm authorized to do anything necessary to keep this ship secret, and that includes venting you if you give me one iota of trouble. Does that sound unfair? Well, it is. It is also your new reality."

Lincoln's unforgiving gaze slowly swept side to side. She held up a second finger.

"Item two. In Fleet's mind, understand that you're already dead." She paused, letting that sink in. "Fleet has pre-prepared cover stories for each and every one of you. A training accident. You're MIA. You're AWOL. You were executed for the crime you may or may not have committed."

Lincoln lowered her hand. She was like no warship CO Anne had ever met. The captains of ships that ferried Anne around the galaxy had been stern yet polite, radiating an aura of calm authority. Lincoln, on the other hand, seemed like a tiger in a deer pen—well-fed but waiting to see which herbivore might piss her off and be the next meal.

"I've survived three patrols on the *Keeling*," Lincoln said. "If you're lucky, so will you. Until your two years are up, take my advice— forget your pasts. They are as dead as you are. There is no *going home* because you *are* home. The *Keeling* is your life now."

She turned, looked down into the hatch, nodded.

Three sailors clambered out. One white-haired woman and two men—the first handsome, fit, with a short red beard, the second so wide and tall Anne was surprised he'd made it through the hatch. All three wore gray coveralls as stained and beat up as Lincoln's. The woman carried a handheld metal detector. Both men held stun sticks.

"On *Keeling*, you'll wear many hats," Lincoln said. "Warrant Ledford here is our propulsion chief—" the red-bearded man, a

Warrant Officer JG, nodded "—Bradley Henry is our lead culinary designer—" the hulking Spec-3 raised his stunstick in greeting "—and Lieutenant Hammersmith is our ship's doctor." The white-haired woman showed no reaction at all.

"I trust none of you are dumb enough to try and sneak contraband aboard my ship," Lincoln said. "There are no personal weapons allowed."

Anne heard someone cough out the word *bullshit*. More than one Raider stifled a laugh.

Sands turned, his face instantly red, and stared at a Raider who had his hand near his mouth—Spec-2 Nitzan Shamdi.

"Sorry, Master Sergeant Sands," Shamdi said. "Scratchy throat."

Sands's face turned so red Anne wondered if he might have a coronary right there on the spot.

When Ellis ordered everyone to give up personal weapons, people had complained—the Raiders most of all. Anne's favorite knife would soon be on its way to her father, who would hold it for her until she could get it back.

She felt naked without a blade on her person.

"Time to board," Lincoln said. "Doc Hammersmith will scan each of you before you step into the umbilical. Henry and Chief Ledford are here to make sure you do as Doc asks. Once you are scanned, you will cross over to my ship, where Chief of the Boat Eloi Sung will be waiting. Master Sergeant Sands, pick five Raiders to go across first." Lincoln pointed at Shamdi. "And make sure that one is at the head of the line."

12

In the Cloister, they'd told Nitzan he was chosen.

Chosen for what purpose, he often asked.

The High One will someday make his purpose known, he'd been told.

That day had come.

The ship, the Union's secret weapon... it wasn't of man.

Not *alien*, exactly, at least in the way of Harrah, the Sklorno, the Ki or any of the Low One's demonic minions. This felt different. Important. *Ancient*, in a way that transcended the alien races, perhaps even Humanity itself.

A hand on his shoulder.

"You okay, pal?"

It was Bennett. A Spec-3, yet he was older than Nitzan's dad. Or, at least, older than his dad would have been had the piece of shit not put a gun in his mouth at Nitzan's tenth birthday party.

"Old-timer," Nitzan said, "you better move that hand."

Bennett didn't get angry, he simply let his hand fall away. The guy had kind eyes. How the fuck could a Raider have kind eyes?

"You spaced out a bit," he said. "Keep moving forward, we're blocking the umbilical."

Mafi, the Raider in line behind Bennett, leaned to the side enough to make eye contact with Nitzan.

"Get moving, cumstain," Mafi said. "If I have to do any PT because of your little coughing stunt, I'll take it out of your hide."

High One, but Mafi was a big bastard. And his eyes? Not nice. Not nice at all.

"Lucky for you I feel like walking now," Nitzan said. "I'll save kicking your ass for later."

Mafi smiled.

Bennett sighed.

Maybe threatening the big bag of stupid was a bad idea. Mafi looked like a tree stump that had grown tree stump arms and tree stump legs, then put on fatigues and started walking around like a man.

Nitzan continued down the umbilical.

He would be the first Raider to enter the Keeling. Abshire was next, then Bennett, then Mafi, and finally that waste of a skull Beaver Perry. Perry had all the brains of a steamy shart.

Nitzan stepped out of the umbilical and into a tight compartment with one hatch leading forward, one aft, and a circular one in the deck. A pockmarked warrant officer wearing a peaked white cap grinned wide. Guy was obviously of old-Earth Asian descent.

"Ah, it's the joker with the throat tickle," he said. "Captain called over and told me to make sure I took real good care of you. The rest of you jizzies get your fat asses in here."

Bennett, Mafi and the others filed in around Nitzan. Everyone was shoulder to shoulder, bangers to butts, six people in a space made for two lovers or an extremely awkward threesome.

"I'm Eloi Sung," the man said. "Chief of the Boat."

Perry waved. He actually *waved*.

"Hi, Chief! I'm Jim Perry, but you can call me—"

Bennett grabbed Perry's shoulder; the old guy was far faster than Nitzan would have guessed.

"Beaver," Bennett said, "this is one of those times where you should be quiet."

Perry's eyes widened. "Oh, yeah. Thanks, Bennett."

Sung shook his head. "And to think when I said bringing a jizz platoon aboard would scuttle the ship's overall intelligence scores, they told me I was crazy."

He knelt next to the hatch.

"You're inside the superstructure," he said. "Two levels of relative normal enjoyed by wardroom types, gun crews, and spooks. You lot ain't any of those, which means you'll spend your days in the ship proper. The only way into the ship proper is through one of these."

He lifted the hatch.

Nitzan and the others leaned in, stared down at... what the hell was it? A meter-wide circle of bright copper-colored metal, but it had the flowing lines, ridges, and curves of a living thing.

"Looks like a butthole," Abshire said. "A really big butthole."

"Close," Sung said. "Officer types call it a *sphincter*. Those of us who work for a living prefer to call it what it is—a space anus. *Spanus* for short. All right, throat tickle, you're first. Stand on it."

Nitzan stood straight. "How about *fuck no*, sir. Enough with the hazing. Where's the real hatch?"

"You're going through this spanus, and that's that," Sung said. "The whole ship is sealed up tighter than a gnat's cooch. We got spanuses bow bottomside, aft bottomside just forward of the tail section, and topside fore and aft." He reached down, rang his knuckles on the pucker of metal. "This one here's the aft topside spanus."

Perry leaned over, stared down. "Why don't they just cut a hole in it and install a regular hatch?"

"Because the hull is hard to cut through," the chief said. "That's something you'll be grateful for soon enough. Shamdi, I'm ninety-seven-point-five percent certain that you've slithered into more than a few anuses in your time, so take a deep breath and step on that circle, *right now*, before I get angry."

An angry COB could cause endless grief for a Raider. Five years in Fleet had taught Nitzan that all too well. He looked down at the man-sized pucker but stayed where he was.

"Get moving, cumstain."

Nitzan felt a big hand on his back, felt himself falling forward—he stepped onto the circle. Before he could step off, he was yanked down into darkness.

Pressure all around him, pinning his legs together, pressing his arms to his chest. Something hard yet giving pushed against every inch of his being, from his booted feet to his face to the top of his head.

He was being sucked downward...

He was being *swallowed*.

He tried to scream but couldn't open his mouth—the firmness held his jaw shut tight.

The pressure eased up first on his feet, then his legs. Hands grabbed him. He slid free; his boots hit a flat surface.

"Relax, you're safe," a woman said. "Take two steps to your left. Make room for the others."

Nitzan opened his eyes. A fire-control chief—ALABAMA—stood in front of him. Close-cropped strawberry blonde curls, a stack of white towels draped over her forearm.

"First time's a doozy," she said. "I take it Chief Sung didn't warn you?"

Nitzan couldn't think. Something cold on his face, on his hands. Something... *slimy*.

Gently but firmly, Alabama pushed him against a bulkhead just before a pair of booted feet slipped through the sphincter.

Abshire dropped through. Two sailors, a sergeant and a corporal, gripped his shoulders, kept him from falling over. The same men had grabbed Nitzan, but he'd been too freaked out to even realize they were there.

A slimy sheen glazed Abshire's wide-eyed face—not exactly brown, not exactly yellow.

Alabama pressed a towel against Nitzan's chest.

"Clean yourself up," she said.

The coldness on his skin...

He slid his hand across his cheek, looked at it—strands of ochre-colored goo vibrated sickeningly between fingertips and face.

"What the fu—"

The strands snapped mid-word, a blob of it flying into his mouth. He grabbed the towel, spit into it three times fast.

"It's okay," Alabama said. "It's not poisonous."

"It tastes *so bad!*" Nitzan rubbed the towel against his tongue, tried to scrape the slime from his mouth. "What the hell is that stuff?"

"It's a lubricant," Alabama said. "Sort of. The ship only secretes it when we have a lot of people coming on board and the sphincter is going to get a lot of use."

Spanus lube. In his mouth.

"I can see by the look on your face you're less than thrilled," Alabama said. "You get used to it."

Abshire thudded against the bulkhead.

"I wanna go home." He wiped his towel across his forehead. "It's hot. I don't like it here."

Hot... Nitzan had been so freaked out he hadn't noticed the cloying heat or the high humidity. His skin tingled. He'd be sweating in no time flat.

Nitzan noticed the ceiling wasn't flat. Neither was the bulkhead. It had shallow curves and undulations, like the surface of an ice cube that had just begun to melt. Dark bronze in color, with a spotted pattern like that of coral.

Another Raider slid through the spanus—the old-timer, Bennett. The sergeant and the corporal steadied him. Bennett wiped his hand across his forehead, looked at the stringy strands of goo dangling from his fingers.

"Well, that was different," he said. "I bet we won't see that on a recruiting poster."

Alabama handed Bennett a towel, directed him to stand beside to Abshire.

Mafi came down next, a snarl on his face, one eye smeared shut with a thick, jiggling glob of ochre gunk. He licked his lips, immediately dry heaved, then bent over and threw up for real.

Alabama tossed a towel on his puke, draped another one over his shoulder.

Bennett pulled him out of the way.

Beaver Perry dropped down, laughing joyously even before his feet hit the deck. Hands reached to stabilize him, but he didn't need the help.

"That was *awesome!*" His eyes blazed with excitement. "Do we get to do that again? I want to do it again!"

Alabama pressed a towel against Beaver's chest.

"The five of you follow me," she said. "And watch your head. Low ceilings. Things are a bit cozy in here."

13

Hot moisture in the air, so thick she felt it in her lungs. Not quite a sauna, but not that far from it

"Back against the wall, Ensign."

Susannah did as she was told, toweling slime from her hair and coveralls. She was grateful Sung had told her to cover her face with her hands. The stuff smelled bad; Susannah bet it tasted even worse.

That entrance, these walls, the shape of the room...

She'd been inside the *Keeling* for all of thirty seconds. What she saw of its interior confirmed what she'd suspected when she laid eyes on its exterior—this ship was biomechanical, its tech likely on par with the Prawatt.

Who built it? What was it made of? Where and how had it been constructed? So *exciting*.

A pair of booted feet slid through the ceiling sphincter. Two sailors helped the person down. Like they'd done with Susannah, they handed the slime-smeared man a towel then stood him against the wall.

Susannah scrubbed at her face, tried to calm herself. Between rounds of plastic surgery, tattoo removal, healing her Bratchford-induced wounds—and getting an absolutely *horrible* bob, she couldn't wait until her hair grew out—the trip aboard the *Creeper* had been a sleepless marathon of studying both xenomechanics and the background of her new identity. Bethany Darkwater hailed from Bollis-town on Reiger 2. She'd done her engineering undergrad at Vollston Tech, also on Reiger 2. She'd married into money, spent her twenties and thirties doing nothing much at all. That looked good on the record, as there was very little detail for her to memorize.

Then, a divorce. No money. Bethany had joined Fleet reserves. Her xenomechanical background got her into the Academy, where she'd excelled until she'd been caught taking tests for others. Bock had been right—Bethany's fraud, combined with on-paper xenomechanics knowledge, drew the attention of Major Maia Whittaker. Did Bethany want to be kicked out of Fleet for good, or did she want to serve on an experimental ship and—at the end of a two-year stint—be given an officer's commission?

And now here she was, Ensign Bethany Darkwater, xeno mate.

She'd thought she would hate this. She'd been wrong. Whatever this ship was, it was already incredible, and she'd seen so little.

"You Darkwater?"

Susannah lowered the towel. A woman in a tank top stood before her, sweat-stained white fabric contrasting sharply with sweat-gleam-ing, cool-brown skin. The woman wore gray sailor coveralls, but only from the waist down. The arms were tied around her waist, hiding both rank and name.

"Yes," Susannah said. "I'm Ensign Bethany Darkwater."

"I'm Jenn Hathorn. Lieutenant. Lead xeno operator. I'm told you've never been on a warship before. That right?"

"That's correct, sir." Susannah knew in-system civilian ships, but not warships. She was grateful Bock made Bethany's record similar to Susannah's in that regard.

"Unreal," Hathorn said. "As if my job wasn't hard enough already. Now I gotta give a newbie the basics? Come with me."

She walked out through an oval-shaped opening. Susannah flung the towel over her shoulder and hurried to follow, but paused when she saw the opening's edges had the same texture as the pucker of metal that had pulled her into the ship. She ran her hand along the shiny, gnarled surface.

"Does this material expand, like the sphincter I just came through? Is this some kind of a pressure door?"

Hathorn stopped, turned sharply. "You figured out sphincters already, did you? Aren't you a smart one."

A compliment, but in words only, not in tone.

There was a subtle essence of meanness in Hathorn's face, subdued like a jagged rock just below the surface of a rippling river.

"This tech is amazing," Susannah said. "How does it—"

"Ensign, if no one told you not to ask questions on this ship, let me be the first. *Don't ask questions.*" Hathorn gestured aft, down a narrow passageway. "This is deck three. Sailor and non-com berths, infirmary, galley crew mess, storage."

The passageway bent slightly left and right, rose a bit here, dropped a bit there. Patterned, dull copper walls curved up into a patterned, dull copper ceiling. There were flat areas in the walls, but those were Fleet-gray. Cables ran along the ceiling's apex, leading to and from bright lights strung along the length. There were several oval-shaped openings like the one she'd just walked through. In the gray parts of the walls were a few standard hinged doors with lock wheels in their center. Susannah gathered that the dull copper might be original equipment, so to speak, while gray walls had been put in to divide up existing spaces.

Bolted into the wall a few feet away, a metal ladder led down through a hole in the fakegrav flooring.

"Is the sailor berth where I sleep?"

"You sleep in the atrium," Hathorn said. "Just like me and Colonel Hasik."

"Who is Colonel Hasik?"

"Xeno department chief. He's very senior. And didn't I tell you not to ask questions? Make sure your hands are dry. Don't want you slipping on the rungs."

Hathorn went down the ladder, loose strands of her frizzy black hair bouncing in time with each step.

Susannah ground the towel into her palms and fingers, scraping away the last of the viscous film, then followed Hathorn down.

"Level four." Hathorn pointed aft. "Engineering, punch-drives, machining, fabrication, the curvine room. You'll see all of it soon enough. Lincoln likes us to cross-train."

This level was more of the same—undulating, patterned copper material with fakegrav decking, and normal, flat, Fleet-gray walls with normal Fleet-gray pressure doors.

Susannah followed Hathorn forward. This passageway was like the one on level three, gently curving this way and that, slightly rising and falling—more like a beetle tunnel chewed through hardwood than a ship's passageway.

A man came from the other direction. When he and Hathorn reached each other, they both turned their shoulders and slipped past —the passageway wasn't wide enough for two people to pass abreast. Susannah did the same, looking down as she did so as not to make eye contact with the man.

Hathorn pointed to a closed gray hatch on her right. "That's the auxiliary CIC, in case the main one gets toasted. Know what a CIC is?"

Susannah had heard the acronym before but had never bothered to learn what it meant.

"Is the CIC like a bridge, sir?"

"*Bridge?* You've watched too many movies. You'll find out soon enough." Hathorn pointed to a closed gray hatch on her left. "We've got storage space in there, but we keep most of our stuff in the atrium."

The wavering passageway ended at an oval pucker of dark copper —a closed pressure door.

"Welcome to the xeno department, Ensign Darkwater."

Hathorn rubbed her hand on the oval's edge. Hard metal opened like a silent, living thing. Hathorn had to duck a little to go through.

A good four inches shorter than Hathorn, Susannah walked in standing tall—and stopped cold.

"High One," she whispered.

So far, everything had been tight, congested, cramped. This room was anything but. A good ten meters wide, the room was as wide as the ship itself. In the center was a cylinder of sorts, like the trunk of a misshapen tree made from molten glass. It glowed from within as if lit by a cosmic fire, golden-orange light thrumming and pulsing in a random, nonrhythmic pattern. The cylinder rested upon thick polyps of bright, copper-colored metal that rose up from the floor like the contorted, gilded ribs of some long-lost dinosaur.

Elevated metal-grate catwalks ran along both sides of the cylinder.

At the middle and at both ends, three steps connected the catwalks to small, rectangular platforms positioned above the glowing construct.

Susannah glanced up, momentarily disoriented by what she saw—the ceiling was an inverted cone covered with plants, a green waterfall of branches and vines hanging down toward the cylinder's life-nourishing light. Some six or seven meters above, the cone narrowed to a point hidden by thick vegetation. The height meant the cone took up part of level three. Colorful, oversized crops dotted the lush green—tomatoes the size of her head, strawberries as big as her fist, peppers the size of her forearm, huge vendamans, massive eggplants, bloated samilins, enormous bean pods, and leg-thick creepers weighed down by meter-long zucchini.

"What... what *is* this place?"

"This is the atrium," Hathorn said. "It holds the beating heart of the *James Keeling*."

It felt far hotter here than it had in the passageways. More humid, too.

"Is the atrium always this warm?"

"It is," Hathorn said. "You'll deal with it. Ensign Darkwater, you're looking at a trans-dimensional coupler. You're about to learn some shit that will absolutely blow your mind."

Susannah felt a rush of energy, a tingling surge that coursed through her being.

"*Trans-dimensional?* Are you kidding? How does it work? What kind of forces are used? What—"

"Ensign, shut, the fuck, *up*. Your job is to *listen* and learn. On the *Keeling*, and especially in this room, the only questions you can ask are those related to what you've been told. No outside-of-the-box thinking. No giving voice to your scientific curiosity. If you aren't told what something does, don't ask. If you aren't shown how something works, don't touch it. You get me?"

Questions were the foundation of science. Not ask any? That would be hard, but asking too many questions might raise suspicion. For now, she would have to be satisfied with whatever Hathorn and Colonel Hasik were willing to share.

"I get you, sir."

Hathorn pointed to the cylinder's near end, at a man-sized, onyx-black, slightly curved spur jutting up at an angle from the glowing material. A metal-grate platform was built around the spur, big enough for two people to stand on. A waist-high rail ran along the back of the platform—just beyond it was a two-meter drop to the front end of the glassy, log-like construct. A red sound-powered phone was attached to the rail, with both a handset and a speaker protected by a metal grille. Susannah had seen the like on various research ships, but never used one.

The spur looked like it was made of the same material as the construct, but it did not glow. Spikes, bumps, rough knots and knobby protrusions dotted its dark surface.

"Ensign, see that thing that looks like a diseased demon dick?"

Susannah had no idea what a diseased demon dick might look like, but she got the idea.

"I see it."

"*Especially* don't touch that," Hathorn said. "That's the protuberance. It controls everything. Keep your mitts off it unless you want to end up like Pete."

"Who is Pete, sir?"

"Pete ain't around no more. You took his place."

This place frightened Susannah, and yet, the heat she felt wasn't just from the room's ambient temperature—it burned from within her as well. Eagerness. Curiosity. The *need* to learn, to know. In the convent, she'd thought those urges gone, but they'd been there all along, hibernating, waiting for a sign.

This ship was that sign. This *room* was that sign.

"Speaking of questions, I have one for you," Hathorn said. "When you came in here, you said *High One*. You a Purist, Darkwater?"

Susannah's guts flooded with cold. Had she blown it already?

The lieutenant wasn't asking in a lighthearted way. Was she a religious bigot? Or was it that Purists were the Union's enemy, and this ship was the Union's greatest secret?

Susannah had to think fast, and she had to be convincing.

"Actually, I'm an atheist," she said. "Ever notice how atheists don't have a good equivalent of *oh my God* or *High One*? Sometimes, those phrases just pop out."

Hathorn's hard-eyed gaze held for a second, then softened.

"I'm an atheist, too," she said. "I'm guilty of the *oh my God* and more than a few *goddammits* myself. Well, Ensign? Ready to get to work?"

Susannah stared at the coupler, watched the lifelike, golden illumination fade and pulse and swirl inside of it.

"Yes I am, Lieutenant. Yes I am."

14

Trav smelled fresh bread baking away in the wardroom's small, attached galley. Bread, along with something rich and cheesy he couldn't pin down.

The wardroom was similar to those of other Fleet warships he'd served on, only much smaller. Wood paneling. A table with a blue tablecloth and ten chairs—four on each side, one at each end. There wasn't quite enough room to pull the chairs all the way out, which made for a strange, side-saddle shimmy to move in or out.

He sat at that table with Kerkhoffs and Lafferty. Corporal Colin Draper, their tour guide, stood against the bulkhead. He was an odd one, his eyes often squeezing tight like he was trying to wish away a waking nightmare.

Kerkhoffs rubbed a yellow-smeared towel against her too-long hair.

"Those sphincters are disgusting," she said. "But I gotta admit, they're pretty cool. I can't wait to learn how the tech works. It's like metal turns into soft dough."

Trav draped his towel around his neck, relaxed in his chair. He hadn't been ready for the sphincter, hadn't been ready to be *pulled down* like a noodle sucked through pursed lips. And the slime? He could do without that, but he wasn't about to let his disgust show. He was the XO of the *Keeling*—he had to set the bar high.

Apparently, Kerkhoffs and Anne Lafferty didn't hold the same standard for themselves.

"They're *beyond* disgusting," Lafferty said. "The less I have to go through one of those things, the better."

Trav, Kerkhoffs, and Lafferty had been given a lightning-quick, mind-boggling tour of the belowdecks. That's what Draper called the ship's three internal layers.

Deck Three: crew mess, cold storage, a small gym consisting of three treadmills (one broken) and two resistance rigs (one broken); and berths for enlisted and NCOs. Port and starboard guns were also on that level, their barbettes built over sphincters.

Deck four: punch-drive, fabrication plant, environmental systems, curvine room, chemical battery and generator compartment, small arms locker, and a cramped auxiliary CIC. There was also a room called the "atrium," but Trav and the others hadn't been allowed in. Draper said they would see it later, when Captain Lincoln approved it.

And, finally, deck five: a strange, tight hangar big enough for two Ochthera crawlers, their maintenance equipment, and little else. Environmental systems were on that deck, as was access to the fore and aft torpedo rooms, both of which had been built over sphincters. Each torpedo room had a 20-millimeter point-defense turret identical to the one atop the superstructure.

The lower bow extension housed what warship command crews referred to as Raider Land, or what crass enlisted sailors called Jizz Island. It contained the Raider berth (bunks, shower, head, CO's quarters) another small gym (four treadmills in that one, only two of which worked, and six resistance rigs, all functional), and the rig room that held TASH armor and the weapons cage. The rig room had a no-fucking-around reinforced door secured by two deadbolt tumbler locks. No getting in there without explosives. Considering that several Raiders who'd arrived in chains had likely been convicted of violent crimes, keeping the guns under lock and key was a must.

Walking through passageways that weren't quite straight? It was a strange feeling. That, combined with the uneven footing, almost *made Keeling* feel more like a gentle woodland trail than a warship.

Some compartments had normal doors while others had sphincter ovals. Trav had seen at least a dozen smaller sphincters, about waist high, wide enough for one sailor to crawl into. Some of those cubby-holes were too small to be useful for anything other than ad-hoc storage. A few, though, were long enough for crew to sleep in, which, Draper said, was the only privacy to be had belowdecks.

After the tour, Draper brought them back up the ladders to deck three, up through the sphincter—hands first instead of feet first—and into the superstructure, which held the ship's top two decks.

Deck One: signals room, telemetry, spectrometry, encryption, infotech, and a turret with a 20-millimeter rotary cannon for defense against torpedoes, missiles, voidcraft and exo-troops. The heavily armored turret doubled as an observation station. If all sensors went down—camera, signals, and darsat—the turret crew could communicate visuals to the CIC. Similar to the *Ishi*'s bubble, the turret was an add-on, not an integral part of the superstructure. Teams entered through a narrow double airlock, which they sealed behind them. If enemy fire tore up a turret, the solid hull beneath often remained mostly intact.

Deck two: CIC, captain's quarters, officer's berth, the spookhouse, quarters for the BII complement, XO's quarters, officer's galley and mess, and the wardroom, where they now sat, waiting for Captain Lincoln to show. The *Keeling*'s most striking feature—outside of the strange bulkheads, morphing metal, and weird passageways—was its width. Ten meters at its widest, it was *three times* narrower than any Fleet vessel of comparable length. Everything was cramped and overly confining, with equipment and people pressed in tight. Not an ideal setup considering how hot and humid it was belowdecks. The super-structure, at least, had a comfortable temperature.

Lafferty shimmied to the percolating urn built into the bulkhead that separated the wardroom from the galley.

"At least we have coffee," she said. "Last mission I was on, I went two weeks without the miracle juice. XO Ellis, you want a cup?"

Trav nodded. Lafferty returned carrying two white mugs. On any other Fleet vessel, the mug would be imprinted with the ship's name and profile outline. On a ship this secret? Plain old blank white.

She handed him a mug. He was surprised to see it was aluminum with an enamel coating, not the ceramic he'd seen on other ships.

"Better drink it quick," Lafferty said. "The mugs are so thin it will get cold fast."

Kerkhoffs wiped at a stain on the sleeve of her gray coveralls.

"I'm starving," she said. "The smell of zucchini casserole has me hungrier than a tick on a teddy bear."

Trav smiled—that was the smell he hadn't been able to place.

Lafferty's nose wrinkled. "*Zucchini?* What is that?"

"A vegetable," Kerkhoffs said. "You've never had it?"

"Never even heard of it," Lafferty said. "I'm not much for veggies. I'm more of a carnivore. Corporal Draper, when do we eat?"

"After Captain Lincoln speaks with you," Draper said. "She should be here at any moment."

Draper sounded highly intelligent. He also sounded... *hollow*, as if his brain used his mouth to communicate but his full attention remained elsewhere. He probably wasn't a day over twenty. Had he always been like this, or had his one patrol on the *Keeling* changed him? Probably the latter. Combat changed a person. Trav had yet to be told what the ship had endured on its last patrol, but considering the amount of replacement crew, it hadn't been a picnic.

"Corporal," Trav said, "have you gotten used to those sphincters?"

"No, sir, I haven't." Draper's eyes scrunched tight as tight could be, opened just as quickly. "I have to go through them a dozen times a day. But you're officers, you'll be up here most of the time." He snapped to attention. "Captain on the deck."

Trav, Lafferty, and Kerkhoffs stood and saluted as Lincoln entered. With her was a man dressed in sailor uniform pants and a t-shirt. No rank insignia. Thinning gray hair. A graying mustache. A single key dangled from the lanyard around his neck. Black-framed glasses made his eyes look like he was in a permanent staring contest.

"You saluted your captain, duly noted," Lincoln said. "No need to see those again. Corporal Draper, return to your duties."

"Returning to my duties," Draper said. "Aye-aye, Captain."

Draper stepped out of the wardroom and shut the door behind him.

Trav still couldn't fully believe it. Kiara Lincoln. Former captain of the carrier *Xihe*. The hero of Capizzi 7. Her combat tactics were a mandatory course in the Academy. She was one of the most dominant commanders in Fleet, yet she'd vanished. What had happened to her, to her career?

Lincoln gestured to the chairs. "As you were."

Everyone sat, except for Hasik, who walked to the urn. He returned with a mug for himself and one for Lincoln.

"Thank you, Zvanut," Lincoln said. "This is Colonel Zvanut Hasik, xeno department chief. Lieutenant Kerkhoffs, while xeno is technically under the engineering department, the colonel handles his area and is independent of your command purview."

Kerkhoffs nodded. "Aye, Captain."

She looked relieved to learn she wouldn't have to give orders to someone who outranked her by two grades.

"Let's get down to business," Lincoln said. "First, the good news. Our cook is fantastic. We eat like royalty. Now, the bad news."

The only *good news* was the food? This was off to an auspicious start.

"Everything you are about to learn is highly classified," Lincoln said. "I'm not allowed to tell you about the ship's history. I'm not allowed to tell you about past patrols. You are not allowed to ask Colonel Hasik or his xeno crew about this ship or the technology it contains. Is that understood?"

Trav, Lafferty, and Kerkhoffs responded in unison with: "Aye, Captain"

Lincoln took a sip of coffee. She looked tired. The last time Trav had seen an image of her, she hadn't had that scar. She'd put on a little weight, too. All muscle, by the looks of it.

"The Raider platoon is a new addition," she said. "On a ship this small, that's going to take some getting used to. XO Ellis, Chief Lafferty, your predecessors and I handled the triumvirate command structure well, but I will tell you the same thing I told them—this is my ship, and I am in command."

The triumvirate consisted of the captain, the XO, and the intel chief. To relieve any one of them from their position required the vote of the other two. The primary purpose of that setup was to prevent a ship's captain from removing an XO who would not obey an illegal order, such as attacking an allied ship or launching missiles against a planet. While the captain made all final decisions, the

XO's and intel chief's opinions were supposed to be carefully considered.

The secondary—and more frightening—purpose of the triumvirate structure was to allow for the removal of a captain gone rogue. If that happened, the XO became the commanding officer. If the XO was incapacitated, command fell to the intel chief.

Trav didn't know who had preceded him as XO. Lincoln hadn't told him, and he wasn't about to ask. If she wanted to share that info, she would, but it had no bearing on how he would do his job.

"This ship is unconventional," Lincoln said. "For starters, it is capable of significant, unprecedented self-repair."

Was that the reason for the secrecy? The Union had spent decades trying to make self-repairing ships, spending untold amounts on nanotech, self-crystalizing materials, inorganic DNA, and more. They'd tried to emulate Prawatt ships, which could heal hull damage, close punctures, even regrow elements like hardpoints, engine housings, passageways, and compartments. In the end, the only Union tech that showed promise was smart-nano—vast numbers of tiny machines that worked together by following simple, relational rules. For politicians and military leaders alike, though, smart-nano smacked too closely of Prawatt tech. No one wanted to accidentally create a *second* sentient, non-organic lifeform, when the first sentient, non-organic lifeform was responsible for *billions* of deaths.

"Self-repair isn't the biggest thing, though." Lincoln raised her mug to Hasik. "Go ahead, Colonel."

The bug-eyed Hasik rested his elbows on the table.

"I am allowed to give you a few key points," he said. "This ship looks different. Obviously. That is because it is of alien origin. Not an alien species we know of, but something different."

Lafferty seemed surprised. Trav wasn't.

Neither was Kerkhoffs.

"That's what I assumed when I saw it," she said. "Is it biomechanical, like the Prawatt?"

"Yes and no," Hasik said. "This ship is biomechanical in nature, but is vastly different from Prawatt tech. This ship has the ability to enter another dimension of reality, parallel to our own. There, *Keeling* is undetectable to any ship in realspace."

Unsure of what he'd just heard, Trav stared at the man. Hasik stared back, his blinks magnified by his thick lenses.

"Excuse me, Colonel," Kerkhoffs said. "Did you say *another dimension?*"

Hasik shifted in his seat, reached to his back pocket. He pulled out a leather-bound notebook—battered, bent, with colored stickies peeking out from the top, side, and bottom. He pulled a pen out of the spine, then flipped through the pages. They were covered with dense scribblings, equations, and words written in a language Trav didn't recognize.

Hasik tore an empty page free, set the notebook aside, then laid the paper flat on the table.

"You may have seen this explanation before, but bear with me," he said. "The contrasts are important to understanding the big picture." On the paper, he drew a letter A at the top, a B at the bottom. "These letters represent planets that are many light years apart." He drew several arcing lines between the letters. "All objects in the universe are attracted to each other through space-time curvature. It is the harnessing and amplification of this curvature that allows our curvature turbine technology, the curvine engine, to amplify and latch onto this force, propelling itself along."

The same high-level concept was taught to every sailor and Raider, to everyone who crewed a starship. Some compared it to climbing a rope; unless you were pedantic about relativistic theory, the rope didn't move, *you* did. A curvine created a "rope" between the galaxy's combined mass ahead of the ship and the galaxy's combined mass behind, then hauled itself—and the ship built around it—along that line.

"Space-time curvature is also what allows punch travel." Hasik lifted the paper, bent it so the top and bottom edges pressed together. "When planets are within a certain range and have similar specific parameters, we can shorten space-time curvature itself and—" he pushed the tip of his pen through the paper "—*punch* through space-time itself."

He laid the paper flat. Both A and B had a small hole next to them.

"Now I will explain what the *Keeling* can do." Hasik picked up the notebook, held it in one hand. "For explanatory purposes, say this book is the entirety of a three-dimensional universe."

He set the notebook down, flipped to a pair of blank pages. He wrote the letter X on the left-hand page, the letter Y on the right, then lifted Page X between finger and thumb.

"Let us pretend Page X is a two-dimensional surface—which we refer to as a *membrane*—that is within the three-dimensional space that is the notebook. Page Y is *another* two-dimensional surface, completely separate from Page X. Both pages have length and width, but not depth."

He flipped Page X to the right—it covered Page Y.

"Now we have a pair of membranes stacked together. A two-dimensional organism on Page Y could not see a two-dimensional organism on Page X, because two-dimensional organisms would have no concept of *depth*. Page X and Page Y are both part of the same reality, occupying an almost identical area space, but they are *separate*."

Hasik closed the notebook, looked at each person in turn. He spoke slowly, intent on making his meaning clear.

"Some believe we exist in a reality with at least nine dimensions. Length, width, depth, then time, and others I won't explain right now. You may look them up at your leisure. We can't see these dimensions, nor can we detect them in any way, because we are three-dimensional beings, just as two-dimensional beings can't detect the third dimension of depth."

Hasik opened the notebook again.

"Using the same analogy, let's say this notebook is now a *nine*-dimensional reality—" he lifted Page X, wiggled it "—and this page is a *three*-dimensional membrane." He raised Page Y, pinched it and X together between finger and thumb. "Page Y is *also* a three-dimensional membrane. A slight difference between my two-dimensional example is this—the three-dimensional membranes don't just occupy a *similar* area of space, they *overlap*, occupying *the same* area of space, yet they are completely separate."

Trav immediately wanted to ask how that was possible, but knew the concept was beyond him. He didn't want to sound stupid.

"I don't get it," Lafferty said. "How is that possible?"

"The *how* is classified." Hasik picked up the pen, wiggled it. "This pen represents *Keeling*." Still holding the pages by their edges, he made slow, overlapping whorls on Page Y. "Page Y is the membrane we're currently in, what we call *realspace*. *Keeling* can move through the three-dimensional space of our membrane, but also—" he poked the tip through the paper, making a hole in both sheets "—penetrate through to the other membrane, and travel there as well."

He flipped both pages to the left. Starting at the hole, he made a slow, whorling line on Page X.

"Unlike our hypothetical, two-dimensional beings, and unlike us in realspace, *Keeling* can do something astounding."

He set the pen down, then lifted the notebook in his left hand. With his right finger and thumb, he held up Page X and Page Y as one.

Through Page X, Trav could see the curling pen line on Page Y.

"While in the second membrane," Hasik said, "*Keeling* can sometimes detect objects in the first membrane—in realspace—while objects in realspace *cannot* detect the *Keeling*. Those objects include enemy vessels. That is why we are here, *because Keeling* is the *only* ship we know of that can do what it does."

Real stealth. No one had it. Space was big. Big and cold. Trav was no physicist, but he knew the general concept—starships produced heat, heat produced black-body radiation, and black-body radiation was detectible, even in tiny amounts, at great distances.

All major governments had their version of coldships—small vessels that traveled mostly by inertia, their crews frozen solid. The tech was far from perfected, though. If the ship wasn't detected and destroyed while in cold-mode, crews still had to wake up to conduct operations. Massive heat sinks let ships operate undetected for a time, *if* they didn't accelerate or maneuver. Successful missions—mostly ambushes and some long-range recon—were possible, but only under specific conditions. Coldships were not reliable weapons of war.

Everyone tried to field AI ships with no biological crew. No living bodies to keep warm meant far less heat expenditure. The AI ships, though, still had to travel from one place to another, and when they did, they became detectible. A little over a century ago, the League of Planets had gotten close to developing a reliable AI stealth ship, but the game-changing development of weaponized space-time ended that dream.

Space-time curvature manipulation—crudely and commonly referred to as *STC fuckery*—wreaks havoc with the electromagnetic spectrum. Digital and quantum computers rely on precise streams of data. STC manipulation causes bits to flip, alters qubit superpositions, and modifies electron flow in unpredictable ways. No amount of error-correction can keep up. You don't have to *destroy* a computer to render it inoperable, you only have to make the data it used unreliable.

In combat, computers became utterly worthless. That included AIs. To win battles in space these days, you had to do it with sentient, biological beings firing weaponry that used no electronic computers of any kind.

Even if someone eventually defeated the heat radiation issue that made even stealth ships light up like a candle in a pitch-black room, there were still curvine echoes, active EM-spectrum detection, and the fact that every object in the universe generates a gravitational signature. The bigger the object, the bigger the signature, the more detectable it is.

But this? This *trans-dimensional* stuff? Trav didn't need to understand how it worked to know it could alter the balance of power.

Lafferty leaned back in her chair, rubbed her fingertips against her forehead.

"So, this ship is like a submarine," she said. "Is this membrane-hopping a trans-dimensional version of going below the surface?"

Trav saw Lincoln lower her head, trying to hide a smile.

"It is *not* like a submarine," Hasik said. "We can't go beneath the surface because there *is* no surface in a three-dimensional existence."

Lincoln held up a hand to still him.

"I know you hate that analogy, but it works for tactical purposes," she said. "The crew refers to going into the other dimension as a *dive*."

Hasik sat up straighter. "But that word isn't accurate. We *shift*, we don't *dive*."

It was obvious Lincoln had listened to this particular objection many times. Hasik seemed to be typical BST—he didn't understand that sailors, Raiders, and strikers preferred to use the simplest terms possible.

"Colonel, give it a rest," Lincoln said.

He sat back, crossed his arms. Was he *pouting*?

"We're like a sub in two key ways," Lincoln said. "We can go where the enemy can't. They can't see us, but we can see them. Some of the time, anyway. That advantage comes at a price." She rubbed at her wrist. Was that a bandage barely peeking out from her coveralls sleeve? "Going into the Mud, which is what we call the other dimension, it can cause... *damage*. Damage to the crew. No one is allowed in areas exposed to space. That includes the artillery gunhouses and the point-defense turrets. While we're in-dim, those positions are always unmanned."

That was shocking. A blanket order like that potentially left the ship vulnerable.

Trav leaned forward. "Why aren't they manned, Captain? And what kind of damage?"

Instead of answering, Lincoln stood.

"We'll make a transdim hop in one hour," she said. "It's something words fail to describe. You have to experience it to understand the challenges involved."

Keeling's dive would not be as straightforward as a submarine quietly slipping beneath the surface of an ocean, that much was plain to see.

"Captain, I don't understand something," Kerkhoffs said. "If this ship can do all you say, then its technology is priceless. What's Fleet's reasoning for putting *Keeling* at risk on missions instead of just studying it?"

Hasik bristled. "I've been *studying it* for six years, thank you very much."

"Thank you for your time, Colonel," Lincoln said. "You should get back to your area."

Hasik seemed only too glad to leave. He walked out, muttering under his breath.

"You want *reasons*, Lieutenant Kerkhoffs?" Lincoln rubbed at her scar. "Command doesn't give me *reasons*—they give me *orders*. Besides, I'm sure you can figure it out. The war isn't going well. *Keeling* is a powerful asset that is needed right now. Our current mission profile is to use the ship but keep it out of harm's way as much as possible. I have strict guidelines to avoid direct confrontation with enemy warships."

If that was true, why were so many fresh bodies needed? Were those "strict guidelines" a response to a mission gone wrong? One that resulted in a need for almost *forty* crew replacements?

"I need to prepare for the dive," Lincoln said. "Any critical questions that involve your area of responsibility, not our deployment orders?"

"I have one, Captain," Trav said. "How's our torpedo team?"

Modern torpedoes were the most complex system on a warship. For centuries, torps had relied on computer and/or AI for guidance and tracking. STC fuckery scrambled those systems. While all torps could be fired "dumb," using only observations and math, a smart torp needed an analog tracking system. There was only one type of analog system that could compute fast enough to be effective in space combat —a biological brain.

"The torpedo team is... they're weird," Lincoln said. "As are most torpedo teams. Our two torpedo leads both have one *Keeling* patrol under their belt. I'm very comfortable with our bat brains."

The modified brain of a bat operated as a torpedo's tracking system. Because of that, *bat brains* had become the slang term for a warship's torpedo crew.

"That's enough for now," Lincoln said. "XO, Major Lafferty, be in the CIC at oh-nine-hundred. That gives you thirty minutes to eat. Combat Cook?"

Trav heard big feet thumping closer. Bradley Henry, the hulking culinary designer who'd held a stunstick to make sure everyone behaved, entered the wardroom—he had to turn sideways and duck to get through the narrow door. Over his coveralls, he wore an apron that said MASTER CHIEF with a jagged black line marking out the "I." He carried four plates, with forks, knives, and spoons stacked on top.

"The soup is splendiffic, Captain," Henry said. "Are you eating?"

"Not yet. I'll eat a sandwich later."

"I got you covered," Henry said.

He set the plates down in front of Trav, Lafferty, and Kerkhoffs, then laid out the knives, forks, and spoons.

"We dive at oh-nine-fifteen," Lincoln said. "I look forward to serving with you all."

She left the wardroom.

The utensils caught Trav's eye. They were brown. He picked up his fork, tapped at it. It was thin, neither metal nor plastic.

Trav held it up. "What is this?"

"Mycoware," Henry said. "Made of mushroom fiber. Doesn't work all that well, but if it breaks, you can eat it."

Lafferty picked up her knife, stared at it. "We don't get metal silverware?"

Henry set down the last spoon. "No, sir. We wouldn't want any of you to cut yourselves or someone else, now would we?"

He hustled back to the galley.

"*Not even a souvenir spoon*," Kerkhoffs said, quoting Lincoln's speech. "Does she think people will use silverware as a weapon? Holy shit. What the hell happens when we hop dimensions?"

Something bad. That was all Trav knew for certain.

Bradley came back with bowls of soup. The bowls, like the utensils, were brown. More mycoware. Trav instantly knew why—because ceramic bowls could be broken, and the shards could cut deep.

Holy shit indeed.

15

It was the strangest rig room John Bennett had ever seen.

Like the Raider berth and some of the passageways, the room's bulkheads and overhead had that crazy metallic pattern reminiscent of fossilized coral hammered flat. Aside from the fakegrav deck and the small section of bulkhead that held the reinforced door, there wasn't a single completely flat surface or a hard angle to be seen.

Still, the room was rectangular enough to hold the standard gear of a Raider platoon: a weapons cage against the forward bulkhead, two TASH repair tables, and stretching from the aft bulkhead, the rig itself —four rows of ten vertical stalls each. Every stall held a pitch-black TASH armor rig, helmet, webbing, flight pack, spare parts, MG tanks, and a diagnostic deck.

"Fuckballs," Radulski said. "V12s? These are three gens old."

John liked Radulski. People in the platoon were already giving him shit for his blue skin, but he didn't seem to care.

"Try *four* gens," Renee Jordan said. "At least this one is. It's a fucking V11."

She sounded as disgusted as John felt. This was like waking up on Christmas morning, opening your only present, and finding out your mother had gift wrapped yesterday's leftover meatloaf.

Sergeant Jordan's skin was so dark it was almost true black. The compartment's lights played off her head, which she kept shaved as clean as a bullet. She had a calm swagger that came with hardcore combat experience.

"Let's get to work, people," PXO Winter said. "They ain't gonna count themselves."

John wasn't usually attracted to squad mates, but he had a hard time keeping his eyes off Winter. She had a Raider's thick muscle and a butt you could balance a rifle on. And those scars on her cheek... she'd seen deadly action and come out the other side. Very sexy.

He forced those thoughts away. She was above him on the command chain, which meant he was off-limits to her. And besides, who was he kidding? He was probably twenty years her senior. Women like Winter didn't go for fossils like him.

Winter wanted a quick inventory of the platoon's TASH rigs. She'd brought John, Jordan, and Radulski along to do the task, because the four of them were among the platoon's thirteen riflemen with combat experience. The other eleven riflemen were unblooded, straight out of boot or so close to it they'd never been under fire.

While Lindros hadn't said as much, John could tell the lieutenant was unblooded. The combat vets, like Jordan, thought that was a bad sign. John, though, knew an inexperienced commanding officer wasn't always a bad thing. He'd served under green LTs who'd flourished, and also those who'd seen battle but couldn't find their own butthole if they had an extra hand with six fingers on it.

"High-level check only," Winter said. "LT wants to know if we have a full forty. Micromuscle test, bring OS online, check air integrity, CO_2 scrubber, waste processor, and MG levels. Don't bother with flight packs, we'll get those later. Make it fast—orders are to be out of here and in our racks by oh-nine-fifteen."

They had twenty-five minutes to get the job done. Most LTs wouldn't assign a work detail for such a short amount of time. Lindros, apparently, didn't want to let a second go to waste. That, too, could be a good trait or a bad one. Some platoon leaders didn't know how to relax. Some relaxed too much.

Winter assigned each Raider a row.

John flipped open the first stall's diagnostic deck. He had just over two minutes to check each of his row's ten rigs. Not a problem if he worked efficiently.

Tactical Assault Suit Hermetic—*TASH*—armor had changed drastically since John's boot days. His first TASH had been bulky, thick with composite plate. He'd looked like a walking tank. Damn things were difficult to manage under the best of circumstances. During a boarding raid? Half the time the suits didn't fit through internal hatches. Raiders would have to slice up perfectly good hatches just to advance through a ship. That slowed things down, and a slow Raider was a dead Raider.

Advances in protective materials and tech gradually made their way into the rigs. John's first TASH—a V3—weighed in at 120 kilos. By the V10, the weight and bulk, had been cut in half. The V11, V12, and V13s offered almost identical armor protection, weighing between 22 and 26 kilos, depending on load out.

It would have been nice to have V14s, which had a new kind of armor that was thinner than its predecessors yet offered superior protection. But a V12 wasn't exactly a poke in the eye with a sharp stick. The 12s—and even the 11, for that matter—would get the job done.

The first in his row was a V12, serial number 1A76.

The form-fitting TASH was the deep black of a starless void. Multi-layered plates covered non-flexible areas. Overlapping lamellar discs protected the joints and the neck. Hopefully the plate was high-quality. John had lived through two bad batches in his day, where QC failed. Or, more likely, had been ignored altogether, so a contractor or procuring admiral could pad their bank accounts. Hopefully the LT would order live-fire tests on spare plates once the *Keeling* was underway. Better to know of potential armor failure before bullets flew.

The left pectoral plate had a thin crack. John marked it for testing and potential replacement. Stress degradation on right shoulder joint —it would have to be fixed, if not replaced altogether.

He triggered the micromuscle check. The headless suit of armor raised both hands, extended the fingers, made a fist, rotated the wrists, and extended the fingers again. Each leg bent up until the knee touched the chest, then lowered. The feet, hovering just above the fakegrav deck, twisted, toes up, toes down, then hung lifeless.

Micromuscle filaments had been one of the biggest improvements in TASH tech. The all-analog material sensed the wearer's movements, then instantly replicated those movements so quickly it felt like suit and Raider were one and the same. Depending on the rig's generation, micromuscle multiplied the wearer's physical strength by a factor of 1.5 to 1.9. As a self-contained analog system, TASH rigs were immune to blazers, scramblers, corruptors, and the general warping of space-time that fucked up electronics in combat.

The right leg had full flexibility, but the left stopped fifteen degrees from regulation minimum angle.

"PXO," he called out, "we steal these rigs from a bargain bin somewhere?"

"Or maybe a dumpster," Jordan said. "My first one is in bad shape. Goddamn thing is missing a finger, and there's still stickers on the armor from the last sap to wear it. How did we wind up with battered gear?"

"Shut up, both of ya," Winter said. "Stay on-task."

John pulled the rig's helmet off the stall shelf and slid it over his head. He pushed the button behind the right ear—the helmet hummed as the firm interior conformed to his skull, providing an instant, perfect fit. Diagnostic code scrolled down the inside of the visor.

Operating system boot-check, A-okay.

He shut the helmet off and placed it back on the shelf.

John ran the remaining diagnostic tests: air integrity 97%, waste system 0% capacity and functional, O_2 reserves 100%, CO_2 scrubber 82%. Regs said the scrubber had to be at 85% to consider the suit functional. He marked that for repair or replacement.

Finally, he checked the MG levels: 7.5 liters in the suit, a full load. The stall's reserve tank contained another 38 liters.

Along with micromuscle, MG—*magic goop*, a viscous gel that flowed within the suit's material—was the tech that made hermetic rigs so effective in vacuum combat. Goop did several things. It conducted analog electrical signals to the micromuscle, eliminating any need for wires. When impacted hard enough from, say, a bullet or shrapnel, MG solidified, dispersing kinetic energy. That made the armor plating above it far more effective. Magic goop insulated the wearer against the Big Two-Seventy—the negative 270 degrees Celsius of the void—and against up to 500 degrees Celsius, although that kind of heat protection didn't last much more than a few minutes. Last and perhaps most important, MG instantly sealed punctures in TASH material, stopping minor bleeding and protecting the wearer from the vacuum of space.

John finished his check. This rig needed serious work before anyone could hullwalk in it, let alone wear it into battle. Whoever was assigned this rig would have their work cut out for them. A Raider's duties included maintenance and repair of their own gear. As the saying went: *know what to fix before you get in the mix.*

"PXO, TASH one-A-seven-six is sub-optimal," John called out. "Multiple repairs needed."

"TASH one-A-seven-six, sub-optimal," Winter called back. "Affirmative."

A standard platoon consisted of twenty-five riflemen—which included the CO, the PXO, and the platoon sergeant—along with three crawler pilots, three co-pilots, three engineer-gunners, a tech crew master chief, and two technicians. Thirty-seven Raiders in total. Three spare suits made for the "full forty," a platoon's usual TASH complement. Pilots and co-pilots wore their rigs on every mission; if the need arose or their vehicle was a mobility kill, they were ready to fight. In combat situations, even the techs TASHed up—if unexpected visitors breeched the hull while the frontline force was deployed, techs anchored defense against those boarders. If things got bad enough, pilots, co-pilots and techs were ready to step in and fill holes in the frontline fireteams.

Such was the mantra of the force: *Every Raider is a rifleman.*

"This one's got a bullet hole in the hip joint," Radulski called out. "This ain't no TASH, more like *TRASH*, if you ask me."

"No one asked ya," Winter said. "Stay on task."

John moved on to the next suit in his row.

16

Sascha Kerkhoffs ran her hand along the bright, smooth copper surface.

"You said this area was cut just yesterday?"

Propulsion Chief Adam Ledford nodded.

"Yes sir," he said. "The integrator struts were giving way, so instead of hacking one together in the machine shop, we got a new cage from *Ishi*'s stores."

The integrator, a fist-sized, perfect cube of osmium, was a key component of the punch-drive. Unless damaged, a cube could last—hypothetically—for a hundred thousand years. The cage that held a cube had to be anchored in the hull structure. Cages suffered at least some structural damage every time a ship punched-in or punched-out. Anchors eventually weakened and needed to be replaced.

"But this is smooth." Sascha again ran her hand across a patch of copper so shiny she could see her reflection in it. "Did you grind it down after installing the cage?"

"No sir," Ledford said. "The ship does that all by itself. No matter how jagged a cut, within a day or three the rough edges smooth themselves out."

Fascinating. She couldn't wait to know more.

She'd wolfed down her zucchini casserole—it tasted sensational, with zucchini slices as thick as her thigh—then rushed down to engineering to learn what she could before the *Keeling* "dove" into another goddamn dimension.

Sascha stood and brushed off the knees of her coveralls.

"Those shiny patches I saw on the hull," she said. "Were those from exterior damage? What caused it, and how long ago?"

Ledford looked uncomfortable. "You'll have to ask the captain about that, sir. I'm not allowed to say."

It was the third time in the last fifteen minutes she'd heard that same answer. Lincoln didn't like it when people asked questions, something *Keeling* vets obviously took to heart.

"I understand," Sascha said. "I'll take it up with the captain."

She would do exactly that, but not any time soon. She had to focus on understanding her department, its equipment, and her people. She'd never been in battle—if a fight came, she needed to be ready.

Ledford's pale skin looked as if he hadn't seen sunlight in months. His coveralls were smeared with mechanical grease and dotted with the purple stains of curvine solvent. He'd tied his coverall arms around his waist. His white t-shirt clung wetly to him, and his face gleamed with sweat, as did the face of everyone in engineering—Sascha included.

She understood why the engineer crew wore light t-shirts and tank tops. Some even wore workout shorts. Those in regulation coveralls wore them like Ledford did—some with shirts, some bare-chested.

The previous engineering chief obviously hadn't been a stickler for the uniform code. Captain Lincoln didn't seem to care, either. Sascha wasn't about to bust anyone's balls for being as comfortable as they could—she wanted out of her own stifling coveralls in the worst possible way.

"Chief, can you at least tell me why we don't have air conditioning down here?"

Ledford laughed a dark laugh. His eyes had a sunken quality to them, like he'd seen too much, and what he'd seen had corroded him.

"AC is on, Lieutenant," he said. "It's pegged at max-cold. The last guy set it to run nonstop. He could never get the temp in engineering below ninety-five, and that was on a good day. Maybe the new aux chief can do better."

Ninety-five; Ledford used Fahrenheit. That meant he was probably from somewhere on Earth. Ninety-five Fahrenheit equaled thirty-five Celsius.

The auxiliary chief was responsible for operation of most non-propulsion systems, which included environmentals.

Ledford referred to the previous aux chief as *the last guy*—not by name. Sascha had already learned that the few vets onboard didn't like to speak the names of those who'd left the ship. Or who'd died on it. It was spooky. Sailors usually waxed poetic about their former mates—but not here, not on the *Keeling*.

"If the AC is pegged and it's still this hot," Sascha said, "what's the temp when it's *not* working?"

"The record is a hundred and fifteen, sir. It was like that for forty-eight hours. People were dropping like flies. We had to take shifts up in the superstructure to cool off."

One hundred and fifteen degrees—forty-six Celsius—for two full days. Brutal.

"Thank you, Chief." Sascha glanced at the brass clock set into the curved copper ceiling—08:55. "We're diving soon. What's protocol for this department when we, uh, do the transdim thing? Who gets stationed where?"

She would rely heavily on Ledford in the weeks to come. He was one of two engineering staffers on their third *Keeling* patrol, the other being Brian Goldsmith, an electrical mate. There were nineteen people in engineering. Sixteen if she didn't count the xeno department. Of those sixteen, five were on their second *Keeling* patrol, and eight were first-timers like her.

"Nobody gets stationed nowhere, Lieutenant," Ledford said. "Captain's standing orders are we have to be in our racks when we dive. Just in case."

"In case of what?"

His dead eyes stared out. "In case it don't go so well."

There was a *you'll see for yourself* tone in his voice. She would, very soon, and she wasn't looking forward to it.

"If engineering isn't crewed, what happens when the CIC wants adjustments to the curvine or to prep for a punch?"

Ledford shrugged. "We've never punched while in the Mud, far as

I know. Maybe the punch-drive doesn't work there, same as with the curvine."

"The *curvine* doesn't work? Then how does the ship move?"

"With the tails, sir."

She remembered seeing the ship's aft section as three separate elements, wavering like eel tails.

"How do the tails propel the ship?"

"You'll have to ask the captain," Ledford said.

Surprise, surprise.

"Thank you, Chief," Sascha said. "That's all for now."

Ledford shuffled away. He wasn't quite 180 centimeters tall—6-feet, in his terms—yet he had to tilt his head slightly so as not to scrape it against the ceiling's rough, repetitive surface. Being in here felt like being inside a barnacle.

Not counting bulkheads and hatches obviously installed by Fleet, the *Keeling*'s hull material was the same inside and out—a metal-organic framework, or "MOF," made of a beryllium-copper-carbon alloy. She'd worked with MOFs before. The engineered materials had microscopic crystalline structures that possessed massive internal surface areas. If one could unfold a typical MOF and lay it flat, a single gram of the stuff would have a surface area greater than that of three tennis courts. BST types engineered MOFs to separate and store particular gasses or fluids.

What did *Keeling*'s MOF material store?

She'd asked. The answer? *Ask the captain.*

The engineering department had an unusual layout, but the tasks it performed were little different from any other Fleet warship. The punch-drive was just aft of amidships, a hull-wide horseshoe-shaped structure wrapped around the graviton battery, which itself was a horseshoe-shape wrapped around the integrator array. Machining and environmental bays ran along the port side, the fabrication plant along starboard. Between machining and environmental lay the curvine room.

The *Keeling*'s curvine seemed normal. At thirteen meters long, it had the expected hyperboloid shape, like an hourglass with the top and bottom cut off. It lay horizontally in a cradle made of the same metal as the hull and interior, but several shades darker than anywhere else on the ship, even the battered exterior. A curvine needed to be located as close as possible to a ship's overall center of mass—*Keeling's* was. A curvine's mass needed to be five to seven percent of the total mass of the ship it moved—*Keeling's* was.

There was something odd about the curvine room, though. Something *different*, at least. While the punch-drive, battery, machining bay, environmental bay, and fabrication plant were all shoe-horned in, their standard equipment modified to fit into copper hollows, nooks, caves, and crannies, the cradle conformed to the curvine as if it had been custom made for that purpose—no cuts, no adjustments.

In a strange ship where nothing fit quite right, the curvine cradle looked like original equipment. That perfect fit seemed incongruent with everything else she's seen thus far.

The clock hit 09:00—they would dive in fifteen minutes.

17

Anne could have been executed. Her father had enemies in BII and the admiralty. Those enemies had tried to politicize Anne's successful mission, punish *her* to get at *him*, but General Bart Lafferty was too smart for that, too adept at this game.

Instead of being vented, Anne had a promotion and a command position with two operators under her.

As intel chief, she enjoyed the privilege of her own quarters. Sure, her compartment was smaller than most closets she'd had, but she didn't have to share it. If she extended her arms and stretched just a little, she could simultaneously touch her port and starboard bulkheads. She could do the same with fore and aft.

Her bed was a mattress atop a coffin locker, where she kept her uniforms, shoes, and personal effects. The bed and locker combo together flipped up into the bulkhead. When it did, the large monitor mounted to the bed's underside activated. Anne could use it while sitting on the floor-retractable chair at her flip-down desk, which had its own monitor. There was a tiny basin with a mirror above it, and that was it.

Small as it was, her quarters were one of only two private compartments on the ship—the other belonged to Captain Lincoln. XO Ellis had a compartment to himself, but only because he was supposed to share it with Xeno Chief Hasik, who instead berthed in the secret generator room along with his staff, Lieutenant Hathorn and Ensign Darkwater. The XO's quarters were just aft of Anne's.

Anne got the private space because intel department heads planned for covert ops, used special coding and decoding equipment, and often had a higher security clearance than the ship's captain. Conducting spy business in a shared area simply wouldn't do.

She wore the black coveralls of BII. While sailors, strikers and Raiders had varying uniform colors depending on formality, everything BII wore was black—dress blacks, black service uniforms, black coveralls... even the black shorts and t-shirt of their PT gear.

Coveralls were standard attire on any ship during a war patrol. Anne admired the heptagram outline on her rank tab. She was an o4, a *major*. How long until she'd get the solid heptagram of a colonel? The single star of a commodore?

How long until her rank insignia held the two stars of a *general*?

A general like her father.

In the mirror, she gave herself a once-over before joining her direct reports. Her Plain Jane looks were ideal for her line of work. Nothing unusual about her features. Normal-sized nose. Lips weren't too thin or too thick. She didn't have the kind of big eyes that people wanted to gaze into.

Was she attractive? Yes, but mildly so. A seven out of ten, perhaps.

The unremarkable nature of her face made it an ideal canvas for makeup. Anne could transform herself into someone so ugly that no one wanted to look at her, or into a stunner who tickled the libidos of men and women alike. When she wanted to draw attention, her makeup skills took her from a seven to a high nine. Occasionally, seducing people was part of the job.

Now, though, Anne didn't need makeup. She was *in charge*. She would earn respect through her work.

"Thank you, Daddy," she whispered. "Thank you for this second chance."

She stepped out of her quarters into the one-meter-wide passageway that separated the starboard-side compartments from the CIC, which ran the length of the superstructure. Just forward of her quarters was the Intel Operations room, a.k.a. the *spookhouse*. It was the same width as her quarters but twice the length. She stepped through the hatch.

The two men seated at the slate-table stood to attention.

"Major," they said in unison.

A girl could get used to this.

"Good morning, analysts. As you were."

The men sat and returned to their work, studying information they'd called up on the slate. These men—Corporal Jester Gillick and Warrant Officer Akil Daniels—were under her command.

The spookhouse held encrypted communications equipment, a massive database for when the ship could use computers, and a rack of paper reference binders for when it could not. The slate was bolted to the starboard bulkhead, with two seats on the long side and one each on the ends.

Anne slid into the aft end seat, the one traditionally reserved for the intel chief. For *her*. She was in charge of military intelligence on a classified warship. Two years here—at *most*—and her career wouldn't just be back on track, it would be streaking along on afterburners. If that wasn't worth getting sucked through a greasy spanus, Anne didn't know what was.

"The first transdim trip is in ten minutes," she said. "You will both join me in the CIC for it."

"Aye, Major," they said, again in unison.

Like her, they were both new to the ship. The two men shared a berth just forward of the spookhouse. Their bunk coffin beds didn't flip up like Anne's did, but other than that, their quarters were identical to hers.

Gillick had thick black hair, a round face, and a down-angled nose that made him look like he'd grown up in a Sino settlement. Daniels was a year or two younger, perhaps twenty-four. His close-scalp cornrows spoke of meticulous attention to detail, and his hazel eyes held the casual lethality of a bored housecat.

Neither man was anything special in the looks department, but they weren't ugly by any stretch. An unremarkable face was a cornerstone of deep cover work.

"A *trans-dimensional* hop," Gillick said. "I find myself looking forward to this as much as I look forward to a body cavity search."

"Oh, come on, Jester." Daniels pinched a piece of lint off the slate's surface. "Depending on who's doing it, a BCS isn't so bad."

Ah, the old *boys will be boys* shit, was it? Would they have said the same tawdry thing in front of an Intel Chief that didn't have tits?

"This is going to be a challenging assignment," Anne said. "We will execute the three pillars of BII—knowledge, discovery, and protection."

Those words decorated the department's crest. Saying them out loud was a bit officious, perhaps, but Daddy always said a good leader makes expectations known. Anne would ensure that her intel department ran smooth and by the book.

"When the time comes to share knowledge on any and all foreign governments, we will be ready," she said. "When we have an actual intelligence mission, we will excel at discovery. For now, this department's primary and ongoing objective is *protection*—to identify potential spies and to defend against saboteurs."

Daniels sighed. "Permission to speak freely, Major?"

Did bored house cats sigh? Anne wouldn't know; the Laffertys had always been dog people. If house cats *could* sigh, though, she bet they sounded exactly like this guy.

"Go ahead, Daniels."

"We're locked out of personnel records," he said. "This ship is *full* of criminals. We have to assume some of the crew are significant intel risks. When do we find out what everyone did?"

A question to which Anne had an answer, one she didn't like.

"We don't," she said. "Other than name, rank, serial number, and skill qualification ratings, we don't know anything about the crew's histories."

Gillick rubbed at his eyes.

"This is such bunk," he said. "How do we do our jobs if we don't know who did what? We don't even get to know who committed financial crimes? Those are our bread and butter."

He was right about that. BII operated on the belief that if a fleeter would commit one crime for financial gain, they'd commit another. Particularly if there is a *lot* of money involved, and money was something enemy intelligence agencies threw around like candy. Druggies were a related story—once you're addicted to a substance, you are controllable by people who supply that substance.

"I'm not happy about it either," Anne said.

In truth, she was *quite* happy about it. Someone had tried to frame her for war crimes. She didn't need people thinking she was some kind of psycho. Anne was ninety-nine percent certain not even Captain Lincoln knew what happened on Eden—Daddy would have seen to that.

"I'll admit my wrongdoing," Daniels said. "I took a big bribe and got caught. How about you two? What got you entombed?"

Gillick grinned wide. "*Entombed*. Sealed off in the *Crypt*. I like it. As for me—"

"Enough," Anne said. "On this ship, past crimes, if any, are classified information. Do not share yours. I've been specifically ordered to *not* ask crewmembers about theirs. However, you both seem like gregarious types. If you have a casual conversation and accidentally learn the truth about what put a crewmember on this ship, you should quietly inform me about it so I can effectively counsel you on how to keep said information quiet."

Gillick grinned. "We certainly wouldn't want to learn anyone's secrets."

"Of course not," Daniels said. "I, for one, would *never* intentionally pry into the private lives of my crewmates. To do so would be uncouth and unseemly."

Prying was BII's *job*—Jester Gillick and Akil Daniels would start doing so, immediately. They'd get information Anne wasn't allowed to ask for. If someone ratted them out to the XO or to the captain, Anne had full deniability.

"Time to go," she said.

They walked aft to the CIC entrance. Just inside were three stairs to port, which led to the xeno loft, and three to starboard, which led to the intel loft. Anne took her place in a raised acceleration chair at the rear of the intel loft, right behind Gillick's and Daniels's stations, which abutted a rail looking out onto the rectangular CIC.

She'd never seen a rectangular one before. Most were circular, with stations positioned to face a three-meter-diameter crystalium navigation orb. Most were significantly larger, too—even a small patrol ship's CIC was four times the size of this confined space.

Keeling's CIC was twelve meters long but only four meters across. The nature of the narrow space meant most stations were built against bulkheads, with operators facing *away* from the nav-orb, which sat dead center in the long rectangle. That orb was only two meters in diameter—tiny compared to the others she'd seen. There wasn't enough room for a bigger one.

Captain Lincoln and XO Ellis stood side by side at the command slate, which was just aft of the orb. That put their backs to both the xeno and intel lofts. The XO's coveralls looked clean. Lincoln's were a disaster. When had she last laundered them? And that ridiculous black bandana on her head, as if she thought she was a pirate on the ancient seas.

Directly forward of the orb was the navigator's station, where Doug Erickson was seated. He could face the orb or turn his acceleration chair forward and watch the pilot stations, which were only a meter away. On one side of Nav's chair was a slate for when computers were functional, on the other, a manual array for when they were not. The manual array contained a bank of slide rules, the chrono controls, and a roll of paper for manual plotting.

The pilot station had two consoles, one for the pilot, one for the co-pilot. In front of them were large monitors that displayed a myriad of flight data needed to maneuver the ship.

Along the CIC's port side, from front to back, were stations for darsat, signals, and ECM. Anne didn't know those particular operators. She'd hadn't memorized the entire crew but would have that mastered within the day. Aft of the ECM station was the Raider liaison station, where Lieutenant Lindros was sitting.

Along the starboard bulkhead, from front to back: the gun control station, occupied by Dardanos Leeds, artillery chief; the weapons station, occupied by Cat Brown, weapons department head; the bulky analog torpedo data computer station, currently empty; and finally, the ops station, occupied by Alex Plait, operations department head.

Captain Lincoln stood. "Nav, set the timer for fifteen minutes, activate on my mark."

"Setting the time for fifteen minutes," Erickson said. "Aye-aye, Captain."

The CIC had three clock-timer arrays—one mounted near the ceiling halfway along the port bulkhead, one opposite it on the starboard side, and one above the pilot station's monitors. The arrays consisted of two dials, the first being a 24-hour military clock set to standard Earth time, and the second a countdown timer. Utilitarian but beautiful in their simplicity, the brass and crysteel devices operated on wind-up springs that powered internal mechanisms.

The timer had stacked dials that showed days in the innermost ring, then hours, then minutes, then seconds. With no electronics of any kind, the mechanical devices worked flawlessly even when multiple, overlapping STC fields turned digital data into number-sludge.

Clock-timers were Anne's favorite part of any warship or Fleet facility. There was something comforting about their mechanical nature. The same went for the analog gear all Union warships used, gear that made CICs look more akin to their mid-20th Century counterparts than to the sleek control rooms and holographic interfaces found on military vessels of the late 23rd.

Analog computing for warfare reached its first zenith six centuries earlier, when electromechanical fire-control devices altered the course of Earth's Second World War. Purely mechanical devices with hundreds—sometimes *thousands*—of intricately machined parts were developed for tactical and strategic needs. Functions ranged from the two-dimensional calculation of artillery trajectories, to the three-dimensional computations needed for torpedoes and aerial bombsights, to machines that predicted the tides for amphibious invasions. Four to five decades after that war, most analog computational devices were replaced by more powerful and far more versatile digital electronics. Digital remained dominant for centuries.

Analog's second coming was born out of necessity rather than choice. The development of space-time curvature manipulation rendered useless five centuries worth of advancements in digital, photonic, and quantum computing. Ships that operated solely on computers didn't operate at all. No matter how bad space-time fuckery got, though, purely mechanical systems mostly functioned like... well... like *clockwork*.

That was why for every transistor there was a gear, for every diode there was a pulley, for every chip there was a chain drive, and for every massive-multi-processing quantum computer there was a human brain.

Next to each clock-timer, a digital readout displayed the same time span. Digital systems were perfectly reliable outside of combat, but for Anne—like most sailors and strikers and Raiders—nothing beat the tick-tick-tick of cogs and mainsprings.

At his station, Erickson turned manual dials, setting the time. He pressed a button. Hidden gears whirred—the minute hands on all three clock-timers swung to the 15 position.

"Finish your prep, people," Lincoln said. "When Colonel Hasik takes his station, we dive."

18

Master Sergeant Sands' voice boomed through the weird compartment that would be Nitzan's home for the next two years.

"Any clothing you are not wearing must be stored in your coffin bunk," Sands said. "*Especially* boots and socks. We are about to travel to another dimension, which our clam brethren call *going transdim*. When we go transdim, you will stay in your rack. No matter what you see or *think* you see, you will stay in your rack."

Nitzan was already in his bunk. He was scared. He wouldn't admit that to anyone, but he was.

If he only looked up, things seemed normal enough. Another bunk above him, barely a handspan from his nose. His bedding and blankets were the same as he'd had on any other ship. To his left, a meter-wide aisle, then another row of bunks. To his right, though? That weirdly textured, dark-copper metal, which was even darker in the bunk's shadow. He would sleep next to the inner hull—beyond it, the endless, unforgiving void.

He wished he'd drawn the middle row.

He fingered the plastic thread that held his dog tags. The plastic felt so weird. He'd had a metal chain around his neck for so long he'd forgotten it existed.

Nitzan reached up and slapped the frame of the bunk above.

"Hey, Bennett. What do you think it will be like?"

Bennett's head peeked over the side. "I got no idea." He was in skivvies, as was Nitzan and the rest of the platoon. "I'm sure it will be fine."

The guy's voice had a soothing burr to it. Nitzan hoped he was just as calm in battle.

"I think it'll be *awesome*," said the man in the bunk below Nitzan's. "Another *dimension*? How fucking extreme is that, man?"

Nitzan, looked down to the bunk below, into the wide eyes of Jim "Beaver" Perry.

"Didn't ask your opinion, Boot," Nitzan said.

Beaver smiled, nodded, and slid back into his bunk.

Nitzan had seen many soldiers like Beaver, all gung-ho, smiles, and optimism. Once the shooting started, though, once they made their first trip across the gap, once they saw people in their unit transformed from Human to hamburger, the gung-ho went goodbye.

"Fucking clam cumstains."

Mafi again, as eloquent as ever. He was on the middle bunk across the aisle to Nitzan's left. The man was so broad in the shoulders he couldn't even roll over—to flip from his back to his belly, the lummox had to get out and get back in.

"They shoved us into this weird room," Mafi said. "Packed us in here like... like..."

"Like bullets in a box?" Shamdi offered.

Mafi thought for a moment. "Naw, that ain't it. That's fucking stupid."

"You muttonhead," Shamdi said. "It's a perfect analogy."

Beaver's head slid out. "How about those foam peanut things they use to pack stuff?"

"Yeah, that's it." Mafi gave him a thumbs-up. "Thanks, Beaver."

The big idiot thought packing peanuts were a better description than bullets in a box? Whatever.

Mafi was right about one thing, though—the room *was* weird. Long and narrow. The clams called it the *forward lower bow protrusion*. Nitzan couldn't help but think of it as living in the hollow jaw of a long-mawed monster.

Everyone in the platoon, including crawler crews and techs, was packed into three-bed bunks, laid out in three rows of four bunks each.

The population density level was "nuts to butts," as PXO Winter described it. Aft of the bunks and to port, the head and showers, to starboard, Lieutenant Lindros's small compartment, which contained a bunk, a planning table, and four chairs.

On previous *Keeling* outings, Nitzan assumed the long compartment had been used for storage. Definitely not refrigerated storage, that was for sure—he could hear AC units blowing in a futile attempt to combat the heat.

He'd been onboard for all of an hour, and he was already tacky with sweat. So were the other Raiders. Things were going to get quite stinky down here in the days to come.

"This sucks," Mafi said.

"Quit your bitching, Mafi," Sands called out. "If your accretion disk of an ass didn't have its own gravitational pull, you'd fit in your bunk like the rest of us."

The 1MC whistle sounded.

"This is the captain. We are about to transit to another dimension. For our new crewmembers, this is not something you can prepare for. Every individual reacts differently. Some hallucinate. Some experience crippling terror. Remember that this is a training hop that lasts only fifteen minutes, at which time we will return to realspace. During that time, no matter what you see or hear, stay where you are. Remain at your post, even if your post is your bunk. That includes those who might vomit, urinate, or defecate during the process. All bio incidents can be attended to after I release you from your current location. Do not move until I give the order to do so. That is all."

Nitzan's heart beat faster. The not knowing was as bad as those moments right before crossing the gap, wondering if your number was up.

He put his hand on his dog tags, pretended they were the infinity symbol necklace he'd worn everywhere before the Cloister sent him to Thomas 3 to start his new, fake life.

Silently, without words, Nitzan prayed: *High One, protect me from evil.*

"I hope I don't shit myself," Beaver said.

That much, at least, Nitzan and Beaver had in common.

19

Colonel Hasik climbed into the xeno loft. He swayed slightly, slumped into his acceleration chair.

Trav faced forward. "Captain, the xeno station is manned."

"Very well," Lincoln said.

Trav sensed the tension hanging in the CIC. The captain had warned the entire crew that they might piss themselves. The newbs looked rattled. The vets, even more so—not a good sign.

Waiting for Lincoln's next command, Trav focused on the nav-orb, getting his mind around how it was a third smaller than any he'd seen before. An arrow in the orb's center represented the *Keeling*. The arrow never moved—it remained flat, pointed perpetually in the direction of the ship's prow. The rest of the orb represented the area around the ship, zoomed out to a large scale when navigating, zoomed in closer when docking or in combat. When *Keeling* pitched up or down, if it banked or yawed, the arrow's position remained fixed—everything in the orb moved in relation around it.

The command slate was familiar tech. On most ships, the XO and the captain had their own slates—on the *Keeling*, they shared. Trav sat at the slate's left, Lincoln at the right. Between them was the ship's public address system. Good old analog. The 1MC broadcast to all areas of the ship, while other circuits broadcast to individual sections, like engineering or the torpedo room, or to individual compartments, like the curvine room or the infirmary.

In a rack above the slate was a row of sound-powered phones, one for each key area of the ship. They required no external electricity, generating power solely from the speaker's voice. Even if the main circuit system and the ship's electrical failed, the six-century-old technology worked. Sound-powered phones played a critical role in ship-wide communication during combat situations.

"XO, prepare for transdim entry," Lincoln said. "Use the checklist. It won't always be this formal, but for now do it by the numbers."

"Preparing for transdim, aye-aye, Captain."

Lincoln wasn't wasting any time breaking Trav in. He called up the checklist on the command slate. It showed the order of events and who manned each station. The list went counter-clockwise around the CIC, starting with the station located port-forward.

"Darsat," Trav said, "any contacts in our sphere?"

Corporal Kanya Saetang checked her station's displays. DARSAT —*Detection and Ranging, Space and Time*—measured gravitational imprints in a sphere radiating out from *Keeling* to an effective range of 10,000 kilometers, with another 5,000 kilometers of semi-effective range beyond that. While darsat could make an active ping, it was currently in passive mode, reading the ambient curvatures of nearby space-time.

Like with all CIC stations, three people rotated through the darsat watch: Spec-2 Gurgen Hakobyan was new to the *Keeling*, like Trav. Spec-3 Carmel Waldren and Saetang, the Darsat Lead, were on their second patrol.

"One contact, friendly," Saetang said. "The *Ishlangu*. Bearing, port zero-three-five, high. Range is three-one-two kilometers. Logging in-orb. No other contacts in detection range at this time."

In the nav-orb, an icon labeled *Ishlangu* appeared, thirty-five degrees to port at an incline angle of sixty degrees.

"Signals," Trav said, "do we have any communications contact?"

"Zero active communications contacts." Corporal Sara Ellison was the ship's lead signaler. "No incoming communication requests."

Ellison was a first-timer. She seemed calm, unfazed by the hanging sword of the unknown transdim. Trav's and Ellison's last names were close enough to cause confusion, but since he would almost always be referred to as "XO," it likely wouldn't be a problem.

"ECM," Trav said, "status of detection?"

In Trav's opinion, the electronic countermeasures operator—in this instance, Corporal Cass Mollen—was the most important job on any warship. While no vessel was invisible, ECMers had a vast array of high-tech tricks that confused enemy efforts to locate and target Union vessels. ECM also gummed up the works on any smart, self-guided munitions thrown the *Keeling*'s way.

"I'm showing zero detection efforts," Mollen said. "We appear to be in the clear, XO."

Trav looked to Lindros. "Raider liaison, any concerns?"

"No concerns, XO," Lindros said.

Trav turned to face the lofts. "Intel, any political concerns?"

Lafferty stood. "None at this time, XO."

Trav continued down the list. Ops reported all hands were at their assigned stations. Weps reported all torpedo tubes were locked down. Guns reported that all cannons and point-defense were unmanned.

That left only one last check.

"Xeno station, coupler status?"

"Transdim coupler in the green," Hasik said.

The transdim status was reported in five colors: *green* for fully powered-up and a-okay, *red* if it was out of power or non-functional for any reason. *Blue, yellow,* and *orange* took up the middle statuses. That was all Trav had gleaned from roughly ten minutes of prep. He'd learn more about it as soon as he could.

Trav faced forward. This was it. It was really going to happen.

"Captain, there are no threats, pending communications, or political concerns," he said. "The coupler is in the green. We are ready to enter transdim."

Lincoln stepped away from the command station, slowly turned in place as she addressed the entire CIC staff.

"Being in transdim is difficult," she said. "What you're about to experience is enough without also seeing what lies beyond our hull. You'll see the Mud soon enough. For now, one mind-fuck at a time. Ops, take us to blackout mode."

"Blackout mode, aye-aye, Captain," Plait said.

All screens showing the *Keeling*'s exterior blinked out. The orb's data faded away.

See the Mud? What did that mean?

"Xeno," Lincoln said, "ready the drive."

"Readying the drive, aye-aye, Captain." Hasik lifted a sound-powered phone handset. "Atrium, Xeno. Make ready to activate transdim."

Lincoln faced forward, put her hands flat on the command slate. She spoke in a voice so quiet it was almost a whisper.

"XO, a leader knows how to endure," she said. "I expect you to lead by example. Be strong."

20

Susannah watched every motion, mentally cataloging everything she saw.

Lieutenant Hathorn's hands slid across the protuberance in a fast, precise pattern: a push on the blue-green knob, a touch on a gnarled amber bump, a turn of a silvery curve, a stroke across an ivory-red indent, a push on a neon orange ridge, move a gnarled thing on top from left to right, bend a flexible, cucumber-sized, translucent indigo lump from up to down, and, finally, squeeze a gnarled nubbin on the left-hand side.

The thing glowed now, oh yes it did, like a surreal glass sculpture filled with plasma. It was beautiful beyond words.

The tip of the protuberance twisted and swelled. It opened like a morning glory responding to the first rays of the sun. From the opening came a chittering noise, deep and indescribable, so disturbing that Susannah found herself taking one step back, then another.

"That sound means she's ready to dive," Hathorn said. Gently, so as not to introduce a random, extra touch, she took one step back. She lifted the handset of the red phone mounted on the rail "Xeno, Atrium. Transdim coupler ready."

Hathorn pushed a button on the phone, switching the audio output from the handset to the unit's grille-covered speaker.

"Transdim drive ready, aye," Hasik said. "Initiate on my mark."

Hathorn looked at Susannah, a not-so-healthy smile pulling her lips tight against her teeth.

"Hold onto your balls, Ensign. Time to witness a miracle."

Susannah had no balls to hold, but if she did she would have already been clutching them in a protective death grip. None of this was normal. None of this was fine. Everything about it seemed *wrong*.

"Atrium, Xeno," Hasik said. "*Mark.*"

Hathorn reached out and cupped the nubbin. She sucked in a breath, held it, then squeezed.

Susannah floated.

Floated in nothingness.

Weightless.

No sound.

Airless, but that didn't matter, for she no longer needed to breathe.

No light. No variation. Black as far as she could see, in every direction.

Had something gone wrong? Had the transdim coupler exploded or something like that?

Was she dead?

"High One," she said. "High One, please—what is this place?"

A light. The faintest pinprick. Coming toward her. Slowly, so slowly.

A feeling of... serenity. Of *unity*.

High One was in this place. Maybe High One *was* this place.

The light grew brighter, larger.

Something yanked her wrist. How could there be something when there was naught but nothing?

Naught but nothing. What did that even mean?

Another yank.

"*Ensign!* Snap out of it!"

That wasn't the voice of High One—it was the voice of Lieutenant Jenn Hathorn.

Another yank. The nothingness twisted and whorled, turning into somethingness, and Susannah found herself in the transdim compartment, a compartment *flooded* with blazing light.

The light itself trembled, twined, bent and bucked. Beams became *things*. Long, twisting things, each of a single, pure color: raspberry red, opal green, pearl orange, daffodil yellow, all blazing and bright.

The things became snakes.

Snakes of light, with eyes blacker than death.

They looked at Susannah, and she started to scream.

21

John Bennett stared up, wishing he was younger. If he'd been younger, maybe he wouldn't have gotten the top bunk. If he didn't have the top bunk, maybe the odd little creature in the translucent copper ceiling wouldn't be gazing down at him.

He didn't know what it was. He knew his aliens, of course. He'd seen Harrah, Sklorno, Whitokians, Ki, and even Dolphins, if you counted Dolphins as aliens. Some people said they were, some people said they weren't—John didn't give a shit one way or another.

The thing staring at him now? He had no idea what it was, nor did he have any clue how it was looking out at him from within solid metal.

Its knobby, pointed head—at least John assumed it was the head—was as wide as a man's chest, with fist-sized, silvery bulbs on either side. Eyes? Probably eyes. The creature seemed to be made up of joined bits of shell, like a shrimp or an insect, but the shells were covered with mottled tan fur, glossy and short. The fur reminded John of rat hair. Thin, iridescent green growths jutted out from what might be a chin. Were the growths antenna? A fashion statement? Maybe a nasty infection? He didn't know.

John looked at it.

It looked at John.

"You stole my watch, cumstain," it said. "I will eat your fucking heart."

Wait... where was the mouth? John hadn't seen any part of the head move.

"Bennett, help!"

The creature vanished. The pockmarked copper ceiling remained, but it was no longer translucent.

John's ears filled with the sound of moaning Raiders, *screaming raiders*, and the unmistakable grunts of a man being choked. John looked down over the side of his bunk. Mafi had his big hands around Shamdi's neck. Shamdi, on his back, half in and half out of his bunk, was unable to do anything but claw at Mafi's thick hands.

"*Cumstain*," Mafi said. "*You stole my fucking watch!*"

Even as John swung his feet off his bunk and dropped down, he took in the entire berth at a glance: Sands and Abshire, pulling a slobbering, snotting, screaming Dave Starr off a facedown Delaker Oneida; Hotchy Kiene standing alone, slapping himself in the face; Sharma Sarvacharya on her hands and knees between the bunks, vomiting; crawler pilot Biggie Bang pointing at Sarvacharya, laughing madly, dangles of drool hanging from her mouth.

John landed on Mafi's back and applied a chokehold—right arm around the neck, right hand in the crook of left elbow, left hand on top of Mafi's head. John *squeezed*. Mafi was so tall that only the tip of John's big toes touched the deck. John tried to haul Mafi down, but he had no leverage.

Mafi took two fast, powerful steps backward.

The metal bunk slammed into John's spine, knocking the wind out of him, sending a geyser of pain up his back, but he held on tight, kept choking. Mafi's meaty hands gripped John's forearm, yanked at it in an attempt to break the lock.

Someone slammed into them both. They fell to the deck, hard—John lost the chokehold. Mafi pulled free and rolled to his knees.

Even as the big man gasped for air, he stared at John, reddened eyes full of murder.

Beaver slammed into Mafi from behind, driving the big man facefirst into the fakegrav decking. Beaver bent Mafi's hand in a wrist lock and jammed his knee in the small of Mafi's back.

"But my watch." Mafi's face scrunched in pain. "That cumstain took my watch."

John tried to sit up, felt a blast of agony below his left shoulder blade. A broken rib. No question. Hopefully just one. Concentrating past the pain, he rolled to his side, looked around for the next threat.

That threat turned out to be behind him—his ID necklace jerked tight against his throat, digging into his windpipe for an instant before the plastic snapped.

"Oh, wow." Biggie's voice. "Well, you can't really strangle someone with a chintzy cord like that, am I right?" She dropped his ID tags in his lap. "Sorry, Fido. I'll get you a rawhide later."

Hands on his arms, his shoulder.

"We got you, Grampa," Shamdi said.

Shamdi and another Raider—the bleach-white skinned Laior—helped John to his feet. Laior was a helluva lot stronger than she looked, that was for sure.

People were still fighting. Master Sergeant Sands and PXO Winter grabbed brawlers, hurled them bodily into their bunks, ordered everyone who looked sane to hold them down.

Oneida was screaming.

Bang started laughing again.

Something pungent hit John's nose.

"Dangit," Beaver said. "Turns out I shit myself after all."

22

Trav stood stock still. He didn't try to swat away the chest-sized Hercules beetle atop the slate. Just like the one in his grandmother's collection, except the lower horn jutted out farther out than the upper. Too-long front claws reached for his face. The slate's illuminated surface lit up the monstrosity from beneath, while overhead lights reflected in glossy spots on its ebony deep-black exoskeleton.

"There's nothing there, XO," Lincoln said. "Whatever you're seeing, it's not real."

The claws came closer. He clenched his teeth tight and closed his eyes.

Somewhere out there, in space, maybe, or in the nightmare of transdim, he heard Lincoln ordering the ship to "surface," to re-enter realspace.

The beetle would get him before that happened.

Flashes of rapid-fire color played against his eyelids. Real, or more of the *un*real that wanted to tear his body and mind apart?

Trav *heard* the claws before they touched him, a sound like the harsh whisper of two seashells scraping together. Chitinous daggers hooked into his temples and dragged down his cheeks, slicing and tearing through skin and muscle. He stiffened against the supposedly imagined agony, trembled as claw-tips carved through lips and gums, scraped against his teeth.

He opened one eye, just a crack. His blood ran down the beetle's thick arms to spatter against the illuminated command slate. The beast's long top horn gleamed in the CIC's many lights.

The captain was wrong. This was real. *Completely* real.

Trav had to save himself.

He reached up to grab the black arms...

...his hands gripped empty air.

"We're in realspace," Hasik called out.

The beetle was gone. No blood on the slate.

The *pain*, though, the agony of his flayed skin and ravaged flesh...

He put his hands to his cheeks. No blood. No cuts.

Why did it still hurt?

"ECM," Lincoln said, "bring us out of blackout."

Trav distantly heard someone answer her.

Lincoln switched the PA to 1MC.

"This is the captain. All hands, secure from dive. Casualty report, by section."

Trav felt his hammering heartbeat in his ears, his neck, his gut and toes. He realized he was panting, tried to slow his breathing. He took in a long breath, let it out as slow as he could manage.

A hand on his shoulder.

"Not bad for your first time," Lincoln said softly. "Did you hear my commands for bringing us out of dim?"

Trav was too fried to even think of bullshitting. He shook his head.

"We'll review everything later," the captain said. "Do better next time. I need you alert and ready to act no matter what you see. You didn't run screaming, though, and you didn't defecate yourself. My official review is that you did okay."

Okay? If the dive had lasted one second longer, he *would* have run.

"Captain, is it... is it like that every time?"

Lincoln shrugged, let her hand drop to her side.

"It's always different," she said. "Learning to endure it requires experience. Get a casualty report."

Trav became aware of the sound of a woman crying—Ellison, head down on her station, her body shaking with sobs.

The PA board lit up with sections calling in.

Trav switched to 9MC, opening the channel to Raider Land. "This is the XO, give me a casualty report."

23

First, he'd murdered his friend.

Then, he'd been sucked through a greasy spanus.

After that? He'd hopped into another dimension, whatever that meant, and a man-beast named "Mafi" had damn near broken his neck.

And now, Nitzan Shamdi found himself flat on his back on a mess table, with strict orders from Master Sergeant Sands to, quote, *not move one fucking muscle until the docs say it's okay or I will personally reach up your ass and work your mouth like a puppet.*

"This is some bullshit," Nitzan said. "I gotta wait for the pecker-checker to look at me? Just give me some damn painkillers already."

Strong ones, hopefully, that would help him sleep, so he didn't have to think about what he'd done to get here.

"You complain a lot," Grampa Bennett said.

Nitzan rose up on one elbow, fully aware by doing so he might experience a spanus penetration of his own—namely that of a master sergeant's fist hammering up his poop-chute.

The old-timer lay on the table of the booth to Nitzan's right. Uninjured Raiders had brought Bennett, Nitzan, and Starr to the mess. *Keeling's* infirmary supposedly had only two beds, which were occupied by people with more serious injuries.

"Hey, Bennett," Nitzan said. "I, uh... well, thank you."

The old-timer winced from some internal pain.

"Don't mention it," he said. "If it had been you choking Mafi, I would have done the same for him."

The *Keeling* was back in realspace, but Nitzan couldn't shake a vibratey chill from his soul. It was like a switch had been flipped. One moment, the platoon had been in their bunks, the next, the berth turned into a prison riot.

Would that happen every time?

"Hey, Bennett... it looked like some of us were hallucinating. When we went transdim, *you* see anything weird?"

"Nope," Bennett said. "Nothing weird."

The man was a terrible liar.

"I didn't see what happened to you," Nitzan said. "You know, on account of that cro-mag's hands on my throat. Why are you here? What did you hurt?"

"I'm not hurt. I'm just resting my eyes."

Ah, that old Raider mantra. Real soldiers ignored pain.

The mess had five booths lining the starboard bulkhead. Each booth had a table and a pair of bench seats that sat two people comfortably—three, if things got real cozy. A fairly wide aisle separated the tables from beverage dispensers, utensil baskets, and a few bins of self-serve cereal. The aisle led to the stainless-steel serving counter, with tray rail, sneeze guards, and food wells—currently empty. Past the counter, Nitzan could see the cooks in the galley getting ready for the new crew's first onboard meal. The food smelled awesome.

The room looked like someone had taken a standard enlisted mess and crammed it into a low-ceilinged metal cave. Muttonhead Mafi, that watch-loving psycho, had to be almost two meters tall; he might have to duck a bit to fit in here, but anyone shorter than him could stand up straight.

Nitzan was on the end table closest to the serving counter, then Bennett, then a clam machinist's mate, then Dave Starr, who had a pair of female docs working on him. There was a woman on the table past Starr. An ensign? Hard to tell with the docs in the way.

Starr had to be drugged up. One medic—a medic with a *fine* ass—was stitching up his face yet he didn't move a muscle.

Nitzan leaned closer to Bennett.

"Hey, check out the tighty-tight ass on that medic."

Bennett sighed. "Have some class. You should be staring at the ceiling, like I'm doing."

What was Bennett's problem? If his shotgun didn't rack a round at the sight of that medic's posterior, he was even older than Nitzan thought. Old or gay. The latter was more likely—typical blasphemy found throughout the Union.

Or maybe Bennett was just a good person.

Nitzan had been a good person once. Before the orphanage. Before spending years pretending to be like the infidels his people fought against.

Someday he could go home. Maybe someday soon.

"I heard Oneeda got hurt," Nitzan said. "But he ain't in here."

"It's pronounced *oh-nai-duh*," Bennett said. "He's in the infirmary. Master Sergeant Sands told me Oneida took a bite out of Starr's face before Starr put a thumb through Oneida's eye."

What a shit show.

"That was a fifteen-minute punch, and we got four people down," Nitzan said. "What do we do if we have to go into combat in this thing?"

"It wasn't a *punch*. We went trans-dimensional, not into punchspace. And what we'll do is fight like the dogs of war."

Fight like the dogs of war. Another Raider mantra. There were many.

"You an expert on trans-punch-warp-hyper-slip-whatever stuff?" Nitzan said. "I thought you were new to the ship, like me."

"I am new. But when I got here, I shut my mouth, I listened, and I learned. You opened yours and complained."

Nitzan started to say something but stopped. Complaining was *exactly* what he'd done.

Whatever. The old-timer saved Nitzan's life, maybe. For that, one could forgive a lot. And a guy like Bennett might be better as a friend than an enemy.

A friend... like Arimun?

Nitzan pushed the thought away. He'd done what he had to do for his country. He hadn't liked it, but he'd done it.

The medic with the nice butt stepped away from Starr. Nitzan could see the Raider's face—clear surgical thread traced a ragged, rather bite-sized circle on his cheek.

"Look at Starr's *face*," Nitzan said. "Oneeda really fucked him up."

"O*neida*. Delaker Oneida."

"Right. Oneida. That's what I said. They're gonna nail Starr to the wall for that assault. Maybe he didn't arrive in chains, but he'll be leaving in them."

"I don't think so," Bennett said. "Before the dive, I heard LT talking to Sands. People go bonkers all the time here. A sailor does something violent in transdim, they strap them down. When the ship comes out of transdim, they put 'em right back to work. Crew is too small to go shorthanded. I imagine the same rules will apply to us."

So nothing would happen to Starr, or Mafi, or anyone else who'd flipped their lid? That was the Union for you.

"You seem to know a lot, Grampa."

"I don't know shit," Bennet said. "But like I told you, I listen. Try it some time."

The medic strode over, her auburn hair in a tight ponytail, her hazel eyes magnified by blocky med goggles.

"I'm Spec-Three Watson, your medic du jour." She locked eyes with Nitzan. "You know, just another *pecker-checker*."

Nitzan felt embarrassed. He hadn't meant for his comment to be heard by anyone other than Bennett.

"It's a compliment," Nitzan said. "Don't get all butt-hurt over it."

"Who, me?" Watson shook her head. "My *tighty-tight* isn't hurt at all."

Bennett laughed, a sound cut short by his grunt of pain.

Now Nitzan was *really* embarrassed. "You, uh, got good hearing, I guess."

"I'm deaf as a bat," Watson said. "Lie back, let me check your neck."

Nitzan did so. She stared down at him through the smart goggles. Light from the lenses' display cast splashes of faint color on her pale skin.

Watson's hands felt at his neck. Gentle at first, then with more force.

"Does this hurt?"

"Yes," Nitzan said.

"Good. How about here?"

She pressed a spot on the side of his neck; he winced.

"Yes, it hurts."

"Sit up, turn your neck slowly side to side."

Nitzan did as told.

"You're cleared for duty," Watson said. "Take these, then get back to your station."

She put two pink pills in his hand and turned toward Bennett. Pinkies—Fleet's cure for anything and everything.

"But I got *choked*," Nitzan said. "You're giving me ibuprofen? Give me some real pain killers, doc."

Watson spun sharply.

"Spec-Two Shamdi, when there are wounded in the mess, the mess is under medical command," she said. "That means, in here, I am your superior even if I wasn't one spec grade above you, which I am, so take the meds then shake your *tighty-tight* out of here before I get on the 1MC and announce to the entire ship that I need your absolutely delightful master sergeant to come retrieve you."

Sands would not take kindly to that. Not one bit.

Nitzan popped the pills into his mouth, grimacing against the pain of swallowing them dry. He'd seen Watson on the tram to the *Ishlangu*. She'd been in chains, just like he had. What had she done to be sent here? Had she killed someone, too?

Watson went to work on Bennett.

Nitzan slid off the table. As he reached the entrance, he glanced at the woman in the last booth. She was on her back, a bag of ice pressed against her left eye.

Yep, she was an ensign. He didn't recognize her rating badge.

"Hey," he said, "you get punched or something?"

Her right eye opened, looked up at him, then quickly looked away.

"Let me see," Nitzan said.

She outranked him, could have ignored him or told him to fuck off. Instead, she moved the bag—her left eye was almost swollen shut.

"Ouch," Nitzan said. "Looks like someone gave you a mean right hook."

"I blacked out in transdim," she said. "I guess I fell and hit something."

Her mannerisms hit home. Her instant avoidance of eye contact, and that soft, deferential tone in her voice...

Was this woman a Purist?

His handler had told him another Nationalite plant was onboard. Could she be the one?

"Looks painful, sir," Nitzan said. "That insignia, I've never seen it. What department you in?"

"Xeno department."

"What is the—"

"Don't ask," she said. "It's been made clear to me that asking questions outside of your department is frowned upon here."

She wasn't dressing him down, like Watson had, wasn't flexing her rank. She was just talking to him.

Nitzan pantomimed zipping his mouth shut.

"No questions out of me, then, sir," he said. "About departments, anyway. How about we share some grub sometime and I ask you about other things?"

She blushed. "No offense, Specialist, but I have enough problems without being brought up on fraternization charges." She laid her head back on the table and returned the ice to her eye.

"A coffee among crewmates isn't necessarily fraternization, sir. Or might I interest you in my personally selected array of gourmet dried foods?"

She lifted her head. He gestured to the bins of cereal. She let out a quick laugh, blushing again.

"Please go before you get me in trouble," she said. "Maybe... maybe we'll see each other around later."

His simple conversation had flustered her, just as it would for any

Purist woman being spoken to by a strange man. That didn't mean she was a Purist—but she might be.

Nitzan would find out. If she was a plant like him, they had to work together.

"Maybe we will," he said. "I hope your eye feels better, sir."

He left the mess, wondering how soon the injured could be cleared so the cooks could start dishing out chow.

24

There was more to the atrium than Susannah had first seen. The coupler demanded all her focus, held all her attention, and why shouldn't it? It was High One's hand at play, His divine fingers stirring the sands of fate.

She'd missed the xeno crew's simple quarters—a small, natural alcove with three cots and three standing lockers bolted to the deck. The once-gray lockers looked like a Rorschach test of bubbled paint brought on by the constant heat and humidity.

There were three workstations as well. Standard BST affairs: acceleration chair, monitors, and the interface. Unlike the computers she'd used in the past, though, these were made for warships. They also had a rack of slide rules, a row of pencils held in place by rubber clips, and a paper roll dispenser, paper slightly warped by the constant humidity.

Susannah was sitting on her cot, staring up at Colonel Zvanut Hasik, who stood there, staring down at her, his crossed arms covering the single key he wore on a lanyard. That key turned on his workstation—he was never without it.

"Go on, Ensign," he said. "What happened then?"

What to share, and what to hold back?

"Then the beams of light turned into snakes," Susannah said. "After that, I fell and hit my head. When I woke up, we were in realspace. Everything was back to normal. Lieutenant Hathorn sent me to the infirmary to get my eye checked out. Doctor Hammersmith had her hands full with more serious injuries, so she sent me to triage in the crew mess. Medic Watson examined me and said I was fine. No concussion or anything like that, just a shiner that will last until nanocyte salve cleans it up."

Hasik glanced at Hathorn, who sat on her own cot, quietly making notes on a keydeck that was simultaneously recording and transcribing Susannah's story.

"Lieutenant," Hasik said, "did you get all of that?"

"One sec." Hathorn's fingers picked up speed. She finished with a heavy, final *clack*. "Yessir, I got it."

Hasik took off his glasses, used the collar of his stretched-out T-shirt to wipe away steam that perpetually gathered on the lenses.

"All of it, Lieutenant?" He put the glasses back on. "Even the part about Ensign Darkwater *falling* and *hitting her head*?"

Hathorn straightened slightly. "Absolutely, sir. I made careful notes."

Hasik looked at the lieutenant for a few moments more. The way he stared would have made Susannah cast her gaze downward, but Hathorn hadn't spent a decade in a convent being told women were less-than—the lieutenant stared right back at him.

There was some kind of tension between them. Perhaps long-standing tension.

"I hope there are no further accidents," Hasik said. "Anything else, Ensign? Anything you can think of?"

Susannah shook her head. "That's all I can recall, sir."

He'd grilled her on what she'd seen in transdim, on what she'd felt. She'd told him about the colored lights and the snakes but chose not to mention the dark room and the ray of brightness it birthed. That part felt like it was only for her.

"How about you two?" Susannah asked. "What did you see?"

Hathorn set the keydeck down next to her cot. She lay back on the thin mattress, stared up at the green riot of dangling, fruit-dotted vines.

"Lieutenant Hathorn prefers not to discuss her experiences."

Hasik's lips pressed into a thin line. "As for me, I didn't see anything. I never do."

That disappointed him. Ate him up inside.

"So, it doesn't affect everyone," Susannah said. "What causes the hallucinations? And what drives the changes in behavior?"

Behavior that resulted in injuries far beyond Susannah's bonk on the head. One Raider had a *bite* out of his cheek. And she'd overheard that young specialist, Shamdi, say he'd been strangled.

There was something about that man, something Susannah couldn't put her finger on.

"I told the FNG not to ask questions," Hathorn said. "It seems she's not good at taking orders, Colonel."

FNG—*fucking new guy.*

Susannah had left her convent sisters behind, women she loved and trusted, only to wind up spending her days with this bitch? Why couldn't Hathorn just be nice?

"This is *my* department," Hasik said. "I'm the one who decides what questions can be answered, not you."

"You got that right, boss." Hathorn made a low *mmm-hmmm* sound in her throat. "Your department. Hundred percent."

Hasik took off his glasses again, cleaned them like he wanted to smash them.

Susannah stayed very still. Sometimes, men got mad. Hasik was mad.

"To answer your question, Ensign, we don't yet know what causes the hallucinations," Hasik said. "My personal hypothesis is that the laws of nature in the overlapping membranes aren't necessarily the same as they are here. I've been told that others are working on it."

Others? Lincoln was the only *other* on this ship that held sway over Hasik. Someone off the ship was directing his research? Had to be Admiral Epperson. Epperson was the architect of this insanity. At least that's what Admiral Bock thought. What was the truth of it? Susannah couldn't say.

Hasik glanced at the protuberance. It was dark, a lumpy, man-sized burnt-out lightbulb, yet it held his attention, almost as if he forgot Susannah and Hathorn were there.

The colonel's words disturbed Susannah. Different laws of nature? Did he mean the other membrane had different *physics*?

No, not *membrane*, singular—he'd used the plural.

"We've tested," Hathorn said, picking up the thread as if the xeno chief blanking out was as normal as normal could be. "We don't think the cause is biological. We've taken readings while in the Mud. Cognitive tests, blood draws, even tissue samples. We didn't see any aberrations, but we don't know if we *can* see aberrations in the membrane because, in the membrane, maybe they *aren't* aberrations—they're simply what *is*."

Hathorn stared up into the atrium's greenery.

"When we return to realspace, those aberrations—if there were any—aren't aberrations anymore," she said. "They're normal. If we measure a value that's, say, *five*, in transdim, and it's *three* when we get back to realspace, here we don't know if we saw it as *five* there, or it *was* five and the method we used to record that number now shows that number as *three*. How can you measure differences in the laws of nature when what you use to measure those laws can only measure the laws of the nature they are *in*? Honestly, it makes me just want to get drunk."

Getting drunk never solved anything. It certainly didn't help someone tackle a difficult problem like this. Purism forbade alcohol, and with good reason.

Susannah's mind raced, searching for a way to test Hathorn's *differences-can't-be-measured* postulate. If what the lieutenant said was possible, though, if a measurement—and that measurement's documentation—changed depending on where one was, how could one measure potential differences in physics between the membranes?

"Video and audio recording don't work, by the way," Hathorn said. "That goes for computer data as well. When we're back in realspace, we find we've recorded nothing at all. We get hours and hours of blankness. There's no malfunctions in the various recording mediums. We've checked. They simply don't work in the Mud. We don't know why."

Even a subtle change in the laws of physics—a staggering concept in itself—could invalidate the delicate process of recording and storing data. Cracking a problem like this with nothing but paper and pencil? Beyond challenging.

Hasik sat on his cot. He looked exhausted—mentally, physically, and spiritually.

"The brain is a complex structure," he said. "Scientists have been studying it since the seventeenth century. After almost a thousand years of research, we still don't fully understand how memories are stored or how the imagination works. Shifting between membranes shakes those processes up, but with inconsistent effects. Some people have repeating visions. Some have a different vision every time. Some hallucinate once, then never again. Some feel no effect for five, six, even seven transdim trips, then they suffer one so bad they have to be restrained before they kill someone. Or kill themselves."

Susannah saw his anguish, his exasperation, and she felt for him. Consistency of observation was the cornerstone of science. If you do *A*, then *B*, *C* happens. Figuring out which specific *A* and *B* were needed to make a reproducible *C* was always the goal.

But if *A* is inconsistent, and *B* is inconsistent, and *C* is inconsistent, you're screwed until you can replicate two of those consistently—or unless you find out *D* was there all along and you didn't know it, influencing things and generally being a big jerk.

Hathorn rested her knuckles against her forehead.

"Darkwater, I'll give you some advice," she said. "The way we stay sane is to pretend it's all sorcery. We have a magic wand—the protuberance. Give that turgid behemoth a stroke or two, and fucking *magic* happens."

Hasik put his head in his hands. "I wish you wouldn't use the *M* word, Lieutenant."

He *wished* she wouldn't use that word—he didn't *order* her not to.

"Colonel," Susannah said, "I want to learn all that I can about this system. About the ship. About *everything*."

Hasik rubbed at his neck. He stank a little bit, a body odor brought on by hours of light, ever-present sweat. Hathorn stank, too. Susannah probably stank herself; she just couldn't smell it yet.

So *hot* down here.

"You will learn how to operate the coupler," Hasik said. "Then, you'll learn how to operate everything required of this department. At some point, you may have to manage all of this on your own."

Susannah's eyes narrowed. "Manage it on my own? What does that mean?"

Hathorn reached under her pillow, grabbed something. She sat up, a steel flask in hand.

"The colonel means we're entombed," she said. "This is the *Crypt*, Ensign. People die here."

Hathorn took a long pull from the flask, then offered it to Susannah.

Susannah froze. Her religion forbade alcohol or any other intoxicant. She hadn't had a drop to drink in ten years. But if she didn't partake, would that draw attention? Sailors *drank*. It's what they did. Drank and screwed and committed casual sacrilege.

"Relax, Ensign," Hathorn said. "It's not like we're going to tell the XO or the Captain. And what's with that bandana she wears, anyway? We should call her *Pirate Captain Lady*."

Before Susannah could change her mind, she snatched the flask and drank.

The liquid burned her mouth, incinerated her throat. She started to cough, to spit it back up, but a desperation to find common ground with these people made her choke it off. A bit of booze shot into her nose, where it scorched like lava. Her eyes watered.

"Good, right?" Hathorn took the flask, screwed the cap tight, and tossed it over Susannah to Hasik.

He caught it, opened it. "We have casualties on this ship." He took a short sip. "Many casualties. I might die. Lieutenant Hathorn might die. If you're the only one left alive, Ensign, you'll be responsible for taking *Keeling* in and out of transdim. If you fail at that task, your failure means the death of everyone onboard. Yourself included." He took a longer pull. "So, before you worry about being an inquisitive scientist, first learn how to be a hairless ape that pushes the buttons she's told to push."

Hasik handed the flask to Susannah. She took it, dumbly, her eyes still watering from the first sip.

"Go ahead, FNG," Hathorn said. "Give it another kiss. I promise it won't be your last."

Hasik lay back on his cot. Almost instantly, he started to snore.

"That noisy motherfucker," Hathorn said. "Remember how I told you that you won't get used to transdim? You won't get used to his snoring, either. But if you drink enough to black out, you won't notice."

Susannah felt a tingle of dizziness. Was she already getting a buzz? It had been so long she didn't remember what being drunk felt like.

She opened the flask, and she drank.

25

Hasik pointed to the spot where the punch-drive integrator cage anchored to the bulkhead.

"Spec Chen, scrape off that foil," he said. "All of it."

Spec-3 Machinist Mate Ri Chen looked from Hasik to Sascha. Chen wasn't sure what to do. He'd told Sascha he'd scraped off the material in the past, but he didn't know what it was—and neither did anyone else in engineering. In prior patrols, apparently, people had been told to remove it, so they'd removed it.

Just because it had been done before didn't mean it was safe to do again or had been safe to do in the first place. Sascha had called Hasik over, assuming he'd explain. So far, he had not.

"Colonel," she said, "I asked you to tell me what that material is. I didn't ask you to give my people orders."

He outranked her, but she was engineering department head. Xeno was technically part of engineering. Lincoln made it clear Sascha wasn't Hasik's boss, but Sascha *was* the boss of everyone else in her department—Hasik was not.

The colonel removed his glasses, wiped at them with a t-shirt so crusty with dried sweat it could have stood on its own.

"It's a side effect of the hull's self-repairing nature," he said. "Nothing to worry about."

That *side effect* manifested as thin filaments of copper foil extending from the bulkhead and stretching a few centimeters along the cage's tungsten surface. Sascha had missed it at first. Probably because there hadn't been much of it if any at all. One week into the patrol, she saw the metallic fibers all over the department, like little flash-frozen clusters of copper lightning creeping out from anywhere something touched the ship's copper material.

"Nothing to worry about, Colonel?" She was careful to keep her voice level. "We've got an unknown substance spreading through engineering, and you say it's *probably nothing*."

Hasik slid his glasses back on. "It's... wall stuff. Have your people remove it."

"What if it comes back?"

"Then remove those bits as well," Hasik said. "It's a simple concept, Lieutenant."

"What if the material is hazardous?"

Hasik closed his eyes and sighed as if Sascha was a toddler who'd worn him out.

"It's *wall stuff*, Kerkhoffs," he said. "All right? It's the same material that makes up the self-repairing hull. We've tested it. It's fine. We were scraping it off before you got here, and we'll be scraping it off after you leave."

"But, Colonel, we—"

"I'm in no mood for another marathon session of your questions, Lieutenant," Hasik said. "This will *not* be a repeat of you asking how the ship moves while in transdim. Got it?"

Sascha fought back an angry retort.

"Aye-aye, Colonel. I got it."

Hasik left the punch-drive compartment.

Two days earlier, Sascha had demanded Hasik tell her how the ship moved while in the Mud. Hasik told her she wasn't cleared to know. She'd kept asking, which earned her a stern rebuke from XO Ellis.

On every Fleet ship, *propulsion* was part of engineering. Every ship, save for *Keeling*.

"It's not that big of a deal," Chen said. "It comes off easy enough. It just takes some elbow grease."

Chen's pockets perpetually bulged with bandanas. He carried

four or five at a time, rotating through them when the one he wore tight around his forehead became soaked with sweat. He was one of the few sailors in engineering who wore his coveralls as intended, with arms in sleeves. Others wore them with arms tied around their waist. Most, though, didn't wear coveralls at all. With the amount of gleaming, bare chests, sweat-soaked tank tops, and shorts rolled up as far as they could go, engineering looked like a discount strip club.

Sascha called for her crew chiefs. Propulsion Chief Ledford's people scraped the punch array and the curvine room. Electrical Chief Keahloha took charge of clearing fabrication. Lead Machinist Hansen led the machinist mates to clean up the machining area. Sascha joined Aux Chief Marchenko in environmental.

She admired Staff Sergeant Barnes Marchenko. A compact, solid man, he'd been in two battles before being assigned to the *Crypt*. In the second battle, he'd lost his left leg below the knee. Marchenko could have chosen to get a bionic replacement, but doing so would have made him ineligible for warship duty. So instead, he'd machined his own prosthetic and gone back to work. No bionics, no cybernetics, just plastic and metal, springs and hydraulics. No electronics. Making adjustments and refinements to the fake leg was apparently one of his hobbies. And he was good at it, too—aside from a slight limp, you'd barely notice.

"This is some fucked-up shit." Barnes used a scraper to peel foil from a bracket that held the AC unit against the curved copper of the port-side hull. "I'm going to get berylliosis, I just know it."

"No, you're not," Sascha said. "Hasik said that doesn't happen here."

"Hasik says a lot of things."

Sascha focused on scraping the brackets of a heating unit that hadn't been turned on since she'd arrived.

Berylliosis was lung inflammation caused by highly toxic beryllium dust. Considering the amount of cutting that went on inside *Keeling*, especially in the engineering department, toxic dust was a valid concern. Jenn Hathorn—who *did* occasionally answer questions, if they were asked by someone her rank or above—explained that the hull alloy's unique composition of copper-beryllium-carbon made it completely non-toxic.

Almost forty people had been replaced for this patrol alone, and Sascha hadn't been told why, so who knew what was true? She could be breathing in her own death. It wouldn't be the first time a military didn't give two wet shits about the safety of its soldiers, as long as those soldiers got the job done.

She wiped sweat from her brow. She was seriously considering chopping her hair, maybe even shaving it down to stubble like Lafferty did.

"Hotter than Satan's house cat down here," Sascha said. "We're one week into this patrol and you still haven't fixed the AC."

Marchenko stopped scraping. Sweat sheened his pale skin, made his black crew cut glimmer like cheap plastic.

"I keep telling you, Lieutenant—it *is* working," Marchenko said. "Before I got here, if you'd told me I couldn't get an AC unit so cold that your nuts... no offense, Lieutenant."

"None taken."

"...your nuts would freeze up and fall off, I'd have said you grasp HVAC basics about as well as a rock crab juggles marbles. There's nothing wrong with the AC. It should be able to make this place a damn refrigerator. There should be frozen nuts... no offense."

"None taken."

"...frozen nuts sliding around in here like someone spilled a box of ball bearings. But no matter what I do, the temperature *will not* go below thirty-five Celsius. The ship doesn't like it."

Despite the heat, a chill rippled across Sascha's skin.

"What do you mean *the ship doesn't like it?*"

"I mean something is putting out heat to counteract the AC, but whatever that is, I can't find it," Marchenko said. "I've spent my off-duty hours looking. No heat source. I turn up the AC, the ship does something to counter it. What that something is?" He shrugged. "You got me. The ship likes it hot."

Marchenko went back to scraping, peeling away a thin bit of foil with each stroke.

Just because he hadn't found a heat source didn't mean there wasn't one. This was an alien ship that could supposedly defy physics, after all.

"Hey, Eng," Marchenko said. "Can I ask you a question?"

Eng, shorthand for *engineering department head*. Sascha hadn't heard many people use it in her short career, but she was less than half Marchenko's age. There was an old-school feel to all he did and said.

"That depends, Chief—does the question involve frozen testicles?"

"No sir."

"Then ask away."

"What did you do?"

Sascha stopped scraping. "Do about what?"

"Do to get entombed. My Fleet days were over unless I took this post, on account of my leg. A pencil-pusher named *Whittaker* said this was the only warship that would have me, so I jumped on it. But a lot of people are here for doing bad shit. Goldsmith assaulted a superior. He told me so. Phil Eskander—he's a gunner's mate—had five DUIs, put a girl in the hospital on the last one. And then there's Yellowbelly. Everyone knows what that coward did."

Marchenko stopped scraping, glanced up at Sascha. He'd gone too far and he knew it. Still, Ellis was calling for all kinds of drills, really crawling up the crew's backs. Her people had to let off a little steam here and there.

"I'll ignore that comment this one time," Sascha said. "But don't badmouth the XO again. Okay?"

Marchenko smiled, returned to scraping. "Okay. So, Lieutenant—what did you do?"

What she'd done was be stupid and greedy enough to trust Doug Erickson when he said *we'll never get caught*. Erickson had quite a racket going, bribing generals and even admirals to give support and supply contracts to Hunata Industries, a company that operated orbital facilities all over the Union. Those Erickson couldn't bribe, he tricked by paying people in influential positions—such as the engineering department head on the *Krakatoa*—to strongly recommend Hunata when contractor services were needed.

It had been easy money. Every time the *Krakatoa* needed something built or replaced or removed, Sascha gave strong recommendations for a Hunata-owned firm. The *'Toa* got what it needed. Who cared if it cost five times more than it might somewhere else? Who cared if the *'Toa* crew spent their shore leave money at Hunata-owned facilities while the ship took on Hunata-provided parts, or used Hunata-owned repair and removal services? Who cared if Sascha got a five percent cut of the markup fee?

Who cared? BII investigators, that's who.

When they busted Erickson, he named names, including Sascha's.

She'd thought she'd wind up spending a decade in prison. Sascha had been upset about that—who wouldn't be—but she hadn't cried into her beer or felt sorry for herself. It was nobody's fault but hers. She'd done the crime, she'd do the time.

And then, like an angel dressed in Raider service grays, Major Maia Whittaker came to her rescue. Sascha had a year's experience as engineering head on an assault ship. That ship hadn't been sent to assault anything, but that didn't matter—she knew how to run a department. If that knowledge was put to work onboard some mystery ship, Sascha's shortsighted bout of idiocy and avarice would be forgotten.

No jail.

No dishonorable discharge.

It was the only deal she could take, so she'd taken it.

But as far as Sascha was concerned, the past was the past. She didn't need people in her department to know she'd defrauded Fleet. Multiple times.

"Chief Marchenko, the only thing I'm guilty of is being the most kick-ass department head in Fleet history. That's why they put me here."

A smile pulled at the corners of Marchenko's mouth.

"I got you, Lieutenant," he said. "You didn't do anything wrong. I got you."

The 1MC alert sounded.

"This is the XO. Vacsuit emergency drill. I repeat, vacsuit emergency drill. You have thirty seconds."

Marchenko threw down his scraper and rushed for the narrow vacsuit bin bolted to the bulkhead.

"Son of a *bitch*," he said. "Second time today, fifth time in three days. How are we supposed to get our work done?"

Marchenko yanked out a blue one-piece vacsuit and tossed it to Sascha.

Sascha slid her feet through the legs and into the boots. "Shut up and get it done, Chief." She shoved her arms through the sleeves and into the gloves. "If my department gets written up again there'll be hell to pay."

The hood hung from the back of the collar. The design allowed sailors to be suited up and ready, without having their vision impaired by the built-in visor. If and when things went bad, the hood came on and the sailor could continue to work in compromised atmosphere or even full vacuum.

Sascha pulled the hood on, sealed the bottom of it to the matching seam running from collarbone to collarbone. She heard a hiss of compressed air. A soft beep from inside the hood told her the suit had sent an air-integrity signal to the CIC, confirming she was protected.

She didn't mind the drill. In a combat situation, crew had vacsuits on well ahead of time. If there was an accident, though, like a fire or a sudden decompression, getting a vacsuit on fast was the difference between life and death.

"Time," Ellis said over the 1MC.

Marchenko sealed his hood, two seconds too late.

"Son of a bitch," he said. "Is he gonna make us sit through kindergarten again?"

A rhetorical question, because that's what Ellis did.

"All crew who did not complete the drill on time, report to the Raider training area at once," Ellis said. "Bring your vacsuit. That is all."

If Marchenko hadn't thrown Sascha the suit first, would he have gotten his on in time?

"Sorry, Chief," Sascha said.

Marchenko grumbled something unintelligible as he limped out the door.

26

Captain Lincoln's pencil scratched against paper.

Anne Lafferty's pencil scratched against paper.

The two women did their work in silence, decoding the level-one message that had come in minutes earlier.

Anne and Captain Lincoln each had a personal, ten-dial cypher key, which they kept in a safe in their respective quarters. The safes had both data-pad and dial-combination locks. Enter three wrong combinations on the data-pad and/or dial, and everything inside got cooked to a crisp. Not that long ago, Fleet regs specified *two* incorrect combos would trigger the heat, but enough simple, fat-fingered mistakes had occurred to require the change.

It was easy to intentionally destroy the cyphers should *Keeling* be in danger of being captured. Tap a duress code of *1-7-9-3*, and presto-chango, the cypher key became melted plastic and warped metal.

Sara Ellison had been on duty when the signal came in. She'd written down the messages, by hand, and delivered the papers to Fred Madison, the signals chief. Madison had quietly instructed Anne to bring her cypher to the captain's suite. There, Madison handed each woman her respective paper and had gone back to his duties.

Captain's suite. A grandiose term, to say the least. A room identical to Anne's, with a second tiny room that had a desk, a padded couch, and several monitors. Even on the coldship *Silverbill*—the smallest warship Anne had been on before *Keeling*—the captain had enjoyed a good-sized bedroom, a compact conference room, and a cozy office. The size of compartments didn't add much to a ship's mass, and, therefore, didn't greatly affect acceleration or deceleration.

Not so in the *Keeling*'s superstructure. Whoever designed it didn't care about creature comforts. Still, compared to the solo pod Anne used to reach Eden—not to mention the long days spent in the utility duct—Lincoln's suite was like a palatial estate.

The utility duct. That had been a rough time. Anne's job was to get intel. Olivia hadn't wanted to cooperate, at least not at first, but she came around. Such a shame Olivia died when the assault force stormed in. Anne missed her.

Lincoln put her pencil down and sat back in her chair, waiting.

Anne refocused her efforts. She checked numbers on the message, turned the cypher dials to match, got a letter, wrote that letter down, and repeated the process until she finished.

Lincoln picked up her paper in one hand, holding her other hand toward Anne. Anne handed over her message as she simultaneously took Lincoln's.

"I read, you confirm," the captain said.

"You read, I confirm. Aye-aye, Captain."

"TW-6-A4 arrive on July twelfth," Lincoln said. "TY-29-B escorts. Wait for coordinates for pickup of asset Beta-4-12." She looked up. "Do you confirm?"

Anne had exactly the same message.

"Aye, Captain. Confirmed."

A mission. An *intelligence* mission. What could be better? Anne Lafferty, newly promoted, would have *Keeling*'s assets at her disposal to complete the task.

"The twelfth is only ten days away," Lincoln said. "We'll have less than three full weeks under our belt when we depart. We'll have to step up our training drills to be ready in time."

Step up the drills? She already had people running ragged. Lincoln had turned XO Ellis into a bulldog who hounded the crew night and day. Even as he learned all of the ship's systems, Ellis pushed others to learn faster, to *execute* faster, to work harder.

"At least we'll have some familiarity with our escort ship," Anne said. "That can't hurt."

TY-29-B—*Ishlangu*—would escort TW-6-A4—*Keeling*—to the assigned zone.

"*Ishi* can't join us on the final leg, though," Lincoln said. "We'll be on our own. She'll be waiting for us when we get back from wherever it is the brass is sending us, but I've got a feeling we're going to be in the Mud for a long time."

The captain dropped her sheet of paper into the small atomizer at the side of her desk.

"I think we wait to tell the crew anything until the mission date is closer," she said. "The newbies are still settling in. Do you concur?"

Anne nodded. "I do, Captain."

As of yet, Anne had uncovered no spies. Despite Daniels and Gillick quietly buddying up to the crew, sharing meals in the mess, and shooting the shit with off-duty sailors in the ship's numerous copper cubbyholes and metal hideaways, they hadn't sniffed out even a hint of suspicious activity.

Well, no suspicious activity relating to *covert operations*, anyway. Some people had quietly confessed why they'd been assigned to this ship. Pilot Colin Draper had been busted for possession of narcotics. Narcotics provided to him by medic Rebecca Watson. Raider Sharma Sarvacharya had slapped her girlfriend around, put her in the hospital. Lead Xeno Jenn Hathorn was rumored to have blackmailed the intel chief on the PUAV *Grace Hopper*, extorting him for thousands to keep certain sexual escapades hush-hush. Crawler Crew Chief Robin Taylor had been caught red-handed stealing high-caliber ammo and selling it to an arms dealer.

A fine bunch of patriots, *Keeling* crew was.

If there were spies aboard, though, they had no way of getting a message off-ship. *Keeling* was orbiting GTW-57, an utterly dead chunk of rock far from anything and everything. No ships around, Union or otherwise. If a spy learned of the upcoming mission, that spy couldn't send intel to anyone, but they *could* whip up some sabotage to incapacitate the ship. Throw a wrench into the punch-drive, so to speak, and the *Crypt* wasn't going anywhere.

Lincoln was right—best to keep any mention of an upcoming mission as quiet as possible.

"I haven't caught up with you on your first transdim dive, Major," the captain said. "How was it?"

Anne shrugged. "The walls wavered a bit. I saw some... what do you call them... *trailers*? Like comet streamers coming off various lights?"

The captain nodded. "I know what you mean."

"That was it," Anne said. "I had no problems. In fact, the whole trip felt kind of... *peaceful*."

"Let's hope you're one of the lucky ones and it's that way every time. Your operative, Daniels, had an issue. Is he reliable?"

The *issue* was Akil Daniels had pissed himself, right there in the intel loft. He'd mumbled something about *zombies*, then made a wet-spot like a four-year-old who couldn't hold it back.

"I've only known the man for the eight days since we came aboard," Anne said. "Other than a rebellious bladder, he seems solid. There were crewmembers who had far worse reactions than he did."

Lincoln grunted. "You can say that again. We're already down one Raider."

Delaker Oneida wasn't just *down*, he was *done*. Hard to shoot straight with one eye. He'd get an artificial one and be back in business, but as a ground-pounder in the Global forces. Raiders existed only on warships, and in combat, warships endured severe curvature manipulation. Said STC fuckery made all things electronic—like artificial eyes, for example—go haywire. Poor Oneida would probably finish his twenty as a guard somewhere, hoping for a day when the enemy would be kind enough to land on whichever planet he was assigned to.

"Captain, don't we get a replacement for Oneida? When we rendezvous with *Ishlangu*?"

"That's not how it works," Lincoln said. "We transfer him off the first chance we get, but we don't get replacements until this patrol is over. Epperson thinks rushing a last-minute addition is an opportunity for a spy to get onboard."

A strategy Anne could get behind. This was, after all, a ship full of criminals. How could you trust those who'd sold drugs, committed fraud, or murdered people?

Still, this was an opening Anne had been waiting for.

"Finding spies is easier when you know who people really are," she said. "I could do my job better if I could see personnel records."

Lincoln huffed a laugh. "So could I, Major, so could I. Epperson might be a nail-driving son of a bitch, but he's true to his word. Certain aspects of personnel records remain sealed, even for me. I don't know what most of my crew has done. I don't know what *you* have done."

Anne smiled. She'd done nothing other than successfully execute a dangerous mission. Lincoln, on the other hand? What could the Hero of Capizzi 7 have done to wind up entombed on the *Crypt*?

Lincoln gently reached out, took the paper from Anne, and put it in the atomizer. A whir, and the secret message was no more.

"Change your cypher set," Lincoln said.

Both women turned the last dial on their keys. Doing so broke a gear inside, ensuring that the previous code set could never be recovered. Even if someone else on the ship acquired the coded message that had just come in, there was nothing left with which to decode it.

"Thank you, Major. That will be all."

Anne stepped out. She needed sleep. She'd spent most of the day trying to ask crewmembers about other crewmembers, hoping to discover anything unusual that might point to a bad apple. Pretending to like people was the type of work that wore a body out.

She reached to open the door to her quarters when Akil Daniels leaned out of the spookhouse.

"Major? A word?"

"I'll be right there," Anne said.

She put her cypher key in her safe, made sure it was locked. Sleep would have to wait.

Anne entered the spookhouse. Daniels and Gillick were there. So, too, was Jennifer Hathorn, sitting in Anne's seat at the slate.

"Major," Gillick said, as casual as could be, "I believe you've met Lieutenant Jennifer Hathorn, lead xeno. It seems she has a concern about someone in her department."

Anne smelled booze. Either Hathorn got sauced up before coming here, or Daniels and Gillick had provided a few snorts to loosen her up.

"Hello, Lieutenant," Anne said. "How can I be of service?"

Hathorn sniffed. She scratched at her cheek.

"I hate to do this, Major Lafferty, but the ship's safety comes first," she said. "I'm worried we might have a Purist Nation spy onboard."

27

It felt damn good.

Back in TASH armor, mustering with his brothers and sisters, preparing to hullwalk—John couldn't wait. The excitement helped him ignore the knife-like pain in his back. Mostly ignore it, anyway.

Sands, Lindros, and Winter stood in front of the weapons cage. They, along with the rest of the frontline Raiders, were in full armor, helmets on.

"Live ammo will *not* be issued for this exercise." Sands spoke through the platoon frequency, his voice heard in every helmet. "Empty magazines only. Your rifle will be returned to this rack after the exercise, as will your combat knife."

John had spent days dialing in his rig's micromuscle, adjusting it to his way of moving, making it match his actions. He'd double- and triple-checked every last servo, every last plate of armor, every last fastener, anchor, and screw. The suit moved *with* him, not *against* him.

John and the other combat veterans preached TASH expertise to the unblooded, sharing with them the importance of knowing all there was to know about their rigs. Beaver immediately picked up on the need for armor synchronicity, even though he hadn't known what *synchronicity* meant. He was excited to spend every available moment working on his rig. No surprise there, the kid got pumped up about anything.

Neal Abshire understood the importance as well, but from a different perspective; Abs looked at every piece as the probable failure point that would cost him his life in battle. Not a bad way to look at things, really, at least not for a Raider, but he said the quiet parts out loud, and that made the other boots nervous. On top of babysitting Beaver, Sands had asked John to toughen Abshire up a bit, because Raiders didn't complain—complaining was for clams.

After many hours of working on the suits, breaking them down and putting them together again, it was time to test them out. What worked perfectly inside a warship might not work properly outside of it. The only way to find the real problems was to put strain on the system, see what broke, then fix it.

"Carry your weapon like this is the real thing," Sands said. "We train like we fight."

Lieutenant Lindros spun the dial on the cage's combination lock. He entered a sequence, tried to turn the cage handle—it rattled, refusing to open. He spun the dial and started over.

After what went down during the transdim dive, John was all for keeping weapons locked up. If Mafi had found a rifle? If Biggie Bang had found a knife? The platoon would be down a whole lot more than just Oneida. Hell, John didn't even mind that the mycoware made all the food taste slightly of mushrooms. Better that than someone breaking off a plastic fork and jabbing the sharp end through a random jugular.

It wasn't just the fear of other people getting weapons... John didn't trust himself. The silver-eyed alien had seemed so real. If he could hallucinate that, what might he see during the next dive? What if *he* wanted to attack his brethren?

The second time, Lindros got it right. The lock opened. He and PXO Winter slid the door aside.

"Get your weapons," Sands said.

The line of armored Raiders clonked along the rack, happy to finally get their hands on their gear even if the rifles were empty. When John came to his bin, he grabbed his assigned knife scabbard and attached it to the magnetic clamp on his right thigh armor. He lifted his rifle from the rack and kept moving down the line.

The RR-36 Zero-G Recoilless Rifle: semi-automatic, shoulder-fired, 20-millimeter caseless cartridges in 50-round magazines. Just under a meter long from muzzle tip to the mouth of the backblast barrel.

John had spent more years of his life hauling one of these around than not. The rifle's counterthrust rounds let Raiders fire in the void without Newton's third law pushing said Raiders through space with every shot.

"Get in your lines," Sands said. "Clamp your rifles, move to the flight bay."

John hadn't seen the flight bay yet. Only the pilots, engineer-gunners, and tech crews had.

He placed his rifle diagonally across his chest. Magnets on the stock and foregrip clamped onto matching spots on his chest plate. The magnets kept his weapon at the ready, yet left his hands free and relatively unencumbered.

Before he could take his place in line, PXO Winter gripped his forearm, which instantly opened a private touch-channel.

"How's that rib, Spec? It's been a week since you got dinged. You good for this drill?"

"To tell you the truth, XO, I forgot all about it." A lie he wished were true. "They have a bone-melder in the infirmary. Didn't hurt a bit." An even bigger lie.

Ultra-thin mechanical arms had slid beneath skin and muscle to first set the bone, then apply osteoglaze directly to the damaged area. Even with top-notch local anesthesia, the process felt like getting hate-fucked by an angry jackhammer.

"Bennett," Winter said, "anyone ever tell you you're full of shit?"

"Only my mother, PXO."

Winter laughed. "And you didn't ask for even one day off."

"Days off are for clams."

"Ain't that the truth. Get moving."

Winter let go, breaking the channel connection.

John took his place in line, ahead of Beaver and behind Rumenia Laior.

The flight bay was on deck five. It was a short walk aft from Raider Land, through a copper tunnel of sorts that ran through a twenty-meter-long dense area behind the lower prow. Some had asked what the dense area was for, or if it held some kind of computer or machinery used by the strange ship. The answer had always been the same—*stop asking about it.*

The line moved down the tunnel. A single lightcable ran along the arched ceiling. Some of the boots clonked into each other. They'd trained in TASH armor—every Raider did—but drills on a big, spacious troop ship were a far cry from the tunnel's narrow confines.

"Form two lines between the crawlers," Sands said. "Move it, people."

John followed Beaver through the open oval of an internal sphincter and into the flight bay, a.k.a., "the pouch."

He couldn't believe how small it was.

The Raiders filtered past crammed-in maintenance racks, missile storage, chemfuel tanks... all the stuff that kept the platoon's two Ochtheras flying. The techs wore light gray LASH rigs that were thinner than their TASH counterparts and afforded more freedom of movement. Chief Taylor and her people were working on a disassem-bled crawler leg. Torches burned. Sparks flew.

Just past the maintenance area were the Ochthera crawlers, one tight against the port-side hull, one tight against the starboard. Flat black paint made the bulky armored personnel carriers look more like large shadows than high-tech deliverers of death. Their legs were folded up tight against their fuselages. Their wings were retracted—there wasn't enough room in the pouch to extend them. Wings were only needed for atmospheric ops, which Raiders rarely performed.

Behind each APC was enough room to lower the rear ramp, and not a centimeter more. The ceiling was so low it almost touched the topside ball turret. The armored turret's twin .50-caliber machine guns pointed straight forward.

The Raiders formed their lines in the two-meter gap between the crawlers.

Up ahead, things got weird. Weird*er*, that was. Was that the flight bay door? A horizontal line ran from port to starboard, like two puckered copper scars pressed tight against each other. It appeared to be made of the same rounded material as the sphincters.

"Check it out," Shamdi said. "This flight bay looks like a big vagina"

"Then it's your lucky day, Shamdi," Laior said. "You *finally* know what it feels like to be inside a pussy."

The platoon laughed.

"Fuck you, Laior," Shamdi said. "This gaping snatch is virgin-tight compared to yours, I'll bet."

Sands and Winter walked through the lines, bringing the humor to a halt. At the strange doors, they turned and faced their people.

"Listen up," Sands said. "You will keep channel one open, set to receive only. My drill squad will use channel two as our primary. PXO Winter's drill squad, channel three. You will *not* initiate private channels. If something about your TASH concerns you, speak up. That's what this hullwalk is for. Once down, use hook lines at all times. Stay with your assigned buddy. Don't bunch up. All you boots, remember inertia is a thing. Slow and steady wins the race."

It wasn't a combat run. They weren't crossing the gap. They weren't going over the top. Even so, butterflies fluttered through John's guts, a thousand ants tingled across his skin. The sense of anticipation felt the same as it had the first time he'd stepped out of a hatch over thirty years ago.

"Platoon, make ready," Sands said. "Liaison, this is Away Leader One. We are ready to egress."

"Away Leader One, this is Liaison. Opening landing bay now."

John didn't recognize the liaison's voice. Some clam in the CIC. At least it wasn't the LT—Lindros could have stayed behind, but he'd opted to be with his people for the first egress. A good sign.

Red lights flashed, alerting everyone that the flight bay was about to decompress.

Up ahead, the two scars—John thought they looked like pursed fish lips, but from the inside of the fish's mouth—lifted away from each other, one contracting up, one contracting down, both moving with eerie metallic fluidity.

Beyond them, *Keeling's* tail section, and the void.

"Your objective today is as simple as pie," Sands said. "Egress, do a five count, extend your thrusters, and follow your leader."

Past the three black helmeted heads in front of him, John saw Sands throw himself into the star-speckled nothing. Laior followed, then Abshire, then Beaver, and then, John Bennett rejoiced in the weightlessness of the void.

He counted to five, clacked his heels together three times. Four telescoping arms extended from the flight pack at his lower back, forming a thin-armed X with its vertex at his center of mass. At the end of each arm, fist-sized chem-thrusters sparked to life.

TASH thrusters were controlled by foot movements. That left a Raider's hands free to fight. John pointed his left foot down and to the left, which sent him up and to the right, a natural motion mimicking what would happen if he pushed off a hard surface. He pointed his right foot down slightly, triggering a bit of acceleration. He formed up behind Beaver, Abshire, and Laior, who followed Sands in an upward curve, their thrusters glowing yellow-white.

"Weapons ready," Sands said.

John gripped his rifle and popped it free of its magnetic clamps. It didn't matter that the weapon wasn't loaded—jetting through the void, he felt truly at home.

Sands arced his line up around *Keeling*'s port side. The Raiders following him kept about twenty meters of space between them.

"Standard spread landing pattern," Sands said. "Nice and easy. Don't forget to retract your extensions and activate your gripfield before you hit."

The gripfields built into TASH armor worked on the same technology as fakegrav plates. Boot soles, knees, hips, elbows, forearms, and gauntlets were all lined with strips that provided roughly one G of pseudo-gravity. The more points of contact you had, the better you could weather sudden events, like a warship performing a hard pitch or roll or yaw to shake off attached crawlers. The name of the game was to land, then stay attached—and alive—long enough to get inside.

With the ease of a soldier who's done it a thousand times, Sands descended to the topside area aft of the superstructure. Fifteen meters out, the fist-sized thrusters at the end of his X arms reversed orientation, firing away from his front instead of away from his rear. With a weightless grace, the master sergeant slowed. His extensions retracted an instant before he touched down on the rounded hull as if he'd been gently lowered there by the hand of God. Sands dropped to one knee, put his rifle over his shoulder, scanned left to right as if this were a real boarding.

Laior managed to reverse her thrusters, but she put too much *oomph* in her deceleration—instead of landing, she accelerated backward away from the ship.

Abshire had the opposite problem.

"Abs, more deceleration," John said. "You're too hot."

The boot smacked into the hull. He would have bounced right off if not for his gripfield, which stuck him there like a bug splattered on a windshield.

John glanced to Beaver, assuming a similar warning was necessary, but the kid's deceleration was almost as perfect as that of the master sergeant's. Beaver touched down like a pro.

And then, like an idiot, he stood there, his thruster arms still extended.

A moment before he landed, John clicked his heels together three times to retract his extensions. He dropped to one knee, shouldered his rifle, and covered an arc of fire to Sands's right.

"Beaver, retract and get *down*," John said.

"Aw shit, I forgot." Beaver retracted his extensions, dropped to one knee, and covered his assigned arc. "I got all excited."

The rest of the Raiders descended with varying degrees of success. Some hit hard. Some over-compensated for counterthrust and, like Laior, pushed themselves away from the ship and had to make a second approach. Radulski touched down a little on the heavy side, but he was in perfect position, already covering his arc. Fred Abeen somehow managed to hit headfirst. Dave Starr spun as he landed, snapping off one extension and bending another. Nitzan Shamdi had the best descent of all—the guy operated his rig like he'd been born in it.

Within seconds, the floaters figured out their thrusters and touched down on the hull.

"That was *not* magnificent," Sands said. "Not magnificent at all. I'd call that a shitshow, but comparing you jokers to a pile of shit might hurt that pile of shit's feelings. You dumb fucks do a self-check, then we're going again. Bennett, help Abshire learn to not destroy a perfectly good TASH by smashing it against the hull."

"Aye-aye, Master Sergeant."

John slid one foot across the irregular surface, then the other, never lifting either completely free of the hull. He knelt next to Abshire, who had rolled to his butt.

"Abs, you okay?"

"I'm good. I feel dumb as hell, though. What's with that ice-skater walk?"

"Always keep at least two points of contact," John said. "Three if you can manage it."

"But in boot they told us as long as we have one foot down, we're fine."

"Never mind what some drill sergeant told you," John said. "You never know what direction the hull beneath you is going to go. With two points of contact, you're effectively part of the ship—when it moves, you move with it. Do something idiotic like try to *run*, and a sudden acceleration or deceleration can shake you free. If that happens, you'll find yourself floating alone as the ship accelerates away."

John knew there were physics behind the practice, but he'd never bothered with them beyond the simple math of *one point bad, two points good, three points better.*

"We train like we fight," John said. "When we're in the mix with a dozen overlapping STC fields going off, and a grav-tether cuts a ship's velocity in half in the blink of an eye, and there's body parts floating around you, and pretty clouds of frozen blood drifting everywhere, you need to have these fundamentals *down.* If you don't, you'll wind up dead. When you're on a hull, even in a drill, always—*always*—act like everything is exploding and a bunch of assholes are trying to shoot you in the head. Got it?"

Behind his visor, Abshire's eyes were wide and white.

"Yeah, I got it. Thanks, Bennett."

John thumped Abshire's shoulder plate. Hopefully the man was *hearing*, not just listening.

"Form up," Sands said. "We have enough time to do it again before we have to be in our racks for the scheduled tail-flip drill. Shamdi, help that moron Starr get back to the pouch. Abeen, pull your head out of your ass. Everyone, fall in behind me."

Sands leapt upward. With his gripfield off, he rose and rose. He extended his thruster arms and shot away. It looked fast—relative to the ship, anyway—but John knew the man was using only a tenth of his flight pack's max acceleration. A TASH could haul serious ass.

John stayed close to Abshire, made sure the man got off the hull okay. Beaver went up next, and then, once again, John Bennett enjoyed the thrill of flying through absolutely nothing at all.

28

"You've got to be shitting me," Hathorn said. "You've never done a tail-flip drill before?"

Hathorn and Hasik stared at Susannah like she was another species altogether, one they'd never seen before and couldn't quite comprehend.

"No," Susannah said. "I haven't. I told you I've never been on a warship. I don't see the big deal—commercial ships decelerate all the time."

Hasik pulled off his steam-clouded glasses.

"You handle this, Lieutenant," he said. "I will be at my station. Kindly keep my ensign from going splat."

Going splat?

Hasik strode to his workstation. With his lanyard key, he turned the hardlock that activated his computer. He used his sleeve to wipe mist from a monitor, then sat and got to work.

Susannah looked at Hathorn. "I'm not trying to be a pain in your ass or anything, Lieutenant. Honest."

Could someone who lied all day, every day, be *honest*? Susannah didn't know.

"It's cool, Darkwater," Hathorn said. "Not your fault no one showed you this stuff, right?"

Susannah waited for a biting follow-up comment, something about how dumb she was, most likely, but the follow-up didn't come. Hathorn was smiling—an understanding smile.

"No, I suppose not," Susannah said.

"Come on." Hathorn reached out and took Susannah's hand. "Let's sit together by the heartstone."

When Hathorn gently tugged, Susannah almost pulled away. Hathorn was being... *nice?* It seemed odd. Welcome, but odd.

They sat at the edge of the long, glowing heart, close to the protuberance and the metal-grate deck built around it. The atrium rose above, its apex lost in the thick tangle of dangling greenery. Many of the plants were in bloom, flowers happily coexisting with oversized fruit and giant vegetables.

Susannah glanced over at Hasik, who was fixated on his monitors. "What kind of work does the colonel do on that station, anyway?" The question was out before she realized she'd asked it. She braced for impact.

"To be honest, I don't know," Hathorn said. "He's got special sensors and data collectors spread out all over the atrium. They're embedded in blocks of titanium. You can't get at them. I've tried. They feed into his private station."

"What do they measure?"

A ripple of bitterness washed over Hathorn's face. "You're not the only one who can't ask questions." She forced a smile. "All right, Ensign, let me walk you through this."

Hathorn pulled a pencil from her coveralls. She held in front of her, parallel to the deck.

"Say this is a warship. It's curvine is spinning merrily along, which accelerates it along the fabricated space-time strand." She moved the pencil slowly from left to right, as if the tip was the prow. "If you want to slow the ship down, what do you do?"

She offered the pencil to Susannah.

Susannah took it. This much, at least, she knew from her years of driving a hauler.

"You gradually slow the curvine spin to zero," she said. "That reduces acceleration. When there's no spin, there's no more acceleration, and you're moving along on momentum alone. Then you reorient

—" she flipped the pencil 180 degrees so it pointed the other way "—and slowly restart curvine spin. That gradually reduces forward momentum—which is now *backward* momentum, relative to the ship's orientation—until you reach your desired velocity or come to a stop."

Hathorn took the pencil back.

"Exactly," she said. "That works fine for civilian ships. In warships, though, in a battle, sometimes—" she held her free hand like a claw out in front of the pencil point, wiggled her fingertips "—you have all kinds of nastiness coming your way. Missiles, torps, other ships, exo-troops like Raiders, you name it. Things are coming at you and you need to reverse course, *fast*. So without slowing your curvine, you—" she turned her hand so that the eraser pointed toward the wiggling fingers "—flip it and rip it."

Susannah leaned back, surprised.

She'd made sudden course alterations during her trucking days. Especially near ports where there was a lot of traffic. But computer-assisted collision-avoidance systems interacted in real-time with nearby vessels, and even a dense shipping area was still mostly empty space. A vector adjustment of a few degrees, a subtle increase or decrease in acceleration, and everyone was fine. Mid-air collisions *never* happened, which meant there was almost never a reason to effectively slam on the breaks.

"But the previous inertia would be directly opposite the curvine's acceleration," Susannah said. "That would be like slamming into a concrete wall at... well, however fast you're going. If you're not in an acceleration seat, you'd..."

Susannah glanced around the atrium, silently taking in all the places her body might be thrown against, the edges and struts and beams that might fold her in half in the blink of an eye.

Hathorn nodded. "You'd keep moving until you hit something solid, and you'd *go splat*." She tucked the pencil back into her pocket.

The 1MC chime sounded.

"This is the XO. General quarters. Battle stations, guns. Battle stations, torpedoes. Battle stations, boarding action. Tail-flip drill will commence in four minutes. All department heads report to Ops when you've confirmed your people are secure."

Susannah's eyes flicked to her station's acceleration chair.

"Best get hopping, little rabbit," Hathorn said.

Susannah was only fifteen steps from her station, but she sprinted for it anyway.

29

"You've got to be shitting me," Nitzan said. "Really? Not even at Brittmore?"

In the stall to his right, Laior shook her head as she stepped into her leg armor.

"Yeah, no, for real," she said. "The drill sergeant told us there were budget cuts or something like that. We never did a tail-flip drill."

What the hell were they teaching Raiders these days? Nitzan hoped the newbs got their shit together before it was time for a real fight.

Across the aisle, Abshire let out a moan of stress and despair.

"I can't get my TASH to work! Bennett, can you help? I don't wanna get splatted."

The old-timer was in the stall next to Abshire, sliding on his boots.

"Stay calm, Abs," Bennett said. "You know how to do this. One step at a time. It's a drill, they're not going to flip and rip until everyone is buttoned up."

"Done!" Beaver, in the stall to Nitzan's left, slammed his helmet down and flipped the lock to seal it. "First! Fuck yeah! Is that a platoon record? It's gotta be. Hey, Bennett, what's the plat—"

"Beaver *shut your cake hole!*" Master Sergeant Sands strode down the aisle in full TASH, his helmet under one arm. "Jesus Christ, son, you talk more than a street preacher hopped up on kermiac extract."

"Yeah, Sarge, but the platoon record—"

"There is no record," Sands said. "Bennett, what do you call the last Raider to TASH up before a tail-flip?"

"That Raider is called *alive*, Master Sergeant," Bennett said.

"*Magnificent*," Sands said. "Shamdi, what do you call a Raider who does *not* TASH up before a tail-flip commences?"

Shamdi knew this bit of dialogue by heart. "That Raider is called *meat*, Master Sergeant."

"*Magnificent*," Sands said.

Abshire tried to seal up his leg armor, wound up dropping a gauntlet and kicking it across the aisle.

Sands shook his head. "Ho-lee-shit, Abshire. Calm down and follow your training. I'll help you."

Up and down the stalls, the platoon quickly and quietly armored up. It wasn't rocket science, but some of the boots were stressing themselves out to the point of making things complicated.

"Move it, people," PXO Winter called out. "Sixty seconds until tail-flip."

The noise of hurry and bustle increased.

A tail-flip wasn't the only maneuver to fear, just the one to fear the most. In Nitzan's two battles, he'd seen G-forces kill one person and badly injure two others. Human bodies didn't handle sudden changes of direction all that well.

Raiders had two ways of riding out harsh maneuvers: in-TASH or in-bunk.

Beneath every mattress lie fakegrav plating, the same stuff that lined every deck of every ship in Fleet. Unless they were assigned in-ship combat stations, the call of *general quarters* put Raiders in their bunks. During harsh maneuvers, bunk gravity increased from a standard 1g to 3gs. In an instant, Nitzan went from weighing 90kg to 270kg—almost 600 pounds, as many in his homeland counted things. The extra 2gs made it a bit hard to breathe, but it held people firmly in place. The weight—combined with a head-toward-prow orientation that put feet flat against a bunk's aft-facing end—meant it took one hell of a violent maneuver or impact to knock a Raider out of bed.

When *battle stations boarding action* was called, though—as

Yellowbelly had done minutes earlier—Raiders rushed to the rig room and TASHed up.

Nitzan sealed his chest plates. He grabbed his helmet and was about to put it on when an armored glove tapped his shoulder.

"Hey," Laior whispered, "give me a hand?"

Her collar was off-kilter. Unreal.

Nitzan was going to get stuck on a fire team with her. He just knew it. Well, with all these newbs, maybe that wouldn't be so bad. He had combat experience. They'd probably make him a team leader, if not a full squad leader. He'd have to show these heathens how to do things right.

"Thirty seconds," Winter called out. "Button it up!"

Plenty of time.

Nitzan slid his helmet back into its stall slot.

"You know how to do this," he said, gripping Laior's collar. "You've done it with a drill sergeant's stinky mouth splattering spit all over your face, right?"

He twisted the collar free and re-seated it.

"Yeah, no, for sure," Laior said. "But, like, we're really doing it now. It's different."

He clicked the collar into place. It was just a drill, but he saw the fear in her eyes.

"It's the same," he said. "What did they tell you to do when things get hot?"

"Stay fierce, stay frosty."

Another Raider mantra. There were many.

"Fifteen seconds," Winter said. "Section leaders call in."

Nitzan gave Laior's shoulder armor a thump. "You're good. Finish up."

He pulled on his helmet, sealed the lock, then put his back against his stall's aft wall. He activated his gripfield, which would keep him in place no matter how harsh the maneuvers.

"Time," Winter said. "Anyone not in-TASH and secure against an aft-facing wall is now lumpy soup in a can."

Nitzan heard the chime of the platoon channel in his helmet.

"That was a sub-par performance," Lieutenant Lindros said. "Some of you were not ready in time. You had four minutes notice.

We need to be ready in *two*. Everyone de-armor and get back to your bunks. PXO Winter, run them through the drill again while XO Ellis tears me a new one."

Well, at least Lindros wasn't a screamer. That was something. You never knew with LTs. Nitzan wasn't sure what to make of Lindros just yet. Time would tell.

"*I'm the first one out of my armor,*" Beaver yelled. "That was like *seventeen seconds*! Gotta be a platoon record!"

Nitzan sighed and pulled off his helmet.

He was probably going to get stuck on a fire team with that numb-nuts, too.

He just knew it.

30

Trav hated being the bad guy.

Lincoln wanted the crew ready to fight. It was Trav's job to make that happen. He drove them mercilessly. Battle stations drills. Fire-fighting drills. Hull breach drills. Boarder repelling drills. Crawler combat launch drills. Torpedo run drills. STC field drills. Artillery drills. Point-defense drills. Darsat drills. And his favorite—emergency dive drills to prep for an escape into transdim.

All drills were of the three-to-one variety: three without computer assistance to every one with. Crew members had to be able to operate their station at the analog-electromechanical level. Computers and AI were wonderful things when they worked. In combat, almost always, they did not.

Keeling followed the standard 18-Earth-hour schedule of a Fleet warship: on watch for six hours, station maintenance and training for six, six hours for sleep. On most ships, station training and mainte-nance didn't take up the full six hours—whatever was left over went to downtime.

Trav's murderous schedule included cross-training in other departments, and surprise drills that came at all hours of the day. *All hours* included everyone's downtime. Lincoln wanted her people to know how to do their jobs when deprived of sleep, so Trav deprived them of sleep.

Through it all came the little comments. The disrespectful stares. The whispered insults. Any and all references to and synonyms for the color yellow. He'd tried punishing that disrespect, but how hard could he discipline people who effectively served on the Fleet's flying prison? What was he going to do to them—sentence them to serve on the *Keeling?*

The crew despised him. He didn't blame them. For the most part, he endured the jibes.

Angry and frustrated crew members complained to their department head. Department heads complained to Trav. That was why, when he finally had a few hours of downtime, he wasn't surprised to see Sascha Kerkhoffs at his door, her eyes simmering with anger.

"XO, may I have a word?"

He didn't want to have a private chat. He wanted to sleep. Constant drills and surprise inspections took their toll on him just as much as they did the crew. He was exhausted, but listening to the needs of officers was part of his job.

"Of course," he said. "Have a seat at my desk."

She entered and sat as he shut the door.

Kerkhoffs had chopped her long hair. With a pipe-saw, maybe—it stuck up in sweat-slick clumps. Her coverall sleeves were tied around her waist. Sweat stains and grease smears dotted her T-shirt. The buttoned-up and polished Lieutenant he'd met on the *Ishi* was no more.

Trav sat on the edge of his bunk. "So, Lieutenant, what can I—"

"You've got to back off, XO. The drills are out of control."

She'd skipped right past the *permission to speak freely?* prologue. So be it. If Trav had been the major he should have been, he wouldn't have tolerated such boldness from a person seven years his junior. But he wasn't a major. He and Sascha were both lieutenants, although as XO he technically outranked her.

"I want the crew ready," Trav said.

He wasn't going to blame Lincoln for the drills. It was his job to implement her orders and absorb any fallout that came with.

"My people aren't getting good sleep," Sascha said. "I don't want them making mistakes."

Good sleep. If Trav had said, *tell me you've never been in combat without telling me you've never been in combat,* the words *good sleep* did the job.

"That's one of the things they need to be ready for," Trav said. "A battle can last several hours. Sometimes even *days*, depending on the number of ships involved."

She shook her head. "But, XO, if they can't—"

"How many people have you seen die?"

Sascha blinked. "What?"

"In combat," Trav said. "Have you ever seen a bulkhead painted in blood? Ever had to apply pressure to an open wound with one hand while paper-plotting a torpedo solution with the other? Ever heard someone begging for their mother to save them? Ever smelled a human being cooking alive?"

She leaned back, eyes wide.

He hadn't meant to bring such intensity, but he was just as sleep-deprived as everyone else and his patience was thin, especially from an officer who should have known better.

"No, XO," Sascha said. "I haven't."

Kerkhoffs looked so *young*, like she was just another fresh-faced engineering spec toiling away in the ship's bowels.

"I'm only looking out for my people," she said.

"I know."

She opened her mouth to speak but said nothing. She glanced at the door.

"XO, there's something else bothering me."

"Let me hear it."

"It's about..."

She trailed off, clearly wondering if she should continue.

"It's fine," Trav said. "I want to hear your concerns."

He waited. She absently rubbed the top of her head, debating internally, then she again met his eyes.

"There's something off about the people who were on this ship when we got here," she said. "Those who already have a *Keeling* patrol or two under their belt."

"Define *off* for me."

"My people won't talk about what happened on previous tours."

Trav had noticed the same thing.

"They're not supposed to," he said. "Previous patrols are classified."

"I know, I know. It's just that... they won't say *anything*. No coy remarks about previous runs. No teasing about how much better the last guy did the job. Hell, they won't even *mention* the last guy. No off-shift stories told in confidence. Nothing."

Trav shrugged. "Gillick and Daniels are trying to be best pals with everyone. Maybe your experienced people are waiting things out, getting a gauge of what gets who in trouble."

Sascha sighed. "Gillick and Daniels. How anyone can't see they're disingenuous con men is beyond me."

"If people could identify con men, politicians wouldn't get votes. People believe what they want to believe long before they'll accept what's real."

She thought for a moment, her left eye scrunching slightly.

"You're right," she said. "About all of that. But sailors *talk*, XO. I understand them not sharing classified info, but aside from discussing their duties they won't talk about *anything* to do with the ship. It's weird. I can't even get them to tell me about materials, how the various native equipment works—things that matter to my job and should be part of this ship's knowledge base. I need to find out what's going on, XO."

Sascha Kerkhoffs had a stubborn streak, that was for sure.

"Lieutenant, is this going to lead to another *stop asking questions* discussion like our one about Colonel Hasik?"

Hasik had complained to Lincoln about Sascha's constant questions. Lincoln had told Trav to make it stop. Trav had told Sascha to stop. Because shit rolls downhill.

Not that Sascha was wrong. She was the engineering head—she *should* know everything about the ship. Trav could tell Lincoln felt the same way, but the captain deferred to Hasik on that topic. Why? Did he have some power over her? Maybe he was close to Admiral Epperson.

"I've stopped trying to talk to Hasik," Sascha said. "He doesn't give a damn about anyone who isn't in his xeno department. And I'll tell you something else, XO—Colonel Hasik is full of shit."

Say one thing for Sascha Kerkhoffs—she was quite subtle.

"How do you mean, Lieutenant?"

For the second time, she paused, wondering if she should continue.

"I probably shouldn't have said that, XO."

"Probably not."

Which was true, and yet Trav had his own bad vibes about Hasik. The man was on his *seventh* patrol. Why was he the only one on board with that much experience?

"Lieutenant, if you change your mind and want to share your thoughts regarding Colonel Hasik, I promise you it will be in the strictest confi—"

The 1MC chimed.

"This is the captain. All department chiefs to the ACIC, immediately. That is all."

Sascha was up and out of his quarters in an instant.

Trav stood, looking wistfully at his bunk. This was his downtime, but sleep would have to wait.

31

After the first day aboard, everyone was expected to manage the sphincters on their own—no helping hands to guide you through. Within three days, Anne had acclimated to the process. She gave no more thought to going through one than she did taking an elevator or riding an updown. It wasn't as disgusting anymore, either; when there weren't fifty-plus people going through the sphincters in short order, the ship produced lubricant in such small amounts it was barely noticeable.

That lack of smegma—as Akil Daniels so eloquently called it— meant those descending from the superstructure into the ship proper didn't look that much worse for the wear.

The Auxiliary CIC was in one of the ship's natural spaces, with bulkheads and the low, curved ceiling textured in that weird coral pattern. Much smaller than its counterpart up in the superstructure, the ACIC's overall shape was more a suggestion of a rectangle than an actual one. No intel or xeno lofts here—there wasn't room. Signals and Darsat were located in a separate compartment, aft of the ACIC. The Raider liaison station wasn't accounted for at all.

Even without those stations, the room was a claustrophobic crush of terminals and acceleration chairs. The nav-orb was two-thirds the size of its CIC counterpart, the command slate, half the size. Anne's station was a natural indent in the copper wall barely wide enough for a stool and a mini terminal.

No air conditioning down here. The ACIC was *hot*.

Anne's undershirt clung to her skin. She hadn't shrugged off her coverall sleeves yet, but it wouldn't be long before she did. She sympathized with shipmates who had to spend all their time belowdecks. Olivia would have liked it, though. Olivia had always preferred close, cozy spaces.

"We have our orders," Anne said. "The *Ishlangu* will accompany us through unclaimed space." She lit up the course inside the maneuvering orb. "It's a three-punch course that will carry us around Purist Nation's territory to a specified demarcation point. From there, *Keeling* will go transdim and travel beyond the border to a point near Mining Colony Three."

The orb's light played off the faces of the people staring into it: XO Ellis, Sascha Kerkhoffs, Alex Plait, Cat Brown, Chief Sung, and Lieutenant Lindros. Captain Lincoln stood at the command station a few meters aft of the orb.

Another encrypted message had come in. The mission remained the same, but the start date had moved from July 12th to July 3rd—two days from now.

That changed cut ten days' worth of training and prep, a rough thing for a crew this new.

Most of the CIC crew weren't cleared to hear what the mission involved, which was why Lincoln used the ACIC for the briefing. She'd left Nav Chief Erickson in command. Lincoln let Anne handle the briefing. It was an intelligence operation, after all, and Anne was intel chief.

"This mission is of critical importance," Anne said. "We don't know what intelligence we're obtaining, but we've been told it's critical to the war effort."

"Important?" Sung shook his head. "Gee, I would have never guessed the brass would send us deep into enemy territory for something *important*."

Sung was an asshole. He always had to have a smart-ass comment.

"Let the Major finish," Lincoln said.

Anne would have rather Lincoln properly dressed Sung down, but this was Fleet, and in Fleet, senior noncoms got away with murder.

"We will enter realspace well away from the mining colony," Anne said. "Then, we wait for our asset to come to us. When the asset is aboard, we go transdim, travel back across the border, rendezvous with the *Ishlangu*, and head to Gateway Station to deliver the asset. We are not to engage the enemy. The *Keeling* is considered a higher value asset than the intel we're sent to recover."

Some frowned, some sneered. Sung, Kerkhoffs, and Brown looked disgusted. Anne wasn't happy about the orders, either—real soldiers wanted to fight the enemy, not run at the first sign of danger.

"That's right in the Purists' backyard," Kerkhoffs said. "This is some dangerous work."

Her hair looked ridiculous. She should just shave it, or at least turn those clumps into a crewcut.

Sung crossed his arms. "It's not the destination that's dangerous, it's the trip. Captain, how long will we be in the Mud for this?"

"Four days, total," Lincoln said. "Two in, two back out."

Plait, the Operations Department head, stared into the orb, rubbed his cheeks.

"The longest I've been under is eighteen hours," he said. "Can we survive two *days*?"

Plait had one *Keeling* patrol under his belt, as did Sung and Brown. Lincoln had three. The rest? Zero.

"We'll survive," Lincoln said. "On my second patrol, I was under for five and a half days."

"*Five* days?" Plait glanced at Sung and Brown, who looked as shocked as he did. "For real?"

Lincoln's face twitched, as if a bad memory rushed into her thoughts and did its damage before she pushed it aside.

"Five and a *half*," she said. "And Colonel Hasik was once under for fifteen days. He's still alive."

Sung huffed. "Anyone else from that particular patrol still alive?"

Lincoln came out from behind the command station. She stood with the others, stared into the orb.

"We have three days before we begin this mission," she said. "We need to season up the newbies. Tomorrow, we'll launch a drone target, then go into the Mud and track the drone for thirty minutes. We'll come back into realspace, do a torpedo run at the drone, then go back into the Mud for an hour. XO, you'll command the entire exercise. I'll step in only if necessary."

XO Ellis looked at Lincoln, his odd amber eyes brimming with doubt.

"Captain, I haven't commanded a dive yet," he said. "I request a short dive so I can acclimate to commanding the ship in transdim before I have to command a full torpedo run exercise."

"Request denied," Lincoln said. "We don't have time to tap dance. The fastest way for me to see what you don't know is to throw you into the deep end. If you can't cut it, I'll get someone who can."

Would she really relieve Ellis as XO? If she did, she'd need Anne's approval.

"We have two days to identify who can't handle a long trip through the Mud," Lincoln said. "We'll restrain those people for the trip in and the trip out. Lindros, I need cross-training on manual artillery operation and point-defense completed by eleven hundred tonight, and your first mock crawler landing and boarder defense exercise completed by oh-eight-hundred tomorrow."

Lindros stiffened. "Captain, we've only been on board for ten days. Most of my people are on their first deployment. I'm still assembling fire teams and drilling basic maneuvering. I request more time to cover the fundamentals before we go into mocks."

"Request denied," Lincoln said. "Complete the exercise and get me a detailed report on how every Raider operated. Understand?"

"Aye-aye, Captain." Lindros said. "We'll get the job done."

"Uh, cap," Sung said, "if we're going to wind up in transdim for forty-eight hours, should the virgins get a chance to take in the sights before that happens?"

Lincoln stared into the orb, thinking.

"You're right, Chief," she said. "On the next dive, we'll let the CIC staff see what the Mud looks like."

32

I wear the Raider black, because I ain't so clever.

But standing on a hull, I can see forever.

The old marching cadence played through John's head even as he watched the instruction for the Type24 gun. It was hard to keep his mind from wandering, both because he was long-since certified on the weapon and because of the view. Here, calm and comfortable in his armor, he truly could see forever.

John stood with Beaver and Abbas Basara atop the starboard-side 24's armored gunhouse, looking down through an open access hatch. Inside, Artillery Chief Dardanos Leeds trained Abs, Shamdi and Laior on the weapon's operation. Four armored people in a space designed for a crew of three made for a tight fit.

"The dual-purpose Type Twenty-Four is fully independent of the ship's interior," Leeds said. "All elements are self-contained within the barbette below us, including gunhouse foundation, rotation system, and ammunition."

Basara grabbed John's forearm, instantly opening a touch-channel.

"Bennett, what's *dual-purpose* mean?"

The big youngster was another spec-1 fresh out of Brittmore. He must have had a religious exemption that allowed facial hair—his black beard was so thick it pressed against his TASH visor.

"It means you can use it against both ships and voidcraft," John said. "And also torps, and decoys, and exo-troops... pretty much anything that moves."

Basara nodded and let go, breaking the channel.

Leeds continued. "The gun is fed by a bottom-loading system operated by the turret master. Munitions vary based on tactical need, but all rounds have rear-venting counterthrust that matches the force generated by the projectile. Any remaining directional momentum added to the ship is easily corrected by attitude chem-thrusters."

This time it was Beaver who grabbed John's arm.

"I can't *wait* to shoot this beast, Bennett. Scream, aim, and fire."

Beaver thought a 127-millimeter gun was a *beast*? He'd probably cum in his pants if he saw the 460-millimeter Type80s on a heavy cruiser like *Chicago* or *Khartoum*.

"If you're part of the gun crew in a battle, that's bad," John said. "It means the weapon's crew are dead or injured, and Raiders have to fill in. Now, pay attention to your instructor."

Beaver let go of John's arm and stared down into the gunhouse like a devout follower fawning over his prophet.

John drifted off again, gazed out at the void. Such a view. The Type24's seven-meter-long barrel aimed out into a star-speckled eternity.

"The turret has three-hundred-and-sixty-degree rotational axis parallel to the hull's length," Leeds said. "The barrel has an elevation of plus-seventy-one degrees. Because of the barbette, which provides three meters of distance between the weapon and the hull, the barrel also has a minus-ten declination, creating an overall firing angle of eighty-one degrees. Mechanical governors prevent the barrel from pointing in any direction that might cause rounds to hit the ship."

That made the '24 somewhat idiot proof. *Somewhat*, because no military in history had ever fully proofed itself against idiocy.

Leeds walked through the controls. As he did, he gave an overview of the instant calculations needed to hit targets moving at insane relative velocities. A good gun crew had to learn a specific bit of complex trigonometry, then turn that math into instant-reaction instinct.

While the Type24 had computerized targeting, it was rarely used. In a fight, the typical computer system's operational efficiency was about ten minutes, fifteen at most, and only then at such ranges the enemy had gobs of time to avoid incoming rounds. When your computer pals went kaput, you still had to deliver projectiles on-target. You did if you wanted to live, anyway.

Firing the weapon manually was surprisingly easy for the three-person gun crew, which consisted of a *pointer*, a *trainer*, and a *turret master*. The pointer, who sat left of the barrel, used handwheels to control barrel elevation. A hydraulic foot switch fired the weapon and cleared the spent shell. The trainer, who sat right of the barrel, used hand wheels to rotate the gunhouse. Both pointer and trainer used identical optical sights to spot and track targets. The turret master stayed in communication with the CIC and selected which type of munition to load: flak for enemy voidcraft, incoming missiles, torpedoes, and exo-troops; high-energy explosive rounds designed to penetrate ship armor; or STC blazers, which let the *Keeling* initiate space-time fuckery from a distance.

While *firing* was easy, *hitting* was another thing entirely. It wasn't like operating artillery on the ground or a naval ship, where there was a constant horizon, a constant *up* and *down*. In a space battle, ships changed pitch and yaw on a whim, they accelerated and decelerated, they rolled—any and all of these movements instantly altered what the gun crew could see and impacted the relative velocity of any target.

"Pointer, elevate fifteen degrees," Leeds said. "Trainer, rotate to ninety degrees. Turret master, load an AP round."

Abshire, the trainer, spun his hand wheels, quickly rotating the gunhouse so that the barrel was at a ninety-degree angle to the *Keeling*'s centerline. As he did, Laior, the pointer, elevated the barrel. It always amazed John how fast manual gears could make a big-ass gun move. Shamdi clearly had prior training—he worked the loader mechanism like a pro and had the round in place before the gunhouse stopped turning.

"Fire now, now, now," Leeds said.

Without a sound, a funnel of orange flashed from the barrel, there and gone in an instant. A plume of smoke billowed forth, expanding to an ever-thinning cloud. From the opposite counterfire barrel, a far bigger, far denser smoke column shot out into the void, a ballooning puff that slowly stretched to nothing.

What a sight to see.

John heard the ping of someone opening a transmission on the platoon channel.

"Bennett, this is the PXO, do you copy?"

Katharina Winter addressing him on the platoon channel.

"Bennett here, PXO."

"Meet me forward of the superstructure," Winter said. "On the double."

"Affirmative, PXO, on my way."

John extended his thrusters and stepped off the gunhouse. He flew topside. To port, he saw both Ochthera crawlers practicing combat landing approaches. One pilot, two co-pilots and one engineer-gunner had zero combat experience—Biggie Bang was putting them through their paces.

Winter was kneeling in front of the superstructure's forward armor, one fist down. Even on a stationary ship with no sign of even debris nearby, her at-rest position gave her three points of contact. A sure sign of a combat vet.

John landed next to her and assumed the same position.

"Bennett, the LT assigned you as a team leader."

With all the boots in the platoon, John realized he should have seen this coming, should have gotten ahead of it.

"I'm not much of a leader, PXO. I excel at following orders, not giving them."

"Master Sergeant says different."

Sands had sold him out. Dammit. If anyone knew John didn't want responsibility, it was Sands.

"Let's skip the part where you tell me you don't want it," Winter said. "Because I don't care. Renee Jordan is Alpha Squad leader. Corporal Sarvacharya leads alpha fire team one, you lead alpha fire team two."

Maybe Sands wasn't a total asshole. The guy could have easily recommended John as squad leader. Better to be responsible for only four other people as opposed to ten.

"Awesome," John said. "Who do I got?"

"Beaver, Shamdi, Abshire and Laior."

A fire team where only he and Shamdi of the Always-Running Mouth had combat experience? Wonderful. Just peachy.

"I'll do my best, PXO. What's the mission?"

Winter kept a blank expression. "What makes you think there's a mission?"

John gestured toward the starboard Type24 and to the crawlers doing mock flybys.

"LT just turned on the training afterburners," he said. "Some of these kids shouldn't be allowed to *look at* a twenty-four, let alone fire one. My guess is we depart for an operation in two, maybe three days?"

The corner of her mouth crinkled upward.

"I don't know what the op is," she said. "But you're spot-on. We depart in three days. You help me get these kids ready, okay?"

John nodded. Raiders helped Raiders. It was part of what made the service so special.

"I have something else to say, Bennett. It's personal. That all right with you?"

"Personal? Sure, hit me."

"I like the cut of your jib," Winter said. "I've heard rumors that Captain Lincoln isn't all that worried about fraternization. If that turns out to be true, and if LT doesn't have a stick up his ass about it, maybe you and I can have a tussle."

She wanted a piece of him? Fraternization wasn't easily dismissed —she must have heard wrong. Still, he was flattered. Winter wasn't young, but she was younger than he was. By a lot.

"I'm old enough to be your father."

"Good thing I got daddy issues," Winter said. "Mommy issues, too, but that's another story. A girl needs her therapy. We get some off-hours, you and I can discuss it. Unless you're not interested?"

Oh, he was interested, all right.

"PXO, you make sure we don't get brought up on charges, and I'll be the best damn therapist you ever had."

Winter's grin told him he would be in for a grand time.

She stood. "Good. We're back on the clock, Spec Bennett. Go inform your team you're their boss. We've got trench training in thirty minutes."

33

Susannah's body hurt.

Not just her eye, which had turned horribly purple and yellow, but also her back, her arms, and her legs, all sore from the constant scraping.

"I know this sucks, Ensign," Hathorn said. "But keep at it."

The lieutenant was on her knees, using a steel scraper to pry copper film from the base of a workstation.

Turned out Hathorn wasn't that bad after all. She just needed a little time to get used to new people. Hathorn's icy exterior had warmed, and now she was treating Susannah—or, rather, treating *Bethany*—like a shipmate.

"Thank you, Lieutenant." Susannah stopped scraping a monitor housing to adjust her already sweat-soaked headband. "Was it like this on the last patrol?"

Hathorn paused. Susannah realized she'd messed up—she wasn't supposed to ask about previous patrols.

"Yeah," Hathorn said. "Except it didn't spread as fast. Finish up and drinks are on me."

Feeling like she'd dodged a bullet, Susannah started scraping again. Could she get away with asking small questions here and there? Could that get her enough information to make Admiral Bock happy?

Maybe. If so, liquor would help. Hathorn drank. A *lot*. So did

Hasik. And so did Susannah. She had to fit in, didn't she? If she wanted them to open up, to tell her more about the ship and how it worked, she first needed to be accepted as part of the team.

The hull material was obviously automatonic. The metal-organic framework formed into an equivalent of cells. Those cells self-replicated. How they did that, she didn't know, and wouldn't know until she could get some under an electron scope and start experimenting. Whatever the mechanism, the material grew quickly, spreading out in thin filaments that spread onto equipment, terminals, cots... even *shoes* if they sat in one place long enough.

She desperately wanted to study that phenomena, but Hasik forbade her from even asking about it.

And besides, between learning the basics of the transdim system, going through the XO's endless drills, and all the cross-training, Susannah's plate was full. For three hours a day, Hasik gave her to Lieutenant Kerkhoffs. Susannah was learning how to operate the curvine, how to use the fabricator, even how to machine parts the fabricator couldn't produce. Punch-drive operation and maintenance, though, was a different animal altogether—she wasn't allowed near the thing.

Susannah hated cross-training. Not counting the three-person xeno team, the engineering department had five women and eleven men. When she trained with those men, she felt eyes upon her. Eyes filled with lust. Some, like Corporal Salvatore and Staff Sergeant Marchenko, had the decency to look away when she caught them checking her out. Others—like that perv-eyed electrical tech, Brian Goldsmith—kept on staring. Staring, and *smiling*, in a way that wasn't at all about happiness or joy.

Those hungry gazes... Susannah knew where they might lead. What if she wound up alone with Goldsmith? Or with Michael Camp, a spec-1 machinist mate, who always found a way to brush up against her.

Susannah didn't feel safe around those men.

But if she said so to Kerkhoffs, or the XO, or the COB, or even the captain, how would that go? Would they believe her? If they did and took action, would those men know it was Susannah who ratted them out? She was going to be here for a long time—she didn't need to make enemies who would try to get her alone, try to assault her the way Bratchford had.

Maybe Hathorn had insights on how to manage unwanted attention.

"Lieutenant, can I ask a question?"

"Is it about the ship?"

A friendly warning in that tone—Hathorn had let one question go, she did not want to be asked another.

"It's not about the ship," Susannah said in a rush. "It's about the crew."

"If you're going to ask me what so-and-so did to get assigned here, that's almost as bad as asking about the ship itself. Other people's pasts are not your concern, Bethany."

Bethany. Not *Ensign Darkwater* or *Newb*, but *Bethany.*

"No, not that, either," Susannah said. "When I'm in engineering, some of the men... they... um..."

"Mike Camp rubs up against you any chance he gets?"

Hathorn smiled. A *real* smile.

"Yeah," Susannah said, a little stunned. "And it's not just him."

"Let me guess—Goldsmith and Montgomery?"

Sal Montgomery was a propulsion mate, spec-3.

"Goldsmith, yes," Susannah said. "He's creepy. I haven't had any problems with Montgomery."

"Oh, you will. That guy's cock is a stray dog in a rainstorm looking for any porch he can crawl under."

Hathorn understood. She'd endured the same things. That realization flooded Susannah with a sense of relief. To have someone on this ship, *anyone*, who was on her side would make things vastly better.

"What do you do about it?" Susannah asked.

Hathorn returned to scraping.

"Depends on the guy," she said. "I was alone with Goldsmith in the fabrication bay. He tried to come on to me, told me not to make any noise or he'd hurt me. I punched him in the throat. While he was struggling to breathe, I told him if he tried it again, I'd wait until we were in the Mud, then I'd find him and slice his sack clean off."

Susannah's jaw fell open. "Oh my goodness. Did he stop?"

"He sure did. Hasn't bothered me since."

"What about Montgomery? What did you do to him?"

"Him I screwed rotten."

Susannah's scraper ground to a halt. "You mean you had *sex* with him?"

"I sure did." Hathorn leaned close to the terminal's base, scraped hard at a resilient bit of foil. "Have you *seen* that man? He's gorgeous."

Susannah couldn't believe what she was hearing.

"But he's enlisted and you're a lieutenant. Isn't that fraternization? What if the captain finds out?"

Hathorn stood. Hands on hips, she leaned left, then right, working the kinks out of her back.

"If the department head doesn't care, the captain doesn't care," she said. "People are stuck in this hell hole for two-year stints. When the ship is in port at Gateway Station, we all get put in the same barracks. There's no real liberty, because of *oh so many secrets*. For the most part, all we see is each other. Think the captain wants to tell a bunch of horny eighteen and nineteen-year-olds, a bunch of people in their early twenties, that they can't get laid for *two years*?"

Susannah hadn't had sex in over a decade. She didn't see the problem. But then again, she'd been nineteen once—things had been different back then.

Back when she'd been with Melanie.

Susannah forced the thought away. She wasn't like that anymore. She'd *never* been like that, not really, she'd just made mistakes in her youth, mistakes she prayed High One would forgive.

"Montgomery's got a cannon, but he's terrible in the sack," Hathorn said. "I was hooking up with Fuentes, but we stopped until we figure out how Kerkhoffs feels about people in her department getting it on. Why do you ask, Bethany? You like Goldsmith? Montgomery? Because if you like Fuentes, I got dibs."

"I don't want Sergeant Fuentes," Susannah said. "I don't like anyone in that department."

"Fair enough." Hathorn hung her scraper back up on the bulkhead. "Other than the engineering guys, anyone else been sniffing around you?"

Right after the dive, while in triage, that Shamdi fellow had seemed interested. There been something... *familiar* about him. Not him personally, but rather the way he spoke, the way he carried himself. She still couldn't put her finger on it.

"Well, there was this Raider. When I was in the mess after I fell and hit my head. He was... well, he wanted to have coffee with me."

Hathorn grinned a grin that would have looked right at home on Goldsmith's leering face.

"*Coffee*, huh? I'll bet that's what he wants. He look like he's hung?"

Susannah's cheeks instantly burned hot. She stared at the monitor bracket, unable to look at Hathorn.

"Sorry, Beth," the lieutenant said. "I gather you're not quite as open about sex as I am. That's cool."

Not as *open*? How about not as *crass*? Not as *wanton*?

"It's not a big deal if you want to spend some downtime with a Raider," Hathorn said. "If his LT doesn't care, no one cares. Just don't think you can use the atrium for a quick fu... I mean, don't bring him here for hanky panky."

Susannah's face felt like it was about to catch fire.

"I'd just want coffee," she said. "That's all. I'd just want to talk."

Hathorn walked to her bunk and dug under the mattress for her flask.

"Then you're home free." She took a swig. "No one cares about two crewmates having coffee. If it becomes more than that, though, I can tell you where to go. Even on a tiny ship like this, there's spaces where you can spend some private time with an interested party. Looks like you're done with that monitor bracket." She held up the flask. "Want a snort?"

Susannah did *not* want a snort. The booze went straight to her head, and then came the hangovers. But she had to fit in. She had to be like the others.

"Yes," she said. "I could use a drink."

34

"I hope I don't get killed this time," Abshire said. "I think there's something wrong with my suit."

There probably was something wrong with his suit—there was something wrong with *everyone's* suit—but that wasn't why he'd been killed. In a platoon full of sacrilegious dumbfucks, Abshire was the dumbest. And, oh joy, he was in Nitzan's fire team.

"You died because you forgot your training," Bennett said. "This time, remember it. The name of the game is *repel boarders*. Keep inside the trench curve, stick to the ribs. If comm goes out—and it will —remember your hand signals. And never, *ever*, leave your notch until you're ordered to."

It was amazing that last bit even needed to be said, yet Abshire had poked his head out—*twice*—and eaten a simulated bullet both times. He wasn't the only moron in team Alpha-One; Laior couldn't seem to understand the concept of a backblast. She kept standing directly behind someone instead of behind and two steps to the side.

Beaver, though... he was good. Surprisingly so. Although if Nitzan heard Beaver say *scream, aim and fire* one more time, he might shoot the guy in the face.

Nitzan was pissed he hadn't been named squad leader, or at least a fire team leader. Whatever information he gathered here was of no use to the Nation if he got dead. The best way to get dead? Be the guy ordered to move toward the bullets instead of ordering others to do so.

It wasn't that bad, though—Grampa Bennett knew his shit. He'd seen more action than anyone in the platoon. By far. Bennett had boarded enemy vessels *four times*. Anyone who could do that and keep on breathing was worth paying attention to. Nitzan had boarded just once. He'd lost two squad mates, even though the enemy ship had been mostly under control.

Boarding was *always* dangerous.

The double-beep of a CIC transmission sounded inside his helmet.

"APC incoming, starboard-high, bearing zero-six-zero." Nitzan didn't recognize the voice. One of the signalers, probably, manning the Raider liaison station. "Gravitational signature is that of a Kloos-class armored personnel carrier. Launching ECM. Point-defense, free-fire."

It obviously wasn't a Kloos, Purist Nation's main APC model. It was a *Keeling* Ochthera, loaded up with Bravo Squad.

"Alpha Squad, stay down until my command," said Sergeant Jordan on the squad channel. "If you peek your head out, the APC gunner will take it off for you."

An Ochthera had both a front-mounted six-barreled minigun, operated by the co-pilot, and a top turret with twin .50-cal machine guns, manned by the engineer-gunner. Even in the worst STC fuckery, those weapons could wipe a hull clean of any enemy troops.

Three rapid clicks—Bennett opening up Alpha-Two's channel.

"Alpha-Two, the APC will drop munitions," he said. "Stay in your notch until you get the green light. I repeat, *stay in your notch*."

Nitzan was already in his notch, tucked in tight. Above him, an illuminated red light, and a green light that was off.

A trench was an insane thing that just plain worked. Being on the outside of a ship during combat was mad-risky no matter how much armor and firepower superiority your side had, but being outside held one key advantage—your soldiers can't be stuck inside by a jammed hatch if they're not inside to begin with. Once curvature maneuvers drew an enemy ship in close and rounds started landing, ships took damage, damage that led to exterior hatches getting bent, warped, or outright destroyed.

"APC two klicks out and closing," the liaison said.

Three-meter-diameter tubes of armor with horizontal slots along the top, *Keeling*'s trenches ran port and starboard along the superstructure's base. Stored below each trench, four tightly bundled lifeboats that could self-pressurize and provide temporary shelter for twenty-ish people. That was a worst-case scenario, obviously—few people in lifeboats lived long enough for help to arrive.

While in a trench, a Raider was mostly protected from small arms fire, anti-personnel munitions, fighter flybys and APC gunners. In a ship-to-ship battle, getting munitions through the top slots was damn near impossible, even when computer-assisted targeting was functional, which was never. Only torpedoes or artillery could punch through the thick armor with one shot.

The slots were a meter wide, just enough room for a fully armed and armored Raider to crawl through.

Inside the trench, internal ribs provided instant cover, meaning bombs, missiles, or grenades—*especially* grenades—that found their way through the slots couldn't scrape a platoon clean like a wire brush through a gun barrel. Between every other rib was a deep notch with a firing port, through which a Raider could shoot at incoming exo-troops while remaining almost fully protected from enemy fire.

Contact wiring laced through the trenches connected touch-comm networks. If wireless comms crapped out—which was almost always—a hand, foot, or helmet pressed against any of hundreds of white comm-dots created an instant voice connection.

"One klick out," the liaison said. "Point-defense failure. APC will land. Repeat, APC will land."

No surprise there—it wasn't much of an anti-boarder exercise if the enemy APC never reached the hull.

It wasn't real combat, yet Nitzan felt his heart beat faster. He couldn't lie to himself—when he finally went home to the Nation, he was going to miss this Raider shit something awful.

Real or not, it was time for the silent dance.

Nitzan fought the urge to slide out of his notch and take a peek. There was something stunning about watching an assault craft come in hot. No noise. Nothing but the flashing of autocannons, the fire blossoms of detonating munitions, the clouds of dissipating smoke, and the rain of shrapnel spreading out, traveling on and on forever, still sailing through the void long after the empires that launched them had crumbled into the entropy of the past.

"APC making a landing approach," the liaison said. "Touchdown in fifteen, fourteen, thirt—"

The comm filled with screeching static that was instantly damped by his helmet's internal systems. The crawler—or possibly the *Keeling* —had activated a STC corruptor, which, among many other functions, scrambled wireless signals.

Nitzan touched his palm to a comm-dot.

"—under cover." Jordan's voice. "Repeat, stay under cover. Alpha-One, when enemy deploys, engage from cover. Alpha-Two, prepare for delayed flanking attack on my signal. If the APC lifts off, *Keeling* will pitch-roll away, so keep your gripfields *on*."

Alpha-One was in the port-side trench, Alpha-Two in the starboard. Jordan hoped to catch the "enemy" boarders in a crossfire.

"Alpha-Two, sound off," Bennett said.

Nitzan did, as did Beaver, Abshire and Laior. Nitzan heard Alpha-One sounding off as well.

"APC touchdown," Jordan said.

In his HUD, Nitzan saw his pulse rate rising. He calmed himself. At that moment, he wasn't a Nationalite, he wasn't a Unionist—he was a soldier, and his only hope of staying alive was to be part of the team and kill the enemy before the enemy killed him.

High One, see me through. I offer my body as a sacrifice to your glory.

He made that prayer before going into any battle, even a fake one. It was his personal mantra. But there was another mantra, a Raider mantra—there were many—that was just as sacred.

Every Raider is a rifleman. My rifle, without me, is useless. Without my rifle, I am useless.

There was more to the creed, but that was the only part he cared about. The Union had trained him how to kill, and kill he would.

He pulled his RR-36 rifle free of his chest clamps.

"Alpha-Two," Bennett said, "clear the trench."

Nitzan took his hand off the wall, returning him to absolute silence save for the sound of his own breathing. He shouldered his rifle and looked down his notch's entrance. An explosion flashed in the trench. His visor compensated instantly, saving his eyes.

He stepped to the mouth of his notch and leaned out, looking left to clear aft as was his assignment.

Abshire was stuck to the trench wall, his TASH frozen, his grip-field locking him in place. Blue lights pulsed on his suit, showing he'd been "killed." Stupid fuck had come out early—*again*—and got hit by a grenade. Past Abshire, Laior also aimed aft.

To Nitzan's right, forward, he saw Bennett and Beaver aiming upward, RRs on their shoulders. They fired simultaneously, backblast smoke billowing off the trench's curved wall. Airburst rounds angled up, detonating as they exited the trench slits. In real combat, those rounds would launch a thousand metal bearings that punch through personal armor. In this fake fight, they launched hundreds of tiny sensors that delivered modeled force information to any TASH rig they hit. The suit extrapolated the damage, slowed down struck limbs to simulate wounds, or even—as in Abshire's case—froze a suit alto-gether to simulate death.

Nitzan waved for Laior to close the gap left by Abshire. At least this time she didn't line up directly behind Nitzan—good to know someone was actually learning.

Inertia yanked Nitzan back and to the right. His feet stayed locked to the trench floor. Through the slit above, the crawler moved away from the *Keeling*, seeming to flip backward and twist right all at once, out of sight in the blink of an eye. Perceived motion only, probably— the Keeling had pitched down and rolled starboard, trying to separate the boarders from the crawler's supporting fire.

The Inertia ceased as *Keeling* hit a consistent attitude and veloc-ity, which it had to do to let Raiders move about on the hull.

"Alpha-One in position at port-aft superstructure," Jordan said. "Fire on my command. Alpha-Two, throw AP grenades, four-count, come up swinging."

Wireless comms were back. In real combat, *Keeling*'s EMC oper-ator would wage a constant war against his or her counterparts on other ships, trying to route communications around enemy interfer-ence. Battles usually involved a constant, flowing skirmish of brainiacs adjusting EM frequencies and curvature modulation, with neither side able to maintain clear control for more than a few minutes at a time. Not the kind of fracas Nitzan wanted to fight—he'd rather trade bullets any day.

He clamped his rifle to his chest, pulled a mock armor-piercing grenade from his leg armor. He thumbed the detonation time ring to one second. He'd practiced throws like this a thousand times, used them in actual combat a half-dozen more, and knew that one-second timer would detonate the grenade when it was over the heads of Bravo Squad troops.

"Throw," Jordan said. "Now, now, now."

Bennett cut his gripfield and leapt the three meters to the trench slit. Beaver did the same—the kid moved like he'd been doing it all his life. Nitzan cut his own and sprang up, reactivating it when his left palm hit the thick slot's underside. He flicked his grenade through, angling it up over topside.

There was no loud explosion, no tinkling of the hundreds of sensors scattering down across the hull. There was only counting, *one... two...*

"Alpha-One," Jordan said, "open fire."

At *four*, Nitzan unclamped his rifle and used his left hand to pull himself up—only the RR's barrel and his eyes peeked over the slot's edge. Blue-flashing TASH-suited bodies littered the topside hull, stuck in place by their maxed-out gripfields, their "deaths" coming at the hands of Alpha-Two's grenades or Alpha-One's fire.

Most of Bravo Squad's was down on the hull or floating away, their lights pulsing blue. The two survivors fired back at Alpha-One, who were hitting them from port, but the Bravos fell still as recoilless sim-rounds from Bennett, Beaver, and Nitzan found their mark.

Nitzan realized he'd seen no fire coming from his left.

He glanced into the trench, saw Laior stuck to the wall, red lights on her suit flashing madly.

Nitzan pressed his palm to a white dot.

"*Cease-fire, drill-stop,*" he said. "Cease-fire, drill-stop! Medic to starboard-aft trench, Laior is down!"

35

Captain Lincoln stayed in the CIC while Trav did the hard work.

Laior had made a basic mistake. For reasons unknown, she'd turned off her gripfield early. When the *Keeling* pitched down hard and rolled to port, Laior's inertia had effectively kept her in place while the trench roof smashed against the top of her helmet.

With a TASH rig in perfect working order, a hit like that was 95% survivable. So much so, a Raider might be scattered for a moment, give her head a shake to clear the cobwebs, then jump back into the fight.

Laior's rig had not been in perfect working order.

Two of the four inertial dampening cylinders on her TASH collar had failed. The other two cylinders were overwhelmed, letting her head bend so sharply that her C_1 vertebrae shattered, severing her spinal column.

That death—and Lincoln's questionable choice to pass the buck for this important ritual—had Trav in a vacsuit, standing atop the aft torpedo bay, giving last rights for Spec-One Rumenia Laior.

"I didn't know Rumenia well," he said. "But she was Fleet. She was a Raider. While she never got a chance to fight the enemy, she was ready to do so, ready to do her duty."

He faced aft, toward the bottomside of the *Keeling*'s barbed tail. At his feet, a green body bag with a Union flag pinned to it. Behind him, forty-four vacsuited sailors—all those not on duty—stood in ranks at attention.

Just past Laior's body bag, the torpedo bay dropped off at a sharp angle, leading down to the scarred copper hull where the armored Raider platoon stood in sharp formation. Her fire team was in front in a missing-man line—Bennett, Perry, a space where Laior would have been, then Shamdi and Abshire.

In many ways, this ceremony was thousands of years old. Change a country here, a flag there, and what Fleet did now was little different from what had likely happened since the moment mankind left the safety of shore and set out to conquer the ocean blue. Spacefaring militaries had even kept the name—while there wasn't a drop of open water within a dozen lightyears, they still called it *burial at sea*.

All deaths were hard to take. Non-combat deaths, though, were harder. Fleet was a dangerous place. Accidents happened. People could, and did, die without an enemy firing a shot.

An accident, yes, but a preventable one. If Laior's TASH had been newer, without defective parts, she'd still be alive. The mission was days away. Her training had been rushed. Maybe if she'd had more time to learn from the older hands, she wouldn't have wound up in a position where those defective parts meant her death.

There wasn't much to say, and even less time in which to say it. Lincoln wanted everyone back inside for the torpedo run drill.

"We commit our comrade's remains to the void," Trav said. "We wish her peace and tranquility until the inevitable day that the flesh that is alive, that is *us*, follows her into the dark."

He bent to one knee, slid the stiff body bag off the edge and guided it down the torpedo bay's slope. Lindros and Winter took it. In Raider tradition, they carried her flag-covered body through the platoon as every soldier reached out for a final touch goodbye.

Winter removed the flag and handed it to Bennett and Shamdi, who quickly folded it.

Lindros pushed the body out into space. He removed a detonator from his webbing. As unit commander, he would complete the ceremony.

Sailors and Raiders alike watched the stiff green bag drift farther and farther away from the ship.

Trav saluted. The Raiders saluted, as did the sailors behind him.

Lindros triggered the remote.

The body of Rumenia Laior flared with flame, then blazed a blinding white. For the briefest moment, her body burned as brightly as any of the countless stars and galaxies that stretched out in all directions.

One dead. If *Keeling* wound up in battle, there would be more. Trav honestly didn't know if he could face combat again—*Schild*'s sights and sounds and smells remained with him. When *Keeling* faced danger, would he want to stand and fight, or would he want to run?

"Return to your stations," he said.

It was time to get back to work.

36

Susannah still didn't like the taste of alcohol, but she was starting to appreciate its effects.

Music played. Her head spun. And if she weren't drunk, Hathorn's bawdy story might not be funny. But she *was* drunk, and the tale was a gasser.

"So then he comes into my bedroom," Hathorn said. "Just walks on in, wearing nothing but a toilet brush he'd rigged up to hang over his dangle like a fig leaf."

Susannah took a quick swig from the flask. The liquor still burned going down, but not as much as it had the first five or seven sips.

She passed the flask to Hasik, who was in his bunk, lying on his back, so tanked he was slurring his words. Steam clouded his glasses. He didn't try to wipe them off.

"So he's standing there," Hathorn continued, "and then I ask him, *are you here to fix the toilet?* And he looks me dead in the eye—I swear, *dead* in the eye—and he says—" she made a fist at her crotch, waggled it as if she was waggling a sword "—he says, *what makes you think I'm a plumber?*"

Hasik let out that peculiar laugh of his, like a stuttering trumpet with a dented bell.

"Wait... wait." Susannah tried to process the logic—or *illogic*, maybe—but the booze gummed up her gears. "He *wasn't* there to fix the toilet?"

Hathorn rolled her eyes. "No, my dear Ensign, he was there to... to... oh for fuck's sake, never mind. Colonel, toss me that juice."

As the flask arced over Susannah's bunk, the joke hit home.

"*Oh!*" She burst into laughter. "He was there to have intercourse with you! After all you told him, Hernando really came out of character like that?"

Hathorn screwed the top on the flask, wiped a dribble of booze from her chin.

"True as the day I was born," she said. "Hernando was a terrible lay, but goddamn he was funny. Okay, Bethany—your turn."

"Me?" Susannah's eyes went wide. "I don't have any good stories."

Hasik raised a hand. "I told a shtory, Hathorn told a shtory, now you tell a shtory." He let the hand drop back down. "Thish how things work, Enshin."

Hathorn tossed the flask into Susannah's lap.

"Take a real good belt," the lieutenant said. "For courage. Your *I'm a shy flower* bit is getting old, girl. Even a shitty story is better than no story at all."

Why didn't Hathorn and Hasik just want to *sleep?* Xeno training, constant drills, and cross-training didn't leave many free hours. Susannah felt wrecked. If she could have asked questions, if she could have *really* studied the miracles around her, she wasn't sure she *could* have slept even if she got the chance. Now eleven days into the patrol, Hasik hadn't shared any knowledge beyond what Susannah needed for her specified duties.

She was a hairless ape that pushed the buttons she was told to push. An exhausted, *drunk* hairless ape.

And now she had to tell a story?

Susannah knew Bethany's background like the back of her hand, but Bock's people hadn't bothered to fill the fake identity's history with funny anecdotes. Susannah was always careful to stick to what she'd read. She didn't want to make things up from scratch and introduce a random detail she'd later forget.

"I got nothing," she said. "Besides, how am I supposed to follow up that... that... that—" she lost the thread, and almost lost her balance just sitting there, then remembered what she wanted to say "—that thing with the plumber?"

"Tell a story," Hasik said. "Thash an order."

An order? Susannah had to follow orders. But what could she say?

"And make it dirty," Hathorn said. "If there isn't a cock, a pussy, or some other genitalia involved, you'll do the scraping all by yourself for the next week."

Susannah didn't have any dirty stories. She didn't even want to *think* about sex, because that brought up memories of Major Bratchford trying to rape her... of Major Bratchford with a Bunsen burner sticking out of his eye socket.

Bratchford attacked her because she was a Purist. Now Susannah's ship was possibly heading deep into the Nation. Would her work in this weird, sweaty jungle of a room contribute to the death of other Purists?

The Nation had been her home for a decade. She missed her sisters in the convent. She missed her old job. For reasons she couldn't explain, when she was on her route, piloting that hauler, she didn't think of the past. She didn't think of...

...wait a minute. The hauler. There was that time she'd ferried Reverend Blightly along on her shipping route. He'd kept coming to the hauler's pilot cabin, whipping out his penis and telling Susannah she'd wind up in hell if she didn't go down on him. Susannah had turned on the hauler's recorders without him knowing, then given the footage to Sister Sara, who played it during worship services.

Blightly hadn't bothered Susannah again.

There was nothing funny about the incident. At all. But it *was* dirty, and it *did* involve genitalia. Maybe she could try injecting some humor into it. Not her strong suit, but hell, she was feeling pretty good. As long as she changed the location, she wouldn't compromise her cover.

"Okay, so this one time, I had this boss who tagged along on a run I did between Jupiter and Saturn." Susannah tried to mimic Hathorn's jokey cadence, tried to make the words bouncier. "He really wanted me to... to..."

She blinked, shook her head. What had she been talking about?

"He *what*, Ensign?" Hasik asked.

Susannah looked at him. "Huh? What *he*?"

Hathorn shook her head and snatched the flask back, unscrewing the cap. "Wow, this is going to be a *great* story." She took a swig. "Your boss, Beth? The one who tagged along on your run between Jupiter and Saturn?"

Oh, yes, that was it. The whole story wormed up through Susannah's drunken brain. She'd swap out a "corporation" for the church, change Blightly's name, make him some mid-level manager. How about that? This wasn't just going to be *funny*, it was going to put Hathorn's story to shame.

"So, my boss, he really wanted to get in my pants, and he wasn't my type, you know? We were departing from the Jupiter Net Colony, and here's what happened."

37

"Actuator is fried," John said. "Go get me a spare."

Abshire shuffled away from the TASH repair bench, head hanging like a dog who'd been yelled at for eating garbage.

Shamdi shook his head. "I swear, that guy—"

John shot Shamdi a look, a look that stopped him from saying whatever he was going to say.

Shamdi gave a half shrug. "Yeah, well, you know what I mean."

John knew. All the combat vets knew.

As the rumor of the mission spread, some of the boots—Abshire included—already assumed they were going to die. Maybe while boarding, maybe while repelling boarders, or maybe *Keeling* would eat some artillery and go tits-up without the Raiders getting to fire a shot.

After all, they didn't call her the *Crypt* for nothing.

Unblooded jitters were nothing new. John had seen the same thing many times during his career. Laior's death, though, made it worse. Sometimes boots didn't really understand what death was. Who at eighteen does? Those who had just given a goodbye-pat to a flag-draped mate, that was who.

Laior's training accident brought renewed focus on the shoddy TASH rigs. Lindros ordered combat vets to go over every centimeter of every suit. John ran one table, examining problems with Alpha-Two's rigs, while Sergeant Renee Jordan, the squad leader, ran the other table for Alpha-One's. She was bent over a disassembled gaunt-let, her smartglasses centimeters away from an exposed inertial damper.

The rest of the squad hung around, working on bits of kit, cleaning rifles, and generally shooting the shit. Just as it had for the last few days, casual conversation drifted to everyone's favorite topic—*what did you do to wind up here?*

John knew he was the exception rather than the rule. Most people were on *Keeling* because they'd fucked up right proper.

"Your turn, Mafi." Corporal Sharma Sarvacharya, Mafi's fire team leader, squinted at the disassembled trigger array of her RR. "You ready to share yet?"

Mafi was on his butt, back against the bulkhead, cleaning empty mags, checking each and every spring for proper tension.

"Yeah, sure," he said. "Why not? I... I killed a guy. He tried to take my parking space. He took a swing at me. I didn't mean to kill him, but... you know. It just happened."

John knew Mafi's story, because he'd heard the same kind of story from dozens of people over the years. Most Raiders were young and naturally aggressive. They liked to fight. Fleet trained these gung-ho teenagers how to take life with their bare hands, how to throw deadly strikes from muscle memory alone. Raiders were trained killers—no real surprise that trained killers sometimes killed, whether they meant to or not.

"Murder, eh, Muttonhead?" Shamdi said. "The guy who took your parking spot say something bad about your fucking watch or something?"

Mafi started to rise, violence in his eyes, the empty mag clutched in his big hand.

"Stay there, Mafi," Jordan said quietly, not bothering to look up from her work. "I mean it."

Mafi sat back down, grabbed another empty mag.

"Let me tell you something, Shamdi," he said. "You're a—"

"A cumstain," Shamdi said. "I know."

As fire team leader, Sarvacharya should have been the one to keep Mafi's anger in check. That was what the E4 Mafia was supposed to do—quietly keep lower enlisted in line so they didn't become a problem for noncoms or officers. Sarvacharya seemed intimidated by Mafi, though. Hopefully, Sands would get her straightened out soon, or give the squad leader position to someone else.

Not that John had room to criticize—everyone on Sharma's team was still alive.

"Hey, Sarge," Sui Jun said, "what's the mission? You gotta know, right?"

Jun was one of the six unblooded Spec-1s in the squad. Good with TASH maneuvering and a steady shot, she showed real promise.

"Hell if I know," Jordan said. "I'm on the mushroom diet, just like you guys."

A mushroom: kept in the dark and fed shit.

Abbas Basara laughed. "With that mycoware, we really *are* on a mushroom diet. Fuckin' everything Combat Cook serves us tastes like mushrooms."

"Don't complain," John said. "You boots got no idea. All the fresh veggies we get? You don't see a lot of that on other ships."

A general grumble of agreement from the vets: Jordan, Sarvacharya, Mafi, and Shamdi.

"Yeah, but those veggies probably gonna kill us," Shamdi said. "I hear they grow them in the secret engine room. Shit's probably radioactive. Gonna kill us inside a year."

"Can't be," Jordan said. "Nothing can go through punch-space and still be radioactive. Besides, even if it was, you don't need to worry —a whiny grunt like you won't make it six months, let alone a year."

A few laughs, mostly uncomfortable, mostly from the boots.

Jun made a yummy noise. "You guys seen that little MILF ensign they got in there? I'd like to glaze her donut, that's for sure."

"Have some fucking respect," Shamdi snapped.

The other Raiders exchanged glances. Nitzan Shamdi took offense to a lewd comment? Nitzan Shamdi talking about *respect*? The guy didn't respect anything.

"Hey, Mafi," Beaver said. "Laior was in for murder, too. She told me before she croaked."

John cringed inside. Leave it to Beav to be oblivious of the situation and open up a scab that hadn't even begun to heal.

"I still can't believe Laior bought it," Fred Abeen said. "Not surprised, though. Lindros and Lincoln are driving us too hard, man. Drill, drill, drill."

If John had to guess who would be the next to die, it was Abeen. No combat experience was one thing, no common sense another altogether. Some Raiders were born with a crosshair on their forehead—Abeen was one of them.

"You think drills are bad, boot?" Sarvacharya slid the trigger array into her rifle, locked it home. "Just wait till the bullets fly."

Maybe Mafi intimidated her, but Sarv was no slouch. She'd seen surface action on Rodina. She'd never boarded, but she had repelled PN boarders while aboard the *Richthofen*.

Abshire returned with the actuator. He handed it to John.

"Abeen's right," Abs said. "We're so tired we can't even see straight. Maybe if we got more sleep, Laior wouldn't have fucked up like that. She died on a stupid training exercise."

Sergeant Jordan stood straight. "There is nothing *stupid* about training, Spec." She slid her smartglasses down her nose, glared at Abs. "This is Fleet. Think Sklorno or Purists will let you get your beauty rest? You're going to be tired, and you'll have to fight anyway." She looked at John. "Laior's death is on Laior. If she'd paid attention during all of fucking boot camp training, she'd still be here."

The squad fell quiet, focused on their work.

John appreciated Jordan's effort. She was right, he knew, but that wouldn't chase away the guilt he'd carry for a long time to come. In a full company, Laior's death would have resulted in John being removed as fire team leader. Jordan would have been removed as squad leader, since she was responsible for her squad's well-being. But here, with only a single platoon and already two Raiders down, Lindros didn't have many options.

The awkward pause didn't last long—in general, Raiders were not silent types.

"You ain't got it so bad, Mafi," Jun said. "I mean, intentionally or not, you wound up here because you killed someone. I'm here because I got a stupid FUI."

Flying under the influence was a serious crime, but serious enough to put her on the *Keeling*? She was likely leaving something out of the story.

"At least you two did *something* wrong," Abbas Basara said. "This is my first deployment. I didn't do nothing to nobody."

Basara had said that before. Several times.

"You arrived in chains, you big dumb fuck," Shamdi said.

"So did you, Shamdi," Basara said. "What did *you* do?"

Shamdi put his hand on his chest. "Me? Why, all I did was give some good, sweet loving to a lovely girl. And her twin brother. Who both *swore* to me they were eighteen and did *not* inform me their daddy is an admiral."

People groaned at the joke, even laughed at it. Shamdi was a loud-mouth, sure, but he had a knack for lightening the mood.

"Hey, Bennett," Abshire said. "What's it like crossing the gap? In real combat, I mean."

The soft rattle of equipment slowed, then stopped altogether. Everyone looked at John. He glanced at Jordan, half expecting her to tell people to get back to work, but she was again bent over the TASH, peering at one part or another.

The kids wanted to know? Fine. He would tell them true.

"It's the greatest thing I've ever done," he said. "It's also the worst. When you're out there, alive only because of your armor, you understand how... how *small* we are. You understand how *big* ships are, and you also see that they're just grains of sand against the endless void. Sometimes you get lucky and there's not much defending fire."

He closed his eyes, and for a moment, he was in his TASH on top of a crawler because there was no room inside it, clutching at webbing to keep from being flung off by the pilot's desperate attempts to avoid incoming missiles and exploding flak. His first crawler had been hit, killing half his platoon. He and the survivors had hopped on another, somehow survived the Sklorno destroyer's point-defense fire long enough for the Ochthera to sink its claws into the ship's armor. Then came the firefight on the hull, watching more of his friends die.

And all of that before the crawler opened a breech and John went inside, where the bloodbath of passageway combat began.

"Most times, though, there's so much defensive fire it's like flying into metal rain," he said. "You'll see your brothers and sisters get dead in the blink of an eye. In the void, spilled blood foams up, then becomes little free-floating blobs. When fresh blood comes out and hits cold outer armor, though, it crystalizes, freezes, makes these weird shapes. To me, they look like red flowers. Flowers that used to be your mates."

He stopped talking; only then did he see the expressions of those around him. They were scared. Good. They needed to become friends with fear, because fear did not go away, not with all the experience in the universe.

"*Flowers*," Abeen said. "That's fucked up. What do you do when that happens? I mean... what do you do?"

John slotted the actuator into its chamber.

"You fight," he said. "Fight like the dogs of war. You move forward. You follow orders. You kill. That's how you come back. Kill the enemy, and *keep* killing until there isn't any enemy left."

For a moment, the only sound was the stretchy squeal of John pulling strands of micromuscle and pinning them to the actuator's inserts.

"Back to work," Jordan said.

The squad returned to their tasks.

38

"It's a terrible story," Gillick said. "That's supposed to be funny?"

Lieutenant Hathorn shrugged. "Darkwater seemed to think it was."

"Well, it's *not*," Daniels said. "Lieutenant, I don't find workplace sexual harassment humorous in the least."

Hathorn threw up her hands.

"You guys wanted me to get her talking, so I did, Darkwater isn't a puppet. I can't control what comes out of her mouth."

Anne thought of letting the process go on for a third retelling. Gillick and Daniels were following BII protocol, which was to get the informant aggravated, then ask them to repeat what they'd said. Three times through a tale was usually enough to figure out what was real and what was bullshit, but Anne had heard enough.

"Lieutenant," she said, "what was the name of the shipping company again?"

Hathorn's face scrunched as she tried to remember.

"Colbinson," she said. "I think that was it."

Anne looked at Gillick. "That's one of the biggest shipping companies out there."

"*The* biggest," he said. "You see their ships everywhere, especially in the Sol system."

Anne was getting to know her team. Gillick and Daniels seemed sharp. Gillick, a little more so. She could tell just by the look on his face that he'd picked up on the same thing she had.

"It's still not funny," Daniels said. "Hopefully Darkwater is better at her job than she is at telling stories. How's her training coming along, Lieutenant?"

Hathorn's head dipped, just a little.

"Really well," she said. "Hasik likes her. I think Darkwater already knows the xeno system better than I do."

Hathorn was jealous. That was good. She feared Darkwater might get fast-tracked ahead of her. Unless the ship took on more personnel, Hathorn or Darkwater would likely replace Hasik if he moved on. Taking over as department chief was a big deal. Even in a fucked-up place like the *Crypt*, a promotion to department chief would boost a career once the two-year stint was up.

"Thank you, Lieutenant Hathorn," Anne said. "We appreciate you informing us. Keep Darkwater talking. Keep listening. Tell no one of this, including Colonel Hasik. *Especially* Colonel Hasik."

Daniels opened the door and leaned out. Seeing no one in the passageway, he waved Hathorn through, then stepped back inside and shut the door.

"That was a waste of time," he said. "So someone waggled a schlong at Darkwater, so what?"

Anne looked at Gillick. "Is there something more than that, Corporal?"

"There is." He grinned wide. "Darkwater doesn't have pilot certification in her skills list."

Daniels realized he'd missed that. "Well, maybe she's just full of shit." He sat. "Maybe she wanted to fit in, so she made up a story about being a trucker for the biggest shipping firm out there and having a perv-dog boss. Telling a tall tale doesn't make her a spy."

If it was a tall tale, it was harmless. An intel chief's job, though, was to assume the worst and act accordingly.

"Or she really was a pilot, and it's not in her record," Anne said. "Which would mean Darkwater either lied about her work history when she joined Fleet, or she's not who she claims to be."

There was zero evidence either way. Lying about your past to Fleet was frowned upon, but usually wasn't considered a crime, especially not for something as mundane as being a hauler pilot. Anne had nothing to go on other than the hunch of a jealous—and often drunk—department rival.

Except... except something about Darkwater didn't feel right. The woman was lying. About what, exactly, remained to be seen.

The *Keeling* was soon to penetrate far behind Purist Nation lines. If Darkwater was a Purist spy, that was when she'd likely strike.

"Daniels, go over her record again," Anne said. "Find me any discrepancy, no matter how small."

He raised an eyebrow. "I'm sure the seventh time I go through it will produce something I missed the first six times."

"Just do it," Anne said. "If she's a spy, the moment one of us even *talks* to her she'll assume we suspect. I need more info first. Gillick, I want you to quietly observe her. When she leaves the atrium, find out who she talks to, and what she talks about."

"Will do, Major," Gillick said. "But I admit I'm with Daniels on this. I think she made up the whole thing because she's as boring as white toast and wants to fit in."

Fitting in—exactly what a spy would want to do.

39

Trav rubbed at his chest, fingertips pressing into coveralls and undershirt. He was too young to have a heart attack, but not too young to recognize the nearly crippling anxiety that seemed to pull his ribs together from the inside, frayed ropes and rusty pulleys drawing the bones closer to his heart.

He was going into transdim again. This time, he'd have to stay sharp and focused, because he would be the one giving orders. Failure was not an option. If Lincoln replaced him as XO, he was finished in Fleet. Finished. He'd be busted down to crew chief in one department or another, and after the one year, eleven months, and three weeks remaining in his *Keeling* stint—if he survived them—the best job he could hope to land would be navigator of a garbage scow.

How would Molly feel about that? It might be another twenty-three months before he saw her again, which would make *twenty-nine* months away from his wife. Away from his family. His unborn daughter would be two years old before he saw her in person. And—

"XO," Lincoln said, "is there a problem?"

He looked at her blankly.

She nodded toward his chest.

His fingers were still pressed in hard, a monster claw trying to find the meat hidden inside.

"Oh, no sir. Combat Cook's breakfast burritos aren't agreeing with me, that's all."

She stared her impassive, tired stare.

"Whatever your issue is, Lieutenant Ellis, get over it. Fast. When we're in Nation territory, I need to know my number two is rock-solid. Be sharp today. Epperson will see my post-action report."

No *do your best*, or, *you can't make an omelet without breaking a few eggs* platitudes from Lincoln. But that was good. That was right. In Fleet, mistakes cost lives. A commander that couldn't execute properly under impossible pressure was no commander at all.

Lincoln's eyes flicked aft. There, Trav saw tiny Ensign Darkwater climbing the steps to the xeno loft.

"What's she doing here?" Trav asked. "Is Hasik training her?"

Lincoln turned back to the command slate.

"I believe the ensign is adding to your challenge," she said. "It appears she'll man the xeno station for this exercise."

Darkwater looked around the loft area like this was the first time she'd seen it. Because it probably was.

"Captain," Trav said, "this is... Hasik should be here for this, sir."

He'd almost said *this is unfair.*

"Let's play pretend, XO." Lincoln tapped the slate and called up a training report. She read it even as she kept talking. "Say Hasik is injured. Or dead. Or stark raving mad and in the infirmary, strapped down in a straitjacket and being fed spoonfuls of tapioca pudding. Let's pretend you're going into combat with the crew you have available, and you can't hit the pause button and ask for a change of cast. Darkwater is your Xeno. If she fails, *you* fail, so make sure she doesn't."

Lincoln flicked the report away, called up another.

Trav turned. He stepped up into the xeno loft.

"Ensign Darkwater," he said.

She jumped a little. "Oh, XO Ellis." Eyes as big as saucers. "I... I'm manning the xeno station for the torpedo exercise. Colonel Hasik's orders."

The ropes heaved, the pulleys squeaked—Trav's ribs pulled in tighter.

"Did he train you on this station?"

249

She opened her mouth to speak, looked down at her hand. She held a napkin. A napkin with pen scribbles on it.

"He told me it was easy," she said. "All the real work is done in the atrium. That's what he told me."

Trav held out his hand. "Let me see that napkin, Ensign."

She handed it over. Damp spots smelled faintly of alcohol. Scribbled on the napkin were the steps for calling down to the atrium and taking the ship into transdim.

One hundred and five lives on the line, and Hasik didn't care.

"I'm sure I can do it right, sir," Darkwater said. "It doesn't seem that complicated."

Trav hadn't spent any time with her. She was always hidden away in the atrium with Hasik and Hathorn.

Trav still hadn't been told what, exactly, went on in that strange, beautiful compartment. He didn't have the necessary security clearance. He, *the executive officer*, still wasn't allowed to know how a key part of the ship worked.

Keeling was Hasik's ship—Trav, and even Lincoln, were just along for the ride.

Trav glanced around the xeno loft, trying to push thoughts of venting Hasik out of his mind. The station had a standard main circuit dial-switch and handset. Three sound-powered phones, small labels beneath them reading ATRIUM, CURVINE, and PUNCH. A terminal for when the ship had power, a slide rule panel, rolling pad of paper, and pencil bin with sharpener for when it did not.

"Ensign, I need you to be solid for this," Trav said. "If you have trouble performing your duties, tell me. I'll order Hasik to the CIC immediately."

Darkwater's lips flattened.

"I'd recommend you call for Lieutenant Hathorn instead," she said. "Colonel Hasik is, ah—" she gently took the napkin back, tapped at the damp spots "—busy gathering data."

The colonel was drunk. That's why he'd sent Darkwater in his place.

This forty-year-old ensign had just ratted out her CO, in a way that she could deny if someone called her out for it. At the same time, she'd taken a risk in telling her XO the truth.

Trav liked her.

"Thank you, Ensign. Carry on."

He returned to the command station.

40

Binder tucked under her arm, Anne entered the CIC. One step up into the intel loft, she froze—Bethany Darkwater sat in the xeno loft. No Hasik, no Hathorn, just a person who might be a Purist Nation spy in the combat information center of the Union's most-secret vessel.

Darkwater must have sensed the stare, for she locked eyes with Anne.

"Good morning, Major Lafferty."

"What are you doing here, Ensign?"

"Colonel Hasik instructed me to man the xeno station for the torpedo exercise."

Did that drunk have no clue what could be going on under his watch? He wasn't BII, true, but how could he miss the obvious signs that Darkwater might be a spy? Or...

...or what if Hasik was a spy himself, and he and Darkwater were in it together.

"Ensign, you've been on this vessel for eleven days," Anne said. "You're qualified to man this station?"

Darkwater cleared her throat, swallowed audibly.

"Colonel Hasik ordered me to be here, sir. If the Major likes, I can call down to the atrium and ask him to come up, so you can address the issue directly with him."

This smart-mouthed little bitch. Anne had power on this ship, but she did not outrank a colonel who'd been sprinkled with the fairy dust of Fleet's most-powerful admiral.

"Major Lafferty," XO Ellis said, "Ensign Darkwater is manning the xeno station."

He stood at the command slate, staring straight through Anne with those weird amber eyes of his. Lincoln was next to him, hunched over the table, her back to Anne. The captain had undoubtedly told Ellis to intervene, then pretended it was all beneath her notice.

"I see," Anne said.

She took her station in the intel loft.

Ellis... who did he think he was? A lieutenant, an old one at that. A *disgraced* one. Using a commanding tone with *her*? XO or not, Anne outranked him. He'd have to be taught to treat her with more respect.

And speaking of age—a forty-year-old *ensign*? Maybe even older? Rare, though not unheard of, especially in the sciences. But still, one more red flag about Darkwater.

Maybe someone should do something.

Do something about Darkwater.

Maybe someone should kill her.

Faint, so faint it almost went unnoticed, Anne felt the tiniest bit of tapping at the base of her skull.

No. Not that. Never again.

She opened her binder and focused on it.

The binder held datasheets with key intel on Union allies and adversaries alike. In a battle, a skirmish, even shadowing a cargo freighter, you could never count on computers to work consistently. STCCM—space-time curvature countermeasures—technology had become so prevalent, so *affordable*, that civilian shipping companies put corruptors on many of their vessels. Corruptors created a sphere of warped STC that bent, scattered, and diffused wavelengths, which made electronics do unpredictable things. Even non-military-grade corruptors altered observable data. From ten thousand klicks away, a ship the size of *Keeling* would appear so distorted that its target profile would be as large as that of a small moon.

STCCM was the reason war had changed so much in the past fifty years. If you wanted to target something, you had to get relatively close. If you wanted to kill something, closer still.

Kill something. The tapping.

Anne hadn't felt it since Olivia.

It frightened her.

But there was no reason to be scared. Not anymore. Anne was better. One couldn't expect to wipe out feelings like that overnight. They might always be there in one degree or another. The trick was to catch and control them, as Anne just had. The trick was to master the urge, not let the urge master you.

There, that was better. No tapping. No *itch*. Hell, Anne probably just imagined it anyway, a phantom echo of the person she'd once been but was no more.

"This is the captain speaking."

Anne heard Lincoln directly, as the captain was only a few meters away, talking into a handset, but also in faint, tinny choruses as her voice emanated from speakers all over the ship.

"We will enter transdim space in five minutes," Lincoln said. "We will be there for thirty minutes. Remember what is real. Remember that the strange things you see while we're under are *not* real. Everyone in this crew has to learn how to control themselves while in transdim. Control themselves, and still do their job. When we surface, we will conduct a live torpedo run on an automated target."

Lincoln paused. She gazed into nothingness. The handset's curled cord vibrated, wobbling in place.

Was she trying to remember something?

Whatever the thought was, Lincoln shook it off.

"Don vacsuits immediately," she said. "Those of you who were ordered to be physically restrained, I appreciate your understanding. Keep in mind that if you refuse, I've authorized the use of force, up to and including lethal force. Stay calm. Follow your orders. Do your jobs. Nothing less is acceptable. That is all."

The seat of every station doubled as a vacsuit storage bin. The CIC crew donned the one-size-fits-all rigs. Anne did as well. The collapsible hood lay flat against her back and shoulders. Some put gloves on. Some, Anne included, left them magclipped to their front thighs. She knew she could don both helmet and gloves in under four seconds.

"Nav," Lincoln said, "start the clock."

Erickson started the clock-timers' five-minute countdown.

"CIC complement, listen up," Lincoln said.

Anne closed her binder. She'd been waiting for this, excited to see what all the fuss was about.

"When we dive, we will not be running black," Lincoln said. "Those of you with passive external sensors will be able to see what is outside the ship. In addition, the orb will paint an accurate picture of our environment. While any strange things you may see *inside* our hull are not real, your view of the *outside* very much is. Stay calm. Communicate. Do your jobs. Everything you see from this moment on is considered classified. Do not discuss it or share any part of it with the enlisted crew or any noncoms you do not see present in the CIC at this moment."

Lincoln glanced up at the starboard clock-timer.

"Four minutes until dive," she said. "This is an attack run. Get to work."

The CIC crew focused on their stations. Whatever the Mud might be, Anne would get to see it in the loft's monitors and in the orb, but she'd watch something else as well.

She'd watch Darkwater.

41

He shut his eyes, but that didn't make the voice go away.

Traaaaavisssss.

He wanted to put his fingers in his ears, but he knew that wouldn't work.

Traaaaaavissssss, you ungrateful cocksucker. You missed my funeral.

It was her voice, her inflection, her foul words—Marge Ellis, the grandmother who'd raised him.

"XO, you still with me?"

Trav opened his eyes, glanced right—maggots burrowed in and out of Lincoln's face. They wiggled within her tongue, twitched with annoyance when she spoke. She didn't seem to notice. Most people would probably notice maggots digging through their skin, so he was fairly sure that part wasn't real.

"Aye, Captain," he said. "I'm here."

Lincoln nodded once, faced forward. When she did, a maggot slid free from a bloody hole on the back of her hand and dropped to the deck. She stepped on it without noticing. Greenish goo squirted out in a jet, splattering Trav's vacsuited foot.

He fought against his rising gorge—he could *smell* the maggot's guts—and turned to face the orb.

"You're all about to see the Mud," Lincoln said. "Signals, put optical in-orb."

Spec-3 Grant Wright manned the signal station.

"Aye-aye, Captain," he said.

The orb flared to life, showing the *Keeling*'s surroundings.

The maggots weren't real, but what he saw in the orb was?

Space was called that because that's what it was—mostly empty space. The Mud was anything but.

The arrow representing *Keeling* sat in the orb's center. All around it, stretching off in every direction, were dense, fibrous strands of an opalescent haze that appeared to coagulate into roiling streams of crimson and ivory, into shapeless rivers of impossible size, into vibrating, coiling veins of glistening fog. The intangible material pulsated with irregular thrums of dim light, the colors of which Trav couldn't begin to describe. The Mud undulated and wavered, intertwined and separated, twisted and flowed, seemed to course along in slow, gentle motions, but he knew the scale of what he was seeing—the strange ballet of smoke moved at incredible relativistic speeds.

His brain fought to apply some sense to what he saw, some comparison to the things he knew, but nothing in his experience came close. Mud looked like a nebula, maybe, if that nebula was everywhere all at once. Mud looked like a drugged-out artist's 3D rendition of brain neurons, maybe, if those neurons were ethereal, shifting in form, and stretching out to eternity.

There were *things* in that turbulent haze—tiny dark spots moving with or against the currents, leaving hazy, infinitesimal trails curling in their wake.

"Signals," Lincoln said, "decrease orb range by seventy-five percent."

"Decreasing optical range by seventy-five percent," Wright said.

Someone in the CIC started to cry. Another quietly mumbled about how he wanted to drive a shovel through the guts of his mother-in-law, quietly repeating the phrase "that cunt's gotta die" over and over again. Was it pilot Lars Nygard or co-pilot Colin Draper? Trav didn't know their voices well enough to tell.

The orb's distance rings expanded outward, vanishing one at a time as the display range zoomed in. The area around the *Keeling* became more defined. The ship left a trail through the haze, a reverse-image comet tail of black through... through *what*? It wasn't smoke. It wasn't mist. It was neither fluid, solid, nor gas.

"The Mud," Trav said. Captain, what's it made of?"

"I don't know," Lincoln said. "No one does."

A maggot crawled out of her left nostril, twitched once, and fell to the command slate's flat top. There it wiggled, slime smearing the glass as it searched for dead flesh upon which to feed.

"Those moving dots out there," Trav said. "Are they ships?"

Captain Lincoln slapped at the air above the table, as if she'd instinctively reacted to seeing something vile and dangerous.

"We don't know that, either," she said.

They didn't know. If they weren't ships, what else could they be? Were they... *alive*?

"I hope you've been studying, XO." Lincoln again slapped at the invisible threat. "The torpedo run is yours to command." She straightened, spoke louder. "Intel, remove the co-pilot from his station. Ops, get a replacement."

Neil Plait snatched up his operations station's handset.

Lincoln took two steps backward, putting her butt against the intel loft.

"The XO has the conn," she said.

Trav was in command. For the first time since his failure with Williams aboard the *Schild*, he was in command.

"Aye-aye, Captain, I have the conn."

You're gonna fail, you worthless pile of shit. I told you you'd never amount to anything.

Meemaw sounded so real, like she was right behind him, leaning on her walker, a vapestick dangling from the corner of her mouth.

Trav found himself wishing for the beetle to come back. Anything was better than listening to that crusty, child-abusing bitch speak from beyond the grave.

She wasn't real. No matter what his ears and his heart told him, she wasn't real.

He looked at the clock-timer—ten minutes until they were due to re-enter realspace. Lincoln had taught him that while some electronics still worked in the Mud, those that did failed to do so consistently. The all-mechanical equipment that functioned in combat also functioned in transdim.

"Nav, increase orb range to maximum," Trav said. "Put our course in-orb."

"Aye-aye, XO," Erickson said. "Increasing orb range to maximum. Bringing up our course."

Red circles shot in from the orb's equator, settling into ten rings marking distance. A green course-line traced from one side of the orb to the other, running through the arrow that represented the *Keeling*. Trav could still see things moving through the Mud, but at this scale they were minuscule dots, little more than thin, fuzzy scratches wriggling through the crimson-white streams.

The two intel operatives—Gillick and Daniels—carried a prone Colin Draper past the command station. Trav hadn't noticed them enter the CIC.

"A shovel is the only solution," Draper said, his voice calm and dreamy. "I tell ya, that cunt's gotta die."

They dragged him out the aft entrance.

Trav heard someone dry heaving.

Another sailor ran into the CIC—Corporal Sora Garcia, Draper's replacement. She hustled to the co-pilot station and strapped in.

"Pilot station fully manned," Plait said.

"Very well," Trav said. "Darsat, activate system and begin DTR sweep."

DTR—*Darsat to Realspace.*

"Activating darsat, aye-aye." Spec-3 Carmel Waldren manned that station, for which Trav was grateful. This was her second patrol; she was more seasoned to the insanity of transdim.

According to Lincoln, sometimes darsat worked while in-dim, sometimes not. Hasik said the Mud produced some kind of variable interference, but he had no idea what it was or how to counter it. Lincoln compared it to flying a terrestrial aircraft through a storm of jammers, except you didn't know what a jammer was. Hasik had a simpler analogy: he called darsat-to-realspace detection "temperamental."

If darsat saw the target drone, Trav could track it. If it didn't, he'd have to guide *Keeling* out of transdim, suffer through the blind period as ship systems and crew returned to realspace, then acquire the target.

"Darsat activated," Waldren said. "Realspace detection strength is... moderate."

Trav had been trained that cross-membrane detection strength fluctuated and was therefore unpredictable. Darsat operators used a six-point relative scale: *very strong, strong, moderate, weak, very weak,* and *none*. At *very strong*, DTR showed a bogey's location and provided passive identification of the bogey's gravitational signature. *Moderate* showed rough locations, but no grav-sigs. At *none*, DTR detected nothing at all.

"Very well," Trav said. "Detection range?"

Just like darsat in realspace, range was determined in a radius outward from the *Keeling*. DTR had a maximum range of around 400 klicks.

"Detection range is about one-zero-zero kilometers," Waldren said.

A hundred klicks. Against the expanse of the cosmos, that was nothing. But even with DTR's significant limitations, it was a game-changer—*Keeling* could detect a small area of realspace, while anything in realspace couldn't detect the *Keeling* in any way.

"In-orb," Trav said.

The orb display shifted from strands of grayish mud to a field of white-black static. Trav looked for purple icons that marked objects in realspace. There were none.

Where was the drone? Was it near, and DTR wasn't catching it, or was it outside the system's range?

Realspace. What was *real*, anyway? Thanks to the tech of an alien ship, he was in another dimensional membrane. How many other membranes were there? Could the *Keeling* go to those as well?

"Contact acquired," Waldren said. "Average bearing, starboard zero-two-five. Average elevation, zero-one-five. Average range, three-zero-one kilometers."

Average was a new term for Trav. On top of unpredictable variations in overall strength, darsat-to-realspace detection produced inconsistent location results from one instant to the next. The darsat operator's job was to quickly average out these readings, giving a CO a best-guess location.

I wanted flowers at my funeral, you skinny fuck. You weren't there. No wonder your parents chose to die instead of take care of you.

Meemaw's voice cut like a rusty knife. Trav had been at the Academy when she'd died. He could have taken bereavement leave, but he chose against it. He'd never wanted to see her scowling, hateful face when she'd been alive—he definitely didn't want to see it when she was dead.

He caught himself drifting and, forced his focus back to the exercise.

"Put the contact in-orb," he said.

Tiny purple diamond-shapes appeared in the orb, port-forward-low. They flickered, appearing first in one place, then another, as if the signal couldn't be locked down. At this scale, two flickers that were close enough to touch edges were actually tens of kilometers apart.

Trav glanced at the clock-timer: five minutes, fifteen seconds remained until the *Keeling*'s scheduled surfacing. As the CO, he could elect to come out sooner, later, or right on time.

"Nav," he said, "calculate a course to provide a dead-ahead shot at scheduled surfacing time. Pilot, implement course when it's ready."

"Aye-aye, XO," Erickson said. "Calculating zero-minute dead-ahead intercept course."

Erickson went to work with parallel rulers, divider, and pencil. He had to calculate the pitch and yaw necessary to point *Keeling* at where the target would be in five minutes, based on the target's relative direction and velocity.

Trav had asked how, exactly, propulsion in the Mud worked. Hasik told him he wasn't cleared to know. Lincoln backed Hasik up. Just one more ludicrous command decision on a ship that seemed to be made of them.

Erickson finished his calculation, spoke quietly to Nygard.

Trav imagined the *Keeling*'s long, flowing, barbed tails curving, somehow forcing the copper hull to angle up and to the right. He couldn't decide if the imagined sight was beautiful or horrifying.

In the orb, the sparkling cluster of purple diamonds rotated until they were ten degrees to port, level on the horizon.

"Course implemented," Erickson said.

"Very well," Trav said. "Darsat, mark the target as *Zulu*. Classification?"

Unknown contacts were labeled via the military alphabet, in reverse order. If another bogey appeared, that one would be labeled *Yankee*. If a ship was positively identified, its actual name was used instead. The temporary letter-IDs reset at the end of an engagement, meaning the first bogey in a future conflict would also be labeled *Zulu*.

"*Zulu*'s classification unknown," Waldren said. "I don't have enough data. Contact is fading in and out. I'm having trouble keeping track of it."

A hand cupped his elbow.

"That's normal," Lincoln said softly. "Sometimes we get a full read. More often than not, we get nothing. Make the most of what you have."

War games could and did sharpen skills and instincts, but in an exercise like this there weren't many variables—they'd come to this sector of space looking for a drone, which meant *Zulu* was that drone.

He knew it. Lincoln knew it. Everyone in the CIC knew it. But wargame protocol demanded he go through the same procedures he'd use if he did *not* know what *Zulu* was.

"Our intelligence sent us to this location to target a Purist Nation Alanson-class combat drone," Trav said, loud enough to be heard by all. "We will proceed assuming *Zulu* is that drone. Intel, current status of relations with the Purist Nation?"

While Fleet did the dying, politicians ran the war. Regulations specified a check-in with BII every time a target presented itself, in case of changing allegiances, potential embedded spies, or a dozen other reasons that left ship commanders operating with one hand tied behind their back.

"For the purposes of this exercise, we have full approval to initiate hostile action," Lafferty said from her loft.

"Very well," Trav said. "Weps, load forward tubes one through four with Mark16s."

Cat Brown repeated the order back to him, her words clipped and fast, like the staccato report of a machine gun.

Trav glanced at Waldren. Her darsat station was forward-most on the port side, an arm's reach from the pilot. A trickle of blood ran from Waldren's temple down her bronze skin.

"Darsat," Trav said, "are you wounded?"

"XO, I'm able to man my station," Waldren said.

How had she been hurt? *When* had she been hurt? Was anyone else wounded?

He needed to replace Waldren.

"Ops," he said. "Bring in a replacement for—"

Lincoln gripped Trav's wrist.

He stiffened against the maggots that crawled from her rotted hand onto his sleeve. The captain's left eye collapsed as if punctured by a nail. Sickly green ran down her cheek, coursed over the wiggling carrion-eaters crawling through her skin.

"When in the Mud, use common sense," she said quietly. "Your darsat operator told you she can man her station. Do you believe her?"

Trav tried to block out the rotting face and hand as he recalled Waldren's words, her tone of voice. She sounded sane and in control. Stressed, yes, but in control.

"I do," he said.

"Then she's fine. Always remember that when you order someone to be relieved, the next person in line might already be worse off. Better the devil you know than the devil you don't."

He understood. Waldren wasn't flipping out, wasn't mumbling *that cunt's gotta die*. She didn't need to be removed.

Lincoln released his wrist, leaving behind a handprint of sloughed skin. She again faded back to the intel loft, leaving Trav standing alone at the command station.

He looked at the clock-timer: two minutes until scheduled real-space surfacing. If he surfaced at that time, *Keeling* would still be a hundred kilometers or more away from where the target would then be—twice the ideal distance for firing a torpedo.

He could stay in transdim for longer than scheduled and try to get closer, but if he did so and the drone changed course, *Keeling* might wind up even farther away. Worse, if darsat dropped the connection, he might lose the drone altogether. He'd have to initiate a widening sweep while still in transdim—and hopefully reacquire the target—or surface to realspace and hunt for it the old-fashioned way, likely at a vastly greater distance than he was now.

His choices: surface when scheduled and take a long-range shot, which gave the target more time to react and defend, or stay under to try and shorten the distance, which might result in losing the target altogether.

He glanced back at Lincoln—half her face was gone now, scraps of flesh dangling to reveal muscle, crawling maggots, and blood-smeared bone.

She mouthed the words, *your call.*

Ninety seconds until scheduled surfacing.

Trav faced forward.

He could hold on. He *would* hold on. He'd ready the crew for the scheduled surfacing but keep the ship in-dim to tighten the distance and increase his odds for a kill.

"Xeno, prepare to bring us out of transdim on my mark," he said.

Darkwater repeated the order back to him.

Trav wished they could shoot torpedoes from within transdim. What an advantage that would be. Lincoln had told him previous missions attempted exactly that, but so far nothing that wasn't in contact with the *Keeling* made it back to realspace.

The clock-timer's second hand reached the bottom of its arc, started to swing up. Thirty seconds until scheduled exit from transdim...

The orb's diamonds weren't flashing as much, which meant the probe's probable positions were growing fewer in number. The DTR signal seemed consistent and strong. Trav did the math in his head—if he stayed under for another five minutes, perhaps ten, he could surface at fifty kilometers or less from the target. Even factoring in the blind period coming out of dim, the *Keeling* would be so close the drone would have almost no chance to avoid incoming torps.

Trav heard a dull slap, followed by a grunt.

He looked in the direction of the sound, to the signals station, and saw Grant Wright punch himself in the face, rocking his head back. A third punch broke his nose. Blood ran down. He hit himself a fourth time, moaned in pain.

"Intel," Trav said, "remove Signaler Wright from the CIC. Ops, get a replacement in here."

Gillick and Daniels again rushed into the room. They grabbed at Wright's arms. He managed to give himself one more good shot to the mouth before they dragged him away.

Almost as soon as Wright was out of the signals seat, lead signaler Sara Ellison slid into it.

Two people down already. Every position was staffed three deep—Trav might need his last replacement for pilot or signals at any moment. And for all he knew, either sailor could already be hallucinating, trying to strangle someone, or be otherwise out of commission.

Traaaaaaavisssss, you stupid turd of a boy. Why even try? You know how this will end.

The voice sent shivers down his spine. Meemaw. She was going to lock him in the basement again, just another item in a crazy old lady's collection of oddities and dead things.

Someone threw up.

The smell of half-digested baked zucchini filled the CIC.

Traaaaaaaaavisssssssss...

His crew couldn't handle another five minutes in this shit, and neither could he.

He grabbed the handset.

"This is the XO. We are returning to realspace. Prepare to release restrained crew."

He moved to hang up the handset, but it clung to his hand—it had become a hornet as long as his forearm, heavy and thick, black and angry yellow. It stared at him, onyx eyes brimming with hunger.

Trav couldn't face this madness any longer. He had to get out, had to get out.

He sat in his acceleration chair, the thick insect still clutching his hand and arm.

Maggoty Captain Lincoln quietly slid into her chair.

"Xeno," Trav said, "take us out of transdim."

"Taking us out of transdim, aye-aye," Darkwater said.

Wings flicking and twitching, the hornet crawled up his forearm, clawed feet piercing through vacsuit and coveralls to puncture the skin beneath. The creature moved to his elbow, then his biceps... and then it vanished.

The orb filled with a crazy multicolored static. The first time he'd come out of transdim, he'd had his eyes closed, trying to deal with a giant beetle shredding his face. He'd seen those colors through his eyelids. Now he saw them with his eyes open, and they brought forth an unexpected flashback to his Academy days, when he, Vesna, Hiroshi, and Skinny had gone to a dance club. Skinny got so drunk they carried him back to barracks.

Hiroshi and Skinny. Gone forever. Maybe because of the chicken-shit choice Trav made at X7. Maybe.

"We're in realspace," Darkwater called out.

In the orb, white static fluttered and jerked.

"Darsat offline," Waldren said. "System is rebooting."

Trav tasted blood in his mouth. He'd bitten his tongue. The hornet had been so real, and yet here he was, uninjured, the handset still gripped in his fist.

He stood. It took every ounce of courage he had to place the handset to his ear.

"Man battle stations guns." He put the handset in its cradle. "Weps, give me visual as soon as you have it."

In situations where overlapping STC fields scrambled electronic detection, or—like now—darsat was unavailable, the point-defense gunners and artillery crews were a ship's eyes.

Lincoln still hadn't told him why guns were unmanned while in transdim. Maybe the visions were worse for those who could literally reach out and touch the Mud.

"Turrets manned and reporting in," Brown said. "No visuals yet."

That wasn't unexpected, even at this relatively close distance. Coated in EM-absorbing material, the drone they hunted wasn't much bigger than Trav himself. Human eyes were critical when battles closed to murder range, but a hundred kilometers or more, even with high-powered optics, there wasn't much to see.

"Simulated missile fire incoming," Sara Ellison said. "Port zero-two-five, declination zero-one-zero, range two-two-zero and closing, ten seconds to impact."

Trav started his stopwatch before Ellison finished saying the word *seconds.* To the uninitiated, ten seconds didn't seem like much time, but in combat it was a significant amount.

"ECM, launch countermeasures," he said.

Cass Mollen at the ECM station echoed his order.

"Darsat online," Waldren said.

In the orb, the static vanished. *Zulu*'s icon reappeared, along with the drone's newly changed trajectory. Too far out for an artillery shot.

"Incoming missiles trajectory deflected," Mollen said. "Counter-measures successful."

Trav reset his stopwatch to zero.

"Darsat signature acquired," Waldren said. "Grav-sig is that of an Alanson-class combat probe."

"Torpedo solution ready," Brown said, her words a rapid-fire, snare drum roll. "Evaluating sig data to establish homing lock."

When a warship acquired a target's specific grav-signature, that profile was transferred to the modified bat brain in a torpedo's cone. The bat brain's darsat-modified echolocation ability did what it had done for millions of years—targeted prey in a 360-degree environ-ment. The tiny, non-sentient, analog biocomputer reacted to darsat pulses, or *pings*, constantly reorienting the torp toward the programmed grav-signature.

"Homing locks acquired," Brown said. "All four fish."

Even after mankind moved warfare into the void, *fish* remained a slang term for *torpedo.*

"Launch tubes one through four in five-second spreads," Trav said. "Fire."

He started his stopwatch, felt a slight tremor beneath his feet as the first torpedo launched. Every five seconds, another flew.

With an internal curvine drive, a Mark 16 torp was a starship unto itself. It had its own small darsat dome, along with two STCCM decoys and a point-defense system to protect against missiles aimed its way.

"Torpedoes fired," Brown said. "All fish running hot, straight, and normal. First torp time to target, thirty-seven seconds."

Torpedo icons reached out from the arrow representing the *Keeling.* Four blue lines showed the trajectories, each fish taking a slightly different route to the fleeing probe. A ticking timer appeared with each torp, but Trav used his stopwatch—one could never rely on a digital countdown.

The torpedoes' acceleration was greater than that of the drone, which meant the drone was toast unless it could get all four fish in its rear, interrupt their tracking with ECM, then destroy them with countermeasures as they tried to reacquire. Trav had forced the drone along a particular trajectory—a trajectory *Keeling* could intersect with the proper angle.

"Nav, evaluate *Zulu*'s current straight-line course." Trav looked at his stopwatch. "Adjust our course for artillery mid-range intersection in fifty seconds."

Erickson repeated the order; his hands were a blur at his station.

"Guns, ready port and aft batteries," Trav said. "I want a blazer in port, flak in starboard."

"Blazer port, flak starboard, aye-aye," Dardanos Leeds said.

The blazer would scramble space-time near the drone, hopefully disrupt the drone's systems long enough for it to fly straight into a well-placed cloud of flak.

Trav watched the dance play out in the orb—the drone fled at full acceleration while the torpedoes closed in on it.

"*Zulu* launching countermeasures," Brown said. "Torpedo one... torps one *and* two are off-course. They're trying to reacquire. Torps three and four unaffected. Twenty seconds to impact."

In the orb, two blue trails turned orange as they veered off in different directions. That made them an instant threat. It was unlikely the bat brains would lock onto *Keeling*'s grav-signature, which was quite different from the drone's, but that had happened to other ships before.

"Weps, detonate torps one and two," Trav said.

"Aye-aye, detonating torps one and two."

"XO," Leeds said, "turret masters report visual confirmation of target. Currently a mid-range shot, closing to short-range."

Exactly what Trav had been hoping to hear. If the torps didn't get the drone, artillery would. He'd won—it was only a matter of time.

In the orb, the drone altered course, trying to veer away from the angle of intersection where *Keeling*'s guns would be at short-range. In doing so, the drone's angle changed in relation to the torps—the blue line of torp four closed in and intersected.

"Direct hit," Brown called out.

"Darsat," Trav said, "status of *Zulu*?"

A hit didn't always mean a target was destroyed.

Waldren's face wrinkled with concentration. Blood continued to trickle down her temple.

"*Zulu* appears to have broken up," she said. "The three largest pieces are on different trajectories at a constant velocity, showing zero acceleration. XO, I have high confidence the target is destroyed."

A cheer erupted in the CIC. Trav felt the rush of victory. After his disastrous command of the *Schild*, this was the win he'd needed. Only a test, sure, and against a drone, but he'd been thrown into the deep water. He'd not only avoided drowning, he'd swum like a champ.

Go fuck yourself, Meemaw.

"The exercise is complete." Lincoln stepped to the command station. "Nice work, people. I have the conn. Remember that you are not to share anything you've seen during this drill. Weps, try to recover that last extremely expensive torpedo. XO, order the stand-down from battle stations, and get me a casualty report."

She lifted the handset, spoke on the 1MC.

"Attention, *Keeling* crew. This is the captain. Congratulations on a successful torpedo run drill. Culinary staff, prepare to splice the mainbrace."

42

Nitzan didn't know the origins of the ancient phrase *splice the mainbrace*, but he'd been in Fleet long enough to know what it meant —it meant *beer*, a reward for a job well done.

Off-duty crew crammed into the mess. From the scent in the air, this celebration was more than beer. Did his nose deceive him, or did he smell cake?

"Let me in there," he said. "I can't see."

He tried to push his way through the packed wall of bodies ahead of him. The mess could seat twenty people comfortably, four each to the five booths, but now at least forty, maybe forty-five people were crammed into the cave-like space—Raiders and sailors, enlisted and noncoms alike.

Nitzan tried to slide through, wound up shouldering the man in front of him. That man turned—it was Dave Starr.

"Knock it the fuck off, Shamdi," the corporal said. "If I have to drag you out of here and I miss out on cake, that's your ass."

Ah, so it *was* cake.

"Sorry, Corporal," Nitzan said. "I get too excited for my own good."

Starr sneered. The bite-sized divot on his face had healed some, but still looked horrible. Nitzan realized for the first time that Oneida probably swallowed that chunk of flesh.

"Me and Mafi and some others are getting tired of your mouth," Starr said. "You should shut it before we shut it for you."

Shamdi felt a hand on his shoulder.

"Let it go, Corporal," John Bennett said.

Starr eyed the man up. "You might be old, Bennett, but you're still a spec. Don't give me any shit."

"No shit from me, Corporal." Bennett thrust his chin toward the serving counter, barely visible behind the packed bodies. "I'll take care of Shamdi, you keep your *eyes* on the prize."

Starr's nostrils flared at the dig. He claimed he didn't even remember the fight with Oneida, let alone poking the man's eye out.

"You're a real smart ass, Geezer," Starr said. "Next time LT has us spar, maybe you and I should go a few rounds."

Nitzan felt a big hand on his other shoulder—Beaver's hand.

"I'll spar with you, Corporal!" Nitzan winced at Beaver's loud voice, which seemed to be right up against his ear. "I'd love to learn some of your fighting skills!"

Starr's angry stink-face melted away, replaced by a combination of respect and a heaping helping of *no thanks*. He refreshed his sneer, which wrinkled that nasty, fresh scar where some of his cheek had once been, then he faced forward.

Nitzan gave Bennett and Beaver a quick nudge of thanks.

"We got your back," Bennett said, quietly.

"Fuck yeah we do." Beaver's volume level sounded normal, which meant he thought he was whispering. "Never fought in a mess before, so if you start a dance, I'll—"

"No fighting in the mess." Bennett *was* whispering. Even when he whispered, though, he didn't have to say something twice.

Beaver had skills. He was just a boot, but he'd already become the heavyweight champion of the platoon. Everyone had bruises from his fists, feet, elbows, and knees. He'd even beat Sands, although not every time. When Beaver did lose to Sands, you could bet next month's pay that whatever dirty trick the master sergeant used to win the match, Beaver would integrate it into his arsenal and unload it on whoever he trained with next. The kid was dumb as a broken rock, but man, could he brawl.

Bennett and Beaver had taken Nitzan's side, no questions asked.

They were ready to throw down in the blink of an eye. *We got your back.* It was a magical feeling. They were good dudes.

But they were still Unionites. They were trained to kill Nationalites, *paid* to kill Nationalites. Nitzan had to remember that, someday, he might have to kill these men.

Just like he'd killed Arimun.

Nitzan would do what must be done. His role was to serve his people, free them from the constant threat of warmongering Union infidels. High One had chosen him. He was ready and willing to die for his country, but sometimes—like when your new pals back you up—it was hard.

The mass of bodies slowly shuffled forward.

"Lord almighty, that's a cake," Beaver yelled. "We get *cake?*"

A few people in front of Nitzan drifted to the side, a plate with chocolate cake in one hand, a tall bottle of beer in the other. The bottles were plastic. No surprise that glass ones weren't allowed on the *Keeling*.

Nitzan saw the serving counter, and the sheetcake tapestry just behind the glass.

"That's beautiful," Bennett said. "I'm impressed, Combat Cook."

Lead Culinary Designer Bradley Henry stood behind the counter, putting slices of cake on mycoware plates, a smile on his face as grand as that of an ancient king casting benedictions upon beloved subjects.

"Much appreciated, Bennett," he said.

A quarter the dessert had already been served up, but what remained was still a masterpiece: three layers of vanilla cake, separated by and topped with icing as black as the void. Candy stars dotted the surface and sides. A milk chocolate *Keeling*—now half gone—fired orange-frosting torpedoes at a fondant probe.

"That's brilliant," Beaver yelled. "You're like an art genius, Combat Cook."

On any ship, in any fleet, anywhere in the galaxy, there was one unified, guiding principle—*be nice to the cooks.* Beaver might have shown just as much enthusiasm had the cake been made of broken glass greased up in goose shit and sprinkled with minced tapeworm, but in this case, the sentiment was genuine.

"Take your cake," Henry said. "I got more mouths to feed."

Nitzan took his plate. "I was told there would be beer."

"Ah, I almost forgot," Henry said, in a way that made it clear he hadn't forgotten at all. "Courtesy of our favorite war hero, Captain Lincoln, every good boy and every good girl gets a brew."

He reached behind the counter and came up with three cans, which he handed over.

A beer was always a good thing. When one had been on a coffin of a ship for eleven days, training and drilling nonstop, a beer was a *great* thing.

The booths were full, most with three people crammed into bench seats built for two. Standing room only, and not much of that. Sailors and Raiders laughed and talked, enjoying a brief break from Lincoln's relentless schedule and the XO's constant urging to do things better, smarter, and faster. Music started up over the 1MC. Some of that queasy-rock garbage coming out of Rodina.

"This is a great party," Beaver yelled. "I *love* this song."

Bennett kept his cake close to his chest, protecting it against an inadvertent bump from this body or that.

"I'm heading back to Raider Land to enjoy my treats in style," he said. "You guys coming?"

Beaver nodded enthusiastically, but something caught Nitzan's eye—Ensign Darkwater trying to work her way through the packed bodies.

"I'll catch up with you guys later," Nitzan said.

Bennett glanced at Darkwater, then back to Beaver, and nodded. He led Beaver out of the mess, and just in time, too, because Beaver started sing-screaming the awful song as if he'd already pounded ten beers.

"Hey, Ensign Darkwater," Nitzan said. "You come here often?"

She turned, surprised, then laughed as the joke hit home.

"Only when I'm wounded." She nodded at his beer. "Can you believe they're serving alcohol?"

Serving alcohol. A strange way to phrase it. Not *they have beer for us,* or *the captain had brews stashed away somewhere,* but rather that accurate-yet-stilted phrase.

A phrase a devout Purist might say.

"Hey, you lugheads," Nitzan said, "make some room for the ensign."

People turned and looked, first at Nitzan, then down at the far smaller Darkwater. Eyes widened. People pushed against each other, making a little room for her. Out of courtesy for her rank? Or was it distrust, possibly even fear—what went on in the atrium was a mystery to most.

Darkwater got her cake, but she didn't grab an offered beer. She walked back to Nitzan, plate in hand.

"No brew for you, Ensign?"

Darkwater winced, her nose wrinkling. "The less alcohol I have to drink, the better. The stuff messes with my head." She glanced around the packed mess. "Pretty crowded in here. I know a place we could go."

Well, wasn't this getting interesting?

He leaned closer. "The atrium?"

Darkwater laughed. It was a beautiful laugh.

"No way," she said. "You're not cleared for that."

Nitzan hid his disappointment well. "Then lead the way, Ensign Darkwater."

She hesitated, perhaps reconsidered, then leaned in close.

"Follow me," she said softly.

They worked their way through the passageways of deck three. It was easy for Darkwater—with her tiny body and holding only her plate—to slide by sailors going the other way. For Nitzan, with his bigger frame, it was a challenge to manage both cake and beer, to not get some of either on passersby.

They descended to deck four, Nitzan pinning his can of beer under his arm to manage the ladders. Darkwater walked toward the atrium. Nitzan had a brief burst of hope she'd changed her mind about taking him in there, but she opened a sphincter door on her left and stepped into a small compartment. A bulkhead rack held boxes, containers, and several pieces of equipment Nitzan didn't recognize. Science stuff, probably.

"Check this place out," he said.

"It's the xeno department's storage area." Darkwater sat on a plastic crate. "No one comes in here but us. A friend told me this is a good spot to... um... to have a chat."

She'd left the sphincter door open. With it closed, this would be a fine spot for some good fucking. Was that what she wanted?

"Have a seat." With her foot, she pushed a second crate closer to him. "Enjoy your beer."

He sat, cracked the tab, and did just that.

Consuming alcohol was forbidden in the Purist religion, but those who wanted to imbibe were usually able to find a spirit of choice and drink in private. While in the Cloister, training for this holy mission, his instructors taught him how to drink like the infidels. As a Raider, that training came in handy. He'd never enjoyed the harder stuff, but he had a hunch he'd never be able to fully shake the taste for beer.

He tilted his can toward Darkwater. "Sure you don't want some?"

She made that face again. Something about it made him think she'd drank recently, and it hadn't agreed with her.

"You tie one on last night or something, Ensign? There's a rumor going around Raider ranks that Hasik is blitzed more often than not."

Darkwater huffed a laugh. "You know how rumors can be."

She hadn't denied it. Nitzan filed that detail away. Hasik was a drunk? Another possible angle to get a look inside the atrium.

He reached out, touched her hair. She shrank away, not quite cringing but not far from it.

"Sorry," he said. "Too soon?"

If so, it was a shame.

"Yes," she said. "I guess it is. Maybe."

Did she not want sex? Maybe she hadn't put together how long she'd be on this ship. Of course, as a woman—even an older one—she basically had her pick of the horndogs on board.

Most women Nitzan hit on were more receptive. Not all of them, though, not by a long shot. But if Darkwater wasn't into the Raider type, why had she brought him here?

Unless...

"If you're not into men, I get it," he said.

Actually, he didn't get that. At all. But as long as he was on assignment, he had to pretend to be like a Unionite, and Unionites didn't give a damn about that type of blasphemy.

"I am," she said. "Into men, I mean. I am."

He felt a surprising flutter in his chest. Not *excitement*, at least not of the sexual kind, but rather... he wasn't sure what it was. There was something about this woman. Something he liked.

"Maybe it's the things I saw in transdim," she said. "I mean... it was bizarre stuff. At least for me. Did you see anything while we were under?"

He had not. He almost wished he had, as it would make for more info to give to his handlers when he got out of here. But at the same time, he wanted nothing to do with the hallucinations that had people crying, screaming in terror, shitting themselves, *biting* each other. It was the work of the Low One, of that there was no question.

"All I saw was Raiders going crazy," he said. "What did you see?"

Her expression softened.

"Nothing much," she said. "Some colors and weird stuff like that. I'm not ready to talk about it yet."

Whatever she'd seen, the memory of it didn't bother her. No fear in those eyes. She seemed at peace.

Nitzan suddenly felt so very stupid. Why had she brought him here? Because she was the other Purist Nation spy. Had to be. He didn't want to rush things, but at the same time he couldn't be certain if he'd get one-on-one time with her again. He had to take this chance.

"Praise High One for blessing your journey," he said.

Darkwater's eyes snapped up. Fear in them now—the fear of being found out.

"Why would you say that to me?"

She hadn't returned the greeting. Doing so would be a simple thing for a spy, a subtle, deniable wink-and-nod that they were on the same team. Was she telling him it was too early? Or did she think he was working with BII, perhaps, and trying to trick her into revealing herself?

He didn't know. What he *did* know, though, was that Bethany Darkwater was a Purist, or at least had been. He knew one other thing —she was a terrible actor. No way she'd been Cloister-trained.

Nitzan offered his most comforting smile.

"It's all right," he said. "I won't tell anyone."

She shook her head slightly, an automatic reaction.

"But I'm not religious," she said. "I'm an atheist."

"Being a Purist isn't against the law." He put his hand on hers, gave it a light squeeze. This time, she didn't pull away. "Religious freedom is guaranteed in the Union."

"Funny, I think I'd have heard about a Raider being openly Purist. Because that seems safe."

Nitzan laughed. "Good point."

The longer the war dragged on, the more Purists in the Union suffered prejudice, hate, and violence. In Fleet, most kept their religious views to themselves, but if people knew you were a Purist, it was an invitation to a blanket party. Or worse. Usually *much* worse.

Technically, "Nitzan Shamdi" wasn't a Purist at all. He'd never practiced any religion. Admitting belief carried significant risk. At the same time, deep secrets bound people deeply. In the Cloister, they'd taught him to use any lever he could to build key relationships.

"No, I'm not doing my midnight prayer while facing Galactic Center." He glanced over his shoulder to see if anyone was outside the sphincter, made a bit of a show of doing so, then he leaned closer to Darkwater. "I keep my beliefs to myself, as is my right. But it sure would be nice to have someone to talk to about it. When others aren't listening. You know?"

The *want* in her eyes. Not a lustful desire, fueled by her body's needs, but rather from the spirit, from her soul.

"Yes," she said. "I know."

Nitzan saw her need for a deeper connection. In a ship packed so tightly with bodies there was almost no privacy to be had, Bethany Darkwater was *lonely*.

He understood.

Bennett was a solid guy. As was Abshire. Beaver was an idiot, but also a bulldog who would not quit, not ever. Nitzan liked them, yet he knew they'd all burn in the Low Place unless they repented and asked High One for forgiveness. He couldn't allow himself to *truly* be friends with them. Not down deep, where it counted.

Yes, he was lonely, too. He had been for a long, long time. This woman might be the one person on this ship who could truly understand that loneliness.

But he couldn't focus on that. Until he verified that Darkwater was a Purist Nation plant, he had to consider her as nothing more than a source of information. He had to get what he could out of her.

He dug his fork into his cake. "So, tell me what you do in the atrium."

"I can't tell you much," she said. "A lot of it is classified, even from the XO."

He put the fork in his mouth. The cake was rich and sugary sweet but tainted by the flavor that permeated everything on the ship.

"Imagine that," he said. "Dessert that tastes like mushrooms."

She took a bite, chewed and thought.

"A little, sure." She set her fork on her plate, pinched off a bit of cake and popped it in her mouth. She closed her eyes and smiled. "Don't use the mycoware and it's perfect."

He stared at her plate, wondering how he'd never thought of that, how none of the Raiders had thought of it. So obvious—eat with your hands. Don't put the utensils-made-from-mushrooms in your mouth, and things don't taste like mushrooms.

He pinched off a piece of his own, careful to not get any that had touched his plate. *So good.* The Combat Cook knew his business.

"It's fantastic," Nitzan said.

Bethany nodded. She seemed pleased he was enjoying himself.

Nitzan pinched off another morsel, spoke while he chewed.

"So, tell me the stuff you can tell me. It gets boring dealing with stinky Raiders all the time. Tell me what your typical day is like, but without the secret bits."

Bethany smiled. A soft, *small* smile, but one that told Nitzan he could, and would, become this woman's close friend.

"I'd rather know what you think about the rumor," she said. "With you *not* being a Purist, and all."

"Rumor?"

"About the mission."

Nitzan shrugged. "Oh, that. We fight where they tell us to fight. I hope it's Sklorno, but if it's Nationalites, it's Nationalites."

Her eyes narrowed. "Obviously we're fighting Nationalites. You haven't heard the rumor about *where* we're going?"

He shook his head.

"Hathorn, in my department, told me we're going into Purist

Nation territory," Darkwater said. "Like, *way* into it. Maybe as far as Micothree."

Later, Nitzan would give himself a pat on the back for maintaining his cool. He kept the conversation going, picked up a few details about the atrium that Bethany let slip, but his mind didn't stray far from what she'd said. If Bethany was right, the *Keeling* might be heading to Mining Colony Three, a place only Nationalites referred to by the amalgamation of abbreviations: Mi. Co. 3—*Micothree*.

The *Crypt* would be deep in Purist Nation space, undoubtedly alone.

If Bethany was right, he might have the chance to escape and bring his intel home.

Or, maybe, bring the *entire ship* home.

43

Sascha put the last forkful of chicken and yam casserole in her mouth and bit off the end of the fork. Some crewmembers bitched about the taste of mushrooms, but not her. She chewed, enjoying the crunch the fork added to the soft dish.

"Another home run from Combat Cook," she said.

"You can say that again." XO Ellis had already cleaned his plate and was snapping off fragments of it, popping them into his mouth like little crackers. "He really grew all of that in the atrium? Besides the chicken, I mean."

Anne Lafferty nodded. "The yams, yes. And the chia in the chia-buckwheat bread, but not the buckwheat."

"So full." Ellis leaned back in his wardroom chair, rubbed at his belly. "I hope I get some real sleep before we rendezvous with *Ishi*."

Sascha hoped for the same. The *Keeling* would punch-out in another twelve hours. The *Ishi* rendezvous was scheduled to be short, maybe not even an hour, then both ships would punch-in for the FTL trip to the mission demarcation point. After that, *two days* in the Mud. Would there be any crew left when they reached the Purist Nation?

Lafferty stood. "I've got work to do."

She walked out, leaving her mycoware plate and utensils for someone else to clean up. Only the XO and Sascha remained in the wardroom.

"I don't like her," Sascha said.

"She's BII." Ellis rubbed his belly again. "Nobody likes BII. Not even other people in BII." He glanced toward the galley. The serving port door to the galley was closed. He leaned forward, elbows on the table. "The other day in my quarters, there was something you wanted to tell me. Is that thing still on your mind?"

It was on her mind all day, every day. She had one hundred and two weeks left to serve on this bizarre ship. She couldn't talk to people in her department about her fears—a department head's concerns about command decisions went *up* the ladder, never *down*.

Could she trust Ellis? Might as well find out.

"There's something weird about this ship," she said.

He laughed. "Oh? I hadn't noticed."

"I don't mean just the *Keeling* itself. I mean the command structure. Only one person, Hasik, supposedly knows how the ship actually works. What happens if he dies? There's no redundancy, XO. It's a critical failure waiting to happen."

Ellis grew serious. "*Supposedly?* Are you trying to say Hasik doesn't know how this ship works?"

Sascha hesitated, wondering if she should continue. Screw it—if the XO was going to burn her, he was going to burn her.

"Hasik knows how to *operate* it," she said. "But as for *how* it accesses other membranes? Or what the hull material really is? What this *ship* really is? Maybe someone in Fleet knows, but if so, it ain't Hasik."

The XO studied her for a moment.

"That doesn't make sense," he said. "Hasik knows how it works. How could we perform transdim dives if he didn't?"

Sasha pulled Lafferty's empty plate closer. She bit off a bit, slowly chewing it as she talked.

"You're not a gunner, but could you operate our artillery?"

Ellis nodded. "I'm rated on the Type24 system."

"You could load it and fire it?"

He nodded again.

"Say we capture a Sklorno warship," Sascha said. "Have you ever been on one?"

"I have not."

"Say you were, and your job was to figure out how to operate that ship's artillery. There's no manual. No tutorial. No one to show you how it works. But you still have to figure out how to load it and fire it. Could you?"

That made him think. He broke off a piece of his own plate, turned it in his fingers.

"Probably, yeah. Shell diameter, bore size... figuring out what goes where would be simple enough. Find the trigger mechanism, learn how to move the weapon. Then trial and error, test firing until you got it down. If I had enough time, I could figure it out."

"So you could learn how to fire alien weaponry," Sascha said. "But could you mine the ore to make the shell casing? Could you smelt it to the right tolerances? Could you cast it with the exacting measurements necessary so it doesn't blow up when you fire it? Could you identify the explosives used, then mix those chemicals correctly to make new rounds?"

"Highly doubtful," he said. "I know trig—I don't know chemistry. Or metallurgy and mining, for that matter."

"Then, you could *operate* alien weaponry, but you don't really know *how it works*."

He frowned. "I get what you're saying, but that's pretty simplistic compared to jumping into another dimension. Or membrane. Or whatever the Mud is."

Ellis wasn't judging her, wasn't placating her. He seemed like a genuinely good person. Despite the albatross of cowardice hanging around his neck, Sascha knew she could learn from the XO. But could she make him see what she saw?

"Yes, it's simplistic, but the principle still applies." She leaned closer to him. "Someone found this ship. Through trial and error, most likely, they figured out how to operate it. Was Hasik part of that? We don't know. But even if he was, it doesn't mean he truly understands the science involved."

"What about all that stuff he said about membranes and universes and dimensions?" Ellis leaned back, crossed his arms. "He described what the ship can do, then the ship did those things."

"I don't think he showed us *facts*," Sascha said. "I think he showed us his hypothesis. His or someone else's. He's bullshitting us. He's trying to build an explanation from observed data, but he doesn't *know how it works.*"

The XO thought that over.

"If you're right, Hasik isn't that different from the rest of us," he said. "Hasik pushes the buttons he's told to push. The people who have the real knowledge aren't here. So what?"

So what? A good question, one she hadn't thought to consider. She'd focused on her instinct that Hasik was full of shit—she hadn't thought about what him being full of shit truly meant or if it even mattered.

"I know something's wrong, that's all," she said. "And there's one more thing."

Ellis sighed. "This better be important. You're cutting into my full-belly-sleepy-time."

He was still listening, but not for long.

"There are areas of the ship that aren't listed on the deck schematics," she said. "The lower bow that holds Raider Land, that's hollow, but the upper bow is solid. And that big chunk of deck five, between the pouch and the lower bow, that's solid, too."

The XO shrugged. "It's probably structural. Right? It holds the ship together, or something like that?"

"I don't think so. I scanned the tail section. It appears solid, *completely* solid but it's not—it stretches out when we're in-dim. If the tail is malleable, are the other solid sections as well? Does Hasik know? Does anyone?"

Ellis sighed, stood.

"No one told you to scan anything, Lieutenant, so I'll pretend I didn't hear what you just said, and you will *stop* scanning. Let's worry about surviving the mission. If we do, you and I can talk about this some more."

He left the wardroom.

Sascha grew irritated with herself. Had she thought the XO would have answers? He'd only been here two weeks, same as her.

Her job as engineering chief was to know every part of the ship inside and out, yet she knew nothing about the atrium, nothing about the material the xeno department sometimes called *the heart* and other times *the heartstone,* and nothing about the solid-but-not-solid sections.

Understanding those things could mean the difference between life or death.

She didn't know when, she didn't know how, but one way or another, she was going to get answers.

44

John ran a gun brush through his rifle barrel, back and forth, turning the brush slightly each time.

"So, Bennett," Abshire said. "You still banging Winter? Haven't seen you two canoodling about town lately."

Fire team Alpha-Two used Shamdi's bunk as a table to clean their weapons. A hand towel marked each man's work area. If John had to go into battle with these guys, he'd make damn sure their rifles were in perfect working order.

"Abs, make sure your mag-catch is properly slotted." John looked down the disassembled barrel of his rifle, eyeballing it for significant wear or potential problems. "If you can't put a mag in properly, Sands will rip the whole team to shreds. You should be focusing on your weapon—not my love life."

Love life. As if love had anything to do with it.

"We can multitask." Beaver set his reassembled weapon on the bunk, held his hands up palms out. "Platoon record! Gotta be. Right? I'm the fastest at this." He grinned at John. "Come on, Grampa, tell us if you're getting some cooch."

John set the barrel down on the long towel that contained the parts of his RR. "Speed records don't matter." He picked up the firing selector switch, examined it closely. "What matters is that your rifle works properly when you need it."

"You're ducking the question," Shamdi said. "You banging that wide ass or not? Considering Winter's anger issues, though, maybe she's the one banging *you*."

John was almost as old as the three of them combined. They were young, dumb, and full of cum. He'd been that age once. Back then, he'd thought about sex a whole lot more than he did now.

But that was easy to say when he was the one getting laid.

"Any interpersonal communication between the Warrant Officer and me stays between me and the Warrant Officer," John said. "I've never been on a ship that allows this kind of open-secret camaraderie. If I was you, boys, I'd stop asking questions before Lincoln gets reminded she's letting an occasional tandem tummy-rub go down. It's my experience that captains do not like to have the privileges they allow thrown back in their face."

Shamdi slid his barrel into the receiver, spun it to thread it home.

"Grampa is right about that," he said. "Let's all shut the fuck up about fucking, lest *not* shutting the fuck up fucks up our fucking."

Beaver's face lit up. "Sham, that's *got* to be a platoon record for using *fuck* the most times in one sentence."

Abshire shook his head. "I don't think the platoon tracks that record."

Beaver started breaking his weapon down again.

"That's bullshit," he said. "It would be a good record."

"I'm changing the subject." Shamdi slotted his cleaned and reassembled trigger array back in his receiver. "We're supposed to come out of punch-space in three hours. Then we rendezvous with *Ishi* and start the mission. Anyone think we'll see action?"

By *anyone*, Shamdi obviously meant John. Beaver and Abs didn't know their butt from a burnt biscuit when it came to second-guessing command.

"I assume we will," John said. "I know you guys heard where we're going, just like I have."

Lindros hadn't been forthcoming with the mission objectives, but Raiders found out, as Raiders often do.

"The fucking Purist Nation," Abs said. "Can you believe my first hop is into enemy territory?"

Abshire carried his dread of combat like a toddler carries a threadbare blanket. There wasn't much John or anyone else could do about it. Until the kid popped his cherry and found out what combat was like, that fear would haunt him.

"I can't wait," Beaver said. "Can. Not. Wait. I hope I get to shoot a churchie right in the face, so they can see it coming. How about you, Sham? You fought churchies before?"

John's fingers knew how to put his weapon together—he didn't need his eyes. He watched Shamdi's reaction. There was something peculiar about the guy. John couldn't nail it down. He wanted to better understand the man before they fought side-by-side. Only John and Shamdi had combat experience; it was up to them to keep Beaver and Abs on-task when the shit hit the fan.

"Yeah," Shamdi said. "I fought them once."

John heard the coldness, the *hollowness* in the man's voice; Shamdi lost friends in that fight.

"Speaking of open secrets," Abs said, "how about that spinner-milf ensign you been hounding, Sham?"

Shamdi set his partially assembled weapon on his towel. He stared straight at Abs. The look on Abshire's face showed he knew he'd said something wrong.

John tensed, ready to jump between the two men if violence blossomed.

"Her name is *Ensign Darkwater*," Shamdi said. "When you talk about her, you will give her the respect she deserves. Or better yet, how about you keep her name out of your shit-sipping mouth?"

Abshire tensed, sensing the anger coiled up inside Shamdi. John didn't fault Abs for that. There is a vast difference between a threat spoken by a man who hasn't taken life, and one who has. Body language, the tone of voice, a lack of doubt... it's just different.

"Wait a minute," Beaver said without looking up from assembling his weapon. "Sham, weren't you just asking if Bennett was hooking up with PXO Winter, or versa visa or whatever?"

"Not the same thing." Shamdi stared at Abs. "Not even fucking *close*."

Beaver, it seemed, did not have Abshire's ability to read the room and sense the obvious.

"Let's all leave it alone," John said. "No more talking about who is associating with whom. Got it?"

Abshire nodded.

Shamdi glared his dark glare for a few more seconds, then he did the same.

Beaver set his reassembled weapon down, raised both hands, palms out.

"Even faster! That's *got* to be the platoon record!"

45

"All hands, general quarters," XO Ellis said. "We're exiting punch-space in three minutes. That is all."

Anne watched him hang up the comm handset. She was growing quite used to her perch in the intel loft. From here, she could observe everybody. And so many people needed to be observed.

"Pilot, prepare to bring us out of punch-space," XO Ellis said. "Darsat, I want any and all contacts the moment we punch back in."

Anne admired Ellis's command style: calm, patient, but with backbone. Hard to believe he was the same guy who'd turned tail and fled a battle, but you don't know who a person truly is until you see how they act when someone is trying to kill them.

Hasik was in the xeno loft, although he appeared to be dozing in his acceleration chair, his chin on his chest. Shameful. An utter lack of discipline. But, Anne had to admit, a sleeping Hasik was better than an awake Darkwater.

The mousy ensign was likely in the atrium, gathering priceless secrets about how *Keeling* worked. Gillick had spotted Darkwater in the xeno supply room with Nitzan Shamdi, a Raider spec-2. Gillick thought he was trying to get in Darkwater's pants.

And why shouldn't Shamdi try to get a little? Lincoln didn't care about fraternization, yet another tick in the *doesn't know how to lead* column. Gillick and Daniels reported that several crewmembers were hooking up. Crawler Master Crew Chief Taylor was shagging Eloi Sung. Nav Chief Erickson and pilot Lars Nygard slipped away to one of the ship's little copper cubbyholes when their schedules permitted, which wasn't often. PXO Winter apparently had a thing for older men, that fossil of a Raider, Bennett, in particular.

Why Lincoln allowed it was beyond Anne. Regulations existed for a reason. Anne had relationships while on missions, of course she did, but not with any Union military personnel serving in her area of operation. Anne had developed a strong friendship with Olivia, but they hadn't been *lovers*, for God's sake.

At the command slate, Lincoln whispered something to Ellis. He nodded, then faced forward.

"Pilot, take us into realspace."

It was funny to think that some on the *Keeling* had probably complained about punch-space travel before they got here. Punch-in and punch-out brought on the "shimmer," which made everything seem to waver like a reflection in a rippling pond. Sooner or later, that phenomenon made everyone queasy to one degree or another. Compared to a transdim dive, though? Punch-space travel was as onerous as lying on silk sheets while a nubile young lover fed you peeled grapes.

"Punching-out," said Nygard, the pilot. "In three, two, one..."

Anne watched the slight wavering of the CIC and everyone in it as the *Keeling* left punch-space behind.

"Conn, two darsat contacts." Gurgen Hakobyan at the darsat station. "I repeat, *two* contacts."

Anne sat forward in her seat. Only *Ishlangu* had been scheduled to be at these coordinates.

She had her doubts about Hakobyan. There was a weasely air to him. She had a hunch his crimes were sexual in nature. A rapist? A pedophile, perhaps?

"Identify contacts," Ellis said.

The orb flashed to life. Two icons appeared, both to port and high, one close, the other quite a ways off.

"Contact one is the *Ishlangu*," Hakobyan said. "Bearing, port zero-three-zero. Elevation, zero-four-five. Range, fifty kilometers. Second contact is the *Akathaso*. Bearing, port zero-five-five. Elevation, zero-four-zero. Range... three-zero-five-one kilometers."

The *Akathaso*—the flagship of Sixth Group.

Admiral Epperson's ship.

"XO, *Ishlangu* is hailing us." Corporal Ellison manned the signals station. She seemed all right. So far. "Audio only, XO."

Ellis straightened, gave his coveralls a tug. Not a normal mannerism for him. Anne filed it away.

"Put it through," Ellis said.

"*Keeling*, this is *Ishlangu*. Welcome to the party."

The voice of Vesna Jakobsson, *Ishi*'s captain.

Trav glanced at Lincoln, silently asking her if she wanted to be the one to greet Jakobsson. Lincoln shook her head.

"Thank you, *Ishlangu*," Trav said. "We weren't aware you'd have company at this time."

"Someone came to see us off," Jakobsson said. "Admiral Epperson requests the presence of the *Keeling*'s captain, XO, and intel chief. The meeting will take place on the *Ishlangu*. We are sending a shuttle to retrieve you now. ETA, ten minutes."

Ellis turned, looked up into the intel loft at Anne.

She shrugged. She had no idea what was going on.

"Thank you, *Ishlangu*," Trav said. "We'll be ready."

46

No mere ensign this time. Master Warrant Officer Sheila Drummond, who'd introduced herself as Epperson's aide-de-camp, led Trav, Captain Lincoln, and Major Lafferty through *Ishlangu's* passageways.

Drummond's service uniform—light gray blouse with black trousers—was spotless and in perfect order. Trav, on the other hand, wore the same stained, rumpled gray coveralls he'd been wearing when Vesna's request came through. The last time he'd met an admiral, he'd been in his dress whites. Granted, he'd been on trial for cowardice in combat, but still.

Lincoln, too, wore coveralls. Trav suspected that even if she'd had ample time to change into dress whites, she wouldn't have.

Lafferty, on the other hand, looked sharp. In the ten minutes it took *Ishi's* shuttle to arrive, she'd somehow managed to don her BII service blacks. She looked sharp, which made Trav even more self-conscious about his grungy appearance.

"I do the talking," Lincoln said. "You two will speak only if I ask you something or if Admiral Epperson directly addresses you. Clear?"

"Aye-aye, Captain," Trav and Lafferty said in unison.

Lincoln was on edge. Trav would be, too, if he'd been the CO. Hell, he was on edge and he wasn't even in command.

Drummond stopped at the door to Vesna's suite.

"You're lucky," she said. "The admiral is in a good mood today. I suggest you don't say anything to change that. Good luck."

She let them in and shut the door behind them.

The three *Keeling* crewmates snapped to attention and saluted, because that's what you did when you met one of the most-powerful people in Fleet, if not the entire Planetary Union.

"Admiral Epperson," Lincoln said. "Colonel Kiara Lincoln reporting as ordered, along with my XO, Travis Ellis, and Anne Lafferty, my intel chief."

Epperson was in his early sixties. Pale skin, mostly bald with a temple-to-temple ring of brown hair and a smattering of freckles on his exposed pate. He wore a pair of thin, wireframe reading glasses. His service uniform was meticulous perfection, gleaming where it was supposed to gleam, flat and smooth where it was supposed to be flat and smooth.

The four stars of his rank insignia screamed of accomplishment and power. He was a full admiral, outranked only by the five stars of Master Admiral Devon Hildred.

Epperson was in the same seat Vesna had sat in when she'd met with Trav. The admiral read from a tablet. A mug of coffee on the table, a carafe next to it.

Without looking up, he casually returned the salute.

"At ease," he said.

Trav spread his feet, put his hands behind his back, and waited.

And waited.

And waited.

Epperson sipped at his coffee and continued to read.

Trav waited some more.

Finally, Epperson set the tablet down. He folded his hands on the table and stared out with deep blue eyes.

"This mission is critical to the war effort." His voice sounded a bit too deep for someone of his moderate size. "*Keeling* is the only ship that can pull this off. Major Lafferty, I'm told you know Colonel Mac Cooley."

"Yes, Admiral. I met him when I was younger."

"He's the asset the *Keeling* will retrieve from Purist space," Epperson said. "You will do everything he asks."

"Yes, Admiral," Lafferty said. "I won't let you down."

"I hope not, Major." Epperson tilted his head slightly. "Lincoln's reports say you're doing well. Keep it up. The only reason you're alive is because I owed your father a favor. You've got a long way to earn out, Lafferty. Understand me?"

Out of the corner of his eye, Trav saw Lafferty stiffen, even though she'd already been ramrod straight. Epperson's words hit her hard.

"Yes, Admiral." Lafferty's voice had lost its ring of confidence. "I understand."

Epperson turned his attention to Lincoln. "How are you holding up, Kiara?"

"I'm tip-top, Admiral," the captain said. "Never been better."

Epperson laughed. "Yes, I'll bet." His eyes swung toward Trav, bore in. "And how is your XO doing?"

"XO Ellis is figuring things out," Lincoln said.

Epperson's left eye twitched. Not a *wink*, more like a *tic*.

"Ellis, Lincoln won't helm the *Keeling* forever," the admiral said. "Your direct experience with the ship means you're next in line to be the CO."

Command of a ship. Being a captain. It had been Trav's goal for as long as he could remember, even before his parents died, before he'd gone off to live with his grandmother. He would never command a carrier, there was no chance of that now, but could he actually command *Keeling*?

"I've been going over Lincoln's after-action report for the torpedo exercise," Epperson said. "You strike me as the kind of person who takes the easy way out."

The comment caught Trav off-guard.

"Sir, I—"

"It wasn't a question," Epperson snapped. "If it isn't a question, you are not to respond." His eyes narrowed slightly. "Don't get all weepy about it, Ellis. My job is to be the one who sees things as they are, call them like they are. I don't think you take the easy way out as a conscious choice, but you and I both know what happened at Asteroid X7." He tapped the tablet resting on the table. "And from what I've read about your torpedo run, you should have stayed in transdim

294

longer so you could get closer to the drone. How do you explain your actions?"

Anger flared, but Trav controlled it. He would never be free of his choices at X7. He might as well get used to that. The exercise, though? That had gone well.

"Admiral, we exited transdim at the scheduled time and we bagged the bogey. We satisfied the mission objectives."

"I didn't ask you for a summary of things I just read in the report, Lieutenant. I didn't ask you your thoughts on mission objectives. What I *asked* was, how do you explain your actions?"

At that moment, Trav understood there was nothing he could say that would satisfy Epperson. This was a pissing contest to establish dominance—Epperson was a Saint Bernard who'd been kept inside for twelve hours, and Trav was a fire hydrant.

"Does the Admiral have specific actions he is enquiring about?" Trav asked.

Epperson slapped the table. "Don't play dumb with me, Ellis. There are places worse than the *Keeling*. Understand me?"

Trav would believe that only if he saw it, but considering how bad the *Keeling* was, he didn't want to find out.

"I understand, Admiral."

"Then tell me why you chose to exit transdim so far from your target," Epperson said. "When you reach your deployment area, *especially* in transdim, a proper commander evaluates the environment and adjusts accordingly. You should have stayed under until you were right on top of the probe."

Trav's anger shifted to shame. Epperson was right.

"Sir, the crew was on edge. There were... problems. I didn't think it prudent to stay under any longer than we already had. I felt confident I could enter realspace and eliminate the target. Which we did."

Epperson stared at Trav. Trav stared at the bulkhead behind Epperson.

"Concern for your crew is a fine thing." The admiral spoke in a calm, matter-of-fact tone. "But your first priority is to limit danger to the *Keeling*. Because you exited transdim so far from the probe, it had time to see you, get a target solution on you, and fire a simulated shot. Had your foe been Purist, Sklorno, League, or any hostile force anywhere in the galaxy, it would have been more than one shot, and it would have been real. If you are called upon to engage the enemy, Ellis, you have to get *close* before you reveal yourself. If you can't get close, you—" he slapped the table, emphasizing each word "—*do... not... engage.* You get the hell out of the area, no matter how long your crew has to stay under, or how many *problems* they have. Understand me?"

Trav felt lost. He was supposed to say *yes, Admiral, I understand,* but he didn't understand at all.

"Admiral, are you saying that even if I have a tactical and technological advantage, as I did with the probe, that I should *not* engage the target I was ordered to engage?"

Epperson's smile blazed with self-satisfaction.

"That is correct, Lieutenant," he said. "*Keeling* is a high-priority asset. If you face a combat scenario that you can't win before the other side gets off a shot, then you run. You understand running, don't you, Ellis? Why the hell do you think you're here?"

Trav went cold as stone. He finally got it. This assignment wasn't a chance to redeem himself of cowardice in combat—he was here *because* he was a coward.

He and Williams had probably been assigned to *Keeling* before their trial even began. He and Williams had *both* chosen to leave the battlefield. When Williams opted for death over serving on the ship, Fleet had been only too happy to put Trav in his place as XO.

"Lieutenant Ellis," Epperson said, "I asked you a question."

No, it wasn't *Fleet* that entombed Trav on the *Crypt*—Epperson had.

"I think I'm here, sir, because you want people in command who prioritize *Keeling*'s safety above everything else."

In other words: *I'm here because you* want *me to run away.*

"Now you've got it," Epperson said. "There are some missions for which we have no choice but to send the *Keeling*. Even then, you are to remember your primary order—do not engage. Repeat that order back to me."

Humiliation so thick it was hard to breathe.

"Admiral, my primary order is *do not engage.*"

Epperson looked at Lincoln. "You're right, Kiara. Your XO *is* figuring things out. We expect zero resistance on this mission. You get in, get Cooley, get him back to me. You run into trouble, you get out of there. Cooley's intel is important. *Keeling* is more important. Don't let me down."

"I won't, Admiral," Lincoln said. "We'll get the job done."

Epperson picked up his tablet in one hand, his coffee cup in the other.

"You better," he said. "Ellis isn't the only one who can get busted down. Dismissed."

Trav, Lincoln, and Lafferty left the captain's suite.

All the way back to the *Keeling*, they didn't say a word.

47

John slammed Warrant Officer Katharina Winter's face against the deck. The impact stunned her—the bloody copper shiv she'd been holding fell free, clattered against the fakegrav tiles.

"Her legs," Sands said. "Abeen, get her legs!"

Sands was on his butt, leaning against a bunk, his eyes glassy, blood streaming from the ragged hole in his cheek.

Scrawny Fred Abeen threw himself on Winter's legs and wrapped his arms around her thick thighs. John grabbed one arm, put her in a wrist lock. Radulski locked onto her other arm, leaned his weight on her shoulder.

Sands stood on wobbly legs. "Sergeant Jordan, get flexicuffs on her." He grabbed the copper shiv off the deck. "Right now."

"We're out of flexicuffs," Jordan said. "I told you that two crazies ago, Master Sergeant."

"Then *get some more!*" Sands tried to wipe the blood from his cheek, but all he did was smear it around a bit before more pumped out of the ragged hole. "They're in the rig room!"

Jordan rushed off.

Despite carrying the weight of three Raiders and being packed in between the rows of bunks, Winter fought like a demon and growled like a rabid animal. John didn't dare relax his hold on her wrist—she thrashed about so hard he wondered if he'd have to break it to keep her down.

And still, Winter struggled, right up to the point where Master Sergeant Francis Sands stepped up and kicked her in the head. Winter, finally, fell limp.

Jordan returned moments later with flexicuffs. She slid the loops on Winter's wrists, pulling them tight.

"Get Winter in her bunk," Sands said. "Nikula, bring Bennett some zipstrips, make it fast."

Beaver rushed over, helped John haul the cuffed warrant officer toward her bunk, passing by other Raiders tied to theirs—most with plastic zipstrips, but others with socks, and even one with bootlaces.

Raider Land echoed with moans and screams, the damned of hell calling out for mercy. People were seeing things they couldn't handle, things that terrified them.

At least they weren't seeing a flat-headed, three-eyed rat-shrimp-thing staring back at them. Because the rat-shrimp-thing could kiss off into the sky, for all John cared.

"This is really wild," Abeen said. "This place ain't nothing like Nebraska."

John didn't know where *Nebraska* was. An orbital in the Newton Web Colony, maybe.

"There's her rack," John said. "Hurry before she gets her bearings."

They set the unconscious platoon XO facedown in her bunk, keeping a hand on her in case she woke up.

Nikula rushed in with a fistful of zipstrips. The engineer-gunner's eye was swelling shut—she'd taken a punch somewhere along the line. She quickly bound Winter's wrists to the bunk frame, then did the same with her ankles.

"*Platoon,*" Sands called out, "sound off if you're fit for duty, by squad, frontliners first, then crawler personnel!"

Even as John's eyes swept across the berth, looking to see who might go batshit next, he tracked the names as they were called out. Bravo-One was down to two people. Bravo-Two had four, thanks to Oneida getting transferred over to *Ishi.* Alpha-Two, John's squad, was full, if you didn't count the previously atomized Rumenia Laior. Alpha-One had only a single member call out.

The Ochthera crews struggled as well. Three of the six pilots were restrained, as was one engineer-gunner and two of the three-person maintenance team.

Counting Winter and LT Lindros, fifteen of the platoon's thirty-three active members were out of commission.

"Abs," John said, "what's the time?"

Abshire limped over, his right arm tight to his chest. Clifton Bishop had broken it when he'd tackled Abs, who'd been trying to restrain Karl Chennault, who had gone batshit after *he'd* been attacked by a batshit Viktor Alyona, a crawler co-pilot who was now wrapped up tight in four blankets like some kind of a Raider burrito.

"Six hours until we're back in realspace," Abshire said. "It's getting worse."

John almost said *no shit*, but he was tired. He'd spent the last four hours managing comrades driven to temporary insanity by the trans-dim. *Hopefully* temporary, anyway. Even if everyone got their gray matter in order, he'd seen at least three Raiders injured badly enough that they would need medical attention before they'd be fit for duty. That included Abs and his broken arm.

"Shamdi," John said, "get over here and keep an eye on the PXO, make sure she doesn't get loose."

John wanted his fire team close. Winter wasn't going anywhere. Lindros was buck naked and chained to the weapons cage. That made Sands the platoon's CO, although the master sergeant was dealing with a rather unseemly hole in his cheek.

Shamdi arrived and, like the veteran he was, tugged sharply on every bit of plastic holding Winter in place, making sure they were strong enough do the job.

"You suck, Bennett," he said. "Why do I gotta do this? She's playing bouncy house on your dick, not mine."

"*Just fucking keep her there,*" John said. "This ain't the time for your jokes."

The freak-outs had come in progressive waves. During the first four hours of the forty-eight-hour trip, only Biggie Bang needed to be restrained. From there, John watched things grow progressively worse, with Raiders flipping out one, two, even three at a time. Some recovered their senses and were let loose, but most stayed where they'd been restrained.

The moaning and crying ebbed, the volume easing off just a bit. That, too, had come in waves. Seemed everyone saw something different, but the intensity of their hallucinations were synchronized.

"Speaking of dicks," Beaver said, "who would have thought LT had that fire hose?"

Shamdi groaned in disgust.

"Beaver, shut the fuck up," he said. "It's already going to be a challenge to scrub that mutant schlong from my memory."

Someone let out a wail, the kind of desperate, lost-soul sound that reminded John of dying Raiders with their limbs blown off, with their guts spilling out onto the deck of an alien ship.

"I wanna go home," Abshire said. "Someone's gonna die before this is over."

The 1MC *all-alert* tone blared.

"Uh... I need some... assistance." A woman's voice. John didn't recognize it. "I need help in the atrium."

"That's almost right above us," Abshire said.

Shamdi sprinted out of the Raider berth.

"Hey," Beaver said. "He's not supposed to leave, is he?"

John had never felt so untethered. This stuff wasn't exactly in the Raider rulebook.

He looked at his platoon's second in command, strapped to her bunk with zipstrips. Sitting on top of her was a rat-shrimp-thing, iridescent green mouth-bits puffing away on a meter-long, blue glass bong in the shape of a Rogalinski rifle. Big, silvery eyes stared at John. Tan-furred cheeks puffed—one, two, three perfect smoke rings, slowly expanding outward.

The creature flipped John the bird. It only had two fingers, so one finger and the thumb were tucked, but John knew what it meant.

"Fuck you, too," John said.

Beaver looked at him. "You okay, Bennett?"

No. No, John was not okay. He should have retired. He should be on a beach somewhere, drinking something, not waving away smoke rings his brain told him were as real as his own hands.

"I'm fine," John said. "Beaver, protect Abs and watch Winter. I'm going after Shamdi."

48

Susannah and Hathorn stood on the protuberance platform, staring at the blood-streaked blade of rough-hewn copper pointed in their direction. Corporal Jester Gillick held the duct-tape-handled shiv in his shaking hand. His eyes swam with madness.

"Hang it up," he said. "And turn off the comm."

Susannah froze. She shouldn't have called for help. Gillick was going to cut her just like he'd cut Hasik.

Hathorn gently took the handset from Susannah's hand, put it back in its cradle, and flicked the heavy power switch to *off*. Hathorn's nose looked broken. Blood trickled from an upper lip that had already swollen to twice its normal size.

Had someone heard Susannah's call for help? Was someone coming?

"You both saw it," Gillick said. "Right? You saw him pull that magic wand on me. Right?"

Susannah had seen no such thing, and if there was ever a time where she might actually see a magic wand, it would be now, when the mist-filled atrium was a pulsing cacophony of colors that no Human had ever experienced before.

"You neutralized the threat," she said. "Put down the knife, Corporal."

She was terrified—why did her voice sound so confident? It was like someone else was talking through her.

"You're right." Gillick nodded, wide-eyed. "The threat is neutralized."

The *threat* was Colonel Zvanut Hasik. The *magic wand*, as far as Susannah could tell, was Hathorn's flask, from which Hasik had been drinking before he'd slipped a gear and started bashing it against Hathorn's face.

Susannah's heart swirled and thumped in time with the madly flashing light. She knew the special colors she saw were for her and *only* her.

Hasik was sitting on the platform's bottom step, his face aglow in the spastic luminosity, he stared at the blood spreading through the thigh of his coveralls.

"I think I might be hurt," he said. "Quite badly, actually, and yet, I feel no pain. That seems incongruous with the observed data, ergo, all this rather important fluid leaving my body."

Hasik needed to shut his damn trap. Did he not see the BII spy/assassin/thug standing a meter away from him? Someone had to do something, fast, or the only person who really knew how *Keeling* worked would bleed out and die.

"I think I should eliminate the threat," Gillick said. "*Further* eliminate, I mean."

The sneaky bastard had been lurking near the atrium for days. When Hasik started beating Hathorn, Gillick had rushed in. Turned out that—surprise surprise—intel people could open the atrium sphincter. Just pop on in any time you please, really. Kick back. Take your shoes off. Sit a spell.

"You can't further-eliminate," Susannah said, her voice still oddly calm, oddly controlled. "It's not mathematically plausible."

Gillick's face wrinkled in confusion. He absently scratched at his temple with the point of the shiv, not even flinching when it opened up a streaming wound.

"Huh," he said. "You're right. But if I cut off his head, that settles the matter for sure."

A man strode into the atrium, the glowing mist parting before him —Gillick hadn't closed the sphincter.

"I heard this is where the party's at," Nitzan Shamdi said. "Love what you've done with the place."

A good Purist man. Nitzan would fix this. He would make the problem go away.

Gillick turned to face him. "Back off or I'll slice you to the bone."

Hasik rubbed a hand against his wound, raised one shaking, blood-smeared finger. "I assure you, he's not lying about that." He flung his hand, sending red splatters flying through the air.

A few drops splashed against the heartstone.

In those spots, the glassine surface began to blaze with the intensity of a new star.

No one but Susannah seemed to notice. Nitzan certainly didn't—he grinned wide.

"Mate, if there's going to be any cutting, I'll be the one to do it." He put his hands behind his back. "Come on, you BII ass-wipe. Come get some."

Gillick rushed him, lunged with the shiv.

Nitzan sidestepped. The bloody tip missed his throat by no more than a whisker. He drove his forehead into Gillick's nose. The man dropped. As he did, Nitzan snatched the jagged blade from his limp hand.

Gillick lolled on the floor, defenseless, blood streaming from a nose bent sideways.

The heartstone flared brighter than ever, beams of lush light streaming up from its curved surface.

Nitzan stood over Gillick, stared down with murder in his eyes.

"You threatened my friend." Nitzan's voice sounded different now. Huskier. *Deadlier.* "Know what that means? It means you can kiss your candy ass goodbye."

He raised the copper shiv...

"Stand *down*, Spec. Now!"

Susannah's blood ran cold. Color faded from the room. That voice was the sound of the void itself, the sound of *evil*.

A Raider stepped through the mist. She'd seen him before, the craggy one old enough to be her father. He looked different now. A vibrating black haze coated him in an umbra of death and destruction. He looked... *empty.*

"But he's gotta die, Bennett," Nitzan said. "He's gotta die."

The empty man stepped closer. "Let go of the blade, Nitzie."

The nickname hit Nitzan like a punch in the gut; breath slid from him in a slow, sad hiss. He relaxed his hand.

"Good work, Raider," Empty Man said as he gently took the shiv. "Secure the corporal. Do not hurt him any further."

Nitzan nodded blankly, knelt next to the bloody, confused Gillick.

Then, Empty Man looked at Susannah. His eyes raged with long tongues of ebony flame.

She felt a fear she'd never before known, not even when shrapnel decapitated her lover.

"Ensign," Empty Man said, "apply pressure to Colonel Hasik's wound. Do it now."

Susannah dropped the handset and ran to Hasik, unsure if she was going to help him or use him as a shield.

A shield against the emptiness.

49

Sascha Kerkhoffs hadn't just failed, she'd failed spectacularly. Because of that failure, a sailor was dead—one more casualty for a crew that had yet to see a moment of combat.

"Spec-One Sui Jun is catatonic," said Polly Hammersmith, *Keeling*'s top doc. "She has no physical injury, yet she's unresponsive. She might come out of it, she might not. We don't have the equipment needed to properly analyze her condition."

Lieutenant Hammersmith had both an unusually wide neck and thin shoulders, giving her an almost oval shape. She spoke in a gruff monotone. Maybe she'd been more emotional before her time on the *Keeling*—this was her third patrol—or maybe she'd always been this way. Sascha didn't know.

"We set Spec-One Neal Abshire's broken arm," Hammersmith said. "I recommend he go easy on it for a few days. As for Master Sergeant Sands, his wound was superficial. He's cleared for duty. Platoon XO Katharina Winter has a mild concussion. One day of bed rest, mandatory. That's it for the Raiders."

They were packed into the wardroom: Sascha, Hammersmith, XO Ellis, Lindros, Lafferty, Chief Sung, and ops head Alex Plait. Coffee mugs abounded. Everyone looked ragged, as was to be expected after two days in the Mud. The *Keeling* was back in realspace, deep in

Purist Nation territory, doing as little as possible, waiting for the signal from Colonel Cooley.

"Abshire will have to buck up," Lindros said. "We're down three frontliners. He'd be the fourth."

Lindros seemed like a different person. Far less confident. He slumped in his chair instead of sitting up straight as he'd done before. Barnes Marchenko had told Sascha the Raiders were calling Lindros "Dork" behind his back. Sascha wasn't sure of the context. Some people could embrace a pejorative nickname, own it in a self-depre-cating way—Lindros did not appear to be one of those people.

"I'm keeping three people in the infirmary," Hammersmith said, "Xeno Chief Hasik's leg wound requires another day of observation, and medic Rudello's concussion requires at least three more days. I repaired Corporal Gillick's broken eye socket and freed a trapped muscle, so he'll see straight again, but I still need to reconstruct his nose. If there's nothing else, Captain, I'd like to return to my duties."

"Thank you, Doctor," Lincoln said. "You're dismissed."

Hammersmith left the wardroom.

Lincoln's anger sizzled on the edge of flame. She kept her voice low, but that didn't hide the rage burbling within.

"Ops," she said, "who is replacing Gunner's Mate Eskander?"

Spec-2 Philip Eskander, part of the port Type24 team, had taken his own life. The second death of the two-week-old patrol. His was even harder to take than Rumenia Laior's. Less than ninety minutes from surfacing to realspace, Eskander used a crude blade made from hull material to slit his own wrists.

Sascha now knew Eskander's death was on her hands. Partially, at least.

"We're moving Spec-Three Jessica Painter into the port gun crew," Plait said. "She's a fire controller but cross-trained as a gunner. Turret Master Ling will bring her up to speed."

"Very well," Lincoln said. "Find what duty you can for Portland, as long as he's nowhere near a station if we enter combat."

Spec-2 Sensor Operator Levi Portland had suffered a heart attack. He was nineteen years old and in prime shape. What had he seen? No one knew. He wouldn't talk about it. Doc Hammersmith said his heart would probably recover, but if he had another, similar event, he could drop dead.

"That brings us to the next item," Lincoln said. "Kerkhoffs, bring in Chief Marchenko."

Sascha stepped out of the wardroom. Down the passageway, Marchenko stood alone, visibly trembling.

"This way," Sascha said.

She led him into the wardroom, his limp slight but noticeable.

Marchenko stood at attention.

"Staff Sergeant Marchenko," Lincoln said. "One crewman dead. We almost lost another. A third requires multiple surgeries to repair his nose, a wound suffered because he had to be disarmed. You've had time to think. What can you tell me about your actions?"

With his left hand, Marchenko tugged absently at a bandage on his right thumb.

"I still don't remember making the weapons, Captain," he said. "I remember the two days in transdim. Eating, sleeping, working... but not making the knives."

Lafferty had quickly uncovered the facts. The copper shivs were sliced from a natural strut in the fabrication bay. Gillick and Winter admitted getting theirs from Chief Marchenko, although they were fuzzy on the details. Eskander, obviously, couldn't speak for himself any longer. Marchenko had cut the metal, polished it, then used a grinder to give the irregular shapes razor-sharp edges.

All of this without Sascha—Marchenko's department head—knowing anything about it.

"Some things can be excused in transdim, and some can't," Lincoln said. "If I had a brig, you'd be in it. Instead, I'm stripping you down to corporal. You will be restrained for every transdim dive, no matter how short, and you will *stay* restrained, no matter how lucid you may seem. Dismissed."

Marchenko hurried out of the wardroom.

Lincoln had knocked him down two full ranks, from E6 to E4. A hammer-blow to Marchenko's career, especially at his age.

Sascha braced herself—now it was her turn.

Lincoln didn't bother to hide her anger and frustration.

"I am promoting Corporal Zhen Smith to sergeant. He is now the auxiliary department chief." The captain pressed her pointer finger hard against the table. The first joint bent back so far it looked like it might break. "At the moment, Lieutenant Kerkhoffs, I don't have anyone I trust enough to replace you as engineering department head. That issue will be rectified the instant this mission is over. Until then, I suggest you spend your time focusing on your *job* and your *people* rather than on asking questions you've been told not to ask. Get out of my sight."

Sascha left the wardroom even faster than Marchenko had.

Lincoln was furious, and Lincoln was right—if Sascha hadn't been trying to solve puzzles, if she'd focused on her job, would she have caught Marchenko making the shivs? Would Eskander still be alive?

Questions that would forever remain a mystery.

50

"The op is so simple, a nutless monkey could do it in his sleep."

Sergeant Renee Jordan had such a way with words.

Nitzan Shamdi wondered, as he often did, if sergeants in the Purist Nation's Crusaders acted like sergeants in the Planetary Union's Raiders. Maybe sergeants were sergeants all over the galaxy. Maybe it had always been so.

He and the rest of Alpha Squad were TASHed up and packed into Ochthera-One's troop compartment, their rifles secured in brackets to the right of each seat. His team, Alpha-Two, was still down one member. From rear ramp to front, it was Nitzan, Beaver, Abshire, Bennett, an empty seat where Laior would have been, then Sergeant Jordan.

Abs was a boot, but he'd impressed everyone with his toughness. That bone-melder in the infirmary was no walk in the park. Abs' arm was so swollen from the process, Bennett was forced to widen his TASH's forearm to make room. As long as the guy could pull a trigger, that was all that really mattered.

Sands and Bennett had some kind of a past. Nitzan didn't know what history they shared, but it was clear the master sergeant relied on Bennett for important jobs. That was why Alpha-Two was the away team, and Alpha-One would fly backup.

Rear to front, Alpha-One was Mafi, Basara, Abeen, squad leader

Sarvacharya, an empty seat where Sui Jun should have been, and finally Akil Daniels, one of the BII pukes. Jun was in the infirmary. Nitzan had heard she was conscious, but all she could do was repeat the last two words anyone said to her. Whatever she'd seen in-dim, it had cooked her brain.

Her brain wasn't the only one that went rogue. Nitzan had come so close to dusting Gillick. The asshole pointed a shiv at Bethany Darkwater. Reason enough to kill him, but that hadn't been the only reason—something had *compelled* Nitzan to do it. Not a voice in his head, exactly, more like an emotional rush deep in his heart. *Bloodlust.* Bloodlust that hadn't been his. Not all of it, anyway.

Thinking back on that sensation, it scared him. He hadn't been in control. He'd succumbed to a devil on his shoulder, whispering in his ear. If not for Geezer Bennett, he would have sliced Gillick's throat.

Nitzan had never felt so powerless. The *Keeling*... it did things to people. This op got him off the ship for a few minutes, probably an hour at most, but he wanted off for good.

"Too bad Lieutenant Dork isn't with us," Mafi said. "We could all take cover behind his baloney pony."

Abeen and Basara laughed.

"Stow it, Mafi," Jordan said. "Everyone listen up. Ochthera-Two is flying standby, loaded with Sergeant Blanding and Bravo-One if we need backup. Master Sergeant Sands and Bravo-Two will be in the trench, ready to cover our landing if things go tits-up."

Nitzan wished Sands had been bumped up to platoon comman-der. Lieutenant Dork—a nickname Abshire came up with because he'd read somewhere that a *dork* was a whale's dick—was a blithering idiot. PXO Winter, second in command, was still recovering from a boot to the head.

"Warrant Daniels," Jordan said, "you have the floor."

The operative stood. With his cornrows hidden under the helmet, he had a bit of a babyface.

"We are well inside Purist Nation territorial borders," Daniels said. "Everything we do needs to be precise and intentional."

Nitzan was home, but he couldn't do anything about it. Even if he could kill his squadmates and seize control of the crawler, the *Keeling* would blow him to bits before he got far.

On top of that, he didn't know enough yet to make his mission worthwhile. He'd seen the atrium and the heartstone but didn't know what those things were or how they operated. He'd saved Bethany's life, and thanks to that, he knew she'd open up to him in the days to come. In addition, now he had a chance to find out what intel this Colonel Cooley had. Who knew how important it might be to the Nation?

"The ship we're boarding is a Tammilton MX series," Daniels said. "It's an in-system hauler, a little more than twice as wide as this crawler, a little less than twice as long. It's designed to carry standard cargo containers. The hold should be empty. Our package is Colonel Mac Cooley, BII. He should be alone. This is a cakewalk, people."

A red light came on in the troop compartment ceiling. That meant the pilot—Danielle Bang—was beginning her boarding approach.

"Attention, friendly fliers," Bang said on the squad channel, "the target is maintaining a steady course. Boarding should be as easy as pulling a train on Mafi's mom."

The platoon laughed. All except Mafi, who glowered behind his visor.

"Biggie, you're a cumstain," he said.

"Silence on the channel," Bang said. "Sergeant Jordan, get 'em ready to rip."

Jordan stood. "Raiders, arm up."

Everyone removed their rifle from its bracket.

"Check safety," Jordan said.

Nitzan did so.

"*Safety on, Sergeant*," he said in unison with his squadmates.

"Check barrel for obstructions," Jordan said.

Nitzan looked into the backblast mouth and down through the barrel. Unobstructed and clean as a whistle.

"*Barrel is clear, Sergeant.*" That chorus wasn't quite as unified.

"Lock and load," Jordan said. "Safeties on. I repeat, keep your safeties *on*."

Nitzan pulled a magazine from his rifle bracket. He had four more in his webbing. He'd loaded the mag himself, but still eyeballed the clear plastic to make sure it held a full 50-round load. He slotted it into the groove atop his rifle body, then gave the magazine a sharp slap to lock it home.

His HUD registered it, displaying 50 in the upper right corner.

"*Locked and loaded, Sergeant,*" came from every Raider.

Every Raider except Abeen.

"Magazine jam," he said.

Abeen—what a fuck-up.

"Team Leader Sarvacharya, help Abeen with his weapon," Jordan said. "The rest of you, up and make ready, fix weapons in jump position."

Nitzan stood, adrenaline flowing even though this was supposed to be an easy run. Of all the wonderful things a Raider got to do—and there were many—jumping out of a perfectly good voidcraft was at the top of the list.

"Twenty seconds," Bang said.

Nitzan pressed his rifle to his chest armor; the magnetic clamps at his right shoulder and left hip locked it firm.

"Sarv, status?" Jordan asked.

"Jam cleared," Sarvacharya said. "Alpha-One ready for deployment."

"Very well," Jordan said. "Alpha-Two, you will jump first and escort Daniels to the target. Alpha-One will deploy at a standard crossfire spacing of ninety degrees to provide cover. Alpha Squad, face aft."

Nitzan turned, faced the rear ramp.

"Ten seconds, my lovelies," Bang said.

The ramp lowered, exposing a window of star-speckled space.

The light turned from red to green.

"Time to fly," Jordan said. "Go, go, go!"

Nitzan took three running steps down the ramp and launched himself out of the crawler. He counted to five, then clacked his heels together three times. He felt the vibrations of his thrusters extending to form their thin-armed X.

Nitzan pointed his left foot down and left, sending him up and right. Beaver, the next out, would go right and level. Abshire would go right and down. Bennett would be last, following Nitzan's path, with Daniels close behind him.

Nitzan had done this enough times to know he had five or six seconds until Bennett called for the squad to form up. He took advantage of those seconds, gazing out into the glory of infinity.

Millions of stars.

The glittering ice of creation itself.

The *vastness* of it all, stretching out in distances the Human mind couldn't even conceive of, let alone comprehend.

And to think there were those who didn't believe High One existed. How could anyone see this and *not* believe?

The hauler was only a hundred meters away. Bang was bringing the crawler around. Nitzan saw Alpha-One—tiny at this distance—leaping out the open rear ramp and spreading out to form a firing line.

If the hauler tried to skedaddle, Bang would lock onto it with a STC tether—that wouldn't stop the hauler, but it would slow it down significantly.

"Alpha-Two, form up on point," Bennett said. "Shamdi, lead us in."

Nitzan accelerated toward the freighter, felt that grinding fear in the pit of his stomach every Raider feels upon approach. If the freighter was in unfriendly hands—and if it had active point-defense—he and his squad were sitting ducks. In a combat situation, Raiders usually weren't deployed until corruptors, blazers, and decoys filled the engagement area, and the LZ had been at least strafed if not punched full of holes. In a weird way, it was less dangerous to go exo in a guns-a-blazin' multi-ship battle than it was to approach a lone vessel in a police action—like this.

"Angling to the freighter's rear," Nitzan said.

"Copy," Bennett said. "We're covering."

Nitzan wasn't thrilled about being the first in line, but he understood. Bennett thought he was the team's best soldier. It was a compliment. Even spies have pride.

He closed in. Fifty meters and closing.

The crawler came around and rolled right, giving the top gunner an unobstructed angle. If shooting began, Alpha-One had a clear field of fire against the hauler's starboard side, Alpha-Two against the rear, and the crawler against the topside. All three elements could free-fire without fear of hitting each other.

There wasn't much to the hauler. A forward pilot cabin with actual windows, as opposed to a CIC buried deep within a warship's hull. The boxy cargo area could hold four forty-foot-long cargo containers in side-by-side stacks of two. A curvine compartment above the cargo hold, directional chem-thrusters at each rear corner. Countless micrometeoroid strikes had turned the hauler's once-white finish to a dirty gray.

Twenty-five meters out.

"Reversing thrust," Nitzan said.

"Copy," Bennett said. "Alpha-Two, decelerate to match point's velocity."

Nitzan tapped his feet together twice. The thrusters at the end of each arm reversed, pointing forward rather than aft, gently slowing his momentum as he closed in.

At the hauler's rear loading doors, a red light started to pulse. Below it, a man-sized airlock door swung inward.

"Abshire," Bennett said, "send in a bee."

"Aye-aye," Abshire said.

Nitzan slowed to a stop just starboard of the open airlock door. His thrusters didn't exactly match his motion to that of the hauler; he let loose intermittent microbursts to stay in place.

Using a bee was a rarity. In zones thick with STC fuckery, remote-controlled drones were worthless. Here, with no blazers or corruptors, the fire team could send one in to see if any armed surprises were waiting.

A window appeared in Nitzan's HUD. He saw himself from behind, his thruster arms extended, his rifle stock at his shoulder, backblast vent pointing behind him, barrel aimed toward the airlock in case someone was dumb enough to come out armed.

The fist-sized drone generating the picture zipped past him and through the open airlock door. In his HUD, the cargo hold looked empty, save for one man in a vacsuit, his arms wide with fingers splayed.

"That should be our package," Daniels said.

"Beaver, Abs, form up on Shamdi," Bennett said. "Standard clearing pattern."

Seconds later, Nitzan felt a gauntleted hand thump twice on his shoulder plate—Beaver, letting him know the team was in place.

Nitzan clacked his heels together three times. His extensions retracted, leaving his thrusters behind each shoulder blade and at each hip. That made maneuvering less responsive, but his extensions wouldn't get caught against doors or cause him issues in small spaces.

He drew in a sharp breath, held it for an instant, then thrust through the open airlock. Internal fakegrav caught him immediately— his feet hit the deck. He turned right, looking for targets, knowing Beaver would aim straight down the hold and Abshire would aim left. It was non-intuitive to look away from the only visible threat—the vacsuited person standing there—but that was how Raiders were trained.

"Clear," Nitzan said, seeing nothing in his area of responsibility.

Beaver and Abs called out the same.

Nitzan turned his back to the cargo hold bulkhead, aimed at the man that was supposedly the package. Bennett entered and moved toward the man, Daniels a step behind.

"Crawler-One, this is Alpha-Two lead," Bennett said. "Hauler cargo hold is secure."

Nitzan lowered his rifle.

Jordan's voice came back. "Copy that, Alpha-Two. We're here if you need us."

Daniels stayed a step behind Bennett. Smart. The operative was no stranger to small unit tactics.

The man they'd been sent to retrieve had the warm eyes of a helpful preacher, and a blond beard so thick it mushed up against the inside of his vacsuit visor. He and Basara could trade grooming tips.

"Y'all are a sight for sore eyes," the man said. "Colonel Mac Cooley at your service, but you can call me *Stone Balls*."

Stone Balls? Well, wasn't this asshole full of himself.

"I have to search you, Colonel," Bennett said.

Cooley raised his hands higher. "Have at it."

Bennett magclipped his rifle to his chest. He patted down Cooley's upper body, the motions steady and methodical. The old fossil was steady and methodical about everything.

"You look a little old for your rank," Cooley said. "What's your name?"

The old-timer patted down the left leg. "Bennett, sir." Then the right.

"Bennett," Cooley said. "*John* Bennett?"

"That's right." Bennett patted down Cooley's back, then stepped aside and again held his rifle in his hands. "He's clean."

"Colonel Cooley, your recognition code, please," Daniels said.

"Kilo, five, charlie, seven, seven, tango, romeo," he said. "Yours?"

"Kilo, golf, six, tango," Daniels said. "Please hold still while I do a retinal scan." He pulled a scanner from his webbing, stepped closer and pointed it through the man's visor. "Identity confirmed. Colonel, do you have any exomobility devices?"

Cooley's eyes narrowed. "I got escape wings up in the pilot cabin. Why? Are you asking me to fly myself back to your crawler?"

"I'd be happy to tow you, sir," Daniels said. "If you'd prefer that."

"Sport, there must be some confusion," Cooley gestured to the ship around him. "My intel is embedded in this hauler. We need to take the entire thing with us."

Daniels looked around the cargo hold. "Please tell me you're joking, sir."

"No Joke," Cooley said. "It's got to come with us, and right now."

Nitzan's spirits sagged. The entire hauler? Would it even *fit* in the *Keeling?*

"Fucking hell," Abshire said.

Cooley clapped his hands twice.

"Chop-chop, Daniels," he said. "We don't have long before a couple of patrol ships carrying Crusaders come after me, and I'd rather not be around when they arrive."

Nitzan closed his eyes. Would he have to fight his own countrymen yet again?

"Fuck," Daniels said. "Crawler-one, this is Alpha-Two adjacent. Radio back to actual—we have a problem."

51

The first time Anne met Mac Cooley, she'd been all of nine years old. He'd been twenty-two, perhaps twenty-three, already a lieutenant and a rising star of BII, so much so that the director himself—Anne's father —invited him to a family dinner. Even at a young age, Anne thought Cooley an insufferable jackass.

That impression hadn't softened with time.

"Why are we discussing this?" Cooley looked around the wardroom, as if asking each person in turn. "My mission was ordered by President McKinney himself. Get my hauler in here and let's vacate the premises, post haste."

When he'd come aboard and started making demands, Lincoln put XO Ellis at the helm and called an emergency meeting with Anne, Kerkhoffs, Hasik, Chief Sung and Lieutenant Lindros.

The meticulously planned operation—*Anne's* operation—was in danger of going down in flames.

"We're not a carrier," Lincoln said. "Your superiors were fully aware of that when they sent us, so they clearly didn't expect us to retrieve an entire hauler. Where do you think we're going to put it, Colonel?"

Cooley was still wearing his vacsuit, the collapsed helmet hanging against his back.

"Your flight bay, Captain. It will fit."

He had the same friendly eyes Anne remembered from way back when, now with far more creases at the corners. The "friendly" bit was as fake as lab-grown leather. Cooley could dial in any emotion he liked, any time he liked. His thick beard, the same blond as his matted, shoulder-length hair, was new. At least to her. He would have blended in with dock workers or long haulers just about anywhere in Human space.

"Flight bay's full," Chief Sung said. "We can barely fit our two crawlers in there."

"Then *ditch the crawlers*." Cooley raised his hands in exasperation. "I barely got out of the mining colony alive. MIM agents were sniffing around. That's why the extraction date got pushed up. I was within hours of being arrested and put in an inquisitor's torture chamber. By now, they've put out a system-wide alert for my hauler. We need to get out of here, pronto."

MIM—the Nation's equivalent to Fleet's BII. The Union might have a technological edge in the war, but MIM, sometimes known as the Cloister, had been running circles around BII for years.

"My top priority is the safety of this ship," Lincoln said. "If I even sniff Purist forces coming toward us, we're gone, with or without your hauler. So get your intel off of it—*pronto*."

Cooley reached inside his vacsuit, came out with a cigar and a lighter. The pompous jerk was going to spark up, like this was some photo shoot?

"The hauler *is* the intel," he said. "Some of it is hidden in the curvine array. Some is embedded in the airlock between the pilot cabin and the cargo area, some in the fakegrav plating. Some is hard-encrypted in the ship's data processor. *All* of it is rigged to smoke itself if not removed correctly. I need time to properly extract it."

Kerkhoffs leaned on the table. "How long will that take?"

"At least twenty-four standard hours." He lit the cigar. "I can't tell you what the intel is. None of you have clearance. What I can tell you is that if I don't get my information back to Fleet, we're going to lose this war. No question, *we lose*. So, Captain, you better reevaluate your priorities and do it fast."

Lincoln and Anne exchanged a glance. Could Cooley's intel be that critical? Yes, it could. He'd been embedded in the Purist Nation for over a year.

"I'm intel chief on this ship," Anne said. "I'm in charge of the intelligence aspect of this mission. You can tell me privately what you have, and I'll help prioritize our actions."

Cooley rolled his eyes. "You are *not* in charge of the intel aspect. I am. In fact, if I choose to be, I'm technically in charge of this ship's entire intelligence department. Right now, I do not choose to be." He blew a smoke ring. "I know about transdim. Figure out how to get my hauler back to Union space before a Purist patrol comes looking for it."

Anne's anger swirled like the smoke expanding through the ward-room. Cooley didn't give a damn about how much she'd sacrificed to be here, how hard she'd worked to earn her rank and her position.

He knew about transdim. What else did he know about the ship? Was Cooley one of Epperson's trusted people, like Hasik was? Like Anne was *not*?

She felt it, ever so light, barely there at all—a tapping at the base of her skull. Anne recognized it as an echo of her former self reacting to this unexpected insult. Nothing more, nothing less. She controlled it, then let it go.

Anne Lafferty controlled her emotions; emotions did not control Anne Lafferty.

"Maybe we could tow it," Kerkhoffs said. "Drag it through transdim with us?"

All eyes turned to Hasik. He looked pale, as might be expected of someone who'd been minutes from death only a few hours earlier. Artificial blood had him back on his feet, although Hammersmith had given him a crutch and told him to avoid putting pressure on the wounded leg.

"Towing won't work," he said. "We've run experiments. In every one, the thing we towed was lost. *Lost* as in *never to be seen again*."

Cooley gestured to the wardroom bulkheads, the ceiling. "We're inside a superstructure that's attached to the hull. How can that make it through but something towed cannot?"

So, there were limits to Cooley's knowledge of the *Keeling*. That was something, at least.

"The ship generates a near-field effect, but only for things in direct contact with the hull," Hasik said. "If we secure the hauler to the hull, that might work."

"*Might* work?" Cooley shook his head. "I'm not authorizing that. Ditch the crawlers, get my hauler in your landing bay, and let's skedaddle."

An expensive option, considering crawlers cost around thirty million each. Compared to potentially losing the war, though, it was a pittance.

"We need them," Lindros said. "The *Ishlangu* rendezvous is in unclaimed space. If we run into trouble, we need the combat flexibility the Ochtheras provide."

"Fuck *flexibility*," Cooley said. "You want the Ochtheras? Then strap *them* to the hull."

Lincoln glanced at Sung. "Will the hauler fit in the pouch?"

"If I break down the maintenance racks, yeah," Sung said. "It'll take about ninety minutes."

"You have forty-five," Lincoln said. "We dive in sixty. Grab anyone you need. Kerkhoffs, assist him. Store the rack parts anywhere you can, but make sure they're labeled. When the hauler is off our hands, I want them reassembled ASAP. Go."

Sung and Kerkhoffs hurried out of the wardroom.

Lincoln again faced Cooley. "Do we need to take the hauler apart to get your intel?"

"Not if the crawler tech crew assists me," he said. "We take the embedded bits out one at a time, and she'll fly just fine. At the rendezvous, I might even set her on autopilot and send her in a random direction. Let those Cloister bastards chase their tail for a while. Look, Captain, I can get my end of the job done in twenty-four hours, easy—as long as no one goes crazy and starts smashing things. I've been told that's an issue on this boat."

Cooley knew about the hallucinations. He didn't hold all the cards, but he held more than Anne did.

"Lindros, get the crawlers out of the pouch," Lincoln said. "Hasik, figure out how to secure them to the hull so they survive transdim. If the crawlers aren't secured in forty minutes, we're leaving them behind. Go."

Hasik hurriedly hobbled out. Lindros followed, leaving Anne alone with the captain and Cooley.

Anne had to admit, Lincoln made decisions fast and she did not vacillate. She was a captain for a reason.

"Colonel," Lincoln said, "I strongly suggest you read Major Lafferty in on your intel. You know a thing or two about *Keeling*, but there's a big difference between being briefed on it and being *here*. Bad things happen in transdim. If something happens to you, consider what would be lost if you don't make it back to report."

An understanding smile crinkled Cooley's friendly eyes.

"That's good counsel, Captain," he said. "I'll share what I can."

That seemed to satisfy Lincoln. She stood.

"Then I'll leave you to it," she said. "Colonel, I'm doing everything in my power to accommodate your mission. I hope it's worth the risk."

She left the wardroom.

Anne sat silently.

Cooley puffed on his cigar, making her wait a few moments before speaking.

"Look at you," he said. "You've come a long way since we first met."

"Thank you, sir. I completed some demanding missions."

"I bet you did." He rolled his cigar between finger and thumb. "How old are you?"

"I'm twenty-six."

"Twenty-six, and already a major." He nodded to himself. "Helluva career track you're on. And you're the intel chief on a classified vessel? Pretty big assignment." He took a puff, let out another smoke ring. "Did your daddy arrange it for you, you little shit?"

The tapping hit so hard her vision blurred. The itch, the *urge*, it blossomed, *exploded*, filled every bit of her brain.

"Major Lafferty, I asked you a question."

Anne focused on her breathing. She wouldn't let this man yank her thoughts around and destroy all the work she'd put in.

"I earned this position, Colonel."

"I'm sure you did. I'll share what I can about *my* mission, Major, but first, I'm awful hungry. Go tell the galley to whip me up something." He pointed his cigar at the coffee urn. "And have them brew me a fresh pot. That's not too *demanding* of a task for you, I hope."

Being spoken to like that? She was a *major*. She was the *intel chief* on this ship.

"Yes, sir," she said. "I'll get right on it."

Anne stepped out of the wardroom. She could have used the wardroom comm to call the galley, but she needed to get away from that smoke. Get away from Cooley.

She hadn't felt like this since...

...since Eden.

But she was better now.

She could control it. She could make the tapping go away, make the *itch* subside.

She was better now.

She was better.

52

"Hey, Bennett," Beaver shouted. "The stuff that goes on in this ship... would you say it's the craziest stuff you've seen outside of combat?"

The card game came to a stop. Beaver, Abs, and Shamdi looked at John, as if he might say, *no, not at all—I've been on ships that make mass hallucinations, fratricide, and jumping into other fucking dimensions look like going down to your local for a pint.*

"Yeah, Beaver," John said. "I'd say this is the craziest stuff I've seen outside of combat. Queen of hearts."

John tossed his card. It rose up, spinning slightly, and hovered there, started flapping like a piece of frying bacon.

Nothing crazy about this place. Nope, not at all.

"Hope you've got better aim with your rifle." Abshire pantomimed picking up a card off Muttonhead Mafi's midriff and putting it atop the five of hearts resting on Mafi's sternum. "Because you suck at throwing cards."

John stared at his hovering, sizzling card. "So you're telling me the queen of hearts is *not* floating in mid-air?"

Now it even *smelled* like bacon.

Shamdi tapped the stack of cards on Mafi's chest. "Yours is right on top, Geezer. You can't see it?"

And just like that, the sizzling card—which smelled *delicious—*

was gone. John's card had actually landed on Mafi's midriff. Abshire had moved it.

Beaver put down the ace of spades. "Got you *nailed*, Bennett!"

Holy hell was the kid bad at this game.

Mafi started to lurch against the canvas restraints holding him tight to the bunk. Shamdi put a hand on Mafi's chest—more to keep the cards from shifting than to comfort the man.

"Hey, Mafi," Shamdi said, "you looking for your watch, buddy?"

"That cumstain took my watch. He took my—"

"He gave it back," Abshire said. "Your watch is in your locker, next to your toothbrush. We checked on it, ol' buddy ol' pal."

Mafi stopped struggling.

"Thanks," he said, then returned to his status as a non-moving substitute table.

Shamdi played the four of hearts.

Abshire played the nine of hearts. "Wow, Beaver, good thing you took that trick with the most-powerful card in the game, amiright?"

"Scream, aim, and fire, motherfucker." Beaver gathered up the cards. "That's how this dog hunts."

Somewhere in Raider Land, a man let out a long, haunting moan. John wondered what the man had seen. Then John remembered he didn't want to know. Not one bit.

Abshire stared off in the direction of that moan.

"Why'd they do this to us, Bennett?" he asked. "I volunteered, you know? I didn't get drafted. I worked hard in boot. I wanted to serve the Union. I didn't do anything wrong, yet I wind up in the *Crypt*. Do they know what this place does to us? Do they even care?"

They was the common pronoun for *the Admiralty*. The people who pulled the strings and sent sailors and Raiders to die. The people who'd filled this ship of nightmares with the guilty and the innocent alike.

"I don't know, Abs," John said. "I just go where they tell me to go."

John hadn't known exactly what he was getting into, but he knew he was signing up for a lethal deployment option. Several Raiders on their first-ever deployment had done no such thing. Abshire hadn't chosen this. Neither had Sui Jun, who was still in the infirmary, still repeating the last two words anyone said to her and saying nothing more. Neither had Delaker Oneida, whose Raider career was over almost as soon as it began. Neither had Fred Abeen, Beaver, Bishop, Chennault, or Ochthera engineer-gunner Silja Lehtonen—they were all fresh out of boot, and as far as John could tell, had done nothing worthy of being entombed.

"We're here because we're fucking *awesome*," Beaver said. "That's why."

Abshire shrugged, tried to play off his emotions. He changed the subject.

"Seems like everyone is handling transdim better on the return trip," he said. "Forty-four hours in and only a couple of small fights so far."

"And a whale's penis," Shamdi said.

"And a whale's penis," Abs agreed. "But this ain't nothing compared to that trip in. It's like people are getting used to it, you know?"

That was one way to look at things. Almost half the platoon was restrained, either by choice or because Lindros ordered it before he stripped down and ran laps around Raider Land until he himself was restrained by Sands and PXO Winter.

Winter's troubles on the dive in had, so far, not manifested on the return trip. She was fine. She'd tried to get John to slip away somewhere to screw, because she wanted to know what it was like to fuck while in transdim. John avoided her. No way did he want to do that. He'd just hallucinated playing-card bacon—what if, in the middle of a good bonk, Winter turned into the rat-shrimp-thing, or a giant trout, or some other mad shit like that?

Sorry, ma'am, I don't fuck fish.

"Neither do I," Abs said. "Not that there's anything wrong with it."

John looked at him. "Did I say the part about fish-fucking out loud?"

"You did," Abs said.

The men looked at the cards remaining in their hands. Beaver took the trick, so it was his lead. He was in no hurry. The point of the game was to pass the time, so no one really cared.

"It's quiet," Shamdi said.

Abshire nodded. "Like Christmas Eve, you know? That kind of quiet. With all the snow."

"I fucking *love* Christmas," Beaver shouted. "Maybe when we surface, we'll get presents. I fucking love presents."

The skin of Mafi's face turned crimson. Blood-smeared horns burst through his temples, cracking bone, spilling wet-red on his pillow. The big man lifted his head. Blazing orange eyes stared out at John.

"You know you won't get presents tomorrow," Mafi said. "You know all these kids are going to die screaming for their mommies. They'll beg you to save them and you won't. Because you can't. You never could. You know they're going to piss themselves, shit themselves. That they'll—"

John winced—Shamdi had punched him in the shoulder.

"What was that for?"

"Play your card," Shamdi said

John looked at Mafi's chest. On it lay a five of spades, topped by a ten of spades, topped by a jack of spades.

"Maybe I should have saved my ace," Beaver said.

"S'matter?" Shamdi waved his fingers in front of John's face. "You seeing something weird again?"

Devil-Mafi smiled wide. A too-thin, too-long tongue slid out of his mouth and into his left nostril. It wormed around in there, struggling to get deeper before sliding back into Mafi's mouth.

"Nope," John said. "I don't see nothing at all."

Devil-Mafi became Table-Mafi. All was back to normal. But what Devil-Mafi had said...

Goosebumps ran along John's arms.

"Game over," he said. "Everyone in their rack. We need all the rest we can get."

Beaver laughed, shook his head. "The dangerous part of the mission's over, Bennett. We're home free. Don't quit now, I'm winning."

Beaver was, in fact, not winning.

"I'm out, too," Shamdi said. "I'm supposed to go chat with Bethany before we surface."

Beaver and Abs busied themselves cleaning up the cards. They didn't say anything, but neither did they hide their lascivious grins.

"Fuck you guys," Shamdi said. "Fuckin' pervs."

Beaver and Abshire started laughing. Abs made a gesture of locking his mouth and throwing away the key.

"We didn't say nothing," Beaver shouted. "Nothing at all."

Shamdi glared at them.

The fire team—as well as the rest of the platoon—had learned that making any suggestive or humorous comments about a certain xeno department ensign would not end well for anyone. Tough Guy Shamdi had a soft spot for her. He didn't take kindly to anything he perceived as an insult.

"In your bunks." John glanced at the brass clock-timer on the bulkhead. "We're four hours out from realspace. Not you, Sham—go do your thing, but don't stay too long. Tomorrow... tomorrow might not go as smooth as we hope."

Shamdi stared back. "Bad feeling?"

John nodded.

"I hear you," Shamdi said. "I won't be long."

If Shamdi didn't feel the danger himself, he recognized someone who did. It was a bond that unblooded Abshire and Beaver couldn't understand. Not yet, anyway.

Shamdi left the berth.

John climbed into his bunk. He closed his eyes, praying he would see no more insane stuff. When he opened them, a rat-shrimp-thing stared down at him through the now-translucent copper ceiling.

"Not tonight, Margaret," John said. "I've got a headache."

And with that, John Bennett rolled over and went to sleep.

53

Susannah had never been a drug-head. She'd always looked down her nose at those types. Always judged them. But if what drug-heads experienced was a teeny tiny fraction of what she saw while in-dim? Then maybe she'd been missing out all along.

She dusted off the crate where Nitzan would sit, even though she'd dusted it off three times already. The little motes that kicked up flashed in the light.

So many pretty colors.

She'd seen rainbow snakes slithering around two or three times during the two-day dive out from the Purist Nation, but they weren't quite as frightening as they'd been at first. They were actually kind of cute.

The colors and the snakes were interesting, but what Susannah really wanted was the silent room with the light. That, and the voice. *The voice.*

High One himself, talking to her. Did he speak in riddles? Maybe. If so, Susannah figuring out those riddles was all part of His plan. High One had *everything* planned out, timed to the last nanosecond. He gave you experiences to make you stronger. He showed you lessons if your eyes were open to learning, to *believing*. He helped you through your troubled moments, all to get you to one particular point where you had to make a *choice*.

If you chose correctly—and you kept passing His tests—you might someday be by his side in body and soul.

Was Nitzan Shamdi a test? Susannah thought so. He was a good man. A Purist. He was interested in her. *Very* interested. Was Shamdi a test to see if Susannah had truly given up her past ways?

Maybe. Probably. If so, she was failing that test.

She liked Nitzan. She really did. But she wasn't *attracted* to him. Not in that way. No matter how many times she tried to talk herself into it, she just wasn't.

Maybe things were about to change. Only a few hours left before entering realspace to rendezvous with the *Ishlangu* and head back to Union territory.

Maybe Nitzan would walk into the storage room. Maybe Susannah would close the sphincter, so no one could see in. Maybe Nitzan would look wonderful and sexy in a way he hadn't yet. Maybe Susannah would hallucinate, and Nitzan would be full of beautiful colors, or maybe he'd look like... like...

...like Melanie.

Susannah slapped herself, hard. She did it again, even harder.

Her face stung. Her hand stung.

That was wrong. *Wrong.* She wasn't going back to those ways. She wasn't. When Nitzan walked in, she was going to rip his clothes off and have at him. She would—

Someone stepped into the compartment, but it wasn't Nitzan Shamdi.

"I saw your meathead boyfriend on his way here," Anne Lafferty said. "I told him to go fuck around somewhere else."

She looked almost like a different person. Her wide eyes danced with glee.

"Ensign Darkwater, I think it's time you and I had a little chat."

Lafferty reached out and stroked the sphincter's smooth surface—it sealed shut, trapping Susannah inside with her.

54

What a slobbering mess. Not like Olivia. Olivia had been stronger. Darkwater wasn't like Olivia, or like...

...like Boomer...

...or the nanny...

...Sam Yannis...

...Wanda Hinson...

...or that stranger in the car...

Anne gave her body a shake, chasing those memories away.

"Major? Did... did you hear me?"

The slobbering mess was talking. Ensign Bethany Darkwater, sitting in the tiny storage room, her back against the bulkhead, knees to her chest, her arms wrapped tight around them.

"I got distracted," Anne said.

Who wouldn't be distracted with this tapping in their head, with a resurgent itch bringing back memories Anne had thought long-since buried, like they'd been dropped in a deep pothole that got filled in and paved over.

"Say it again," Anne said.

Darkwater nodded. "I will, Major. But... may I ask you to put down the knife?"

Anne looked at her right hand. Sure enough, she held a copper shiv. Black electrical tape around the bottom made for a handle.

Chief Marchenko said he didn't remember making the shivs, but Anne had found a small note of his with five bloody thumbprints on it. Marchenko had sliced his thumb after completing each blade, marked the paper to show his progress. He didn't remember the note, either. Anne had kept it—along with the shiv she'd found under Marchenko's mattress—for herself, and reported to Lincoln that only three such weapons existed. The shivs used by Gillick, Winter, and Eskander had already been melted down.

One shiv, though, remained missing.

Anne meant to find it during the two-day return dive, but she must have forgotten. It was hard to remember things because of transdim, and because that bully Cooley kept giving her busy work meant for specs, not for a goddamn *Major*, not for a goddamn *intel chief*.

Cooley was asleep. He'd bunked with the XO. While he was out, while Anne could actually *think*, she knew she needed to question Darkwater. Darkwater, who *wasn't* Darkwater.

Anne didn't remember pulling the shiv.

There wasn't any blood on it. Not yet.

No harm, no foul.

Anne slid the shiv in her coveralls, between a flap of canvas she'd turned into a sheath. Electrical tape on that, too. The stuff came in handy. A sheath was important, because details mattered.

"Thank you, Major Lafferty," Darkwater said. "My answer is *no*, I am not a purist spy."

If she was, Anne could kill her now. Take some time with it. Two hours until they came out of transdim. Around half the crew was sedated or restrained. People screamed all the time on this looney bin of a warship. Would anyone hear Darkwater scream?

With a single swipe of her hand, Darkwater wiped away both tears and snot.

"I'm *not* a Purist spy," she said. "I swear it."

"Because a spy would never tell a lie. Isn't that right, Ensign? I'm sure you're as honest as one can be."

Darkwater looked scared. *So* scared. She trembled. Anne could smell her fear. There was something compelling about it, something... intoxicating.

Tap, tap, tap...

Oh, that clutching need, that all-consuming *heat*...

So easy to make it go away.

Anne shook her head, hard, clearing away those thoughts. She was better now.

She was better.

"I'm telling you the truth," Darkwater said. "I'm *horrible* at lying. I really am, Major, I really am."

Anne felt calmness course through her, felt it wash away the urges. She'd been upset, but she had a job to do. The security of the ship was *her* responsibility—not Cooley's. If Darkwater was a Purist spy and Anne didn't find out for sure, she would fail Captain Lincoln. She'd fail her crewmates. She'd fail her father.

Anne couldn't allow that to happen.

Darkwater was going to spill.

Anne squatted, resting her butt on her heels. That put her almost at eye level with Darkwater. Tears glistened on the ensign's cheeks. A bit of snot glimmered on her upper lip.

"I see," Anne said. "You're terrible at lying. Fair enough. Were you *good* at it when you worked that run between Jupiter and Saturn?"

Darkwater shook her head. "No! I was terrible at it then, too! I couldn't even barter, because everyone knew when I was bluffing. I would ... I..."

If Anne could have controlled her grin, the ensign might have gone on longer, but that didn't matter now.

"I guess I need to work on my poker face," Anne said. "Do you know what gave you away?"

Darkwater blinked against fresh tears. She looked more terrified than ever.

"Because... I don't have a pilot history on my record?"

Well, how about that? The old ensign was all kinds of smart.

Anne slowly drew the copper shiv out of its makeshift sheath.

"I'll give you one chance to tell me your real name. If I have to ask twice, you won't be happy."

Darkwater stared at the weapon. She opened her mouth to speak. She closed it. Anne heard the woman's teeth chattering.

Anne grabbed her short hair and *yanked*, cranking Darkwater's head to the side, exposing her neck.

"Susannah Rossi! *I'm Susannah Rossi!*"

An electric rush coursed through Anne, from her hair to her toes and back again.

"Are you a Purist, Rossi?"

The kill would be justified. That would show Cooley, show him good. Anne would be a hero—*again*. Daddy would be so proud.

"Yes, I'm a Purist, but *please* don't kill me, I—"

Anne's hair-filled fist shook Rossi's head.

"Are you a spy, Rossi? Tell me now or I'll cut out your tongue."

"*Yes, but not for the Purists! I'm a spy for Admiral Bock!*"

Anne froze, her fingers still locked in the ensign's hair.

Bock?

Tap, tap, TAP...

The itch tickled in Anne's soul. The want. The *need*.

So easy to make it vanish, but Daddy would want to know this information.

Anne let go of the ensign's hair.

"Say that again, Rossi. Quietly. Slowly."

Darkwater/Rossi drew in a ragged breath, her mussed up hair framing her tear-streaked cheeks.

"I got attacked," she said. "I fought back. The man who attacked me, he's... he's dead. Admiral Bock told me if I didn't pretend to be Bethany Darkwater and find out what the *Keeling* was all about, I'd spend the rest of my life in jail."

This was big. Anne grabbed a plastic crate and sat.

"Admiral Adrienne Bock told you to spy on this ship?"

Darkwater/Rossi nodded.

It could be bullshit. Then again, Epperson kept a tight grip on things. It was no secret the other admirals didn't even know what the *Keeling* was, other than a black hole into which Fleet poured a black budget. Epperson reported directly to President McKinney, and *only* to McKinney, a fact that infuriated the other admirals.

"How do you get information to Bock?"

"I don't know yet," Darkwater/Rossi said. "I was told to learn all I can. They'll figure out how to contact me later."

It made sense. Bock wanted to know what was going on. She'd seen an opportunity to put her own person aboard and jumped at it, even though the details had yet to be worked out. Maybe the contact attempt would come when the mission was—

The 1MC sounded.

"This is the XO. General quarters. We are ahead of schedule and will enter realspace in ten minutes. Vacsuits on. Release everyone who appears calm from restraints. Those that remain agitated, release them the moment we surface. Medics, immediately begin administering counter-doses for those who were sedated. That is all."

Darkwater/Rossi sat there, shivering.

"Here's what's going to happen," Anne said. "You will return to the atrium. You will tell no one about this. You're in a lot of trouble, but remember that I'm the intel chief of this boat. If you help me with my investigation, I'll protect you. You'll come out of this smelling like a rose. Understand?"

Darkwater/Rossi nodded madly, like her head was on a loose spring.

Anne stood and ran her hand along the sphincter door. It opened with a huff of air, bringing with it the sounds of sailors running through the passageway outside. The ship was coming awake.

"Go," Anne said.

Darkwater/Rossi was through the door like a recoilless round, out and gone the same instant.

Admiral versus Admiral.

Anne could pick and choose how to benefit.

Bethany/Susannah Darkwater/Rossi would be the game's first pawn.

55

Trav shifted in place. His vacsuit pinched in the crotch. He turned his body slightly, trying to hide his action behind the command station, then grabbed a handful of the material and gave it two quick tugs.

There, that was better.

Lincoln lifted the command station's handset and spoke on the 1MC. "This is the captain. We will exit transdim shortly. Release restrained crew and report to general quarters. Man battle stations torpedo. Upon surfacing, man battle stations guns. That is all." She returned the handset to its cradle. "Xeno, prepare to surface."

"Aye-aye, Captain," Hasik said. "Preparing to bring us out of transdim."

Hasik still refused to use the dive/surface lingo. He picked up his sound-powered phone to the atrium. Hasik looked like he hadn't slept for the entire two-day return trip. There were smears on his glasses he hadn't bothered to wipe away, and behind the lenses, visible bags under his eyes. What was left of his thin, gray hair stuck up in clumps. His vacsuit was unfastened, arms tied around his waist. His crutch leaned against the xeno loft railing.

Trav faced forward. Almost done with the return trip, and he'd seen no bugs. Nor had he heard the voice of Dear Old Meemaw. He didn't know why he hadn't experienced those things this time, but he was grateful.

"Signals," Lincoln said, "I want confirmation on *Ishlangu* the moment you have it."

Sara Ellison manned the signals station.

"Aye-aye, Captain," she said. "Will confirm *Ishlangu* the moment I have it."

Trav glanced back to the intel loft where Lafferty topped the steps and slid into her seat. While Hasik looked exhausted, Anne radiated energy. She was obviously fired up to leave transdim behind. Trav could relate. *Everyone* could relate.

Akil Daniels and Jester Gillick were already seated in front of her. Gillick had a metal brace that ran from his forehead down his nose and across both cheeks, smears of nanocyte salve visible beneath. The skin beneath it was yellow and purple, remnants of Nitzan Shamdi's headbutt and the two surgeries that followed.

There was a reason smart sailors didn't mess with Raiders.

"Darsat," Lincoln said, "activate system and begin DTR sweep."

"Activating darsat, aye-aye, Captain." Carmel Waldren manned the darsat station. "Commencing DTR sweep."

Lincoln waited for the system to do its work.

"Darsat activated," Waldren said. "Reaslpace detection strength is weak. Detection radius is fluctuating between five-zero and one-one-five kilometers."

Lincoln gave the command slate a small thump of frustration. She wanted a larger range for darsat-to-realspace detection, but the mercurial fates of transdim weren't allowing it.

"Realspace contact acquired," Waldren said. "Bearing, port zero-three-zero. Elevation... can't lock it down. I... contact is lost, Captain."

"Get it back," Lincoln said. "Pilot, turn thirty degrees to port, maintain vertical plane."

Waldren's brief contact blip was likely the *Ishi*. Lincoln directed the *Keeling* toward it, hoping to get closer. Trav felt only the slightest pull of inertia as the ship angled to port. In the orb, the Mud rotated to starboard.

He hoped he'd get to see Vesna again. Even if she thought he was a coward, she was a link to the past and happier times. He wanted to tell her about the briefing with Epperson. Would she agree Trav's trial had been a sham? Or would she think he was getting what he deserved? Vesna's opinion mattered. It mattered a lot.

That trial. A sentence of two years on the *Keeling*. Two weeks down, a hundred and two weeks to go. How long until Trav could see Molly again? He had no idea.

"Realspace contact acquired," Waldren said. "Bearing, port zero-two-five, our directional change has it angling toward zero-zero-zero. Range... nine-zero kilometers."

"Same contact?" Lincoln asked.

"Unknown," Waldren said. "Gravitational signature unavailable."

It was almost assuredly the same contact, but Waldren's job wasn't to make assumptions. If she couldn't identify a ship, or even a ship's rough classification, she wasn't going to say otherwise.

Lincoln rested her elbows on the command slate, shifted toward Trav. He'd learned that gesture meant *I have something for your ears only*. He mirrored her posture. Their shoulders touched.

"Ninety kilometers is closer than I'd like," Lincoln said quietly. "I'd prefer to be a hundred and fifty klicks away, at least. That little bit of extra distance gives you more reaction time if something goes wrong."

Trav nodded. The captain was still teaching, still sharing. Every bit helped.

Lincoln stood straight. "Very well, darsat. Any other contacts?"

"Negative," Waldren said. "Contact signal is weak and fading. I may lose it again."

The *Ishlangu* would be the only ship there to greet them. It had been scheduled to arrive at these coordinates the day before, allowing it time to recharge its punch-drive. The *Keeling* didn't use its punch-drive in the alternate dimensional membrane, so it was fully charged. As soon as *Keeling* came out of transdim, the two ships would punch for Union space. Good old normal, mundane, every-day faster-than-light travel.

Lincoln put her elbows on the slate, leaned toward Trav. Again, he mirrored her.

"What would your call be, XO? Try to get more distance before we surface?"

He'd already thought that through.

"Not while DTR strength is weak," he said. "I'd rather come out now while we know where the contact is."

Lincoln nodded. "I agree." She stood straight, gripped his shoulder. "See, XO? You're starting to think like—"

Her scream tore through the CIC. She backpedaled so fast she smacked hard against the intel loft railing.

"*Get it away!*"

Lips curled, eyes wide, Lincoln stared at the command slate.

Trav stepped toward her, his hands out to his sides, his fingers splayed.

"Captain, it's not real."

"Make *sure*," she said. "Get if *off* of there. Make sure."

Trav waved his arm above the command slate.

"See? Nothing there. It's not real."

Lincoln closed her eyes tight, opened them again.

"It's gone," she said. "It's gone."

The fear in her voice. What had she seen?

Trav glanced around the CIC. Every pair of eyes stared back. Even the chiefs—Erickson, Cat Brown, Alex Plait, Dardanos Leeds—looked shaken. In an instant, the crew was questioning Lincoln's stability, was afraid for what might come next.

"Attend to your duties," Trav snapped.

Heads faced stations.

"Xeno," Lincoln said, her voice sharp, "bring us out of transdim. *Right now.*"

She didn't sound like her calm, cold self. She sounded like a person who'd witnessed something unspeakable and was trying hard to keep her shit together.

As far as Trav knew, Lincoln had suffered no hallucinations on this patrol—until now. Maybe she had and was good at hiding them, but if so, they'd been nothing like this one.

"Aye-aye, Captain," Hasik said. "Bringing us out of transdim."

The orb filled with the multicolored static that made the CIC look like a dance club full of revelers wearing matching coveralls.

"We're back in realspace," Hasik said.

"Rebooting darsat," Waldren said.

Ellison sat up like a shot. "Distress signals from *Ishlangu*! They're under attack!"

Lincoln rushed to her seat. "XO, sound general quarters. ECM, prep standard decoy." She fastened her harness. "Weps, load blazer torpedo in tube one, Mark16s in tubes two, three, and four. Darsat, I'm blind, get me eyes, now!"

A crew's worst nightmare—a friendly ship in trouble and they couldn't see a thing.

"Loading torpedoes, aye," Brown said. "Gunners report visual of a damaged Union warship, eleven o'clock high."

"Signals," Lincoln said, "I need to talk to *Ishi*."

"Can't reach them, sir," Ellison said.

"Darsat contact," Waldren said. "It's *Ishlangu*, grav-sig verified. Bearing, port zero-one-four. Elevation, one-one-five. Range eight-five kilometers. She's launched at least three decoys. The local STC field is soup."

Trav's pulse hammered in his eyes and throat. It was the battle at Asteroid X7 all over again. *Soup*—the local space-time reality was warped and twisted, bent and wavering enough to invalidate any digital or quantum data. The *Keeling* had surfaced into a zone of utter STC fuckery.

The orb's colored static blinked out. Distance rings and rage lines appeared, along with a blue icon labeled *Ishlangu*.

"Visual acquired," Ellison said. "*Ishlangu* showing heavy damage."

"Send to command slate," Lincoln said.

The course chart that had been on the slate vanished, replaced by an image of the *Ishlangu*, vibrating and wavering from the effects of space-time manipulation. One chem-thruster firing, the other broken, twisted, and cold. A ragged hole starboard amidships. A shredded, deep gouge on the bow armor, venting atmosphere.

"Two new darsat contacts," Waldren said. "Identities unknown."

She read off the angles and ranges as she placed them in the orb. Two red icons, no labels, port zero-two-zero low and port zero-three-five low, both just over three hundred kilometers away.

Ishi was engaged two-to-one. There was no way she could perform a straight run needed to enter punch-space without taking heavy enemy fire. Give *any* decent gunner a target like that and they could land nine out of ten salvos inside a twenty-second span. And if *Ishi* got hit during the run? Its approach profile might skew enough that when it hit the window, it would rip into a thousand pieces.

Entering punch-space was threading a big needle—easy as could be, unless someone was shaking your arm the whole time.

"Labeling new contacts *Zulu* and *Yankee*," Waldren said. "Grav-signatures acquired, both match Chanda-class Purist Nation corvette."

"Missiles inbound," Ellison said. "Salvo of ten, port-bow-low, salvo of five at port-bow-low. ETA thirty-two seconds."

Trav thumbed his stopwatch.

In the orb, one cluster of orange dots reached out from *Zulu*, another from *Yankee*, red lines showing an intercept course with the *Keeling*.

"Audio connection with *Ishlangu*," Ellison said. "On channel two."

"XO, get me a sit-rep from *Ishlangu*." Lincoln slid into her chair. "ECM, four blazers, standard spread, midpoint intercept of salvos, fire when ready, follow with decoy." She fastened her restraint bar. "Pilot, execute tail-flip then accelerate at flank speed."

She used the 1MC to warn the crew of harsh maneuvers. Trav grabbed the overhead handset, the one for external comms, and hit *Channel 2*, even as he dropped into his chair to brace himself against the impending course change.

"*Ishlangu*, this is *Keeling*, what is your status?"

Vesna's voice came back scratchy and tinny, warbling from STC interference.

"*Keeling*, we are engaged with three Purist Nation warships."

Trav waved three fingers at Lincoln even as he felt the ship flip along its vertical axis. The image in the orb spun madly—that which had been on top ripped toward the bottom, while that which had been on the bottom ripped toward the top.

Inertia pulled at him, pulled hard. He held the handset tight to his face.

"Multiple casualties," Vesna said. "Curvine at three-fourths power. One chemjet down, the other has fifteen minutes of fuel left at max acceleration. Enemy has a partial tether on us, but we're countering it. Bottom line, we can't outrun them. Three of six lifeboats inoperable. Can you engage one of the corvettes?"

The flip completed—the pitch rotation stopped.

Keeling's chemjets fired and the curvine engaged—Trav was slammed back hard against his seat. The CIC rattled and shuddered. Bits of paper fluttered through the air as if blown by a stiff wind. A loose pencil whipped past his head to clack against the xeno loft. It was like being in a car dropped backward to slam against the ground, with the point of impact stretched out continuously, second after second after second, pulling the skin of his face tight against his skull.

"Captain," he said, "*Ishlangu* has multiple casualties, chemical engine damage, curvine power at three-quarters. She's requesting we engage one—"

"*Third missile salvo incoming,*" Ellison shouted, her words hard to hear over the cacophony of rattling material and vibrating gear. "Port-quarter-high, time to impact fifteen seconds."

Trav's hand slid across his chest; he started his stopwatch. The pressure pushing him into his seat eased, and eased, and eased—the rearward momentum had been countered and the *Keeling* was accelerating forward.

"Weps, point-defense, fire at will," Lincoln called out. She grabbed the comm handset. "All hands, brace for impact."

Trav glanced at his stopwatch—eight seconds...

In the orb, a cluster of five orange dots arced in from port-quarter-high.

"New contact," Waldren said, a touch of panic in her voice. "Starboard bearing zero-three-five, declination one-five-five. Grav-signature indicates possible destroyer or frigate, labeling it X-*Ray*."

Four seconds...

Through his boots, Trav felt the vibration of *Keeling*'s three point-defense guns firing at the incoming missiles.

Dots of orange in the closing cluster winked out—but not all of them.

Two impacts slammed the hull. Everything shook and shuddered in a brief but terrifying rattling sound. Out in space, combat was silent —inside a ship, death made plenty of noise.

There was a suspended instant, one that comes with every impact in battle, where time stops and you wait for everything to collapse, for the curvine to go critical and tear the ship apart, an instant that lasted a fraction of a second and a million years.

And then it was gone.

The *Keeling* was still in the fight.

"Salvo two no longer a threat," Ellison said. "Salvo three partially mitigated by ECM, three to five missiles still inbound, new ETA thirty-five seconds."

"Torpedo launch," Waldren said. "Two fired at us from *Zulu*."

A new pair of red icons appeared in the orb

"ECM, launch countermeasures," Lincoln said. "Shake those torps."

Vesna, in the handset: "*Keeling*, we are leaving the combat area at full possible speed, dropping blazers to cover our rear. It's our only chance. Can you engage one of the corvettes to buy us time?"

"Captain," Trav said, "*Ishlangu* is trying to escape and wants us to engage *Zulu* or *Yankee*."

Lincoln's lips curled into a sneer of frustration.

"Xeno," she said, "can we emergency dive?"

Trav's eyes flicked to the orb, to the icon of *Ishlangu*, now below *Keeling*'s midline and accelerating away at a heading of starboard one-four-five. *Zulu* was turning to give chase, two red lines arcing away from it, signifying the just-launched torpedoes now closing in on *Keeling*. *Yankee* and *X-Ray* angled toward the orb's center, toward *Keeling*. One small cluster of orange dots approached, only seconds from impact.

"Transdim coupler power level at blue," Hasik said. "Ninety percent chance of success."

Lincoln spoke into the handset. "This is the captain. Prepare for emergency dive."

She started her stopwatch. Type24 crews needed ten seconds to vacate their gunhouse and get inside their barbette, which offered no exterior view. There they would stay until stand-down from battle stations, when they would return to the ship proper. The point-defense gunners left their positions as well. *Everyone* had to be inside.

"Captain, we can't dive," Trav said. "We have to engage. *Ishi* is in trouble."

"Our priority is the intel. We need to get clear of this." She looked at her stopwatch. "Xeno, dive when ready."

"Initiating transdim entry," Hasik said.

Trav looked to the orb. Just as the display began to fill with pulsing, multicolored static, the orange cluster closed in.

The CIC filled with light and fire.

56

Susannah heard a scream of pain. The *strangest* scream. She didn't hear it, really—she *felt* it. In her head. In her soul.

The ship shuddered.

She suffered a flash of memory of the only other time she'd experienced enemy fire, when she'd seen the decapitated head of her lover rolling across a debris-strewn, blood-streaked deck.

"Stay with me, Darkwater," Hathorn said. "Watch the power level."

Susannah did as she was told, even as the light around her faded and vanished. She was in the black again. But not all the way this time. There were two spots of light, of reality. In one was Hathorn at the protuberance, hands sliding over the strange, glowing device. In the other, the wavering power-level display on Susannah's monitor.

"It's fluttering between blue and yellow," she said, but it was hard to focus with that screaming in her head, like a baby crying. Someone was hurt bad.

The color gradient was stupid. Didn't yellow and blue make green? Shouldn't it be green, then yellow, then blue? But then yellow and red made orange, and red was worst, so—

"Darkwater! Pick one!"

"Yellow," Susannah said. "Definitely yellow, my mellow fellow."

What a funny turn of phrase. Was she drunk? No, she hadn't been drinking. She didn't think so, anyway.

Well done, Susannah.

"Well done, Bethany," Hathorn said. "Tell Hasik we're in."

Wait a minute... who'd praised her first?

Susannah lost the train of thought. Tell Hasik. Yes, that's what she needed to do. Although he wasn't *Hasik* now, he was *Xeno*, and she wasn't *Bethany*—she was *Atrium*. Whoever was in the loft in the CIC was *Xeno*. That was dumb. Dumber than the colors. People had names, didn't they?

She picked up the sound-powered phone yet. "Xeno, Atrium."

Susannah waited.

"Xeno?"

Still nothing. Usually Hasik would say, *This is Xeno*, and Susannah would say, *We're in transdim*, and Hasik would hang up without saying goodbye or asking Susannah how her day was, because Hasik was kind of an asshole.

"Lieutenant Hathorn, I'm not getting an answer."

Hathorn said something, but Susannah didn't hear it, *couldn't* hear it, not with that mournful wailing in her head, not with the color snakes slithering out of the heartstone, their eyes flashing with hate, their fangs dripping with dark venom...

57

John Bennett stayed calm, because next to being lucky, staying calm was the best way to stay alive.

The XO's endless drilling had paid off—even the boots had donned their vacsuits in seconds. Most had hoods up and sealed, protecting them from the smoke slowly filling Raider Land.

"We gotta take Bishop down or he's gonna kill Torres," John said. "You two ready?"

Beaver and Abshire nodded, the necks of their vacsuits crinkling in time. Behind Abshire's visor, John saw fear and tension written on the man's face. Beaver, on the other hand, looked excited. No, the kid looked *happy*. Did he not comprehend that the *Keeling* had been hit, at least twice, and that something, somewhere, was on fire?

"Abs," John said, "you ever play gridiron?"

Abs nodded again. "Middle linebacker, all-conference."

Perfect.

"Beaver, draw his swing," John said. "Abs, treat Bishop like you'd treat a quarterback that pulled a train on your lover. On three. Three, two, one, *go*."

Beaver rushed down the bunk aisle toward Bishop, Abshire a step behind, John a step behind both.

Bishop, coughing from the smoke drifting into the berth, held a heavy spanner as long as his forearm. He swung it wildly, perhaps slicing an imaginary sword at imaginary monsters. His vacsuit hood lay limp on his back.

At his feet, vacsuited and motionless, lay his team leader, Kimberly Torres.

Bishop saw Beaver coming, swung the spanner at the man's head. Beaver dropped and rolled forward—the spanner missed him by a mile. Abshire drove his shoulder into Bishop's belly in a textbook head-snapping tackle, wrapping him up at the waist and lifting him before driving him down to the deck. Bishop grunted, coughed, and tried to bring the spanner down on Abshire's back, but John snatched it out of his hands.

Spit flying from his mouth, snot streaking his nose, Bishop fought to rise. Beaver jumped on him, fist raised.

"This'll hurt you more than it'll hurt me," he said, then gave Bishop a light, perfectly placed punch to the windpipe.

Bishop coughed and gagged. He clawed at his throat.

"Get him in his bunk," John said.

The three of them wrestled Bishop into his bunk, a middle one. Everyone carried flexicuffs and zipstrips now, as everyone had to be ready to restrain a batshit crazy Raider or sailor. Bishop had been restrained in his bunk, but once out of transdim, the captain had ordered everyone released.

Then the ship took hits. Before anyone understood what was happening, the dive alarm sounded, they were back in the Mud, and several Raiders went stark raving bonkers.

PXO Winter had grabbed five Raiders, Shamdi included, and rushed out of the berth to help fight fires and assist with any wounded. Sands ordered the rest of the platoon—the sane ones, anyway—to restrain those who were *not* sane.

As for Lieutenant Lindros, John hadn't seen him, and he wasn't giving orders. Sands now called the shots.

Abshire yanked flexicuffs tight around Bishop's wrists. John zip-tied the man's ankles to the rack, while Beaver did the same with his hands.

"He ain't going nowhere," Abshire said. "Who do we get next?"

John looked around, trying to spot the most dangerous Raider, someone who might cause more injuries, or worse.

"Bennett, come in." Sands on the platoon frequency, his voice in John's vacsuit speakers.

"Bennett, here."

"Get Lindros," Sands said. "Take him down *easy*, no injuries. And watch out, he, uh... he ditched his vacsuit and is doing laps around the berth."

Oh, the joys of being a Raider.

"Copy that, Master Sergeant," John said. "Beaver, Abs, we got the LT, and Beav, no throat punch this time. Wait... he's coming around now."

They looked down the bunk aisle and saw Platoon Commander Lieutenant Gary Lindros sprint past, naked as a jaybird, his obscene package flopping about like the trunk of a miniature elephant.

"Can I dick punch him, then?" Beaver asked. "Because it'd be kinda tough to miss."

And to think—John could have retired.

"No dick-punching, either," he said. "Let's get him."

58

Doc Hammersmith looked up, angled her head to see through her vacsuit visor.

"She's out, XO. The ship is yours."

Trav stared down at Hammersmith, who was behind the command station, kneeling next to Lincoln. The captain was on her back, her body limp.

Hammersmith beckoned toward the CIC entrance. Two sailors ran in, carrying a stretcher.

"Take her to the infirmary," Hammersmith said. "Be careful lowering her through the sphincter."

Hammersmith moved further into the CIC as the sailors carried Lincoln out.

Trav put his hands on the command station, tried to get his head around the situation. The captain was down. That made him the ship's acting commanding officer.

Just like at Asteroid X7.

He didn't have to look up to know the crew was staring at him, waiting for him to tell them what to do.

Lincoln had given orders to get clear, but *Ishi* and Vesna were in deep trouble. *Keeling* was a small ship. It wasn't a brawler—it stood no chance against three Purist warships.

But while in the Mud, the Purists couldn't see her. Trav had a minute to regroup.

"Ops, get me a damage report."

"Aye-aye, XO," Plait said.

Purist missiles had hit the superstructure, probably three of them in close succession, each driving for the same spot. That was the only way they could punch through Union armor, which had to have happened for damage to reach the CIC. The Raider liaison station had blown apart, tearing monitors to pieces and sending debris flying. A chunk that missed Trav by centimeters hit Lincoln in the head. Fortunately, the liaison station had been unmanned—Lindros had been in Raider Land with his platoon.

The ECM station, just forward of the now-destroyed Raider station, *had* been manned. Cass Mollen was on the deck, Doc Hammersmith now tending to her. Carmel Waldren and Sara Ellison, who'd been giving first aid, slid back into their seats. Their hoods were down, as were the hoods of everyone in the CIC save for Hammersmith.

"Darsat," Trav said, "do we have a DTR window?"

"Working on it, XO," Waldren said.

Colel Citlalmina, a spec-2 first-timer, rushed in and took Mollen's seat at the ECM station.

Trav turned to face the Xeno loft. "Hasik can you—*get your vacsuit on*, now!"

The drunken fool still had the arms tied around his waist. He grabbed at them, pulling them loose.

"I need probabilities," Trav said. "What is our chance of going back into realspace, and once there, diving yet again."

Surfacing into realspace would be the third trans-dimensional crossing in the last fifteen minutes. Returning to the Mud would be the fourth.

Hasik floundered with the arms as he read from his interface. "I can't tell from here." He grabbed for his sound-powered phone. "I'll find out."

"XO," Hammersmith called.

Trav looked her way. Sad eyes behind that visor. She shook her head. No comm needed—Corporal Cass Mollen was dead. Mollen's second patrol on the *Keeling* was her last.

Hammersmith waved to the intel loft. "You, get a stretcher over here."

"Damage report," Plait called out. "Single missile impact port side, deck two, punctured armor at wardroom galley, penetrated to CIC. Fastfill sealed the puncture almost immediately. Air pressure is standard. Raider liaison station inoperable. Single missile impact, port side amidships, deck four, damage to fabrication bay. Fire in fabrication bay, extinguished. Three casualties reported. Engineering is fully manned."

A *single* missile had penetrated topside armor? That wasn't supposed to happen. It certainly hadn't happened at X7. Were the missiles upgraded? Was the armor defective?

"As we went into dim, the top point-defense turret camera showed damage to one of the crawlers," Plait said. "Doubtful it can fly. There's fighting in the sailor berth. Multiple injuries in Raider berth. Raider Lieutenant Lindros is down, Master Sergeant Sands is now platoon leader. Hostage situation in crew galley, Raiders are responding."

The crew was reacting far worse than they had on the calamitous trip into Purist space, or on the somewhat calmer trip back. Had two dives in rapid succession made things worse? That question would have to wait.

Akil Daniels ran past the command station, stretcher in-hand.

"Ops," Trav said, "get Tech Chief Taylor into the top turret for a visual on the crawlers. I need her damage assessment."

Plait turned in his seat. "XO, we're in the Mud. If people see the Mud directly, it... it..."

"Do *not* send her," Hasik said.

Trav turned to look at him. Hasik stood there, his vacsuit on save for the hood. He held his sound-powered phone, his hand over the mouthpiece.

"People seeing the mud with the naked eye have gone insane," Hasik said. "The kind of insane you don't come back from."

He sat and talked into the handset.

Just *seeing* the Mud could drive people to madness? That explained why Lincoln always ordered the gun crews inside.

Trav couldn't evaluate damage to the crawler, or any external area. Great. Just great.

"Ops," he said, "any damage to curvine, chemjets or punch-drive?"

"None reported, XO," Plait said.

The ship had full power, full maneuverability.

"Weps," Trav said, "status of platforms?"

"All operational," Cat Brown said. "No problems reported from gun crews. They're standing by to return to their stations upon surfacing."

Keeling had been hit, but she remained combat-capable.

"XO, transdim coupler levels at blue," Hasik said. "Mid-blue, firm reading."

What the hell did that mean?

"Fuck the color system, Colonel, I asked you for our chances."

"Oh, we have—" Hasik glanced at his slide rule bank "—a ninety percent chance to enter realspace at this moment. After that, my best guess is seventy percent odds of re-entering transdim."

More than a one-in-four chance they couldn't dive a third time.

"If we try to dive and fail," Trav said, "what happens?"

"We're stuck in realspace," Hasik said. "The heartstone's power store drops to zero. If it does, it'll take days to bring it back up."

If Trav surfaced *Keeling*, and couldn't get her back under again, he'd be stuck in a combat zone with three Purist warships.

"Get me more power," Trav said. "Fast."

Hasik focused on his interface.

"DTR connection established," Waldren said. "Connection strength is high. Big window, XO, three-hundred-kilometer radius. I have blips from two ships. I'm trying to acquire grav-signatures."

That was the biggest darsat-to-realspace window he'd seen yet. He could pick and choose where the *Keeling* surfaced, maybe catch the Purists by surprise. If he could disable one enemy ship quickly, maybe engage a second, *Ishi* might be able to fight back against the third.

If he didn't, *Ishi* and her crew were as good as lost.

"In-orb," Trav said.

The orb flickered. The endless, slow movement of milky-crimson mud strands appeared, and with them, two large black blobs, both heading in the same direction. The one out in front had to be *Ishi*. The second trailed behind her, perhaps already close enough for long-range fire.

"Nav, *Ishlangu* will be that lead blip," Trav said. "Get us moving in her direction, we can't let her out of range."

"Aye-aye, XO," Erickson said. "I'll get us close."

59

Ever smelled a human being cooking alive?

Ellis had asked her that, not so long ago.

The stench of scorched rubber and burned flesh found its way through Sascha's vacsuit filters and into her nose, the taste into her mouth.

She had her hands under Ri Chen's knees. A Raider had his armpits. Together, they carried him out of fabrication. Another Raider moved with them, pressing a mass of bloody bandanas against Chen's inner right thigh.

"Over here," Sascha said. "Set him down."

They laid Chen on the deck near the ACIC entrance sphincter.

"He's still bleeding," said the Raider holding the gauze. "Real bad."

Sascha glanced at the Raider's name tag.

"Medic's on the way, Shamdi," she said. "Keep up the pressure."

The other Raider rushed off into the smoke billowing from the curvine room.

Enemy fire had hit the fabrication bay. The copper hull held, but some shrapnel made it through, driving a shard of metal into Chen's leg. Another piece had penetrated into the curvine room, causing something to explode.

Sascha looked up, saw the Raider and one of her engineers carry a man out of the curvine room on a stretcher. His chest smoldered, thin whisps of smoke rising up to mark his path.

They set him on the deck—Brian Goldsmith, electrical mate. He cried out from the pain. His hands clutched at empty air. His vacsuit had burned away at the chest, as had his coveralls, revealing scorched, blistering flesh.

The stretcher-carriers rushed back into the curvine room.

"What the fuck did you say to me?"

The shout made Sascha jump—Shamdi, screaming at the unconscious Chen.

"He's not speaking," she said. "Are you hallucinating?"

Shamdi's eyes snapped up at her. He reared back a little, blinking fast, but kept the bloody bandanas pressed to Chen's thigh.

"I'm fine," Shamdi said. "I'm fine."

Two medics rushed down the passageway. Rebecca Watson knelt by Chen, the other medic, Rudy Rudello, by Goldsmith. Rudello smeared handfuls of nanocyte salve on the burned man's blistered, raw chest—the man screamed as he did. So loud. *So loud.*

Shouts for help from the curvine room. Sascha had to get in there. In the Mud, the *Keeling* used a form of propulsion she didn't understand, but if the ship surfaced, it wouldn't get far without a fully functioning curvine.

"Shamdi," she said, "come with me."

He started to rise, but Watson's hand shot out, locked on his wrist.

"Keep pressure on the wound, Spec" she said. *"Do not leave this man* until I tell you otherwise. Lieutenant Kerkhoffs, we've got this."

Sascha ran for the curvine room.

60

"I said, *I'll swallow your soul,* you Purist fuck!"

Nitzan nodded. He couldn't help it. That was exactly what he'd thought he'd heard. It wasn't the words so much as the person who said them. Correction—as the *thing* who said them.

His first hallucination. Had to be. He was pretty sure this wasn't happening. At least not all of it.

Some of it was real. He pressed blood-soaked bandanas hard against Machinist Mate Chen's thigh. There was a fight in the curvine room. Something was on fire, and no matter what people claimed, burning Human flesh did *not* smell like roasted pork.

What he *wasn't* sure was real, though, what he *prayed* wasn't real, was Chen's head, which—quite convincingly—looked like an angry, man-sized frog head with big, red, faceted rubies for eyes and a sweaty blue bandana tied tight across its green brow.

"You're going to hell, Nitzie! To the Low Place! That's what you get for murdering Arimun! I hope you like a big fat, hot nut sack, you backstabbing motherfucker, because Low One is gonna teabag you with his flaming balls forever and ever and *ever!*"

It looked *so* real, and yet a part of Nitzan's mind told him that someone, anyone, at some point prior to this, would likely have noticed a frog-headed machinist mate.

Nitzan would have heard about such a thing.

358

He finally understood why Mafi freaked out during dives. Why LT, PXO Winter, Danielle Bang, and all the others freaked out.

"You're just a hallucination," Nitzan whispered.

"And you're just a murderer. A *murrrrrderrrrrerrrrr!*"

Nitzan closed his eyes, but when he did, Arimun was there—his friend—blood shooting from a gash in the side of his neck. Smiling Arimun, *trusting* Arimun, who'd never seen the ultimate betrayal coming.

Nitzan opened his eyes.

"I'll swallow your *sooooouuuuullllll!*"

This *was* real. The *Keeling* had been destroyed. Nitzan was dead. Dead and in the Low Place. It was the only explanation. He was going to burn for all time and—apparently—get tea-bagged by Low One's flaming balls forever and ever and ever.

"I got it, Spec," Watson said. "Move aside."

Nitzan did as he was told and stood, staring at the blood on his vacsuit gloves.

"Hey, Nitzie," Frog-Face Chen said. "Kill this stupid bitch. Take one of these blasphemers with you, right? Oh, by the way, you're gonna get gangbanged by demons. I'll swallow your soul, *I'll—*"

An injector's sharp hiss. Ruby eyes sparkled, then closed. The tongue dangled from the wide mouth.

If it was a hallucination, how had drugs knocked it out?

Nitzan was done. *So* done. Done with *all* of this.

"I gotta get out of here," he said.

"Stay right there," Watson said. "I still need you."

He stared at the ACIC sphincter. Anything was better than looking at Chen.

Nitzan knew what was happening. Somehow, his countrymen had engaged *Ishlangu*, then landed a few punches on *Keeling* after it came out of transdim.

His people were out there. If *Keeling* surfaced to realspace, could he find a way to immobilize the ship? Then, somehow, send a signal that would bring Crusaders to board it? Capturing *Keeling* meant capturing all its secrets. And Cooley. And Cooley's intel.

Or would his people blow the living shit out of *Keeling* the first chance they got? And by doing so, blow the living shit out of Nitzan?

Maybe he could escape instead, share what intel he had. He knew *Keeling*'s crew complement and armament. He knew what the ship could do. He'd seen the atrium and the heartstone. He didn't know what purpose those things served, but he could tell other people —*smarter* people—what he'd seen. It was enough to make a difference. Had to be.

A Raider—Hotchy Kiene from Bravo Squad—set a stretcher on the deck next to Chen.

"Get him on," Watson said. "Slow and gentle."

Chen no longer had a frog head. Maybe that hadn't been real after all.

Nitzan helped Kiene place Chen on the stretcher.

"We're taking him to triage in the crew mess," Watson said. "You two are part of medical now, you'll assist me."

Watson had just deputized Nitzan and Kiene. More like press-ganged them, if you judged things by the tone of her voice. With damage control teams busy and the ship to be run, Raiders were the only ones without pre-determined jobs—at least until they heard the call for *battle stations, boarding action* or, far worse, *battle stations, repel boarders.*

"*Now*, Spec," Watson said. "Let's go."

Nitzan grabbed the stretcher handles. He and Kiene followed Watson toward the ladder to deck three.

He wanted to go home.

He'd done his duty.

He had to get off this ship.

He *had* to.

61

"Xeno," Trav said, "talk to me."

"My people are working on it," Hasik said. "They're going as fast as they can."

Trav controlled his breathing, which let him control his anger. Hundreds of lives and two warships on the line, and Hasik didn't know if he could generate power faster? Maybe Kerkhoffs was right after all. Maybe Hasik didn't understand *how* the *Keeling* worked, or what generated the power needed to move from membrane to membrane.

"Get down there yourself," Trav said. "All three of you work on it. I'll call for you when it's time."

Hasik ran down the loft steps and out of the CIC.

"I got 'em," Waldren called out. "Grav-signatures on both vessels. *Ishlangu* confirmed. *Zulu* confirmed." She leaned closer to her screen. "Detecting artillery transients. It looks like *Ishlangu* and *Zulu* are trading fire. Definitely long-range, but *Zulu* has greater acceleration and is closing in."

Where were the other two Purist ships?

Trav tried to call up Chanda-class information, but the command slate was black and refused to respond.

"Ops, find out what's wrong with my slate." Trav turned to face the intel loft. "Do you have a binder on the Purist Nation?"

"Uh, yes sir." Gillick slightly lifted the one he had open in front of him. "Right here."

Trav stepped to the railing, held up his hand.

Behind Gillick, Lafferty stood. "XO, we can—"

Trav grabbed the binder. He took it to the command station and flipped through the pages until he found the Chanda-class overview. Cat Brown and Dardanos Leeds hurried over. There wasn't much they could do at their stations, as there was nothing to shoot at in transdim.

Brown looked at him quizzically. "Are you really going to fight?"

She didn't believe it. No need to ask why—Trav knew what the crew thought of him.

"We have to help *Ishi*," he said.

Even as he read, he caught Brown and Leeds exchange a look of surprise.

Chandas were 123 meters long, 18 meters beam, 16 meters high. A bit wider than tall, typical of Purist Nation design. Bigger than *Keeling*, but then again, almost every warship was.

"Single one-seventy-six millimeter in a top turret," Trav said. "Two ten-tube rocket launchers, four thirty-millimeter point-defense guns, two torpedo tubes."

Keeling had no missiles, but three times as many torpedo tubes. And better torpedoes. She wasn't quite a match for a Chanda in a straight-up brawl, but coming out of transdim, *Keeling* could put a lot of bat brains in flight in a hurry.

Leeds leaned in, eyeing the binder. "They have a variety of missile types." The artillery chief sounded excited—he wanted to fight. "Penetrators, incendiary, and a strong area-effect that spreads a cloud of explosive micrometeorites. Purists like to fire those ahead and let targets fly through—"

He jerked away from the command station, his eyebrows high. Trav knew that look by now.

"Warrant Leeds, are you hallucinating?"

Leeds nodded slowly. "There's like a... boy-sized... *thing* standing on the slate. Big silver eyes. It's... it's smoking a hookah."

Trav whipped his arm over the slate, just as he'd done for Lincoln.

"It's not real," he said. "Can you perform your duties?"

The expression on Leeds's face showed his imaginary creature hadn't vanished.

"I can, XO," he said. "As long as that guy stays where he is."

If *Keeling* surfaced to fight, Leeds's hallucination would vanish. So would any Trav might soon encounter. His grandmother, bugs... they could come for him at any moment. Them or something new.

Ishlangu's curvine was at three-fourths power. She couldn't outrun *Zulu*, and when it closed in, she wouldn't last long.

If Trav was going to act, he had to do it fast.

The other Purist warships were out there, but with this excellent detection strength, even if they were just outside DTR range, they were still far enough away that—if *Keeling* surfaced—it would take them ten minutes or more to get into maximum firing range.

Captain Lincoln was down. At least one *Keeling* crew member was dead, and several were badly injured. If Trav took the ship into battle, would more people die? Highly likely. But he couldn't leave *Ishlangu*. He couldn't leave Vesna.

"Nav," Trav said, "plot fastest possible course to intercept *Zulu*."

Erickson ripped a long piece of paper from his roll.

"Aye-aye, XO," he said. "Calculating."

Something moved at Trav's right—he jumped, dreading a giant beetle or a massive hornet.

It was neither—Anne Lafferty stood in Lincoln's spot, her eyes hard.

"Guns," she said, "return to your duties."

Leeds didn't need to be told twice. He hurried away, casting glances over his shoulder to see if his hallucinated creature was following.

"You, too, Weps," Lafferty said. "Immediately."

Brown gave Trav a glance, then walked to the weapons station.

Lafferty thought she could give orders?

"Major," Trav said, "I am in com—"

She moved closer, a single fast step that brought them toe-to-toe.

"We have orders to clear out, XO," she said. "And that's *exactly* what we're going to do."

62

The beautiful nothing.

Susannah floated through the heavens.

The heavens floated through Susannah.

The screaming had stopped. Or, maybe, she couldn't hear it anymore because she was in the dark place.

This is your home, my child.

The voice. A supernova of love and understanding. Of *acceptance*.

Had she felt contentment like this since Melanie died? No, she had not.

And, truth be told, she'd *never* felt this way. Not with Melanie. Not with the Purist Church. Not in the convent with her sisters. Not anywhere.

This love was on a different level. So explosive and thunderous, there was no word to describe it. It was all-encompassing, permeating her skin, her muscles, her organs, her bones. It made her vibrate. No, it made her *hum*, made her entire being sing in tune to a song of perfection.

This is your home.

"I've searched so long," she said. But she wasn't speaking. Not with her mouth. The words came from within, as if her soul were a tympanum drumming the message across the cosmos.

And I have searched for you. For you, my child.

The Mud. The glorious Mud. It wasn't a different dimension—it was the High Place. *Heaven.* Literally heaven. The dwelling place of High One and his chosen followers.

Susannah ached with joy. How lucky was she? How special?

Snap out of it, you little bitch.

Floating in the non-reality, Susannah felt the love ebb, a tide sliding away across glistening sand and stones and out to a distant sea.

"But why? What did I do wrong?"

Goddammit, you worthless little whore, I need you.

Had she done something to anger High One? Susannah wanted to be needed, *longed* for it, but—

Her head rocked back. Something had hit her mouth, an invisible stone cast out from the nothingness.

"*Snap out of it!*"

That wasn't High One.

Susannah opened her eyes to see Hathorn standing over her, fist clenched, one knuckle split open and freshly wet with blood. Fury and panic etched the lieutenant's face. The atrium was dimmer then normal, the heartstone a faint yellow glow in the mist.

"Get up, Darkwater, or I'll punch you again!"

Susannah's hand shot out, locked hard on Hathorn's wrist.

"You shouldn't have hit me, sinner. You will be punished."

It was Susannah's voice, but also not hers. Darker. Deeper. *Other.*

Hathorn yanked her hand free and stepped back.

"We need power," she said. "Ellis is in command now. Hasik thinks he'll surface us to rescue people from *Ishi,* and we might have to dive right after—that's *four crossings* in a row. I've never done that. We don't have enough power. We have to get more power."

The crash-dive. Susannah remembered it. The missile impacts. Was the ship damaged? Had people died?

If they had, it was all part of High One's grand design—as was putting Ellis in command. If Ellis wanted to add two more crossings, than that, too, was High One's will.

The atrium sphincter opened, and Hasik rushed in.

"Hathorn, man the protuberance," he ran to his workstation. "Darkwater, get your hands on the heartstone. Tell me if my alterations produce any result. And if you have any ideas, now's the time to share then."

"Aye, Colonel," Susannah said.

Her voice was hers again. Almost. A trace of that other deepness remained.

She moved through the mist and placed her hands on the glowing heartstone's firm surface. So warm. Soothing energy seemed to flow through her arms and into her chest. She looked up, into the dangling greenery's hazy dimness.

There was nowhere in the universe she'd rather be.

"I'm ready, Colonel," she said. "I'm ready."

63

"You will return to your station," Trav said quietly. "I'm done with this conversation. *Ishlangu* is under attack. We *will* assist her."

Anne couldn't believe it. He was serious about this?

"Again, XO, our mission objective was to retrieve Colonel Cooley and bring him and his data to Union space," she said. "We have both. Lincoln ordered us to get clear."

His eyes narrowed. She wanted to cut them out of his head.

"I have the conn," he said. "It's my decision."

Yes, he really was serious.

"With Captain Lincoln incapacitated, you and I are co-commanders of this vessel," Anne said. "Not only did she give you an order, we have clear guidance from Admiral Epperson to *not engage* under *any circumstances*."

XO looked at the orb, doubt creasing his face.

"Our choice is clear," Anne said.

He hesitated, then shook his head. "I can't leave them."

But he could. His *orders* were to leave. Didn't he know that? Didn't he feel the tapping?

No... no, the tapping was only her.

She wanted it to go away, knew *how* to make it go away. She could draw that pretty copper blade and slice the XO's leg—not kill him, just draw enough blood to make the tapping *leave her the fuck alone*, and—

"Return to your post, Major," Ellis said.

She couldn't cut him. Not yet. And she wouldn't anyway. Him or anyone else. She was better.

"We can't win this fight," she said. "You know it. We'll throw our lives away. Don't you want to see your family again, XO?"

To her left, Anne saw Akil Daniels return to the CIC. Ellis didn't seem to notice him—the XO focused only on her.

"*Ishi*'s crew wants to see their families, too," he said. "I am in command, and as long as we're combat-effective, we will assist her."

A shriek made them both jump. Colel Citlalmina, the EMC operator, lurched out of her acceleration chair. She fell to her back, hands clawing violently at the air.

"Combat effective?" Anne shook her head. "You've got a crew that's flipping out, you're now down to your last ECM operator, at least one crawler is toast, and your xeno chief is probably drunk. You think we can *fight*? We'll be lucky to survive the Mud long enough to get clear of the Purists."

Her words should have snapped him back to reality. Instead, they seemed to galvanize him.

"Corporal Gillick," Ellis said, his eyes never leaving Anne's, "get Spec-Two Citlalmina to the mess, immediately. Ops, get a replacement in here, on the double."

Gillick hurried down the loft steps.

Ellis wouldn't listen to reason? He wanted to do this the hard way? He didn't know what hard was.

"Corporal Gillick, belay that order," Anne said. "XO, I am relieving you of command of this vessel under Fleet code one-thirty-five. Gillick, Daniels—escort the XO to his quarters."

———

Trav couldn't believe his ears.

Neither could Gillick and Daniels, apparently. They exchanged a worried glance.

Code 135 allowed the intel chief to take command if they felt the CO had been compromised. In the triumvirate command structure,

Anne would have needed the XO's endorsement to use C-135 against a captain. But with Lincoln out, Anne *could* take command.

Trav wasn't going to let that happen.

"I am acting commander of this ship," he said. "You will stand down, Major Lafferty."

Daniels and Gillick probably had good poker faces—they were BII, after all—but now those poker faces were nowhere to be seen. They'd been thrown into the frying pan of what could amount to mutiny, and they didn't know what to do.

Lafferty kept her voice low, but heads were turning—the CIC staff knew something was wrong.

"I gave an *order*," she said. "Take the XO to his quarters."

A sailor ran into the CIC, ran right past Trav, Anne and her intel operatives—Brinson Sorro, the ship's last ECM operator. He stepped over Citlalmina and took his station.

Someone else entered, and Trav's heart sank—big-bearded Colonel Mac Cooley. The crew might back Trav against Major Lafferty, but a colonel, a *real* colonel and not a puffed-up pencil-pusher like Hasik, was a different story.

"I saw that Lincoln is out of commission," he said. "So I come up here and find y'all standing around with your thumbs up your asses. Lafferty, what's the situation?"

———

Anne smiled. Not a big one, but she couldn't help it. Ellis was *not* going to ruin everything by trying to save a ship that was already lost.

"Colonel Cooley, I'm taking command of this vessel, under Code—"

"*Taking command?* What for?"

"I informed the XO we need to leave the combat area," Anne said. "He's considering engaging the enemy. Our objective is—"

Cooley sharply held up a hand, cutting Anne off. He looked at Ellis.

"Is that true, XO? Are you taking this vessel into combat, which would put my mission at risk?"

The XO straightened. Anne had to give Ellis credit—for a guy nicknamed *Yellowbelly*, he didn't wilt.

"Colonel, that is correct," he said. "*Ishlangu* is engaged with two Purist corvettes, and also a probable frigate or destroyer. We may be able to rescue at least some of *Ishi*'s crew. I won't abandon her."

Cooley's blond-bearded face broke into a grim smile.

"I like where your head is at, Ellis. Let's get at 'em."

Oh, *hell* no. Anne would not let these two meatheads fuck everything up.

"Colonel Cooley," she said, each word a low threat, "we have orders from Admiral Epperson to *not* engage, under any circumstances."

Cooley looked at her. "Do you have that order in writing, Major?"

Anne said nothing; she knew she'd lost.

He puffed out his chest, spoke loud enough for all to hear.

"I am Colonel Mac Cooley. Via Fleet code one-fifteen, as the highest-ranked intel officer aboard, I appoint myself *Keeling*'s intel chief. With the captain incapable of performing her duties, Fleet code one-thirty-five allows the intel chief to take full command of this vessel. I am doing so now. As of this moment, I am *Keeling*'s acting CO. My first order is for the XO to assist the *Ishlangu* in any way he sees fit. Carry on."

Heads turned back to stations.

"You two," Cooley said to Gillick and Daniels, "get that screaming sailor out of here and get her some help."

They rushed to Citlalmina's side and grabbed her wrists to stop her futile air-clawing.

"Lafferty, get in the spookhouse and see if we have deck schematics for a Chanda-class corvette, and anything we've got on Purist destroyers and frigates," Cooley said. "Be quick about it."

Just like that, Anne had no say. Cooley outranked her. Her own people weren't backing her up. The only thing she could do about this breach of protocol would be to report it when *Keeling* returned to Union territory.

For now, though, she could do nothing at all.

Cooley had chosen sides. He'd chosen *against* Anne.

Someday, there would be a price to pay—for Cooley and Ellis both —but this was not the time for that.

She hurried out of the CIC, the tapping in her head hammering so hard it made her wince.

64

Cooley stepped to the command station and stood in the XO's spot—Trav remained in the captain's.

"Show me what we're facing, Ellis. Make it quick. I'm familiar enough with the *Keeling*'s abilities—you talk and if I have questions, I'll ask."

Cooley had put Lafferty in her place. He'd also taken full command. Would he second-guess Trav's orders?

"We suffered minor damage," Trav said. "Maneuverability and weapons weren't impacted. *Ishi* and a Chanda-class corvette, labeled *Zulu* in the nav-orb, are trading long-distance fire. *Ishi*'s curvine can only produce three-fourths max acceleration, and she burned all her chemjet fuel. She can't outrun *Zulu*. We saw two more ships, another Chanda, tagged *Yankee*, and a frigate or a destroyer, tagged *X-Ray*, but they're currently outside our detection range."

Cooley stared into the orb. "You think we can take *Zulu*?"

"We get to pick our point of insertion into realspace," Trav said. "*Zulu* has significant momentum. If we surface and immediately launch a torpedo salvo, I think we can take it out before it can maneuver."

"Where do you think the other two ships are?"

"We don't know if *Ishi* landed hits on them," Trav said. "One or both could be damaged and are therefore staying back. As far as the Purist task force knows, *Keeling* popped in out of nowhere, then blinked out of existence. It's possible they fear we could pop in again, so they could be keeping one Chanda to protect the larger ship while *Zulu* finishes off *Ishlangu*."

Cooley thought, absently rubbing at his temple. "You're missing it."

"Missing what?"

The colonel walked around the command station to stand in front of the orb.

"I was a sniper," he said. "A good one. Know how I got the most kills?"

Trav grew irritated—*Ishi* could be taking hits that very second.

"No sir, I do not."

"I'd shoot to wound and incapacitate, not to kill," Cooley said. "Legs were best. If I could pin someone down, have them screaming in pain, calling for help, sooner or later their mates would try to reach them. That's when I'd go for head shots." The colonel pointed to *Ishi's* icon. "They *want* us to come to her rescue. They want *Keeling*. You said the battle was underway before you surfaced?"

"That's correct. The task force must have been on patrol, picked her up and came after her."

Cooley pinched his lips together, which made them vanish within his beard.

"This rendezvous point is way outside Purist territory," he said. "The only way those three ships could get the jump on *Ishi* is if they knew where she was going to be. They connected her to my pickup, maybe... or they knew she was escorting *Keeling*. Could be both. *Ishi* is bait, Ellis. *Zulu* will be waiting to tether you, slow you down long enough for the other Purist ships to come in."

Trav had missed it. The Purist ships were outside detection range, but that didn't mean they were far away. Did they know *Keeling's* DTR range? Probably not. They'd picked a distance and got lucky. Cooley was right—they were close, waiting to spring.

"I want to help *Ishi* as much as you do," Cooley said. "But even if you get *Zulu*, you might not have enough time to evac *Ishi* and get clear before the other ships come in. And if you can't dive, we're screwed. I have to assume those other two ships are untouched. Your *best* scenario is you wind up defending against a corvette and a frigate or destroyer. Unless you have a plan to deal with those odds, I can't justify the risk to this ship and to my intel. I won't let you surface just to lob torpedoes at *Zulu*. I'm sorry."

But there was a way to deal with those odds. A risky way, but it could be done.

"We surface close to *Zulu*, launch a crawler and deploy Raiders," Trav said. "Raiders capture *Zulu* and turn it toward *X-Ray* and *Yankee*. Unless the Purists want to get outmaneuvered, one or both of those ships have to deal with *Zulu*. Maybe that buys us enough time to evac *Ishi*."

Cooley glanced around the CIC. "I haven't felt anything myself, but I see members of your crew losing their minds. How are you going to control the *Ishi* crew you rescue? Where are you going to put them?"

"We'll pack them in," Trav said. "We'll manage as best we can. Better to have some of them going nuts than all of them in Purist hands. We can't let them wind up like the crew of the *Blackmouth*."

The Colonel stared back. Did he know the Blackmouth was Trav's fault? Maybe. It didn't matter.

"How many Raiders you got?"

"One platoon," Trav said. "And we're down to one crawler."

"Is your Raider CO experienced in boarding?"

"Our Raider CO is out, sir," Trav said.

Cooley's eyes narrowed in doubt.

"You want to send one platoon of Raiders, with their CO out, and only one crawler for support, to capture an enemy corvette?"

Trav nodded. "That's right."

The expression of doubt turned to one of admiration.

"And people call you a coward," Cooley said. "If the crawler is supporting the Raiders, how are you going to evac people from *Ishi*? We can't get close enough for an umbilical connection, that would give the Purists a big fat double target."

"We won't get close," Trav said. "Is your hauler back together and ready to fly?"

Cooley grinned and nodded.

"Get your executive staff in here," he said. "And a crawler pilot. And John Bennett—I need to know if he thinks *Zulu* can be taken."

65

"Make way," Biggie Bang yelled. "They want us in the CIC!"

John would have done the yelling himself, but Biggie's voice was almost as powerful as Beaver's.

Sailors flattened themselves against the passageway's copper bulkheads as he and Biggie ran past, headed for the topside amidships spanus.

John had no idea what was going on. The XO had called for him and Biggie *by name*. Biggie, okay, she was the lead pilot, but why him?

"Hey, Bennett," Biggie said, "I never did apologize for trying to kill you, man."

That had been, what, only a couple of weeks ago? It seemed like years.

"Don't worry about it," John said.

"Thanks, man. Winter's right about you—you're a good dude. And she says you're a great lay, too."

Did *everyone* know about his sex life?

At the spanus, Biggie reached up into the weird copper pucker and was slurped through. John did the same. A waiting sailor waved them into the CIC.

It was the first time John had been in the superstructure since that brief moment when he'd first boarded from *Ishlangu*. He had a moment to marvel at how everything looked *normal*, like a regular old warship. Steel and composite. Fleet-gray. Flat bulkheads, flat deck, a flat ceiling.

And... sweet Jesus, was that *air conditioning?*

So this was how the other half lived. Nice.

The CIC was dimly lit. Most illumination came from station consoles and a nav-orb. Maybe this CIC was small, maybe it was big, John didn't know—he'd never been in one before, not once in his almost four decades of service.

Crammed around the command station, a who's who of the PUV *James Keeling*: the XO, Chief Sung, Kerkhoffs, Erickson, Plait, Leeds, Weapons Department Head Brown, Signals Chief Madison, that creepy Intel Chief Lafferty, and the man the *Keeling* had been sent to retrieve, Colonel Cooley.

Where was Captain Lincoln? Was she hurt? Maybe she was tripping out, like so many others.

Ellis glanced over his shoulder, saw John and Biggie.

"Find room," the XO said to them.

Biggie turned her thin body sideways, edged in between Ellis and Kerkhoffs. John stood behind Brown—she was short enough that he could see over her to the paper spread atop the command slate.

"Listen close," Ellis said. "*Ishi* is under fire from a Purist corvette. We don't know *Ishi*'s warfighting capacity, but she can't outrun pursuit and we think she's done for. I intend to surface, engage the corvette, and rescue as many of *Ishi*'s crew as we can. There are two other Purist ships out there, another corvette, and a frigate or destroyer."

Biggie snorted a laugh that, without words, clearly said *of course there are two more enemy ships, of course there are.*

"It gets worse," XO Ellis said. "We're down to one Ochthera."

Biggie shrugged. "Well, we're out of pilots, anyway. Warrant Akagi went batshit with a wrench and caved in Warrant Nessa's skull, Warrant Romauld has a broken clavicle, and then—"

"Biggie, shut up," Ellis said. "Just tell me if we have a full crawler crew."

The woman smiled wide. "Oh, *hell* yeah. Me and Dudgeon are still here, and my gunner Nikula is top-notch. She could shoot the snatch off a sparrow at ten klicks away."

Chief Lafferty put her hand down on the paper covering the command slate.

"This is a schematic for a Chanda-class PN corvette," she said. "Chandas have no Crusader complement as far as we know." She put her finger on a data chart. "Known speed and maneuverability here—" she slid her finger to another chart "—known armament here."

John took in the info. Chandas were small, with a crew of 165. Solid armament. Those 30-millimeter point-defense guns were bad news, but an Ochthera could likely knock them out of commission.

"We need to capture that ship," Ellis said. "What do you think, Bennett? Can the platoon get it done?"

John's gut clenched. He suddenly realized why he'd been summoned here.

"That's not my call to make, XO," he said. "PXO Winter and Master Sarg—"

"Spare me your modesty," Cooley snapped. "We don't have time. I know your history, Bennett. Can you or can you not take control of that Chanda?"

Heads turned toward John, all with quizzical expressions save for Cooley and the XO.

John had spent his military career avoiding situations like this. He was a brawler, not a leader. Sure, he'd taken charge at times, but only when those above him were dead or out of commission.

"I can't make that kind of decision," he said. "I'm just a grunt."

The XO leaned on the slate. He stared at John. No bullshit in those eyes.

"*Ishi* needs us," Ellis said. "Answer the Colonel's question."

John's stomach tightened more, began to churn. He wanted to throw up. First Sands had made him team leader, and now this? John wasn't made for things like this.

But now that he was on the spot, if he didn't do something, the XO might give up, might leave *Ishi* to die.

Out of nowhere, in a split second, over a hundred lives were on John's shoulders.

He bent over the schematic. It was incomplete. The deck plan looked like a best guess, but a warship was a warship, and the CIC was probably in the middle, as it was shown. They'd have an arms locker, people trained to repel boarders. All ships did. But those people were sailors, not Crusaders, not trained fighters—Raiders would cut through them like a hot knife through butter.

"If the crawler can get us on the hull, I think we can take her," John said. "But when we surface, you got to give us a few minutes to get our people together. Some of them are in bad shape from the Mud. We need every Raider we have."

Ellis looked to Biggie. "With just one crawler, can you get it done?"

"No problem, man," she said.

Half of John wanted to believe Biggie, and half wanted her to take a good, hard look before deciding so quickly.

"We'll use Colonel Cooley's hauler to get as many as we can off the *Ishi*," the XO said. "We'll only have time to make one rescue run. Biggie, who do you have that can operate the hauler?"

"Uh, like, no one," Biggie said. "I told you all our pilots are out 'cept me and Dudgeon, and I need her as co-pilot. Besides, crawlers and haulers ain't the same. Get someone who knows how to drive that thing, man, or don't even bother."

John noticed Plait, the operations head, mouth a curse. Plait had probably searched crew records for anyone rated as a commercial hauler pilot and found none. The XO had hinged his strategy on one an Ochthera jock doing the job.

"So, no one can fly it," Cooley said. "No one except me. I'll do it."

A small hand slammed down on the Chanda schematics with a sound like a bullet hitting flesh.

"Absolutely *not!*" Lafferty's eyes raged. Her nostrils flared. The woman looked nuttier than macadamia pancakes. "We're already putting our primary mission at risk. We have the Colonel's physical intel, but the Fleet needs the info in his head. Using him to pilot a *civilian hauler* in an *active combat zone* is unacceptable."

Cooley turned on her, the anger in his eyes enough to make John want to take a step back.

"Lafferty, you need to—"

"She's right," Ellis said, the snap of command in his voice. "Colonel, you're the primary mission. You stay. We'll get someone else to fly the hauler."

"Who?" Cooley spread his hands, jostling the people on either side of him. "A hauler isn't a pleasure craft. It's not a fucking video game. Anyone you get to fly it is likely to shoot past *Ishi* or slam right into her, especially if they come under fire. If not me, who's going to save the *Ishi* crew?"

Lafferty glared back at Cooley, her face tight with hate. Hate, and violence—John knew a natural killer when he saw one.

"I know *exactly* who," she said. "And I'll go with her to make sure the job gets done."

66

"Ensign Darkwater."

Susannah turned in her station chair and looked to the atrium entrance—Major Lafferty stood there, a scowl on her face.

"Come with me, Ensign," Lafferty said. "On the double."

Susannah looked back to Hasik, who was taking readings from the protuberance, and Hathorn, who was on the rigging atop the heart-stone. Hasik said nothing. Hathorn said nothing. Did they have any idea how dangerous Lafferty was? Any clue what the psycho was capable of? Maybe they did know, and that was why they stayed quiet.

"*Now*, Ensign," Lafferty said. "Don't make me come in there and get you."

Susannah did as she was told. Lafferty gripped her by the arm, led her roughly out of the atrium, past the xeno storage room and ACIC, and to the ladders.

"Down to the flight bay," Lafferty said.

Susannah descended the ladder. She stepped off the bottom rung and stood there, for a few seconds feeling oddly like she had as a little girl when she'd done something bad and was waiting for her father to get home.

Lafferty stepped off the ladder and again grabbed Susannah's arm, grabbed it *hard*, and turned Susannah so she was looking into the flight bay. The crawlers were gone. In their place, stuffed in like a white square peg in a roundish copper hole, was a cargo hauler.

"Ensign, can you fly that?"

"Fly it? Why would I..." Susannah's stomach dropped. "You mean *now*? In a combat situation? Are you crazy?"

Lafferty stepped in close.

"Rossi—if that's your real name—you have one chance to tell me if you can pilot that truck. If you lie, and I'll find out if you do, I will cut the skin from your body in long strips. I will make you eat it."

Susannah's breath froze. Bock had her playing the spy, but she wasn't a spy. She wasn't a soldier, either. Anne Lafferty was both; her threats were real.

"Yes, Major. I can fly it."

The 1MC chime sounded.

"This is the XO. Prepare to exit transdim. Battle stations torpedoes. Gun crews to ready stations. Raiders, prepare to gear for boarding action the moment we surface."

67

Cooley was a pig—more so than Anne could have imagined.

The tapping. The fucking *tapping*.

She caught herself rocking back and forth in the co-pilot's seat. Caught herself because of the wide-eyed look of dread on the face of Bethany/Susannah Darkwater/Rossi, who sat in the pilot's chair.

How easy it would be to make that galling expression *and* the tapping go away, all at the same time...

"Face forward, Ensign."

Darkwater/Rossi did.

Food wrappers and empty beer cans littered the sticky floor. Dust covered everything other than the seats and the controls needed to operate the hauler. And then there was the sleeper bin, which was just past the lockers behind the pilot and co-pilot seats—utterly disgusting.

Anne wasn't going to let Cooley get the glory. If survivors came off *Ishi*, hers would be the first face they saw. Even if they were sworn to secrecy—which they would be after being onboard *Keeling*—word would get out about Anne. That, along with her after-action report, would fast-track her for another promotion. With a little luck, *Colonel* Lafferty's career would continue its upward trajectory.

It wasn't just the glory or the career, though. Anne had tried to get *Keeling* out of there, as Epperson wanted, but she'd been overruled. Her ship had committed to the fight. *Ishlangu*'s crew was in trouble.

They were Fleet, just like her. If there was a chance to save them from death, or worse, Anne would risk her life to do that every single time.

Anne had wanted to don a TASH rig for this run. As a BII operative, she knew how to use one, although she wasn't that experienced. Cooley had denied the request, though, stating that the platoon's remaining rigs were needed in case Purists managed to close in on *Keeling*. As much as she hated Cooley, Anne had to admit that was the correct choice.

At least she was armed. Not just with the shiv, which she grew increasingly fond of as the moments passed, but also with a Grall microjet pistol from *Keeling*'s small arms locker. While the .45-caliber, self-propelled rounds would blow big holes in unarmored people, they weren't all that effective against exo-armor unless you could hit a joint or put a round through the visor. Still, it was better than nothing.

A LASHed crawler tech squeezed between the nose of the hauler and the pouch's aft bulkhead. She waved her hands over her head, raised both thumbs, the signal for *you're cleared to launch.*

Darkwater/Rossi was supposed to signal back. The ensign sat there, trembling.

"Answer her, Ensign," Anne said.

"This is insane," Darkwater/Rossi said. "We're going to die. *This is insane.*"

Tap, tap, tap…

Anne reached into her open vacsuit and pulled out the shiv. She kept it low, where the tech couldn't see it. The pilot and co-pilot seats were separated by the communications console, but still close enough that Anne could reach across and cut Darkwater/Rossi without fully extending her arm.

"*Answer her*, Ensign."

Darkwater/Rossi gave the tech a thumbs-up.

The tech saluted and slid out of sight.

Anne returned the blade to its sheath.

Air had been removed from the pouch. As soon as the wide doors opened, the hauler would be shoved out into space.

"We're going to die," Darkwater/Rossi said again.

"Not today, Ensign. Not if you do what must be done."

The tapping made it hard to think, hard to *see.*

Anne glanced back at the sleeper cab, wondering how much of it was Cooley's "cover" and how much was his natural perversion. The cab was built around a queen-sized mattress that rested atop meter-high plastic cabinets. The flat rail holding the mattress in place was just tall enough to prevent a sleeping trucker from rolling out. A meter above the mattress, more plastic cabinets. The whole thing was a cozy, prefab unit.

And everywhere on that unit—on the cabinets, the flat rail, the bulkheads flush around the mattress—was *endless* pornography. Flexi-paper and glossy print both. Scantily clad and naked women, men, and trans.

Just to port of the sleeping bin was the airlock that led into the cargo hold.

Had Cooley pretended to be a deviant in a country where deviants were publicly executed? Had that helped him make the connections he needed to complete the mission? Or was that who he really was, a pervert who masturbated every chance he got?

Anne didn't even want to think about what the rumpled sheets and mattress felt like.

"It's happening," Darkwater/Rossi said. "I can feel it. We're surfacing."

The PUV *James Keeling* was entering realspace.

68

"Battle stations torpedoes, battle stations guns, battle stations boarding action."

The XO's voice on the 1MC rang off the copper bulkheads as John dragged a groggy Clifton Bishop into the rig room.

"Bennett," Bishop mumbled, "what the fuck is happening?"

"Time to fight." John grabbed Bishop's shoulders and stood him up straight. "Get your armor on."

Not even thirty seconds earlier, the kid had been chained to his bunk because he'd freaked out and hit Torres with a wrench. He blinked wildly, like a person awoken in the middle of the night.

"Come on, Bishop," John said, "get with it."

All around them, Raiders were either armoring up or dragging dazed comrades to their TASH bins. Even Torres, with bloody gauze around her head, fumbled with her armor. No exceptions, for anyone. There wasn't time to be nice, wasn't time to coddle.

"Bishop!" John gave the kid a hard shake. "You hear me?"

Bishop snapped out of it all at once and started donning his armor.

John ran to his own bin. Shamdi and Abshire were armoring up. Beaver was already in full TASH and was helping Fred Abeen get ready. Abeen had a bloody lump of cotton sticking out of each nostril. Had someone hit him, or had he hit himself?

At least Abeen and Torres were still alive, their wounds minor.

Another Raider—crawler pilot Bhola Nessa—was dead. Dead at the hands of her platoon mate. Dead because of this ship of nightmares.

"*Move it, Raiders.*" Master Sergeant Sands barked out orders even as he donned his own TASH. "This is not a drill. We are going to engage the enemy."

John realized he'd already put on his leg and torso armor without even thinking about it—decades of practice and drill meant his hands and body did the work automatically, robotically.

"About fucking time we get in the mix," Beaver said. "Scream, aim, and fire! Right, guys?"

The guys didn't answer.

John finished his arms, legs, and torso, vaguely aware he could TASH up in half the time it took for Beaver's *platoon record.*

"Cap Lincoln ain't messing around," Mafi said. "Sending us out to get some."

John knew better than to talk about decisions above his pay grade, but he'd seen the determination in Ellis. The Raiders deserved to know who was in command.

"Wasn't Lincoln," he said. "The XO's running the show. It's his call."

Abshire paused in fastening his torso armor. "What? *Yellowbelly* is sending us in?"

"That's the way I saw it," John said.

Abs and others stared at John, their expressions ranging from confusion to outright disbelief. Ellis carried the brand of a coward. His decision to fight mucked up everyone's preconceived notions.

The introspective moment didn't last long. The platoon got back to the business of prepping for battle.

These men and women—vets and boots alike—all knew this might be their last few hours alive. The boots might know that logically, but they didn't *feel* it deep down. Not yet. That last bit of ignorance would soon be cleansed away by the baptism of fire.

"All you FNGs remember to stay frosty," Sergeant Jordan called out. "Slow is smooth, smooth is fast, fast is final."

John pulled on his helmet. He was barely aware of running systems checks, of topping off oxygen and magic goo, barely aware that his old battery maxed out at a 92% charge and that there were no replacements. His mind was elsewhere.

His mind was on Admiral Epperson.

Epperson was responsible. Responsible for this shitty armor, for this horrible ship that ate people up and spit them out. He didn't give a damn about this platoon or the two Raiders who'd already died. He didn't give a damn about those who'd been hurt, those who couldn't sleep even when not in transdim because they were afraid to close their eyes.

John had thought this would be his last stint. He'd wanted to die. Not anymore. Now he wanted to live long enough to find out the truth behind the *Keeling* and kill whoever was responsible for it.

"Ammo will be live," Sands said. "Ours and theirs both. Listen for my commands, rely on your squadmates, and we'll get you back home."

Sands would lead the assault. Five frontline Raiders had been sedated, but only two came out of it in time to join the sortie. Winter, Dobrevski, and Lindros were still under. Doc Watson was trying to bring them around, but even if she succeeded, they wouldn't be ready in time.

"You may see your friends fall," Sands called out. "You may see them die. Remember that they are Raiders, which means they go straight to Valhalla, and they will be looking down upon you, howling at you to you to advance, advance, advance."

Shamdi, oh he of the always-running mouth, had yet to say a word. Maybe he'd finally suffered a hallucination. John hoped he was all right, *needed* him to be all right, because Shamdi was no boot—he'd fought and killed before.

"Team Alpha-Two," John said, "do your pre-flight checks. Know the state of your gear. And unless your TASH can't hold air pressure, keep any problems to yourself because we're all going."

A clean rifle, a full load of MG, and plenty of ammo. That was all a Raider needed to wage war. At least, that's what the drill instructors claimed when John had been as young and ignorant as Beaver and Abshire.

"Alpha-Two," John said, "activate team channel and huddle up."

Shamdi, Abshire, and Beaver gathered around him, all in their black armor, all looking ready but afraid. Even Beaver was scared, although the gleam in his eyes probably meant he *liked* being scared.

John turned off his other broadcast channels so he could have a fast, private word with his team.

"Good news and bad news," he said. "The good news is, you're going to get the most amazing view of your life. The bad news is, you're getting that because we won't be *in* the crawler, we'll be *on* it. There ain't enough room inside for everyone."

He gave them a beat to process, a beat to let them feel what they were bound to feel. An Ochthera's armor was thin, but it was still armor.

"Bennett," Abshire said, "why'd you let them fuck us like that?"

"I didn't *let* them. I asked for it. Someone's got to go on top. Might as well be those of us who are truly ready to tussle, and Alpha Squad is ready. You boys chew iron and shit nails, and you know it. I would *not* have volunteered for this if I didn't have you three on my team. Understand?"

It wasn't just a pep-talk. John believed in these men. They could all get the job done, and with a little luck, they could all make it back in one piece.

"Listen to Sands," he said. "Listen to Jordan. Listen to *me*. Stay calm. Beaver, Abs, I'll tell you right now what Shamdi already knows —there ain't *nothing* like this. All the people you'll meet during all the years you'll live, if they aren't Raiders, they won't know. You will."

John held out his gauntleted hand. "Scream, aim, and fire."

Beaver lit up like a Christmas tree. "Fuck yeah, Bennett!" He placed his gauntlet atop John's.

So did Abshire. "Scream, aim, and fire."

Shamdi put his on top. "You guys are fucking morons."

"*To the weapons cage*," Sands called out. "Our Fleetmates are up against it. For *Ishi* to live, Churchies gotta die. Get your rifle and form up in the pouch."

69

In a normal situation—if anything on this insane ship *could* be called normal—Nitzan and his team would be inside the crawler, not flying from the open pouch and up the *Keeling's* starboard hull.

"*Move it!*" Sands in the platoon channel. "Alpha Squad on top, Bravo in the troop compartment!"

Nitzan didn't know much of the attack plan, but XO Ellis couldn't have handed him a better way out. If the Raiders reached *Zulu*—and that was a big *if*, seeing as Nitzan could die on the trek there in a dozen different ways—he could fake an injury, fade to the rear of the unit, then start taking his "mates" out from behind as opportunities presented themselves. With a little luck, he'd survive long enough to tell his people who he was, and his Union days would be behind him forever.

Nitzan reached topside, aft of the superstructure. The first crawler was toast—something had smashed in from a port angle, crushing the cockpit and bending the front cannon like a metal straw, then ripping out the troop compartment's starboard side. That same projectile had punched holes in the fine copper mesh that secured the crawler to the hull.

The second crawler looked undamaged. Raider techs in LASH armor pulled its mesh free. Two pilots scrambled up the sides and into the cockpit. Bravo Squad ran up the open rear ramp.

Alpha Squad descended onto the crawler, landing on the titanium netting bolted atop the troop compartment section. No crashes this time, no awkward landings; the endless exo drills had paid off. Even clumsy Fred Abeen made a descent touchdown.

As his squad mates scrambled to clip safety lines to the eye hooks protruding through the titanium webbing, Nitzan looked starboard, three o-clock high, at two blurry dots of dim light—*Ishlangu*, and behind it, the PN corvette that, hopefully, Nitzan would soon board.

Aft of *Keeling* and pulling away fast was Cooley's hauler, already little more than a glowing spec angling to come up alongside *Ishi*. Nitzan had thought Cooley a pompous ass, but that man was flying a commercial hauler to a ship under fire—maybe *Stone Balls* was an appropriate nickname after all.

"Lock in," Jordan said. "If comms drop out, when I jump, all of you jump."

Nitzan took his place at the back, next to Mafi. The rest of Alpha Squad packed in up front and around the armored turret, making sure their safety lines were secure—if the crawler took a hit, their armor's gripfield might not be enough to hold them in place. As long as the crawler flew forward, a heavy, angled shield rising up from the cockpit window would protect the topside troops from micrometeorites and other battlefield debris.

With nine Raiders clustered atop the Ochthera, Nitzan imagined it looked like a black wolf spider with babies on its back. Inside the turret, he saw Dalia Nikula, the engineer-gunner, going through her pre-flight weapons checks.

The crawler's cockpit window lowered and sealed.

"Welcome to Biggie Air, ladies and gentlemen. We'll be taking a delightful sightseeing cruise to visit a fascinating foreign culture."

Bang was such a loudmouth. *Foreign culture.* Not to Nitzan, and not to Bethany.

I̶ ̶ ̶ his heart he wouldn't be able to save her. If *Keeling* e'd have to keep working away in the atrium, hopefully and more intel. Maybe he'd find her someday. Maybe the let him help extricate her. As long as Bethany laid low, ve, might someday find a way out. With High One's gs were possible.

"Alpha-Two, full count, in position," Bennett said on the squad channel.

"Alpha-One, full count, in position," Sarvacharya said.

Only a few seconds more, and it was time to jump out of the frying pan and headfirst into the fire.

A LASHed-up Crew Chief Taylor crawled up the crawler's side, looked over the packed Raiders.

"Y'all keep your heads down," she said. "You're on top, but at least you're not on that piece of shit hauler."

"That Cooley guy has a pair, all right," Mafi said. "And people think what *we* do is crazy?"

"Cooley's in the CIC," Taylor said. "Lafferty's leading the rescue op. Shamdi's little girlfriend's doing the flying."

Nitzan went cold, as cold as the void.

"God bless you all," Taylor said and started back down.

Nitzan grabbed her forearm. "*Darkwater* is piloting the hauler? You're sure?"

"Sent them off myself," Taylor said. "I hope she makes it. Tear 'em up, Shamdi."

Taylor descended.

Bethany wasn't safe. She was going to die. He had to do something, he had to—

"We're cleared to fly." Biggie on the platoon channel. "And away we go."

Before Nitzan could react, the crawler lifted off. In the amount of time it took him to look down, the *Keeling* was already a hundred meters below, streaking toward the Purist Nation corvette.

"I want a career change," Abshire said. "Anyone think we'll make it back?"

"Couldn't say," Beaver said. "All I know is I finally get to kill somebody."

"Cut the chatter," Jordan said. "Get your heads in the game."

"Hold on tight," Bang said. "Max acceleration in three, two..."

Nitzan gave one last look at the dot of light that was the cargo hauler, then Biggie hit the gas.

70

"Darsat rebooting."

"Ochthera-Two away, Hauler-One en route to *Ishlangu*."

"Turning zero-five-one to starboard, declination one-one-zero."

Trav took it all in, feeling strangely calm. His crew had given him the lay of the land—now it was his turn.

"Weps, set tube one STC torpedo solution to close fast on *Zulu*, fire when ready," he said. "Guns, launch blazers in *Zulu*'s forward path, stagger the rounds along its current course."

Putting blazers in front of the corvette would force it to either turn away from *Ishi* or fly through heavy interference that would mask the crawler's approach.

The Raiders. Such bravery. How Fleet could train human beings to do what the Raiders were doing now, Trav had no idea.

"Tube one torpedo solution set," Brown said. "Thirty-five seconds to target. Launching tube one."

Trav started his stopwatch.

"Firing blazers," Leeds said.

The *Keeling* vibrated slightly as both the port and starboard Type24s fired.

Trav looked into the orb, took in the whole scene. Ochthera-Two, out ahead of *Keeling* and accelerating toward *Zulu*. Behind the crawler, *Keeling*, and the torpedo that would pass by the Ochthera in seconds. The hauler, angling for *Ishlangu*.

"You really think we can pull this off?"

Trav glanced left, at Cooley, who stood in the XO's spot.

"I believe in my crew," Trav said.

"The crew you've known for all of two weeks?"

Two weeks. Such a short time. A bunch of misfits, miscreants, criminals, and total rookies that had only two things in common—they were all Fleet, and they'd all wallowed in the Mud.

"Yes," Trav said. "With a little luck, yes."

"Darsat activated," Waldren called out. "Two contacts, *Yankee* and *X-Ray*, range one-zero-zero kilometers and closing fast."

The two enemy warships had been outside of DTR range. Luck on their part, or did the task force commander know *Keeling's* abilities?

Cooley leaned closer. "The trap is sprung."

"In-orb," Trav said.

Existing range rings constricted. More appeared at the orb's hemisphere and shrank inward like a reverse image of a pebble dropped in a pond, revealing blips marked *X-Ray* and *Yankee*. They angled toward a midpoint between *Keeling* and *Ishi*.

At their current course and acceleration, the two enemy ships could cover half the distance before going after either target or splitting up and taking on both. Smart tactics by the Purist task force commander.

"*X-Ray* grav-sig confirmed," Waldren said. "It's a Malag-class destroyer."

That was bad. Very bad.

Cooley leaned in again. "I hope we find some of that luck, XO, because we're going to need it."

Trav sat in the captain's acceleration chair, Cooley in the one meant for the XO. The rest of the crew were already in theirs.

Find luck? Trav was about to *make* some.

"Pilot, perpendicular attack approach on *Zulu*, random acceleration-deceleration to throw off *Zulu's* targeting. Guns, link to pilot station, keep your crews informed of pending velocity changes. Guns, free-fire on my mark. Ops, get Hasik up here on the double."

71

John breathed deeply. He breathed slowly. For the next few minutes, things were out of his hands. He'd seen enough crawlers take a mouthful of missile to know there was nothing he could do but ride.

And what a ride it was.

The enemy corvette was a blurry smear no bigger than his thumb, a smear that appeared to be pointing almost straight down, its perceived orientation shifting as Biggie turned and burned, closing the distance. She changed pitch, and just like that, *Zulu* was below the crawler's equator—John saw nothing but stars.

While *Zulu* was, in reality, in one fixed point in space and time, space-time fuckery generated tens of thousands of "probable locations," locations that overlapped and obscured each other, spread out over a relatively massive area of space. Each possible location was just as valid as the next, or so John had been told. The farther you were from an object viewed through STC fields, the more probable locations you saw. The more *intense* the STC interference, the more probable locations you saw. It was a something-something-square-inverse rule he'd given up trying to understand decades ago.

John made partial sense of it by thinking of STC interference as spiritually akin to fog. From a long way off, fog can obscure the trees of a forest, even block sight of the forest altogether. As you near the edge of that forest, the fog—the very same stuff that obscured everything—

seems to thin. By the time you touch a tree, you can see that tree clear as day. The fog hasn't dissipated, there's just not enough of it between you and what you're looking at.

Biggie rolled. John again saw the corvette, now as long as his arm. The corvette wasn't as much of a *blur* now as it was *fuzzy*, with thousands of probable locations overlapping each other, strobe-flashing on and off faster than the eye could track, so fast it looked like one big, sparkling, multifaceted, endlessly vibrating image.

The corvette's gunners—if they could spot the far smaller crawler at all from this distance—would see a similar cloud of probabilities. With space-time fuckery drowning any digital or quantum assistance, all targeting was done by sight alone. Shooting at a probability cloud and hoping to hit your target was like shooting into a wall of fog and hoping to hit one particular tree. The *Zulu*'s gun crews wouldn't fire for another, oh, thirty seconds or so.

"Here comes a torp," Sarvacharya said. "Port-high."

A brief blur of motion shot past the crawler and streaked toward *Zulu*. Then, from the same direction, the coppery mass of *Keeling* slid into view, rushing forward to draw *Zulu*'s defensive fire. *Keeling* was rotating to starboard, which would present her underside to enemy fire and keep the superstructure out of *Zulu*'s line of sight. *Keeling* was close enough that there was no blurring—perhaps only the smallest bit of waver and vibration, which made it look like a living thing lazily gliding through space.

Keeling's port-side Type24 changed angle and fired. A thin stream of smoke plumed from the gun's eight-meter-long barrel, while a blossoming cloud puffed from the weapon's stubby backblast tube. A marvelous dance of power, equal amounts of force emanating from front and rear cancelling each other out, preventing any torque that might skew the ships' course and require correction.

"That big copper bastard is our shield," Biggie said on the platoon channel. "We got it made, boys and girls."

She had it made, for the purpose of bringing the *Raiders* in close. As for the Raiders themselves, the silent dance was soon to begin.

Inertia shifted as Biggie banked the crawler up and to starboard, putting more of *Keeling* between it and *Zulu*, which was getting bigger and bigger, clearer and clearer.

Logically. John knew the Ochthera was *flying* toward the corvette, but his brain told him he was *falling* toward it, straight down at terminal velocity.

A round from *Keeling* hit *Zulu* amidships, blasting away thick chunks of armor.

"Lord almighty," Beaver said. "Did you see that?"

Well short of the oncoming corvette, *Keeling*'s STC torpedo detonated. Instead of expanding outward, as did most things that went *boom*, the space around the torp seemed to be pulled *inward*. Like an instant black hole, the light of distant stars bending and curving toward it. The torp's power made *Zulu*—now as long as two John Bennetts lying head-to-feet—fuzzy once again.

"Great shot," Sands said over the platoon channel. "We owe a bat brain a beer."

That much interference might let the crawler slip in unnoticed until it was in spitting distance of the corvette. The platoon's chances of success had just gone up.

"Target altering course," Biggie said. "I'm executing correction, then curving around to match velocity for our approach. Alpha Squad, get your best dress on, it's almost time to party."

72

"*Zulu* broke off pursuit," Lafferty said. "The other two Purist ships have appeared, but they're far enough out we can complete our run and get back. We've got our window."

Susannah kept her hands on the controls, guiding the hauler toward the fuzzy cloud that was *Ishlangu*.

"You should hood up, Major."

Lafferty huffed. "Worry about flying, Ensign."

Susannah had hoped the psycho might seal her vacsuit, which would make it harder for her to draw that knife. No joy. That left Susannah the option of venting the pilot cabin but doing so required several steps—Lafferty would see it coming, seal her suit and pull her hood up—and then, most likely, the cutting would begin.

Better to concentrate on flying, as the Major said.

Susannah had never flown through STC interference fields. Logically, the *Ishlangu* was solid within its own sphere of reference, as solid as the hauler in which Susannah now sat, but from her point in space, the blurry warship vibrated and bucked, expanded and contracted in spastic bursts, moving in ways solid matter could not move.

"Now comes the dicey part," Lafferty said.

"*Now* comes the dicey part? What are you talking about?"

"We have to hope *Ishi* tracked us coming out of the *Keeling* and doesn't mistake us for an enemy APC."

Susannah's guts felt like the cold copper of the *Keeling*'s hull.

"You mean *Ishi* could *shoot at us*? Why didn't you tell me?"

"You didn't need to know before. Now, you do. I'll start sending a tightbeam transmission on fast repeat. Let's hope it gets through."

The communications array's small monitor flared to life, lit up with jerking lines and wild static. Lafferty flipped a switch from DIGITAL to ANALOG. The static vanished. She hit the button for TIGHTBEAM—a reticule appeared. Using a small joystick, she centered the reticule on the blurred, wavering *Ishlangu*.

"Transmitting *Union rescue don't shoot*." She tapped a spring-loaded button, sending the tightbeam message in ancient Morse code. "Done. It's on repeat. Step on it, Ensign. The time you save getting us there is extra time we'll have to run for our lives."

Susannah tore her eyes away from the small screen. Her life now depended on a Morse code message getting through shuddering space-time interference before the people she intended to rescue sent a missile her way.

The *Ishlangu* looked bigger now, its form growing less volatile. Steadily, bit by bit, its probability cloud shrank. Some details started to merge.

Susannah couldn't die here. She couldn't. She belonged on the *Keeling*. She belonged *to* the *Keeling*.

The hauler's curvine was already pegged. She gripped the chemical thruster lever and slid it forward—inertia shoved her back in her seat.

73

Zulu had turned to face *Keeling*. Trav knew the enemy captain had no other choice. If the corvette continued direct pursuit of *Ishi*, *Keeling* would have had it lined up in a T-approach—*Zulu's* entire length exposed, while *Keeling*, coming in at an angle, would have offered a far smaller target profile.

With the course change, the ships would pass each other at an obtuse angle. That was what Trav needed; he would buckshot *Zulu's* prow to set it up for the crawler's landing. *Zulu* would undoubtedly try the same tactic, to put a storm of metal directly in front of *Keeling*, but Trav had an ace up his sleeve.

"We've closed to mid-range," Brown called out. "Another twenty seconds to short, another thirty to point-blank. *Zulu* hasn't landed a round on us yet, XO, but they will soon."

"Very well," Trav said.

He had a few seconds more to review the info on Malag-class destroyers. He knew that warship's offensive power first-hand. At X7, one just like it had hammered *Schild*, prompting Antoine Williams to turn and run—an order Trav carried out when Williams went down.

In a head-to-head fight, *Keeling* stood zero chance.

Malags had topside and bottomside twin 130-millimeter guns. With good crews, they could fire thirty rounds a minute. Two forward torpedo tubes, although Purist torps weren't in the same class as the

Union's. Two ship-killer missiles. Two twenty-four-tube missile launchers with a variety of munitions to choose from.

For this battle, the worst stat wasn't the guns, the torps, or the missiles—it was Malag's exo complement. Four platoons of Crusaders, each with a Kloos-class APC. If the Raiders could take *Zulu*, they wouldn't hold it long.

"ECM, be ready to counter any tether attempts," Travis said. "Forward view to command slate."

Zulu, still slightly fuzzy but coming into sharper focus, appeared on the slate. The enemy warship was dead-ahead at ten degrees declination. That attack angle protected the *Keeling*'s superstructure. He could see the trails of artillery rounds fired from *Keeling*'s port and starboard batteries streaking toward the target.

Zulu no longer cared about *Ishlangu*—it fired its main gun at *Keeling*.

"Xeno," Trav said, "current probability of diving and surfacing again?"

Paper rustled in the xeno loft behind him.

"Ninety-five percent chance to enter transdim." Hasik was out of breath after his sprint up from the atrium. "Darkwater figured out how to squeeze all latent energy from the transdim coupler reserves, but that's all the power there is. There's nothing left. Chances of subsequently shifting back to realspace... maybe eighty percent."

Far better odds than before. Hasik and his team had delivered, getting more power into the heartstone.

"*X-Ray* and *Yankee* changing course," Waldren said. "*X-Ray* heading our way, *Yankee* angling for *Ishlangu*."

The Purist task force commander had finally committed. Trav eyed the orb. *Yankee* would reach firing range on *Ishi* in twenty-five to thirty minutes. *X-Ray*'s angle of intersection was longer, perhaps forty minutes, but when it reached firing range, Trav hoped to be long gone.

"Xeno, prep for immediate crash-dive, initiate on my mark." Trav grabbed the handset, spoke on the 1MC. "This is the XO. Prepare to dive. Whatever you see in the Mud, *ignore* it. I need every one of you at your posts and ready to fight when we surface. I'm counting on you. That is all."

He returned the handset to its cradle.

"You mean *if* we surface," Cooley said quietly.

He wasn't wrong. There was a one-in-five chance *Keeling* wouldn't make it out of transdim. If that happened, the Raider platoon, Lafferty, Darkwater, and the *Ishi* and everyone on it were as good as dead.

"We'll surface," Trav said.

He stared down at the command slate.

Zulu grew closer. *Zulu* grew more defined.

74

The tightbeam responder let out a rapid series of beeps.

"They heard us," Anne said. "Getting approach instructions now."

A touch of Anne's fear and anxiety slipped away. *Ishlangu* wouldn't shoot them, but that was only one of the many threats remaining.

She wrote down the message, one letter at a time. Some of it was gibberish, the STC fuckery diffusing the light, but the signal was on fast repeat—Anne wrote a similar line of letters over and over again, slowly eliminating erroneous characters.

"Come alongside... starboard. Match current velocity... and plane. Crew... will evac... manually."

"No way," Darkwater/Rossi said. "They're going to *spacewalk* to us? Can't we clamp?"

Anne wondered how someone so smart could be so stupid.

"If they could accept a clamp, they would have asked us to clamp," Anne said. "*Ishi* has taken a beating."

Darkwater/Rossi was sweating. Anne saw it through the woman's visor.

"What if they launch lifeboats?" Darkwater/Rossi asked. "Do we have time to lock those to the external cargo brackets?"

"If so, they'll have to figure that out," Anne said. "I don't know how to do it, and you're staying in that seat. I'll go into the cargo hold, raise the loading door, and collect as many of the evacuees as I can. You *will not leave* until I tell you to, Ensign. Not a second before. Do you understand me?"

Darkwater/Rossi nodded. "I understand."

She was afraid. Good. People who feared were people who obeyed.

Anne looked out at *Ishlangu*. So close now. So big. The Purists had shot her up real bad: at least four missile impacts on the hull, the bubble shattered, starboard gunhouse shredded, a long gouge amidships that was likely from a torpedo hit.

"Disengaging curvine and reversing spin to decelerate," Darkwater/Rossi said. "I don't trust tail-flipping this thing, even if I'm gentle. It's a real bucket."

That was the truth. A bucket of porn that belonged to Mac "Stone Balls" Cooley.

It wasn't that Anne didn't fear death. She did. *Yankee* was likely closing in at flank speed. Even though *Ishi* was between *Yankee* and the hauler, once the firing began, that little bit of protection wouldn't last long. What she and Darkwater/Rossi were doing was as risky as risky got.

But if they pulled it off? If Anne used Cooley's pornomobile to rescue a hundred-odd fleeters while he stayed behind in the *Keeling*? Whatever accolades he would get for completing his mission, she would get the same.

The Fleet cross for each of them? Why not. Daddy would see to it, and deservedly so.

"Closing in," Darkwater/Rossi said. "Almost in position. You'd better get back there, Major. Jack into an audio port so I can talk to you."

The hauler slid alongside *Ishlangu*'s battered hull. Out the cab window, Anne saw vacsuited crew with handheld emergency personal thrusters accelerating away from the ship, already moving toward the hauler.

"Not one *second* before I tell you," Anne said.

She slid out of the seat, tried to not look at the display of infinite smut as she moved to the airlock door.

75

Keeling's port and starboard guns had fallen into an opposite rhythm—the CIC shuddered every two seconds as a round ripped toward *Zulu*. All targeting was done by eye, a life-and-death challenge for gun crews who had to account for distance and angle, relative velocity, distance to lead the target, and do all of it as *Zulu* seemed to shift and vibrate. Of the thirty rounds fired so far, only three had hit, and only one of those appeared to have penetrated armor and caused visible damage.

Zulu's gunners weren't doing any better—they had yet to land a round on the *Keeling*.

"Conn," Brown called out, "we're entering point-blank range."

Keeling and *Zulu* were about to streak past each other at a shallow angle, both stutter-stepping their approach with alternating acceleration and deceleration, hoping to throw off each other's gun crews while trying to land shots themselves.

Time to set Biggie's approach.

"Guns, canister rounds," Trav said. "Aim directly ahead of *Zulu*. One salvo from each gun, then get the crews into their barbettes. Xeno, the instant the crews are inside, we're diving."

The ship slewed to port. Trav felt a vibration even through the thick padding of his acceleration chair.

A piercing sensation in his brain, as if a sound could be a pock-marked dagger—he didn't hear it with his ears, he *felt* it.

"We're hit," Plait said. "Artillery round, port amidships."

76

John's breath locked in his chest.

A burst of light from the fuzzy cloud that was the *Keeling*, there then gone—an artillery round had landed.

Had the ship been destroyed? Was it a mobility kill, hurtling along on its own momentum? If it was out of commission, the Raiders' only escape hinged on either taking full control of *Zulu* and trying to outrun the other Purists ships, or making a near-suicidal cross-battle sprint for *Ishi* and pray the frigate survived.

Sands on the platoon comm: "Alpha Squad, disembark, now, now, now."

Jordan unclipped and stepped off the crawler.

John did the same.

It wasn't like the movies, where Raiders or other action-heroes leapt clear and were left behind as their ship streaked off for a dogfight with some evildoer. He was moving at the same velocity as the crawler —it was like stepping off a stationary surface in zero-G and gently floating away.

Alpha-One disembarked to port, Alpha-Two to starboard.

Zulu slowly approached. Biggie had brought the Ochthera around to bleed off much of the relative velocity difference between it and the corvette.

With Alpha Squad clear, the crawler dropped down and away so fast John felt like he was flying upward at a thousand KPH.

Sergeant Jordan raised a fist—the signal for *on me, get ready.*

John pulled his rifle free of his chest clamps, saw others doing the same.

He knew STC interference made it pointless, but he tried his team channel anyway.

"This is Bennett, anyone read me?"

He got nothing but haunting, pinching static.

Jordan extended one finger, circled it above her.

The Raiders clacked their heels together, extending their thrusters.

John's heart slammed in his chest. The adrenaline rush made him shudder like a pulsar.

Abs, Beaver, and Shamdi floated there, RRs in their gauntleted hands, thrusters extended. John felt so *proud* of his guys. He loved them. He loved Sarvacharya and her team, too—big Basara, Where's-My-Watch Mafi, and even that moron Fred Abeen.

Shamdi pointed at John, then at the enemy warship. The gesture was obvious: *you want to take the lead, Grampa?*

Yeah. John *did* want to take the lead. Shamdi could bring up the rear. If Beaver or Abshire panicked, tried to bail, Shamdi would calm them down and get them back in the fight.

Jordan pointed toward the oncoming corvette, patted the top of her helmet twice: *Follow me.*

She was a stone-cold killer. John loved her.

Jordan lit her thrusters, streaked *away* from the oncoming *Zulu* in order to bleed off more of the velocity differential.

John followed, angling himself to watch what he knew was coming. Canister rounds detonated in front of the corvette, fireworks worthy of a planet's millennial celebration. The warship ripped straight through the cloud of death, where fist-sized hunks of metal scraped against bow armor, ripping along the hull to slam into any extrusion and extension.

Zulu had fired a similar salvo, but before *Keeling* reached it, a swirl of red, ochre, and the colors of rot formed before her. *Keeling* plunged prow-first through that blazing hole in space, vanishing as it went—but before it dropped from existence, the ship's starboard gunhouse burst apart in a sphere of orange fire.

And then *Keeling* was gone, the decay-colored swirl shrinking to a point, then to nothing at all.

How bad was the damage? Would *Keeling* ever surface again?

For now, that didn't matter—John had a job to do.

The enemy corvette drew abreast, a moving, scarred fortress wall from some ancient tale of knights and magic, bigger than anything had a right to be, and yet, this was a *small* warship. No visual distortion here, no cloud of probabilities—John and his Raiders were too close for that.

From behind *Zulu*, the crawler started an attack run. Nikula's twin .50s and Biggie's front autocannon raged, hurling heat at a point-defense gun already swiveling to return fire. Biggie barrel-rolled away from that gun's retort. Two missiles streaked from the crawler and landed with a surgeon's precision—the PDG popped like a metallic water balloon filled with flame.

Biggie extended the crawler's legs and dropped her beast onto the corvette's hull.

John tore his eyes away from that skirmish and focused on his own. He followed Jordan toward the corvette's port-side bow.

77

Commercial haulers didn't have the kind of tricked-out darsat rigs found on military vessels, but they did possess basic collision-avoidance functionality that identified two important things: large objects nearby—meant to alert the pilot of other ships—and objects that had a possible collision vector.

When the system detected both, like it did now, an alarm sounded. A *loud* alarm. Object detected at port zero-eight-five, elevation one-one-zero. She looked up and left out the pilot cabin window. She saw it. Far away, just a cloud-like clump, but she *saw* it.

"Uh, Major? Hurry it up back there, *Yankee* is coming at us fast."

"Relax, we knew that would happen." Lafferty's voice was scratchy and warbled even though she was jacked into the internal network. "How much time do we have?"

"*Relax?* Are you out of your mind? We have to get out of here!"

"*Ishi* crew are still coming in," Lafferty said. "We are *not* leaving them. Send a tightbeam to *Ishi* CIC, see if they have an ETA for *Yankee* reaching medium targeting distance. Set the message on repeat, then plot an ETA yourself in case they don't respond."

How could Lafferty sound so *calm*? Didn't she understand the situation?

And what was she talking about with *medium range*? An area-effect round fired past *Ishi* could put a dozen holes in the hauler.

Susannah shook. She tried to control it. Tried and failed.

"We have to go," she said. "I did my part. I'm engaging the curvine and—"

"*Ensign Darkwater*, if you leave before I give you the order, I will slice you open from pussy to chin. Do what I say, and you have a chance to live. *Don't* do what I say, and you have no chance at all."

A chance to live? The psychopath was going to kill her as soon as they returned to the *Keeling*. What was the point of it all?

Major Lafferty had a gun, a nasty looking pistol she wore in a holster on her right hip. But she didn't threaten with the gun—she threatened with the blade. Always with the blade.

"Plot the problem, Ensign," Lafferty said. "I need to know how much time we have left to collect evacuees, get clear of *Yankee*, and make it to the pickup point."

Be calm, my child.

Susannah's breath caught in her chest. Her stress didn't vanish completely, but it ebbed, receded somewhat.

"Twenty-five rescuees in and counting," Lafferty said, still maddeningly calm. "I can fit at least fifty more. Do the math, Ensign, I need a time estimate."

Outside the pilothouse window, were dozens of sailors with escape wings approaching the hauler, still more coming out of hatches, and even a few leaving through the holes in the ship put there by Purists weapons.

Come home to me, my child.

Susannah's shivering slowed, then stopped altogether.

Everything would be all right.

She looked for and found a slide rule.

"Calculating ETA, Major," she said. "Assume we have fifteen minutes, max, until we *have* to go or we won't get away. I'll notify you when I have more info."

78

"Darsat rebooting," Waldren said.

Someone was crying. Not crying, exactly, more like *moaning*. Moaning with a rhythm and melody. Someone else was praying, the same short, fierce prayer, over and over.

Trav stared at the nav-orb, the nav-orb that was going to liquify his innards and suck them out like porridge.

It isn't real, it isn't real...

"Hull penetration," Cooley said. "Round entered amidships deck five, exited amidships deck four. Light damage to landing bay, extensive damage to machining bay. Atmosphere vented on impact, but holes are sealed and atmospheric pressure reestablished. Multiple injuries, one KIA."

The brackets that supported the orb had become tucked-in spider legs, the orb itself now glossy black with a blood-red hourglass shape on its underside. A tiny head had formed, curved fangs dripping venom. He couldn't see its eyes, but he knew it was tracking him, waiting to spring.

It isn't real, it isn't real...

"Port Type24 took a direct hit," Brown said, her machine-gun voice heavy with urgency. "The barbette was breached. Gun crew presumed dead. Damage and fire-control teams responding."

The long, thin legs extended. Pointed feet clicked against the deck as the massive arachnid prepared to pounce on Trav.

"Captain Ellis," Cooley said, his voice soft as a running brook, "what do you see?"

Trav's head snapped to the left, saw Cooley looking back with calm, understanding eyes.

"A spider," Trav whispered.

Cooley held up his hands at chest width. "This big? Bigger?"

Trav looked to the orb, nodded at it.

"Ah," Cooley said. "That's bigger, all right. Get behind me, XO."

Trav moved quickly, placing his back to the xeno loft, putting Cooley between him and the monster.

The black widow scurried onto the command slate. It was so *big* that the pipes and wires in the CIC's ceiling pushed down against the black, round body.

Cooley glanced back at Trav. Trav saw him and didn't see him, because he couldn't take his eyes off the spider. His grandmother had one just like it, forever trapped in a block of crysteel. It had been so *tiny*.

"It's not real," Trav said, but he didn't believe a word of it.

I'm real, little boy. I'm real and I'm pissed.

Trav found himself shaking his head, shaking it hard—the spider spoke with Meemaw's voice. It *smelled* like Meemaw, like her cloying, funeral-scented skin lotion.

You're going to die, you worthless nerd. You never came to see me, you abandoned *me, and you're going to pay for it.*

Cooley jumped atop the command slate. Crouching there, he waved his arms, turned in a waddling circle.

The spider's front limbs reached out to snatch him, the fangs stretched to strike—and then the creature was gone.

Trav dropped to a knee, adrenaline raging through his body. He was almost hyperventilating.

"Conn, darsat is up," Waldren called out. "Strong DTR reading, but limited range of five- zero kilometers. Four blips—*Zulu, Yankee, X-Ray,* and *Ishlangu.*"

Trav stood on wobbly legs, his breathing ragged. "You see our Ochthera or the hauler?"

"Ochthera could be too close to *Zulu* to read, clamped to *Zulu*, or destroyed," Waldren said. "Same for the hauler with *Ishlangu*. *Yankee* is on intercept course with *Ishlangu*, ETA ten minutes to be in long-distance firing range. *X-Ray* is angling for *Zulu*."

Hasik leaned over the xeno loft railing, his glasses slowly sliding forward along his sweat-slick nose.

"We're down to a seventy-percent chance of shifting to realspace," he said. "Maybe seventy-five, I don't know."

Every bit of this battle was a gamble, with the odds getting progressively worse.

"Understood," Trav said. "Chances of diving again after that, and then surfacing?"

"XO, you don't understand—"

"*Give me numbers, Hasik. Now!*"

Hasik shoved his glasses back into place.

"Fifty percent chance to dive again," he said. "After that... I can't say."

Fifty percent. A flip of the coin.

If Trav took *Keeling* into realspace and the ship couldn't dive again, they were dead. Cooley's intel, the Raiders, Lafferty and Darkwater, the *Ishi* survivors, and Vesna, if she was still alive—all lost.

"Weps, load tube one with another STC," Trav said. "Set the Mark 16s in tubes two, three, and four to auto-seek *two* profiles, Chanda-class and Malag-class. I know that puts us and *Ishlangu* at risk, just do it. Nav, plot a course with best possible probability to intercept *Yankee*. Everyone remember—what you might see isn't real. Fight through it. We're going to get our people."

Cooley hopped off the command station, took his place at the XO's spot.

The CIC buzzed with activity.

Someone threw up.

Trav stepped forward to the captain's position, put his hands on the slate, looked into the orb—just an orb once again—and watched his ship slice through the Mud.

79

Sascha looked out into the Mud, and the Mud looked in at her.

She held tight to what was left of the machining bay hatch. Her mind told her the ragged, narrow, oblong hole in the hull was death, that she might be sucked out of the ship in an instant even though her HUD told her the machining room was at normal air pressure.

An enemy round had hit somewhere below deck four, ripped up through the deck where it met the bulkhead, then exited halfway up the bulkhead's curve. *Keeling* had been belly-facing *Zulu*—the penetrator round struck a glancing blow up the port side. Someone had been in here when it happened. Sascha didn't know who yet, because the shards of metal cast out by the disintegrating penetrator round had ripped that sailor to shreds.

In the time it took Sascha to get from engineering control to machining, all of about sixty seconds, a strange, translucent film had formed over the hole. She could see through it somewhat, see shapes, *moving* shapes—what might be eyes, eyes as big as her head, six of them, staring through the membrane at her, blinking in different rhythms, each moving independently of the others like goldfish scrambling to get at dropped crumbs.

A hand grabbed her arm. Sascha jumped, started to yank free before she realized it was Marchenko.

"Eng, what in Heaven's name is that?"

Sascha looked back to the oblong hole—the eyes were gone.

"The eyes," she said. "Did you see them?"

"*Eyes?* No, I didn't. Is that some kind of glass? It sealed the tear. Am I hallucinating this?"

Hallucinating. That's what it was. Sascha had been hallucinating. Had to be.

"It's real," Sascha said. "If it wasn't, we'd be dead."

The film's translucence slowly faded, as if the material was thickening. In front of it, stretching out from the inner hull's surface, gossamer threads of bright copper extended across the film, connecting with and melting into the far side. Strands overlapped, crisscrossed. It was happening fast—the hole would be covered in seconds.

Sascha rushed across the machining room wreckage, knowing she was stepping on and through the remains of one of her engineering crew, hating herself for it, but she *had to see.*

At the oblong hole she leaned close, looking through the few remaining spaces. The film had thickened, but from only centimeters away it wasn't yet fully opaque.

Sascha closed one eye, peered out, and for a moment, for just the briefest beat of her pulse, she thought she saw something with four bony wings vanishing into a vast cloud-river of pulsating crimson Mud.

The 1MC chimed.

"This is the XO. Prepare to surface."

80

Anne gripped the safety cable keeping her clipped to the hauler's raised loading door, leaned out and waved her hand inward.

Another vacsuited sailor entered, this one with a carbine slung across his back. That made thirty-five and counting, three of them armed with weapons they'd probably grabbed from *Ishi*'s small arms locker.

Anne didn't have to direct the rescuees anymore. The first ten had quickly organized, packing everyone near the front of the cargo area so there was more room.

Only minutes to go, five at most. *Ishi* CIC hadn't reported on *Yankee*'s ETA to short-range. If it had, Darkwater hadn't relayed the info.

People were streaming out of the *Ishi*, the non-essential combat crew abandoning ship. Even as they did, the ship's lone remaining artillery gun silently fired, plumes of smoke billowing as its crew tried to land a shot on the incoming corvette.

That enemy ship—which Anne couldn't see because Darkwater kept the hauler behind *Ishi*—was beginning to land shots. Big slabs of *Ishi*'s armor spun this way and that, beginning an infinite journey through the cosmos. The hauler remained in the lee side of that storm, protected—for now—from the larger pieces.

"Major, *Ishi* CIC responded," Darkwater said. "They said *Yankee* is already in medium range, sixty seconds to short-range. They've given the order to abandon ship."

Anne scanned the area around *Ishi*'s hull. At least two dozen sailors coming her way. It would take two minutes, at least, to get them all in.

"Hold position," she said. "Don't leave until I give the order."

She waved in another evacuee.

A chunk of armor whizzed past about a hundred meters aft, spinning so violently fragments of it were breaking off—*Yankee*'s shots were beginning to punch clear through *Ishlangu*.

Anne accepted she wouldn't be able to save all the evacuees, not if she wanted to preserve the lives of those she already had.

Another forty seconds... she could get ten more...

Out past the dozens of evacuees flying toward the hauler was one much farther out, moving twice as fast as the others. *More* than twice as fast. TASH armor? Yes, a Raider, rifle in hand. A lucky break. If the corvette had Crusaders—intel was fuzzy on that detail—they might try to board the unarmed hauler. A single Raider wasn't much, but he or she could make all the difference when Darkwater/Rossi accelerated away from here.

"*Ishi* is coming apart," the ensign said, panic in her voice. "Major, we're out of time!"

The little spy wasn't wrong.

Anne looked across the area, did the brutal math of who she'd have to leave behind. Six more would make it before the Raider arrived, and when the Raider did, that was it.

"Not yet," Anne said. "Thirty more seconds."

81

John and his squad plummeted toward *Zulu*.

That was how it felt, like he was free-falling to crash against a massive monster. Sergeant Jordan led the way, moving toward the landing point she'd picked out.

Keeling's canister shot left deep divots and gouges all along *Zulu*'s bow. Four of the dense metal balls had hammered into the ship's port-forward point-defense gun—a wicked-looking, six-barreled rotary cannon—leaving fist-sized holes in the turret's plate armor. The PDG turret moved a meter left, shuddered, moved a meter right, shuddered, moved a meter left again.

It was stuck.

War was part luck, part skill. A jammed turret was all the luck Alpha Squad needed.

John could no longer see Biggie's Ochthera. By now, the APC had likely ripped a hole in *Zulu*'s topside-aft armor and deposited its load of Bravo Squad and Master Sergeant Sands. Any organized defense would be flocking in that direction—exactly as John had planned.

He followed Jordan toward the jammed turret, her four thrusters glowing yellow-white against the endless black. Flashing green lights on the back of her TASH told her squad to follow.

When living and working inside a warship, it was easy to lose track of how big warships were. This corvette—small by military standards—was over 130 meters long and 16 meters at the beam. John and his Raiders looked like ticks by comparison.

Had *Zulu*'s spotters seen them? Just a few seconds more, and the Raiders would be on the hull.

The corvette's attitude thrusters fired—the ship began rotating port-side-up along its axis.

Yes, the spotters had seen them.

John triggered the squad channel. "LZ rotating, watch out for functional weapons."

No response. Either they were still within the STC torps EM-spectrum-warping range, or *Zulu* had activated a corruptor. Maybe both. Whatever the reason, comms remained dead.

The hull rotated, rolling the jammed turret upward—John's relative "upward"—and out of his line of sight. Simultaneously, the matching starboard PDG turret rolled into view from below.

And there wasn't so much as a dent on it.

They were so close to the hull, only seconds now...

The turret swung toward the Raiders.

Jordan abandoned her stealthy approach—the back of her TASH flashed the stuttering yellow/red signal for *evasive action.*

The PDG opened up, flame-tongues spitting out ten 30-millimeter rounds per second, tracer trails painting orange streaks through the void.

Raiders scattered like flying cockroaches fleeing the light, all choosing their own direction while simultaneously returning fire. Rounds slammed on and around the PD turret's armor in a flash-fire popcorn burst.

John banked left, away from the stuttering orange streaks.

Those streaks sliced into Fred Abeen, instantly tearing him into three pieces that spun away in three directions, blood streamers boiling into dissipating foam.

The squad's withering fire engulfed the turret, punching through the armor—the PDG stopped firing.

Jordan's TASH lights flashed alternating green and yellow, telling her team to land and attack.

The sergeant's feet touched down the hull as soft as if she'd been lowered by an angel. Her thruster extensions retracted. John landed a few meters to her right.

He pressed his rifle to his chest mag clamps and crawled on all fours to the hole-filled turret, keeping a careful eye on it in case it swung his way. It didn't. He pulled a shrapnel grenade from his thigh armor, thumbed the timer to two seconds, and shoved it through one of the holes made by the canister shot. He scurried away—the grenade detonated in silence, an explosion marked only by a slight vibration of the turret armor.

Jordan flashed hand signals. Beaver and Mafi each pulled a cutter torch from their calf armor and went to work opening the turret's top.

John felt a slight inertial tug—*Zulu* pitching down and yawing starboard, trying to shake off the Raiders, but it was too late. Everyone was down on foot-knee-foot, three points of contact holding them firm.

John did a quick headcount. Beaver and Mafi at the turret. Abshire to the right, kneeling close to Sergeant Jordan. Sarvacharya to the left, Basara a few meters past her.

Where was Shamdi?

John scanned the space above him, but all he saw were the remains of Fred Abeen, still spinning, slowly moving away from the corvette.

Jordan crawled to him and put her hand on his armor to create a contact-connection.

"Move it, Bennett, we're in."

He glanced to the PDG turret, saw Mafi and Beaver push the sliced-open top out into space.

"I don't see Shamdi," John said.

"We're not looking for him," Jordan said. "We go in now, your team in front. Move it."

John felt a sharp stab of loss along with the deep slash of guilt. He should have been in the rear where the team leader was supposed to be. He pushed those emotions down—now wasn't the time.

He crawled to the turret, grabbed his Rogalinski, and aimed— inside were three bodies wearing the Purist version of LASH rigs, thin armor plates cracked and broken, ripped flesh exposed, red froth bubbling.

John pointed to Abshire and Beaver, then down into the cramped turret. The two boots drew their knives, crawled in, and stabbed the chests of unmoving men who were obviously already dead. John crawled down. The gunner seats and targeting equipment were ripped apart, courtesy of RR rounds that had ravaged the interior even before the shrapnel grenade did its job.

The first airlock door was flat on the deck behind the seats. John pointed to Abs, then to the wheel on the door. John and Beaver took up opposite sides so they could take out anyone unfortunate enough to be inside. Abs spun the wheel. He waited a beat, yanked the door open.

Empty.

A short ladder led down to a second wheeled door. John pointed to Beaver, pointed down. Beaver clamped his rifle to his chest and descended the ladder. From his thigh armor, he pulled a fist-sized breech charge complete with coiled wire and a detonator. He smooshed the charge's soft material against the door, well away from the wheel and the hinges. He jammed the wire's end into the explosive, then ascended the ladder.

John signaled up to Jordan and Alpha Squad—they vanished from sight.

Abs, Beaver, and John moved away from the first door, which was left open.

John gave Beaver a thumbs-up.

Beaver flashed the hand-signal for *fire in the hole*, then pressed the detonator's button.

Air and debris rushed out of the ladder in a brief atmospheric decompression. Interior pressure doors were probably sealed, but anyone caught in that passageway without a vacsuit was in big trouble.

John clamped his rifle and descended the ladder. Beaver's charge had blown a head-sized hole in the door's bottom left corner. John pulled a grenade, thumbed the fuse timer to two seconds, and flicked it through the hole forward. He did the same with a grenade he flicked through the hole aft.

He spun the airlock wheel. It turned, the mechanism working fine thanks to Beaver's smart charge placement.

John pulled the door open, unclamped his rifle, and waved for Abs to join him. The two TASHed Raiders made for a tight fit in the confined space. John stepped through and aft, aiming along the passageway, knowing Abs would be an instant behind, stepping out and aiming forward.

One person in the passageway, on his back, his vacsuit punctured in a half-dozen bloody places. An infinity tattoo on his forehead marked him as a confirmed Purist. The man opened and closed his mouth like a fish gasping for air, which was exactly what he was doing.

He'd be dead in seconds, but Raiders never risked such things.

John drew his knife. He drove the dense blade deep into the man's chest.

The man's eyes widened, a final bit of surprise, of fear, in his last few seconds.

"Rest," John said, even though the man couldn't hear him. "You did your people proud."

John felt a hand on his shoulder armor.

"Get us to the CIC," Jordan said.

John sent Beaver first, Abs after, then brought up the rear. In a tight stack formation, Alpha-Two moved down the passageway, Jordan and Alpha-One close behind.

82

A plume of fire erupted from *Ishlangu*'s starboard side, raging outward twenty meters ahead of the hauler.

Susannah trembled with fear.

"Major, *please*! We gotta go!"

"Ten more seconds," Lafferty said.

Lafferty was still in the cargo area, still bringing in evacuees.

Another explosion drove *Ishi*'s nose downward, briefly leaving Susannah with a line of sight to the oncoming corvette. The enemy warship loomed, a vibrating cloud of possibilities.

She pitched the hauler down, again putting it behind the ravaged *Ishi*.

That glimpse of the corvette delivered a terrifying truth—it was too late. At this distance and relative velocity, no matter which way she flew, she could not outrun *Yankee*.

In minutes, the hauler would be destroyed or captured.

Motion high above caught her eye—in one fixed spot, the void itself seemed to bulge, to *breathe*, as if coming to life...

83

"Major Lafferty, *Keeling* is coming out of transdim," Darkwater/Lafferty said. "I can see it!"

Time was up.

"Last one coming in now," Anne said. "Hold tight."

Out in the void, four tiny engines blazed yellow-white. This Raider was *good*, expertly applying counterthrust against his high relative velocity, decelerating as he approached the hauler. Anne had spent enough time training in TASH to know the difficulties of that maneuver—many Raiders set themselves to spinning wildly, a problem that itself could take minutes to puzzle out.

Mere meters from the open loading door, the Raider retracted his thrusters. Rogalinski rifle in his gauntleted hands, he drifted past her and into the cargo area.

Anne spun the well-oiled wheel that lowered the loading door. Before it closed, she made the mistake of looking outward—a dozen sailors coming her way, two so close she could just make out the look of horror on their faces.

She'd saved forty-five people. She could do no more.

When she turned away from the hatch, she jerked in surprise—the Raider was standing right in front of her.

Anne had time to see the nameplate—SHAMDI—before the butt of his rifle slammed into her stomach, doubling her over and dropping her to the deck.

84

"We're back in realspace."

The orb buzzed with static.

"Rebooting darsat."

Trav couldn't see where *Ishi* or *Yankee* were, but he had to take a chance, had to fire blind and strike now.

"Fire tubes two through four."

"Firing two," Brown said. "Firing three. Firing four."

Three red torpedo lines serpentined away from the *Keeling*. The Mark16s' bat brains were instructed to seek out gravitational waves put out by a Chanda and a Malag, but at this range and with so much signal chaos, they might lock on to anything in the area. If the torps accidentally targeted *Ishi*, Trav had sealed the fate of that ship and her crew.

He still had an STC torp in tube one. "Weps, load tubes two, three, and four with Mark16s."

Brown repeated the order.

"Darsat coming online," Waldren said.

The orb stuttered to life. Icons for *Ishlangu* and the cargo hauler appeared at starboard-aft-low, and for *Yankee* at port-bow-high.

Keeling had surfaced almost directly between the two warships— exactly what Trav wanted.

Two new icons appeared, much farther away at port-beam, ten degrees declination.

"Torp two has locked on to *Yankee*," Brown said. "Torp four as well. Ten seconds to impact."

In the orb, icons for two and four, along with their trailing lines, changed from red to blue, headed straight for *Yankee*. From *Keeling*'s perspective, they streaked up and to port. Torp three continued to wander.

"Signals," Trav said, "put visual of *Yankee* in-orb."

"Six seconds," Brown said.

In the orb, icons and range rings vanished, replaced by a cloud of probability fuzz. Trav had a three-second look at the shuddering, stuttering image, just enough time to make out a few strobe-pulse details of the corvette and the electric blue wake of the two torpedoes streaking toward it.

The first torp broke into pieces, knocked out by Chanda's point-defense battery.

The second came in untouched—*Yankee*'s prow erupted in a bright orange flash.

85

High One, see me through. I offer my body as a sacrifice to your glory.

Nitzan Shamdi aimed and fired, aimed and fired, aimed and fired. He'd heard the phrase *shooting fish in a barrel*, but he'd never really understood it until this moment. Where he aimed, Union sailors died. Three of them had been armed with carbines—he'd killed them first, dropping them before they knew what was happening.

He kept his aim away from straight-on, aft-to-forward shots that might go through the target and penetrate to the cabin, where Bethany was.

There was nowhere for the sailors to run. Two made a split-second decision to rush him—Nitzan scored a chest shot on the first and a head shot on the second. People screamed, begged for mercy, but he couldn't hear them, not in the vacuum, and that made it easier.

The Union had taught him well. When the last of the sailors were down, their blood frothing in boiling puddles on the cargo hold deck, he still had three rounds left in his fifty-round magazine.

He put in a fresh mag, then hauled the heaving intel chief to her feet. High One had smiled upon him—the Cloister would piss themselves with delight. Lafferty was still trying to draw breath as Nitzan shoved her toward the pilot cabin airlock.

When he saw a body still moving, he put a round in it. He wasn't out of the woods yet, but he and Bethany were so close to pulling this off.

So close to being heroes of the Purist Nation.

86

Susannah yanked open another locker, tore through the contents. Clothes, a cracked bracelet, some paper books... but no weapon.

Another locker—two escape wings.

Another locker—a cardboard box. She grabbed it and looked inside. A *dildo*? Was that a riding crop? She dug through the box's contents—ropes and black leather and a chain dog leash, but there was nothing she could use to defend herself.

She crawled into the sleeper area, ripped the pornographic pictures from the bulkheads in search of a hidden compartment. She found none. She yanked the filthy sheets from the mattress, ran her hand in the space between the mattress and the bulkheads, felt nothing but dust and crumbs and something sticky—no guns or knives.

No weapons.

Susannah had heard Lafferty's breathy grunt of surprise and pain, then the signal cut off. Cargo hold cameras showed why—she'd been doubled over on the deck while a black-armored Raider gunned down rescued *Ishi* crewmembers, blowing them apart one at a time with murderous efficiency, a silent horror show taking place in total vacuum.

All that risk, all that danger, all those rescued people...

Wasn't Cooley some kind of super-spy? He *had* to have a weapon in here, didn't he? Where would he hide it?

She heard a beep from the cargo hold airlock—the hold-side door opened. She had to do something, that killer was coming in here to gun her down just like he'd gunned down all those sailors.

Another beep: the cab-side door opened.

Susannah froze. Not by choice—she couldn't move. She was going to die here on this pervert's mattress.

Anne Lafferty stumbled into view, bouncing off a side-locker before slamming against the back of the co-pilot's chair. She fell to the floor, her hands clutching her stomach.

The Raider stepped in after her, booted feet heavy against the deck, his rifle tight to his shoulder. He turned, looked into the sleeper bin, and his eyes locked with Susannah's.

She knew those eyes. She couldn't believe it.

"Nitzan?"

Behind his visor, Nitzan Shamdi smiled.

"We did it, Bethany," he said. "We did it."

87

"I had to get to you," Shamdi said to Darkwater/Rossi. "I know who you are, Bethany. I've known all along. We have more than enough intel. Head for the destroyer, full burn. We can go home again."

Anne struggled to her knees, rage filling her, the tap-tap-tapping so thick it was like being punched over and over again. All those sailors she'd saved—they were dead. She'd *known* Rossi was a Purist spy, yet she'd ignored her instincts to kill the bitch. Shamdi was also a spy? Anne hadn't suspected him at all.

She was an utter failure.

"Bethany," Shamdi said, "we have to go. *Now.*"

Darkwater/Rossi nodded dumbly, crawled out of the sleeper bin. As she passed by, she cast a fast glance Anne's way, a glance full of fear and desperation and... and pleading?

The ensign slid into the pilot's seat.

"Hold tight," she said.

Shamdi clutched the sleeper bin ledge with one armored hand. The other hand remained on his rifle's grip.

He stared at Anne.

"Remember me, Major? Remember when you told me to go fuck around somewhere else? Well, I guess this is that *somewhere else*. You're the icing on my cake, Major. I bet you know secrets about the *Keeling* that even Bethany doesn't know. I tossed your sidearm out the cargo bay door, by the way. Bethany, are there any other weapons aboard?"

"No," Darkwater/Rossi said, her voice barely audible. "I don't think so."

Anne felt the slight tug of inertia as the hauler accelerated away from the dying *Ishlangu*, away from the poor souls still floating out there in space with nowhere to go.

She felt lost. How could she have gotten things so wrong?

Shamdi was a Purist spy. Rossi was a Purist spy.

Anne couldn't think straight. The tapping, *crawling* through her brain—it made her skin scream, made her heart ache.

This Purist meathead had beaten her.

Her death would not be quick.

Anne's end would come at the hands of Cloister torturers.

She would die screaming.

88

Alpha Squadron met little resistance.

The passageways were a bit confusing. The layout John had seen in *Keeling*'s CIC wasn't exactly right, but a ship the size of a corvette offered only so many options. They'd sealed hatches behind them, which allowed sections to repressurize.

John stepped over dead bodies, some vacsuited, some not. Those that weren't wore the blue uniforms of the Purist fleet. Some had tried to fight—those brave souls had big, meaty holes in them courtesy of Beaver and Abs, who'd mowed them down. A TASH-armored, Rogalinski-wielding soldier against a crew member in a vacsuit carrying a pistol? It wasn't a fair fight. And that was fine—Raiders didn't like fair fights.

Some had tried to surrender. John felt bad about those corpses, but what could he do? With only one shorthanded squad of seven Raiders, they couldn't leave people behind, and they couldn't take prisoners. Purist sailors that didn't fight got a knife to the base of the skull, quickly sending them to meet their High One.

War was a bitch.

Through his TASH's external mics, John heard distant gunfire and explosions. Bravo Squadron must have drawn the bulk of *Zulu*'s internal quick reaction force. The two-pronged strategy had worked better than he'd dared to hope.

Zulu had escaped the STC interference, and if there was a corruptor that had been shut off—the squad channel now worked fine.

"Beaver," John said, "CIC entrance should be just ahead on the left."

"I see it," Beaver said.

"Hold position," John said. "Sergeant Jordan, I believe we found the CIC."

John's heart ached for Shamdi, but it threatened to burst from pride for Beaver and Abs. They were unblooded no more. They hadn't panicked. They'd performed like hardened vets, staying patient, communicating well. And, most of all, when a threat presented itself, they turned that threat into hamburger.

"Alpha Squad, let's finish the job," Jordan said. "Move in."

John slapped Abshire's shoulder armor, pointed to the door, extended his fingers in an animated *boom* pantomime.

Abshire grabbed his breech charge from his calf, crouch-walked to the hatch door as John and Beaver covered him.

Abs stretched the explosive putty into a long rope and ran it down the hatch's side, atop where the internal hinges would be. He stuck the detonator lead into the soft material, then backed away, trailing wire.

"I still wanna go home," he said, "but not right now. Fire in the hole."

Neal Abshire, only a few weeks out of boot camp, pressed the detonator button.

The explosion produced surprisingly little smoke. The hatch skewed inward, then tilted and dropped to clang against the deck beyond.

John and Beaver moved past Abshire, who rose and followed. John entered and swept left while Beaver swept right. A large nav-orb ringed by glowing workstations sat in the CIC's center. Some vacsuited Purists lay prone on the deck with fingers laced behind their heads, some dropped to that same position, and others stood there in shock.

A woman raised a pistol—she died instantly as Beaver put a round through her chest.

John reached the CIC's right corner.

Those Purists still standing had their hands up.

He glanced left, saw Sarvacharya just inside the hatch to the left, Abshire just inside to the right.

"On the deck," John said. "Now!"

Those who were still standing dropped to the deck.

"Abs, check them for weapons," John said. "Slow and steady. Sergeant Jordan, the CIC is ours."

89

"*X-Ray* is accelerating," Waldren said. "It's closing on *Zulu*."

Trav hoped the Raider platoon saw the destroyer coming. They had to get out of there.

"*Ishlangu* signal detected," Sara Ellison called out. "The crew has abandoned ship and is requesting rescue."

Which meant Lafferty and Darkwater hadn't gotten everyone. No surprise there.

"Darsat," Trav said, "I don't see Hauler-One. Find it."

A small ship like the hauler could easily drop off darsat, especially in a chaotic, interference-filled engagement like this. That was part of what made fightercraft such a terror—sometimes the only way you knew they were coming is when you saw them with your own eyes.

Odds were, though, the reason *Keeling* couldn't see the hauler was because the hauler had been destroyed. Had it taken on evacuees who were now dead, along with Lafferty and Darkwater?

"Tubes five and six loaded," Brown said. "Calculating *Yankee* target solution."

Trav had turned *Keeling* away from *Yankee*, which left the rear tubes pointed in the corvette's direction. *Yankee* spun wildly, but that spin steadily slowed as its crew brought the ship under control.

"Hauler-One located," Waldren said. "It's... it appears to be headed for *X-Ray*."

In the orb, Trav saw the hauler icon moving away from *Ishlangu*, and moving fast—*too* fast.

"Signals, see if you can reach Hauler-One," he said. "They must have a mechanical failure."

"Contacting Hauler-One, aye-aye," Ellison said.

If there was a mechanical issue, there was little Trav could do to help. He had no voidcraft left to send after it.

"It's not a malfunction," Cooley said quietly. "Someone on that hauler is a Purist. It, Lafferty, Darkwater, and anyone they rescued are as good as gone, XO."

Trav fought to control his frustration. Could there have been a spy onboard *Ishi*?

"ECM," he said, "can we get a tether on Hauler-One?"

Brinson Sorro manned the ECM station. Sweat sheened the man's dark face.

"No, sir," he said. "Hauler-One is too far away."

Trav knew that, but desperation had forced him to ask anyway. If Darkwater and Lafferty were still alive, they were doomed.

"We have torpedo solution on *Yankee*," Brown said.

At least there was something Trav could still control.

"Fire both tubes," he said.

"Firing five," Brown said. "Firing six. Time to impact, thirty-five seconds."

Trav started his stopwatch. "Load tube five with STC, tube six with a Mark16."

Brown repeated the order.

"I'm unable to reach Hauler-One," Ellison said.

Was that because of existing STC interference or was the hijacker just not answering?

Trav watched the orb, focused on the two blue icons streaking toward *Yankee*. If either landed, that might be it for the Purist corvette.

Twenty-five seconds...

"*Yankee* has arrested its spin," Waldren said.

Sorro turned and shouted at Trav: "XO, *Yankee* has lunched countermeasures!"

"Eyes on your station," Trav said.

If they made it out of this, Lincoln would have to do something about Sorro. The man didn't have the mettle needed to work in the CIC.

Fifteen seconds...

The hauler icon continued on a straight line toward *X-Ray*.

"Torp five drawn off by a decoy," Brown said. "Torp six... it's destroyed."

The corvette was back in business. If Trav turned *Keeling* around to engage *Yankee*, he might finish it off, but a straight-up fight was risky. And what would it achieve? If *Keeling* went down, the Raiders were screwed.

The battle had become a numbers game—minutes, seconds, and sailors who would survive to see another day.

His heart heavy, his belly churning, Trav made the only decision he could.

"Pilot, continue course to *Ishlangu*. Weps, set tube five to maximum STC disruption, build solution for midpoint to *Yankee* and launch when ready. Ops, prepare to open the pouch. Let's save who we can."

90

Perversion, everywhere. Pornographic pictures taped to the bulkheads, strewn about the deck. Over the past few years, in order to fit in, Nitzan often had to look at such things, but no longer. Once back in the Nation, he would work with clerics to purge his mind of the unclean thoughts that collected like cancerous lesions.

He pulled the zipstrip tight around Lafferty's wrists, binding them behind her back. As gently as he could, he rolled her to her butt.

"Get against the co-pilot seat," he said.

Lafferty glared at him, but she did as she was told, scooting until her back rested against the rear of the seat.

He'd searched her, found her crude knife. He couldn't believe his luck—Lafferty had provided him with a sample of *Keeling*'s hull material. High One works in mysterious ways indeed.

Nitzan examined the jagged, gleaming blade. "That Gillick douche had one of these." He realized he sounded like a Unionite. A foul-mouthed Unionite. "I mean, Corporal Gillick had one. I'm glad you brought this, Major Lafferty. You turned my mission from a stand-up double to a home run."

Maybe only a triple. A *home run* would have been bringing the entire ship back to the Nation. Still, he knew his handlers wouldn't complain.

He tucked the blade into his chest webbing, then leaned back against the sleeper bin wall. He could watch Lafferty in case she tried something.

Bethany looked frightened, which he understood—they would not be safe until they boarded the destroyer. So beautiful she was. A soldier, a selfless servant to their nation and their faith.

Soon, he'd be able to talk to her without reservation. They could trade stories about their time in the Union. Like him, Bethany's deep cover work was over. They could never return to Union space lest facial recognition software pick them out of a crowd. And forget about operating in the League of Planets—the gene-queens got their hands on Union data almost before the Union did.

He was going *home*. He'd be confirmed in the church. He'd probably never have to fight—or kill—ever again.

His future was bright. Lafferty's was not.

"Let me give you some advice, Major," Nitzan said. "The Cloister's inquisitors are good at their jobs. *Really* good. You're going to talk, eventually. The sooner you give up all you know about the *Keeling* program, the less pain you'll experience."

Lafferty's features twisted with hate. Hate against him and Bethany? No... her expression struck him as *self*-hate. He wasn't an inquisitor, but Major Lafferty looked like she was already broken.

When the hauler reached the destroyer, Nitzan knew someone else would interrogate Lafferty. If he could get some info out of her in the next fifteen minutes, he and Bethany might be able to stay on as Lafferty's primary captors. The more info he could provide to the Ministry of Intelligence, the better off his eventual position would be.

"Cooperate, and you'll find Nationalite hospitality a lot more fun than screaming in agony," he said. "Let me help you, Major."

Lafferty said nothing. She stared at the deck, or maybe at the torn picture of a woman and... was that a *farm animal*?

Blasphemers, these Unionites. One and all.

"Bethany," Nitzan said, "I'm so sick of these people. Praise be we're going home."

"Uh... yes," Bethany said. "Praise be."

It was over. He'd done his duty. He'd *won*. It felt so good. A weight off his shoulders, off his very being.

"I haven't seen Nation soil in seven years," he said. "Can you believe that? *Seven years.* How about you, Bethany?"

She didn't answer right away. She seemed to be struggling with the controls. The screens on the dashboard fuzzed with static. Flying one of these things looked like it was more work than he would have guessed.

"I haven't been gone as long as you have," Bethany said. "But I guess every minute away is one minute too many. Right?"

Nitzan smiled and nodded. Truer words had never been spoken.

"You're just full of surprises," he said. "They teach you how to operate haulers in the Cloister? Oh, I don't know your rank. Should I be addressing you as *ma'am?*"

91

Rank? What was he talking about?

Susannah's thoughts sputtered and spun. She couldn't process what Nitzan was saying. He was a murderer, yet he was trying to chat with her like they were back on the *Keeling*?

As a battle raged around them, he'd ordered her to fly to the destroyer. She'd obeyed. A mistake? She didn't know. What else could she have done? Nitzan thought, somehow, that she was on his team. She wanted to keep him thinking that, lest he turn that gun on her.

"Bethany? You okay?"

Nitzan sounded so *friendly*. He'd just slaughtered forty-four human beings, and he sounded like he wanted to help.

Susannah faced forward, pretended to focus on her flight controls.

"I'm fine. Sorry, there's so much interference. Navigating through it isn't easy."

"I bet," Nitzan said. "I asked what your rank was. You a first lieutenant? A captain, maybe?"

Again with the rank. And he'd asked if she'd learned how to operate a hauler in the Cloister...

It hit Susannah all at once—Nitzan Shamdi thought she was a Purist spy.

Just like him.

She glanced at Lafferty, restrained behind the co-pilot seat.

"I'm a major," Susannah said.

"A major?" Nitzan laughed. "I should have known. You played it so well—I almost didn't know you were a plant at all."

Far out ahead, Susannah saw the blurry image of the Purist destroyer.

Nitzan walked forward, his heavy boots clonking on the deck. He knelt down at her right. He placed his rifle angled against his chest—it stuck there with a click—then rested his gauntleted hand on her seat-back. It was all she could do not to pull away from him.

"I spent two years in the Cloister," he said. "How about you?"

She didn't know a thing about the Cloister. She didn't know a thing about the Purist military. She couldn't let him know that.

Susannah looked up at the handsome face behind that visor. A face full of serenity. The kind of serenity Susannah had striven for, lived in a convent to achieve, served High One and Purism for a decade to reach, yet she'd never really found it.

Not until the *Keeling*.

Not until she'd seen the dark place.

Nitzan nudged her.

"What do you miss the most about the Nation, Bethany?"

"Habanero falafel biscuits," she said, blurting out the first thing that came to mind.

"Oh, *me too*," Nitzan said. "Haven't had the real thing in ages. Close, though. Real close. There was a place on Zackmann Station where Ari and I..."

He stared out at the fuzzy destroyer. "I just want to go home." Such sorrow in his voice. "I want to go *home*. Do you?"

Home. Yes, Susannah did.

But *home* wasn't the Nation. Not anymore. The Nation had kicked her out, made her flee in the dead of night with nothing but the clothes on her back. The Nation had stolen away a decade of her life, wiped clean all her work, all her sacrifice, all her dear friends in the convent.

No, the Purist Nation wasn't home anymore.

Keeling was.

She'd driven a hauler similar to this one for years. She knew what it could do. What it *couldn't* do. Somewhere in between was an area of failure, but if she didn't try now, she'd be lost forever, no matter where she wound up.

If she was going to die, she was going to die by her own choices, by her own hand.

"Nitzan, can you move Major Lafferty to the back? I want to tell you something, but I don't want her to hear."

There was a short pause as he considered it, then he gently grabbed Lafferty's ankle and dragged her to the sleeping bin. Susannah glanced back, saw Lafferty adjusting herself, putting her back against the floor lockers beneath the mattress.

Nitzan stepped forward again.

Susannah looked at her instruments so she didn't have to look at him, so big in that black armor, with that gun he'd used to kill so many people.

He again knelt next to her. "You were saying?"

His armor...

"I'd like to see your face," she said. "Your *whole* face, I mean. Can you take off the helmet?"

Susannah stared out the window. The fuzzy ball that was *Yankee* grew larger.

She heard clasps unfastening.

"I probably stink," Nitzan said. "We sweat a lot in these rigs. Sorry about that."

So friendly... so *nice*.

Susannah glanced at him. Tousled, short hair. Helmet-pad impressions on his forehead. Bright eyes. A beautiful monster.

Now or never.

"I do want to go home," she said. "I was just saying to Major Lafferty back there, just the other day, that when you get what you want, you have to hold on to it. You have to hold on tight. Isn't that right, Major?" Susannah looked over her shoulder at Lafferty. "You have to *hold on tight*?"

Nitzan turned to look as well.

Still looking aft, Susannah flew by feel and memory alone—she quietly increased the curvine's rate of acceleration.

Anne Lafferty stared back at Susannah. Her eyes narrowed, then widened with understanding. She shifted, turning her back to the starboard bulkhead, pushed with her heels to cram her body into a tight space between the side lockers and the sleeper bin.

Nitzan watched Lafferty with a puzzled expression. Then, he looked into Susannah's eyes.

Maybe, at that last instant, he figured it out. Maybe he had time to realize he should have strapped in, maybe enough time to realize he should have kept his helmet on. In that split second, Susannah saw into Nitzan Shamdi's soul, saw an explosion of realization and sadness, of betrayal.

With her left hand, she pulled a lever to disengage the curvine. Simultaneously, she thumbed the pitch control, felt the tug of inertia as the hauler's nose spun sharply upward.

Nitzan reached for her throat.

What had been *up* was now *down*—she released the pitch control and slammed the curvine lever forward, engaging it.

G-forces slammed Susannah against her seat, threw Nitzan aft. Susannah heard the sleeper bin's composite frame crunch and splinter as his heavy, armored body smashed into it.

The hauler shuddered and rattled like it was made of tin. Metal groaned, plastic snapped, seams sheared.

A distant part of her mind did the math. The force was like that of a car dropped ten stories straight down, but with the impact ongoing and sustained—squashing, crushing, a python's slow squeeze of inevitable death.

She couldn't draw a breath. She couldn't think. Spots formed in her vision, spread out, met each other.

As the blackness overtook her, she locked acceleration on full, praying to High One the hauler was pointed in the right direction.

92

John kept his Rogalinski leveled on the CIC crew. Abshire and Sarvacharya had herded the fifteen Purist sailors into a corner, made them kneel with their hands laced above their heads. If he had to, John could kill them all with one quick burst.

Master Sergeant Sands on the scratchy platoon channel: "Biggie informs me we've got company en route. I do not want to be here when it arrives. If Alpha Squad would be so kind as to get to the Ochthera, ASAP, I'd be most appreciative."

"Raider Lead, if we're out, we should scuttle the ship," Jordan answered. "I can try to set the curvine to go critical."

"Negative, squad leader," Sands said. "Biggie's crew has been busy. Inform your new church-going friends they have seven minutes to get off the ship or they'll see their precious High One face to face."

"Affirmative," Jordan said. "Sarge... anyone find Shamdi?"

"Negative," Sands said. "Biggie made a pass around *Zulu*, no joy. Get to the crawler, pronto."

Jordan shot John a glance.

"Affirmative, Master Sergeant," she said. "We're on our way."

Shamdi hadn't entered the ship with Alpha Squad. He or his body hadn't been found outside. What happened to him?

Jordan stepped closer to the prisoners. "Ladies and gentlemen of the Purist Nation, when we leave the CIC, you will stay where you

448

are for thirty seconds." She pointed to a woman in the back. "Lieutenant Major Anderson, you will count out loud to thirty. Count nice and slow. Make sure I can hear each syllable. If any of you peek your head out before thirty, we'll blow it clean off. When your count is done, you will have roughly five minutes to get to a lifeboat and get clear before this ship blows the fuck up."

The prisoners exchanged quick glances. They were in disbelief. Because their ship was done for? Or maybe that they'd live to see another day.

"Alpha-One, take lead," Jordan said. "Make sure no *Zulu* crew took up positions behind us."

Sarv, Mafi, and Basara filed out through the blown hatch.

Jordan backed away from the prisoners, careful to avoid John's field of fire.

"I *strongly* suggest you take my words to heart," she said. "And tomorrow, when you're grateful to be alive, send me a nice thank-you card, expressing your appreciation. Anderson, start counting."

"Thirty," Anderson said.

Jordan and Abs filed out.

"Twenty-nine."

Beaver went out next.

"Twenty-eight."

Rifle still aimed at the Purists, John backed out of the CIC. A slap on his shoulder told him to turn and run. He sprinted along the passageway behind Beaver and the rest of the squad.

Bennett's private channel squawked.

"Hey, Grampa," Beaver said, "what if they stick their heads out before thirty? Shouldn't we have someone there to shoot them if they do?"

Jesus Christ, this kid...

"Just run, Beaver. Just run."

93

"One lifeboat, inbound," Ellison said. "And fifteen... no, *seventeen* free-floaters, incoming."

Was Vesna among them?

Trav grabbed the 1MC handset.

"This is the XO. Lifeboat inbound. Flight bay, signal landing area." He thought of the terrified sailors out there, approaching the ugliness that was *Keeling*, probably aiming for the superstructure because that part looked familiar. "Chief Sung, get people at the topside hatches in case they come in that way."

He jammed the handset back in its cradle.

"*Ishlangu's* curvine just went critical," Waldren said. "She's going to blow."

The two ships were close enough that there was almost no visual interference. In the orb, *Ishlangu* glowed from within, sapphire light streaming through cracks and fissures.

At amidships, a deep blue sphere exploded outward, ripping her into two splintering halves.

"Signals," Trav said, "did the survivors get clear?"

A brief pause, then Ellison answered in a somber voice.

"The lifeboat did," she said. "The curvine explosion caught two free-floaters. Fifteen people still en route."

Trav sucked in a sharp breath. A pair of dedicated sailors had survived the battle, had hung in there till the end only to die so, *so* close to escape.

"Very well," Trav said. "Darsat, any sign of *Yankee*?"

Keeling's last STC torp had put a huge blob of blankness between her and *Yankee*. It gave cover while the crew hauled in the lifeboat and the free-floaters, but not being able to see the corvette made Trav's skin crawl.

"Negative," Waldren said. "STC interference is too strong."

"Conn, Flight Bay." Chief Sung's voice on the 5MC.

Cooley grabbed the handset and switched to that channel. "Flight bay, Conn, go ahead."

"The lifeboat is in the landing bay," Sung said. "We're getting them out now. Free-floaters are entering. We should have all survivors aboard in sixty seconds. Repeat, all survivors aboard in sixty seconds."

"Sixty seconds, aye," Cooley said. "Get the lifeboat clear as soon as possible, the Raider team is inbound." He put the handset in the cradle, glanced at Trav. "XO, the second that crawler is in, we need to dive."

Could they dive? That was still a question. Hasik put the odds at fifty-fifty. A coin flip. Heads, they live, tails, they die.

"Contact," Waldren said. "XO, Hauler-One acquired. Starboard zero-one-five. Elevation zero-two-seven."

The icon appeared in the orb. Its trajectory line showed a slight bow-up curve, indicative of fixed acceleration without attitude adjustment. Was someone asleep at the stick?

"Signals," Trav said, "connect to Hauler-One by any means necessary."

94

Something had punched through her cheek and broken a tooth.

Anne coughed, spit blood.

She hoped the blood came from her cheek, but from the way her body pumped pain, it might be from internal damage. Lungs? Intestines? Broken ribs? Ruptured spleen? All seemed possible.

Her head thundered. A concussion? She'd had them before, but not like this.

She tried to touch her mouth, but her hands wouldn't move. They were behind her back, as though something bound her wrists.

Where was she?

A locker, maybe, tight against her right shoulder. An external bulkhead against her back? Tight against her left shoulder, some kind of flat frame. Wood or plastic, maybe.

In front of her, just past her feet, ruined lockers and a TASH-armored Raider smashed up against a mattress bent in half longwise. Glossy paper fluttered everywhere, descending like wind-blown leaves.

The Raider wasn't wearing a helmet. Blood streamed from his forehead. A finger-sized splinter jutted from his lower lip. His right arm was twisted at a funny angle.

The Raider... his name was Shamdi, maybe... some woman, yelling at her... Darkwater... the *tapping*, the all-powerful itch and the need to make the tapping stop.

Anne remembered. Shamdi had murdered the *Ishlangu* crew and hijacked the hauler. Anne thought she was dead meat, helpless at the hands of a pair of Purist spies.

But Darkwater/Rossi had warned Anne to hold on, so she'd wedged herself into the thin space between the locker and the sleeping bin.

Doing so saved her life—the mousy little ensign had fucking tail-flipped the hauler.

Anne had no idea how many Gs she'd suffered, the unstoppable force smushing her against the sleeping bin's flat frame. But as bad as she hurt, being tight against the frame meant she hadn't built up inertia like Shamdi had—a good four meters of it before his armored body smashed into the bin like a wrecking ball.

Where was Darkwater/Rossi? Oh, up there in the pilot seat. She wasn't moving. Had Shamdi shot her?

The Raider's foot jerked. He grunted in pain. Still alive.

His left hand moved, gauntleted fingers stretching like a blind spider feeling about for prey. He was searching for his rifle—the rifle that was cracked and bent in the middle, uselessly resting atop a glossy picture of a man wearing only a cowboy hat and leaning against a bull-riding machine

Shamdi wanted to hand Anne over to Purist inquisitors, those savage butchers.

She could incapacitate him, make sure he was down for good, but she had to move before he did.

Her wrists...

He'd zip-stripped her.

Anne tucked her knees to her chest. Doing so *hurt*. She lurched forward, bending at the waist, trying to unwedge herself from the narrow space. She lurched a second time, popped free and fell to her right side.

Almost there...

Shamdi tried to sit up. He let out a yelp, stiffened, then lay still.

Focusing her will against the pain, Anne tried to slide her handcuffed wrists under her butt. Inside her body, things ground against each other.

"Bethany," Shamdi said, his voice closer to that of a little boy then a grown man. He moved a bit to the right, a bit to the left. "Help me, Bethany. Help me."

Anne's wrists wouldn't clear. She clenched her jaw, knowing she was inviting utter agony, then rolled to her back and kicked her legs up and over so that only her shoulders and the back of her head remained on the deck. Fighting against the roaring pain, fighting to keep her balance, she cried out as she stretched and stretched...

...her wrists slid under her butt.

Shamdi rolled to his left side. Groggy, he tried to rise.

Anne used her hands to pull her left foot tight to her crotch. She hooked the zip-tie on the outside of her left heel. From there, a yank, a push, and her foot was through.

Shamdi rose to his hip, his armor crinkling Cooley's dirty pictures. He looked at Anne, confusion in his eyes.

She got her right foot through. She hopped to her feet, then landed a snap-kick under Shamdi's jaw. He fell back against the porn-covered mattress.

He didn't move.

Her special knife—the beautiful copper blade was tucked into Shamdi's chest webbing.

Anne straddled him.

Tap-tap, TAP-*TAP*...

She removed his shoulder armor.

95

Sergeant Jordan set down on *Zulu*'s hull. She hustled up the crawler's rear ramp and into the packed troop compartment. Raiders were sitting in there, but also *lying* in there—two of them, unmoving, on the deck at their brethren's feet, and one of them, Abeen, in pieces.

Sands stood next to the ramp, Rogalinski in hand. He saw John flying in, pointed up.

"Alpha-Two on top!"

John retracted his extensions, set down next to Ochthera's armored turret. Inside, he could see Nikula grinning like a fool, her twin barrels aimed at a PDG she'd blown apart. Maybe she thought the dead Purists inside might spring up like zombies and start firing, and she didn't want to take any chances.

John scooted forward, saw wires running from the turret, down the crawler's canopy, and into the TASH-sized hole the crawler had cut through *Zulu*'s topside armor.

Man, oh man—Biggie's gang was going old-school.

Beaver set down behind the turret. Abshire came in too fast, thudded hard against the Ochthera's top. Had there been air, the crawler might have rung like a gong.

"I got him," Beaver said, and helped Abshire right himself.

Abs looked around. "Sarge Jordan ain't joining us up here?"

"Rank has its privileges," John said. "Clamp on, and *face backward*. You'll want to see this."

The three men clipped on safety lines.

Sands on the platoon channel: "Rear ramp sealed. All troops accounted for except Shamdi, but we gotta go. Light it up, Biggie."

"Roger that, Raider lead," Biggie said. "Topsiders, crank up them gripfields and clench those cheeks tight."

Abs and Beaver sat on their butts, facing aft. John watched them increase gripfield settings to make sure they did it right, then he sat and increased his own.

He held his breath, hoping he might hear Shamdi pipe up on the platoon frequency, say *hey, I'm here, don't leave me!*

John heard no such thing.

Raiders fought. When they did, Raiders died. With the probability cloud of an enemy ship closing in, if Sands waited any longer to search for Shamdi, the entire platoon would be lost.

The crawler lifted, yawed to port, then took off like a shot. John saw the glow of chemjets driving the Ochthera forward.

"Lord alm-m-*mighty*," Beaver said. "I thought we w-were accelerating f-f-fast before!"

Sometimes it was hard to talk clearly when acceleration Gs mushed the skin of your face.

Beneath John, the Ochthera rattled and bucked. That kind of vibration meant Biggie had pegged her curvine's acceleration and also maxed the chemjets. Not a good sign. It probably meant there was a countdown ticking away, a countdown that meant *Keeling* was either under fire or soon would be. Biggie couldn't spare a second.

John looked back at *Zulu*, not so large now and shrinking fast. Lifeboats jettisoned away, activating their precious directional burn fuel to get clear.

Beaver on the squad channel: "Sarge Sands? What happens now?"

"Now *Zulu* goes bye-bye," Sands said. "Biggie's crew put seeker missiles inside the dig-hole."

"I can't *wait* to see that," Beaver said. "Lucky we got to ride up top, huh, Abs?"

"Yeah," Abshire said in a deadpan. "I feel so lucky."

A thought popped into John's mind. "Hey, Beaver... did you fire your weapon?"

"Sure did, Bennett! I fired that RR like a real killer!"

That he had.

"Did you aim when you fired it?" John asked.

"Fuck yes I did!"

"So, you aimed and you fired," John said, "but I'm pretty sure I didn't hear you scream."

There was a pause—*Zulu* fell farther and farther away.

"Shit," Beaver said. "*Shit!*"

Far behind them, *Zulu* looked about as long as John's forearm. That small perspective, though, didn't make the view any less spectacular.

A tongue of flame jetted from the corvette's topside.

A split-second later, an expanding ball of fire blossomed and vanished as *Zulu* split in two.

Warship armor was made to stop things from getting in—not from getting out.

"Friendly fliers, we're in a bit of a time crunch," Biggie said. "You might feel a little additional turbulence. Sorry for the inconvenience. Topsiders, lay flat."

John watched Abs and Beaver lie back and straighten their legs, giving them more surface connection. They maxed their gripfields. Satisfied his charges were as secure as they could be, John followed suit.

He stared at the stars. Billions and billions of them.

Another boarding, and—somehow—he was still alive.

"I can't *believe* I forgot," Beaver said. "I got the fucking tattoo and everything."

96

"I got most of it," Zhen Smith said, "where do you want these?"

These. The mangled remains of Corporal Breslav Salvatore; remains that were hurriedly being crammed into a body bag. An arm here. A leg there. A meat-thick chunk of ribcage there.

"Put them in one of those cubbyholes," Sascha said. "And make sure you mark it."

"Aye-aye," Smith said.

Sascha had to hand it to her—she was doing her job quickly and efficiently, despite the shreds of flesh that had once been her crewmate.

Smith picked up a severed foot. One toe missing. The blast had blown Salvatore right out of his vacsuit boots. Smith put the foot in the bag.

Barnes Marchenko and Li Yang were doing a quick and dirty policing of the machining gear, anchoring free bits of wreckage that could become internal missiles if *Keeling* had to do harsh maneuvers, or extra shrapnel if another penetrator round struck home.

The hole had sealed itself. Where she'd briefly been able to look out into the Mud, now only bright, fresh copper remained.

She'd been told the ship could repair itself. She hadn't really believed it. Now she'd seen it happen, and still couldn't fully accept it.

People who looked out at the Mud supposedly went crazy, but she felt nothing of the sort. Had she hallucinated the shadowy thing with the big eyes and the bony wings, or had it been *real*?

"Finish up quick, all of you," she said. "I'm going down to the flight bay to make sure the hole there is sealed."

97

The sound of a slap, a sting on her cheek.

"Ensign, wake up."

Lafferty's voice...

Susannah jerked awake, saw Lafferty on her right, tried to dive away but the pilot seat restraints held her tight.

"Be still, Ensign."

Susannah froze.

Blood dotted Lafferty's face. Blood in her short auburn hair, on her vacsuit gloves and sleeves, blood on the chest coveralls where her vacsuit hung open. Blood on the homemade copper shiv she'd threatened Susannah with back on the *Keeling*.

The tip of that blade was centimeters from Susannah's belly.

"Don't try another tail-flip," Lafferty said. "I'm quite fast."

Was this it? Was Susannah about to die?

"Major... are you going to kill me?"

Lafferty slowly shook her head. "I don't think I have a reason to, but I'll ask you about that in a moment." She tilted her head toward the front window. "For now, I need you to point us at *Keeling*."

Susannah looked forward, saw three large overlapping blurs just as they slid down beneath the window's line of sight.

She gripped the controls. They were sluggish. Things rattled that weren't supposed to rattle. She felt vibrations she wasn't supposed to feel.

"Couldn't do another tail-flip if I wanted to," Susannah said. "Hauler's in bad shape."

She said that mostly to placate Lafferty, so the psycho might move the blade tip away, but it was also true—the hauler was on the edge of coming apart.

Lafferty left the blade where it was.

"The center cloud," she said. "That's *Keeling*. Aim for that."

Susannah had to fight the controls, but she put the *Keeling* dead-ahead.

"What are the other two blurs?"

"*Ishlangu*," Lafferty said. "Her curvine must have gone critical, or *Yankee* blew her in half. Ensign, we don't have long, so I'll ask you one time and one time only—were you working with Nitzan Shamdi?"

Susannah didn't want to look at Lafferty's bloody face, but she had to. The major appeared calm. Almost... stoned. She looked *serene*.

The same way Nitzan had looked when he'd thought his mission was over.

The same way Susannah felt when she was in the atrium.

"No," Susannah said. "I'm not. I wasn't."

Lafferty's eyelids slowly lowered, slowly rose.

"You sound honest about that," she said. "But put yourself in my shoes. Shamdi certainly believed you and he were on the same side."

Susannah glanced down at the shiv. Hadn't there been blood on it a moment before? No blood now. It was clean, gleaming.

In the back of the cabin, Nitzan let out a moan of agony.

"I don't know why he thought that," Susannah said. "I told you, I'm not a spy."

"Not a *Purist* spy, you mean."

So calm. So relaxed. So terrifying.

"Yes, Major," Susannah said. "That's correct."

Lafferty raised the shiv, rested the flat of the copper blade against her own forehead, thinking.

"You could have gone with him," she said. "You didn't. You were loyal. Are you loyal to the Union, Ensign?"

Tell her what she wants to hear, my child.

The Voice. Finally. But what would Lafferty want to hear?

Maybe High One took control, maybe not, but either way Susannah suddenly knew exactly what words to use.

"Yes, Major, I am loyal to the Union. That's why I took action against Shamdi. That's why I'm helping Admiral Bock, because even though I'm a Purist, a *devout* one, I'm a Unionite first."

Lafferty stared at her. A hint of a smile. A dreamy expression.

That moan again. Agonized. Mournful. Lost.

Susannah kept her eyes locked with Lafferty's.

"I believe you," the major said. "If it wasn't for you, I'd be under an inquisitor's knife, not the other way around. I'm going to keep your secret, Darkwater, and you're going to keep mine. This is for your own good. Soon, I'll talk to you about Admiral Bock. How long till we reach *Keeling?*"

Susannah glanced at the controls, looked out the window.

"Six minutes," she said. "Maybe seven."

Lafferty frowned. "So soon? That's too bad. Oh well, when life hands you lemons. Let me know when we're two minutes out. *Exactly* two minutes. I've got to take care of some details, Ensign. Because details matter."

She walked back toward the sleeper bin.

Susannah tried to stop herself from looking, tried hard, but she couldn't help it.

Nitzan Shamdi lay chest-down on the deck in a wide puddle of his own blood. Most of his armor had been removed, the pieces scattered carelessly about the cabin. Lafferty had used Cooley's bondage ropes to bind his ankles. His right arm lay outstretched, a loop of rope around his wrist binding it tight to a locker.

His left arm... High One...

It was severed at the elbow, flesh-spotted bone sticking out, wet strips of meat flopping and swinging when he moved. A black leather strap tied tight at his biceps slowed his bleeding but didn't stop it. He waved the stubby arm about like a toddler trying to swim, the motion splattering lockers with drops of red.

There was blood *everywhere.* Even on the ceiling.

Nitzan's eyes were wide and puffy with agony, confusion, with disbelief that this could be happening to him, and horror because he knew it was.

Thick, gleaming blood smeared his lower lip and jaw.

"Err-raa-ree... hep eee..."

He couldn't form words because Lafferty had cut out his tongue. But Susannah understood what he'd said: *Bethany, help me.*

She couldn't help him. She couldn't. High One gifts every Human with free will, with the ability to choose good or evil. Nitzan Shamdi had chosen evil.

Lafferty knelt next to him, her knee dipping in the blood coating the deck. "Bethany was your friend." She put her hand atop his head. "She's *my* friend now. My best friend."

Major Anne Lafferty started to pet Nitzan's hair.

"Well, Specialist-Two Nitzan Shamdi, I've only got a few minutes more to spend with you," Anne said. "You might say it's all over but the crying. But I think I've heard enough crying for one day."

The major grabbed a pornographic picture from the deck. It dripped with blood. As Nitzan screamed a tongueless scream, she crumpled it into a ball and shoved it in his mouth.

She looked at Susannah.

"Ensign, I think you'd rather focus on where we're going."

Susannah whipped around so hard she banged her elbow on the bulkhead.

Watch where she was going. Yes, then she didn't have to see.

If only she didn't have to *hear*.

"And don't forget my two-minute warning," Lafferty said. "Don't forget."

Susannah's insides tingled with the coldness of oncoming panic. This couldn't be happening to her, couldn't be happening to Nitzan.

A thunderous *bang* came from somewhere below her feet.

An alarm sounded. On the dashboard, lights flashed.

"Major, the curvine disengaged on its own, I think it's toast. We're drifting on momentum."

"Activate emergency retrieval beacon," Lafferty said, as if this were a normal shipping lane and a friendly passerby would soon stop to help.

Susannah pushed a button. "Activated."

Nothing more needed to be said. Either *Keeling*'s crew would see the beacon and send help, or they wouldn't.

She heard Nitzan's muffled scream.

She closed her eyes and tried to wish it all away. Through her eyelids came a pulsing yellow.

She looked—a flashing light signified an incoming tightbeam transmission.

98

"I have contact with the hauler," Ellison said. "Tightbeam message, garbled from interference. One clear word, that word is *drifting*. Their curvine must be out. The message is on repeat, I'll keep working on the rest."

Trav looked at the orb, his mind crunching the harsh math. The hauler was still inbound from aft-low, but if its curvine was out it couldn't decelerate. It was possible to match the hauler's velocity and tether it in, but doing so would require a prolonged, straight-line trajectory that would make *Keeling* a sitting duck.

X-Ray's superior acceleration was starting to show. The destroyer was coming in from *Keeling*'s port quarter. If Trav tried to pick up the hauler, the destroyer would tear them apart long before he could dive.

"Conn, I have *Yankee*," Waldren said. "It's pushing through the interference at full burn. Five minutes until they're in mid-range."

"*Yankee* has launched mimics," Sorro said. "At least four."

Mimics emulated a ship's specific grav-signature. They weren't all that effective, but in STC soup this dense they might very well draw any torps *Keeling* threw at it. For effective targeting, Trav had to wait until the enemy corvette came out of the interference field.

"*X-Ray* has launched two torpedoes," Waldren said. "Putting in-orb. Run time is... nine minutes, twelve seconds."

Trav started his stopwatch. The destroyer had finally entered the fight. *X-Ray*'s torps were far enough out that *Keeling* could easily deal with them. As an opening strike, it was a soft jab, meant to probe *Keeling*'s defenses.

"ECM, launch decoys," Trav said. "Weps, load tubes five and six with Mark15s, plot course to intercept incoming torps, fire when ready."

Mark15 torps contained four scattershot warheads, which the torp automatically launched when it drew near its target. The warheads tracked in unison, interacting with each other to create the widest coverage area possible. With luck, they'd detonate in the right place, forcing *Yankee*'s salvo to streak through a cloud of metal bearing.

"Conn, three torps launched from *Yankee*," Waldren said. "Putting in-orb. Run time is eight minutes, twelve seconds."

Trav started his second timer.

Two torps coming from starboard-quarter-low, and now *Yankee*'s three from directly aft.

Guns from both the corvette and the destroyer would be on the *Keeling* in minutes.

And soon after that, *X-Ray* would draw close enough to launch ship-killer missiles.

Erickson stood up from his nav station and ran to the command slate, leaning close.

"XO, Ochthera-Two is three minutes out. We can get the crawler in the pouch with plenty of time left for an emergency dive, but the hauler is too far away from us. There's no path to reach it that won't have us eating those torps."

Trav glanced at his stopwatch—eight minutes.

Cooley rested his elbows on the command slate.

"You've done all you can, XO," he said. "This is a battle. There are losses."

Trav hung his head as frustration overwhelmed him. Cooley was right.

All they could do now was hope that Darkwater could get the hauler's engine back online.

"Pilot," Trav said, "pitch up ten degrees, turn five degrees to port."

That would angle *Keeling*'s tail between the *X-Ray* and *Yankee*, adding a few more seconds to the enemy torpedoes' run-time.

Trav turned and looked up at Hasik. "Xeno, you have three minutes until we dive."

99

The torturer dragged him into the airlock.

He would not go home.

He would not see his people.

He would not be a hero.

He would not be with Bethany.

The airlock's door shut.

Was this High One's plan? It had to be. Everything was. Nitzan clung to that belief, for it was all he had left.

He'd come so close.

"I'm actually kind of a nice person," his torturer said. "I'm going to do you a little favor. When the airlock opens, I'll get you out the back as fast as I can. You can die in the void. I think a Raider would like that —or a Crusader, if that's what you are."

That was a favor?

Yes, it was. Anything to stop the pain, although the pain had faded somewhat. He was numb, no longer a slave to the agony rippling through his body.

She'd cut off his arm.

She'd cut out his tongue.

She'd cut off his left foot. That one had taken some work. The wicked copper blade hadn't got the job done, so she'd pulled his combat knife—a knife so dense and sharp it would punch through exo-armor—and used it like a hatchet, hacking at the bone and gristle of his ankle. He'd *heard* it when she finally pulled his foot free, a squelching sound like a spoon digging into a hot, fresh bowl of macaroni and cheese.

"It was nice to get to know you a little," the torturer said. "People in our line of work... well, professional courtesy is a must."

He heard her words, but he didn't care.

He'd lost. She'd won.

"If you have any last prayers, make them now," the torturer said.

Nitzan wished he could have said goodbye to his team.

To say goodbye to Abshire, to tell him that fair didn't matter, that he could survive this.

To say goodbye to Beaver and tell the kid that while he'd been so annoying at first, his endless, genuine optimism had worn Nitzan down.

To say goodbye to Grampa Bennett, who—for a Union heathen—was a genuinely good man.

Just like Arimun had been.

"If your afterlife is real, I hope you get to go there," the torturer said. "Bethany, hon? Shut off fakegrav in the cargo hold. Right away."

The torturer pulled a lever.

Nitzan heard air hiss out of the small chamber, loud at first but quickly tapering off as there was no air to carry sound.

The Raiders had trained him about being exposed in vacuum. Like a checklist read off by a drill sergeant, Nitzan knew each effect as it happened.

Fresh agony bloomed in his face as his sinuses struggled to equalize.

Piercing pain as his eardrums ruptured.

Were his muscles cramping from the bends? Hard to tell with the misery that already racked his body, courtesy of his little torturer.

She dragged him out of the airlock by his collar. One hard tug, then a light pull, and he was floating.

The *cold*...

Things were happening to his ruined body but he didn't care, because if there was an afterlife, he would spend it at High One's side.

His eyes stung. His mouth was dry.

The torturer pulled him through the cargo hold, through bodies floating near the deck, through shell casings and escape wings that slowly tumbled through the air.

So many dead Unionites.

Would *they* spend eternity at High One's side?

Nitzan hoped they would, but he knew better. The Union was made of blasphemers and perverts, of sinners and butchers.

They weren't like him.

They weren't like Bethany.

His vision grew cloudy as the wetness of his eyes boiled away. Everything was out of focus.

And then, he was in space, looking back at the hauler's open rear cargo door, at Major Anne Lafferty, Intel Chief of the PUV *James Keeling*. She was so blurry he could barely make her out, but he saw enough to know she was waving goodbye.

100

"Just identified that big fattie cloud at seven o'clock," Biggie said on the platoon channel. "That's a Malag destroyer. It's launched torps."

Beaver grabbed John's arm.

"Hey, Bennett, is that bad?"

"Yes, Beaver," John said. "An enemy destroyer chasing us down and launching torpedoes is bad."

From the looks of things, *bad* was soon to get *worse*. John was no navigator, but his naked eye told him the Ochthera would reach *Keeling* only minutes before the big Malag started shooting the hell out of everything.

Off to port, something caught John's eye. Hard to tell in the STC soup, but it looked like tiny pulses of yellow and orange light.

"Biggie, this is Bennett up top," John said. "I think I see a distress beacon at nine o'clock high."

The Ochthera's turret rotated to port. The cannon elevated.

"I see it," Nikula said. "Got it in my optics... definitely a beacon, and... hard to tell, but that might be Cooley's hauler."

That wasn't where the hauler was supposed to be. Why was it closer to the destroyer than it was to *Keeling*?

"If that's the hauler, it's straight-lining," Biggie said. "No acceleration, no maneuvering, traveling on momentum alone. It will miss *Keeling* by a country mile. Master Sergeant Sands, if those on board bail out, they can grab on to us topside. We can still get to *Keeling* on time, but it'll be close. What are your orders?"

Sands was the mission's commander. Biggie was dumping the choice on him, as she should—it was his call, and his alone.

"Hey, Sarge Sands," Beaver said "Shamdi's girlfriend is driving the hauler. He's gone, but we could save her for him."

A pause.

"Let's get her, Sarge," Abshire said. "We owe it to Nitzie."

"Major Lafferty's supposedly on board, too," Jordan said.

"And maybe people from *Ishi*," Basara said. "We can't abandon them."

"Do it, Sarge," Sarvacharya said.

Another pause.

What an impossible decision for Sands to make. His surviving Raiders were in the clear, but not if he went for the hauler. No way to communicate with the hauler from this far out. Everyone aboard could be already dead, which meant a diversion toward it put the platoon in danger for nothing. Of course the Raiders wanted to go after their own; that was what Raiders did. Sands, though, was responsible for bringing his people home. He'd already lost Fred Abeen, Malik Blanding, and Karl Chennault. Their bodies—at least parts of them—were on the deck in the troop compartment. And Nitzan was lost to the whims of war.

The correct decision was to fly straight for *Keeling* and get out of there.

But John knew Francis "Book" Sands. Knew him from way back when. The man just needed a little nudge, a nudge from someone he respected.

"Master Sergeant," John said, "if we leave without knowing if there's people alive in that hauler, I don't think I'll be able to sleep at night."

John wasn't sleeping at night anyway, a silver-eyed rat-shrimp-thing saw to that, but that wasn't the point.

"All right," Sands said. "Let's roll them bones. Warrant Officer Bang, get us to the hauler. Start broadcasting a tightbeam signal, tell them to abandon ship. Hopefully they receive it as we get closer."

101

"I see it," Susannah said. "I see the crawler!"

"Then get back here fast."

Susannah lurched out of the pilot's seat. She tried to ignore the pornography and the bloody smears, handprints, and footprints that covered the deck. She entered the airlock and shut the inner door.

For some reason, it hadn't occurred to her that the airlock, too, would be bloody.

Susannah checked her vacsuit HUD: sealed and pressurized.

She opened the cargo-side airlock door and stepped out into an abattoir.

Bodies and blood foam floated everywhere, all slowly moving and turning at different rates. Some corpses had big holes in them. Others were missing limbs. Some were missing heads. Here and there, a severed hand, frozen coils of intestine, a few internal organs, even what appeared to be the left hemisphere of a brain in remarkably good shape.

Move, my child.

Susannah cried out as she pushed through the bodies, bodies that were so thick she could barely see to the cargo container's end. The corpses seemed to be alive, seemed to be landing soft kicks, punches, and slaps on her as she moved. She shoved a dead man aside, his left eye staring out, frozen forever, his right missing along with that half of his face.

She should have turned the fakegrav back on, but it was too late now.

A dead hand reached for her, grabbed her wrist and pulled her aft. Susannah *screamed*.

"Relax, Ensign."

Lafferty stood there, two escape wings under one arm, her free hand locked on Susannah's wrist. What looked like a hunk of freeze-dried liver floated above Lafferty's head.

"Take a wing," the major said.

Susannah took one and checked the charge level—down to a quarter full. That would have to do.

The major gripped the handles of her wing, turned to face the open loading door. Bodies and body parts were slowly drifting into space. She stepped out, and the wing's small engines carried her away from the hauler.

Susannah followed her into the silence of the void.

Low and off to the left, Susannah saw the oncoming Ochthera, attitude thrusters sparking at all corners as the pilot fought to decelerate, match velocity, and come up alongside. It felt like driving on a highway, watching a car on the onramp drift closer and closer.

Atop the crawler, a lethal-looking turret, and three crouching Raiders in black TASH armor waving her in.

For a moment, Susannah's mind rejected what her eyes were telling her. They told her she and Lafferty were stationary, that the Ochthera and the reaching Raiders floated closer and closer. She knew, though, that wasn't how physics worked. She, Lafferty, *and* the crawler were hurtling along at some insane velocity.

Raider hands reached up, grabbed Lafferty and pulled her down atop the metal netting affixed to the crawler's roof.

Their black armor... just like Nitzan's...

The hands snatched Susannah, yanked her down.

"Ensign, anyone left aboard?"

There, atop an armored personal carrier, Susannah Rossi pissed herself. It was the Empty Man, John Bennett, gauntleted hands gripping her shoulders, talking to her through a touch-channel. No black flames raging from his eyes, no vibrating dark haze, but she was not fooled—it was *him*.

"No," Susannah said. "We're the only survivors."

"On your belly," the Empty Man said. "Hurry."

Susannah did as she was told. The Empty Man put his arm over her, held her tight to the crawler's top. She couldn't look at him. She turned her head and found herself staring at the blood-speckled face of Anne Lafferty, only centimeters away.

Lafferty stretched out a finger, touched Susannah's arm.

"Isn't this *amazing*, Beth? We might make it after all."

Beth. The butcher called her *Beth*.

Past Lafferty, past the Raider holding Lafferty down, Susannah saw the *Keeling*. Beautiful *Keeling*. Beautiful, even when it was fuzzy and blurred, the copper hull whipping in and out of focus.

Beneath her, the crawler shuddered and accelerated.

Susannah put her visor against the metal netting. That way, she didn't have to look at the face of the Empty Man, nor did she have to look at the beatific smile of Anne Lafferty.

102

The crawler drifted toward *Keeling*'s open pouch. Anne thought it felt like being atop a balloon in a light breeze, flowing forward, floating upward.

Inside the flight bay, Raiders in LASH armor and sailors in vacsuits hovered in place, safety lines attached to their backs.

"Stay flat, Major," Abshire said on their touch-channel. "Not a lot of room between us and the ceiling."

The Ochthera slid into the pouch. Tiny attitude thrusters spouted spurts of vapor as the pilot tried to bring the crawler in without bumping the sides or—more importantly—the top, which might squish Anne's and Beth's unarmored bodies into a meaty pudding.

Anne looked back, saw the pouch closing behind her like a copper-lipped fish mouth. When it silently slammed shut, gravity returned with barely a bump as the Ochthera settled onto the deck.

103

In the orb, three torpedoes closed in on *Keeling*, the first of which was just under four minutes out. The Mark15s had eliminated one of *Yankee*'s torps, and the decoys had taken out one of *X-Ray*'s.

"Crawler-Two is aboard," Cooley said. "Pouch door sealed. One Raider MIA, unrecoverable. Ensign Darkwater and Major Lafferty recovered from Hauler-One, no one else."

Where were all those rescued from *Ishi*? Had the hauler brought no one in after all?

Even if Trav's crew could eliminate the three incoming torps, both *X-Ray* and *Yankee* were close to effective firing range. If *Keeling* wasn't in transdim inside of three minutes, it would be either captured or destroyed.

"Xeno, crash-dive," Trav said. "Colonel Cooley, alert the crew."

Hasik repeated the order down to the atrium. Cooley made the announcement on the 1MC.

"Activating transdim coupler," Hasik said.

Trav gripped the edge of the command slate. What would he see this time? His *sixth* membrane-hop in less than an hour. How would it affect the crew? The Raiders in the landing bay were fully armed. Would they...

Nothing happened.

"Xeno," Trav said, "why are we still in realspace?"

"It didn't go!" Hasik's voice shot up an octave. "I told you the power was low!"

Trav stepped to the Xeno loft and looked up at the man.

"Hasik, get us under, right now, or we're dead."

Behind his glasses, Hasik's tired, raw eyes blinked madly.

"When the dive failed, the coupler's energy reserve dropped to zero," he said. "I don't know what else to do. Neither does Hathorn. Maybe Darkwater does, she seems to have an affinity for—"

Trav stepped to the command slate, took the handset from Cooley.

"This is the XO. Ensign Darkwater to the atrium, *immediately*. Darkwater, you have ninety seconds to get us into transdim or we're all dead." He pressed the handset against his chest to mute it. "ECM, launch all remaining countermeasures. Weps, split remaining Mark15s and Mark16s between *Yankee* and *X-Ray*. Fire when ready."

As his crew repeated his orders, Trav switched the comm to the 18MC—the direct line to the atrium.

104

Susannah stepped off the ladder and sprinted through the strangely curved passageway to the atrium's sealed sphincter. She rubbed her hand along the edge—it opened instantly, spreading apart with a *pop* of air.

She rushed in, the warm steam of an old friend caressing her face.

The heartstone was dimmer than Susannah had ever seen, mere hints of light pulsing within the thick material. Hathorn stood on the protuberance platform.

The protuberance was dark. Lifeless. Like black glass.

Hathorn looked at Susannah, cheeks wet with tears and snot gleaming on her upper lip.

"I can't get it to charge," she said. "I don't know what to do."

Next to Hathorn, the comm unit blared with the XO's voice.

"Atrium, Conn, torpedoes incoming. You have seventy seconds to get us under."

In the blink of an eye, all lives depended on Susannah Rossi, and Susannah Rossi alone.

Everything faded away.

The horror of the hauler's cargo compartment.

The insanity of Lafferty cutting Nitzan into pieces.

Nitzan trying to take her to the destroyer.

Lafferty suddenly, *genuinely* thinking Susannah was her friend.

Bock's blackmail.

Bratchford's attempted rape.

Murdering Bratchford.

Chief Marchenko's secret present.

The lost ten years in the convent.

Melanie's severed head, rolling around the debris-strewn deck.

Lafferty's copper knife...

...the *blood*, both on the knife and then *not* on the knife.

Susannah knew what the ship wanted.

She knew what the *voice* wanted.

"Sixty seconds," Ellis said.

Susannah came back to the moment. Vibrations rippled through the deck—one of *Keeling*'s cannons firing.

She ran to the protuberance, but instead of stepping onto the platform with Hathorn, she dropped to one knee and reached under it. Susannah's cheek pressed against the platform as her hand fished about in the narrow, dark space.

Where was it?

Hathorn screamed in frustration. She sobbed as she repeated the activation pattern, a pattern that would do nothing without power.

Power. Power was life. Life was power.

Susannah stuck her hand farther in, swept it left—she felt it, grabbed it.

She stood, the copper blade low and flat against her thigh, the duct-tape handle cool against her palm.

"Fifty seconds," Ellis said.

Marchenko had given Susannah the blade. In the mess, at breakfast, he'd sat down next to her, hadn't said a word as he slid the blade across the seat. Susannah had taken it and hidden it—first in her coveralls, then under the platform. She hadn't known why then, and until now she hadn't even remembered the exchange.

But she remembered now, and now, she knew why.

You know what must be done, my child.

Yes. Susannah knew.

Hathorn shook her head, screamed again. She punched the protuberance hard enough to split her knuckles, smearing a streak of blood on the dark glass.

Where the blood was, the glass glowed.

"*I can't get it to go,*" Hathorn screamed. "*We're all gonna die. We—*"

"You shouldn't have hit me."

Hathorn turned, looked at Susannah, tears streaming down.

"Hit you? What are you talking about? *Help me!*"

So many people asking for help these days.

"Forty seconds," Ellis said.

Susannah climbed the two steps up onto the platform.

"I remember now," she said. "I remember what you did while we were in the Mud."

Susannah hadn't fallen and hit her head. Hathorn had punched her, thrown her against these very platform rails, bounced her off equipment in this very room. When Susannah had awoken, she'd felt sore all over.

Because Hathorn had *beaten* her.

Just like Bratchford had.

You know what must be done, my child.

Yes. Susannah knew.

She stepped close to Hathorn, who blinked, then shook her head and snarled.

"Who cares if I hit you? Beth, *fix this*! Fix this *or we're going to die!*"

"Only my friends can call me *Beth.*"

Susannah drove a straight right into Hathorn's mouth, felt teeth break.

Hathorn stumbled backward against the waist-high rail, nearly tumbled over it to drop down atop the heartstone's irregular, dim surface.

The lieutenant straightened some, pressed her fingers against her bleeding mouth.

Behind her, the heartstone pulsed softly with new light. Still dim, *too* dim, but brighter than it had been.

"What the fuck is wrong with you?" Hathorn's fingers muffled her words.

"Thirty seconds," Ellis said on the comm. "If you're going to do something, Darkwater, you better do it fast."

Yes. Susannah would do something.

"You pretended to be my friend," she said. "You're a liar."

Susannah took one step forward. Hathorn's eyes went wide, but she froze, didn't move as Susannah's second straight right smashed into her nose. Cartilage and bone crunched. Hathorn's head rocked back. She almost tumbled over again. Her hands clutched the rail, one foot coming off the platform as she fought for balance.

Drops of her blood fell to the heartstone. Where it splashed, the heartstone burst with tiny rays of yellow-red light that lit up the swirling steam.

Susannah grabbed a handful of Hathorn's hair, yanked hard to the side. Hathorn stumbled, slid along the rail as she grabbed at Susannah's hands.

Susannah shoved her hair-clutching hand out and down, bending Hathorn over the rail.

Fingernails dug into Susannah's hand, pierced her skin, sent more bomb-run droplets onto the heartstone. More beams of light appeared, almost solid in the mist.

"Atrium, you've got twenty seconds!"

Love wins, my child.

Love did. In the end, love *always* wins.

"You hurt me," Susannah said. "You don't get to hurt me ever again."

She yanked Hathorn's head back hard, drove the copper blade into the side of her neck. The metal punched deep, all the way to the duct-tape handle. Warm red splattered Susannah's hand. She tried to rip the blade forward, through Hathorn's throat, but she didn't have enough strength. The weapon still buried to the hilt, Susannah sliced back and forth as she pushed outward—severing muscle, cleaving cartilage, slashing arteries—until the blade burst free.

Blood sprayed onto the heartstone. Yellow-orange light erupted, made the hanging leaves and fruit-thick vines vegetables seem to glow from within.

Hathorn stiffened. Still bent over the rail, her palms slapped spasmodically at the hand clutching her hair.

"In your name," Susannah said, "I offer this sacrifice."

She sliced again.

More crimson gushed from Hathorn's throat. Where it hit, it vanished, soaking in or burned away by the holy light.

The heartstone dazzled like the core of a white-hot star. So bright, it filled every bit of the atrium. So bright, it *blinded*.

Hathorn's struggles slowed.

"This is the XO, brace for impact in ten... nine..."

Susannah dropped the knife, let go of Hathorn's hair. The lieutenant lurched, waved her arms one last time—the motion finally carried her over the rail to thump against the heartstone.

"Six..."

Susannah put her hands to the protuberance, which now glowed with the undeniable light of a thousand stars.

"Five..."

Her hands ran through the pattern: push, touch, turn, stroke, push, move, bend.

"Four..."

Susannah made the final squeeze.

The heartstone's light turned the world to white.

"Three..."

She felt the dark place form around her, and she was grateful.

"Two..."

So grateful.

Love wins, my child.

Yes. Love wins. Always.

105

The shimmer washed across the CIC.

"We're in punch-space," Colin Draper said. "Course locked."

"Very well," Trav said. "Nav, start the clocks."

"Starting the clock, aye-aye."

Erickson pushed the button that began the countdown, both on the watch-clocks and the digital displays next to them—seventeen hours, five minutes, and sixteen seconds.

After diving to escape the Purist task force, *Keeling* spent eight hours in the Mud while waiting for the transdim coupler to recharge enough to surface. Things got bad. Violence broke out across the ship. The rescued crew from *Ishlangu* hadn't been prepared for it. Six of them sustained significant injuries, including two who were in critical condition.

Keeling's crew hadn't fared any better. Two more people were in intensive care. Lieutenant Hathorn had died. Ensign Darkwater almost joined her.

Turned out Barnes Marchenko had made four blades, not just three. Hathorn had stashed one away in the atrium. When *Keeling* entered transdim, she'd lost it and tried to kill Darkwater. Somehow, despite severe cuts on her arm and leg, the tiny ensign got the knife away from Hathorn. In a brutal battle of kill or be killed, she'd cut Hathorn's throat.

Over half the crew had succumbed to incapacitating hallucinations. With so many incapable of doing their jobs, Trav had barely been able to keep the ship operational. While stuck in transdim, he'd put the eight hours to good use, guiding *Keeling* to another punch-point, one well-clear of *X-Ray*, *Yankee*, or any other enemy ship that might be stalking them.

Keeling was back in Union territory. Now that the ship was safely in punch-space, Trav could finally let down his guard.

He lifted the handset, spoke on the 1MC.

"This is the XO. We are in punch-space. We will reach Gateway Station in approximately seventeen hours."

He paused, wondering if he should say more. It wasn't really his role to do so, but he felt compelled to let the crew know his thoughts.

"We've had one hell of a shakedown run," he said. "We endured things that no one else in Fleet could possibly understand. We lost good people. We accomplished our mission. I'll be the first to admit that if I had my choice, I'd never go transdim again. But if I have to wallow in the Mud, I'm proud to do it with this crew. That is all."

He put the handset in the cradle.

"Chief Erickson, you have the conn."

"I have the conn," Erickson said. "Aye, XO."

Erickson walked from the nav station and took the captain's spot at the command slate.

Trav left the CIC. He would rest soon, but not until he reported to his commanding officer. Before that, though, he had to see his oldest friend.

He walked to his quarters, a room he hadn't seen in over twenty-four hours. He knocked softly.

"Enter."

She was awake. Finally. Trav opened the door and stepped inside.

Vesna Jakobsson was seated at his tiny desk.

"You're up." Trav shut the door. "That's great to see, Vez."

She looked horrible. A black patch over her right eye. Her left eye showed the burden of an impossible emotional weight. Her left hand in a brace. A blue bandage where her pinkie and ring fingers had once been.

Vesna slowly stood, moving like a woman three times her age.

She saluted him. A formal gesture, heavy with gravitas and deep conviction.

"Lieutenant Travis Ellis, thank you for saving my crew. At least the ones you could. If not for you, all of my people would have been lost."

She seemed to read his mind, to sense the guilt he carried for the *Keeling* crew who perished while under his command, the guilt he carried for the *Ishi* crew he hadn't been able to save.

Vesna knew what he was feeling. She undoubtedly felt the same way about those who'd died under her command. Her salute was part respect for him, part absolution *for* him.

He returned it.

"Thank you, Colonel," he said. "I wish I could have done more."

"As do I, Trav. As do I." She slowly sat back down. "Thank you for lending me your quarters."

"A little privacy is the least we could do for someone of your rank."

"I'm sure you'll find this hard to believe, Trav, but I think you look worse than I do. When is the last time you slept?"

He wasn't sure. Sometime before the battle, near as he could recall.

"I'm off-duty in a few minutes," he said. "I'll sleep then."

Vesna stared off, gently touched her eye patch.

"I need to see my people," she said.

Ishi's crew were stashed all over the *Keeling*—two in the infirmary, some in various cubbyholes located throughout the ship, some in the NCO berth, and some in the aft torpedo room.

"I'll have an escort show you where they are," Trav said.

Every single *Ishi* survivor—Vesna included—had seen the highly classified ship, both inside and out. When *Keeling* reached Gateway Station, what would Epperson do with them?

"In transdim, I... I had visions," Vesna said. "My crew. The dead ones. They kept asking me why I didn't save them. All those faces. It was so *real*."

For the first time, Trav realized there were hallucinations far worse than giant spiders.

Vesna sat up straighter, squared her shoulders.

"Trav, all the things I said, the way I judged you... I couldn't have been more wrong."

His heart swelled with pride and relief. Even though they'd grown apart, he'd always known she believed in him, and he'd always believed in her. Losing Vesna's respect had cut him deep, kicked out from under him one of his last foundational pillars. To know he still had that respect—to know he'd *re-earned* it—gave him a tiny sliver of light in a black hole of exhaustion and self-judgement.

"It's all right," Trav said. "I don't think you were wrong, though. My actions at X7 were... I made the wrong call."

Vesna smiled.

"A call you learned from," she said. "There are sixty-seven *Ishi* crewmembers onboard who wouldn't be alive without your choices."

And several *Keeling* crew members who would have been. But this wasn't the time to talk about that.

"The Purists knew we were there," Vesna said. "Could have been a patrol, but it felt more specific than that. Colonel Cooley visited me. I told him what I knew." She shrugged. "We held our position as long as we were able."

Vesna could have run. Outnumbered three-to-one, she could have opted to preserve her ship and her people. But that wasn't like her. Vesna's decision to stay saved *Keeling* but cost her more than two-thirds of *Ishi*'s crew.

"If you hadn't stayed, they'd have dusted us before we even knew they were there," Trav said. "Because of you and your people, we accomplished our mission."

She looked down, nodded in an absent way.

"Do you think it will matter in the end?"

Trav had no idea.

"Yes," he said. "I think it will."

She again nodded.

"I have to meet with Lincoln and the officers," he said. "I'll come back and check on you after the debriefing."

"I won't be here. You can have your quarters back. I'll sleep where my people sleep."

Vesna Jakobsson was alive, but she wasn't sure if she deserved to be. She'd been *Ishi*'s captain for two years. Even the most callous CO couldn't help but build relationships during a span like that. Especially in wartime. How may close friends had she lost in the battle? How many during Nitzan Shamdi's murder spree?

Trav stepped out and closed the door behind him. He walked to the wardroom. On the way, he passed by the wardroom galley. The Purist missile had punched through here, the shaped charge powerful enough to reach the CIC and kill Corporal Mullen. Repair crews had removed debris. Broken appliances sat twisted and unusable. Thick, hardened fastfill foam gleamed mostly white. Where the fastfill was not, the bulkheads were scorched and blackened. It would remain that way until Gateway.

The wardroom hadn't been hit directly, but the blast caused plenty of damage to the bulkhead separating it from the galley. The never-ending coffee urn was no more. Shrapnel gouges dotted the wardroom table.

At that table sat Kerkhoffs, Brown, Lafferty, Plait, Cooley, Lindros, and—at the head of the table—Captain Lincoln.

Lincoln wore her usual black bandana. A bit of bandage peeked out from beneath it.

"Let's get started, XO," she said. "I know you need some rack time."

Trav sat.

"Raiders first," Lincoln said. "Your current numbers, Gary?"

First names? Lincoln was making this more relaxed than Trav expected.

"We have seventeen frontliners available for duty, including me." Lindros sounded like a shell of himself. "Spec-One Oneida, Spec-One Jun, and Spec-One Dobrevski are unfit to serve and need to be removed at Gateway."

"Dobrevski?" Kerkhoffs glanced around the table. "What happened to her?"

"Spec-One Brogan stabbed her in the thigh shortly after we entered transdim," Lindros said. "Dobrevski was still in-TASH. Brogan's combat knife penetrated her armor. She needs reconstructive surgery."

Kerkhoffs sighed, sat back and shook her head. Sometimes, that was all you could do.

"Ochthera-One remains out of commission," Lindros said. "We need a replacement. We probably need a replacement for Ochthera-Two as well. Biggie pushed it past acceptable tolerances. The curvine is cracked, and there appears to be significant damage to the frame."

He glanced down at a sheet of paper on the table before him, read from it.

"Spec-One Laior died in a training accident. Spec-One Abeen, Spec-One Chennault, and Sergeant Blanding were killed in action while boarding corvette *Zulu*. Warrant Officer JG Nessa was killed in transdim. Spec-Two Shamdi remains missing in action."

"Shamdi is *dead*," Lafferty said. "I told you that."

Lindros nodded. "You did tell me that, sir."

Trav wondered if Lindros would remain as the platoon CO. He'd missed all the fighting. He was a laughingstock among his own people.

"Engineering," Lincoln said. "Where do we stand?"

Kerkhoffs looked even more shook up than Lindros.

"All internal damage fully repaired, Captain. We need some replacement gear in fabrication, but we're keeping up for now. Port-side superstructure armor needs replacement. From what I've been able to see so far, the armor was substandard to begin with. I'll look into that when we get to Gateway."

Lincoln held up a hand. "*I'll* look into it. Get me a full report. You don't say a word about it at Gateway or anywhere else. Understand?"

Kerkhoffs face reddened with anger.

"Aye, Captain," she said. "I understand."

The armor had been substandard? Was that why a single missile penetrated? Was Corporal Mollen dead because of shoddy materials?

Trav hoped Lincoln would get to the bottom of it, and fast.

"As for casualties," Kerkhoffs said, "Corporal Salvatore died during the battle. Lieutenant Hathorn died in a transdim incident. Corporal Goldsmith needs hospitalization due to severe burns. Doc Hammersmith said the rest of engineering's wounded will soon be fit for duty."

Nineteen people in her department. Two dead. Another that would not return.

"Thank you, Lieutenant," Lincoln said. "Weps?"

Brown leaned forward. "We're down to three torpedoes. All

Mark 16s. No STC torps remain. Port-side Type24 gun is destroyed. The barbette as well. The entire array needs to be replaced. As for casualties, Turret Master Ling, Gunner's Mate Canuk, and Fire Controller Painter were killed when the port Type24 was hit. Painter replaced Gunner's Mate Eskander, who is also dead. Doc Hammersmith said Sensor Operator Portland is susceptible to another heart attack, which might kill him. She strongly recommends he be replaced. There were additional injuries during transdim, but nothing that will stop my people from doing their jobs."

Eighteen people in the weapons department—four of them were dead, one medically unfit to serve.

Lincoln turned to Plait. "Operations status?"

"I guess you could say we got lucky, comparatively speaking," he said. "Corporal Mollen was our only casualty. Everyone else is fine. Physically, anyway. Mentally? I couldn't tell you."

The same thing might be said of everyone on the ship.

"Thank you," Lincoln said. "All but Colonel Cooley, Major Lafferty, and the XO are dismissed."

Brown, Kerkhoffs, Plait, and Lindros filed out.

"Colonel," Lincoln said, "final numbers from the *Ishlangu*?"

Cooley had no paper in front of him.

"We have sixty-seven survivors aboard," he said. "Two are in critical condition. Hammersmith doesn't think they'll survive to reach Gateway. Including those two, one hundred and twenty-four members of *Ishlangu*'s crew perished."

Gutting numbers, although Trav had endured a higher death toll at X7. A toll he was responsible for, at least partially.

"And this Nitzan Shamdi business," Lincoln said. "Any progress there?"

"We're working on it," Cooley said. "You've seen Major Lafferty's after-action report. We're questioning the Raiders to find out what they do and do not know. This situation does not reflect well on Lieutenant Lindros." He glanced at Lafferty. "Or on the intel department of this ship."

Trav expected Lafferty's temper to flare, for her to snap back, but she did nothing of the sort. She seemed tired but calm. Maybe she was on exhaustion's edge, just as Trav was.

"There were failures at multiple levels," Lafferty said. "It happened on my watch, and I'll take responsibility. However, I'm recommending a full investigation of *Keeling*'s recruiting process."

Lincoln let out a grunt. "I'll make that request for you, Major."

"Thank you, Captain, but I'll do it myself," Lafferty said. "This needs to go through BII channels."

Lincoln sighed, laced her fingers together.

"Major Lafferty, I can't order you not to pursue this, but I can make a strong recommendation that you leave it to me. I'm well aware you have certain connections. Those connections won't help. You should focus on making your remaining time here go as smooth as possible."

Lafferty stared back at Lincoln.

"I'll take that into consideration, Captain."

"I hope for your sake you do," Lincoln said. "How about the rest of the crew? Do you think there are other spies aboard?"

Lafferty hesitated. "I wouldn't rule it out." She smiled. "If there are, I'll find them."

Calm, sure, satisfied, yes, but had Lafferty lost that predatory vibe? Not in the least.

She'd shown true courage going on that rescue run with Ensign Darkwater. And Darkwater's report about what happened on the hauler—well, that cemented Trav's respect for Anne Lafferty. She was brave, decisive, and committed to doing her duty, no matter what the cost.

"Mac," Lincoln said. "Do you still have your intel? Nothing was damaged or lost in the battle?"

"We have it all," Cooley said. "I'm grateful to you and your crew. They're not the only ones who sacrificed to get this information into Union hands."

Lincoln smiled wanly at him, acknowledging his appreciation.

"Thank you, Colonel," she said. "And thank you, Major. That will be all."

Cooley and Lafferty left, leaving Trav alone with the Union's greatest war hero.

"XO, I'm sure you were keeping score?"

Yes, he had. He'd also been keeping score when Lincoln skipped the burial at sea ceremony, leaving Travis to send the bodies off into eternity.

"Eight sailors died on this patrol, seven of those in the battle," Trav said. "Two sailors are medically unfit for duty. We need ten replacements. One Raider dead in a training accident. Five Raiders died in combat. Three are medically unfit. The platoon needs nine replacements."

Maybe ten, depending on what Lincoln wanted to do about Lindros.

The captain fell quiet for a moment. When she spoke, it was without the steel her voice usually carried.

"For the *Keeling* crew, not counting Raider losses, that's a casualty rate of twelve percent," she said. "Believe it or not, that's one of this ship's most successful missions."

He'd heard of the eighty percent mortality rate. Many had. But coming in well below that mark didn't strike him as a win.

"I feel horrible, sir. I can't stop thinking about what I might have done differently."

She leaned forward, elbows on the table, closing the distance between them.

"What you might have done *differently*, XO, was obey your orders and *leave*."

Trav stared at her, trying to understand.

"Sir, are you saying we should have run? Abandoned *Ishlangu* and her crew?"

"You put the entire mission at risk. If Cooley's intel is as big as I suspect it is, your decision to stand and fight could have cost us the war. And don't forget that *ten* of our casualties were combat-related. I don't include Shamdi in that count. You decided to fight, Ellis. Those ten deaths are on you."

Rage hit him hard.

"Sir, with all due respect, that means the sixty-seven survivors from *Ishlangu* are also *on me*."

"Including your Academy sweetheart," Lincoln said. "Is she why you ordered my ship into battle?"

Trav fought to hold his anger in check. The gall of this person to accuse him of—

Lincoln held up a hand, palm out.

"I'm sorry, XO. I went too far. Yes, sixty-seven fleeters are alive because of your decision. Ten are dead because of it. That's the wicked balance of command. You fought. The crew fought with you. For that, you have my respect."

He felt his fury drain away. Most of it, anyway.

"Unfortunately, my respect won't help you with Epperson," Lincoln said. "I'm sure he'll be at Gateway. You need to prepare for the worst."

Trav could no longer hide his disgust.

"*The worst*? What's he going to do, sentence me to a stint on the *Keeling*?"

Lincoln stared back. She didn't find humor in his joke.

"No," she said. "*The worst* will be his recommendation that your original sentence be carried out. *The worst* is that Admiral Epperson will order you vented."

106

The wounded had finally been moved from the crew mess, and it was about time—said crew was hungry.

John sat at a table with Beaver, Abs, and Master Sergeant Sands. The clams had shown rare respect in that they chose to stand, giving the tables to as many Raiders as would fit.

People were still packing in. Some were quiet, maudlin, thinking about those who'd been lost. Most were loud, energetic, knowing they were lucky to be alive and bursting with the survivor's joy that comes only after combat.

"I can't believe what they're saying about Nitzie," Abs said. "He was a spy? Killed all those sailors?"

Beaver shook his head. "No way. Not Shamdi. I'm a really good judge of character, you guys, and there's no way."

They'd all showered, patched up various bumps and bruises, gotten some rack time, and yet they remained exhausted. Fighting, killing, and dying takes it out of a body. And a soul.

"Chief Lafferty ain't making it up for shits and giggles," Sands said. "Face facts, men—our guy Shamdi was a traitor."

John wished they'd stop talking about it. He didn't want to believe it was true. He'd looked out for Shamdi. Shamdi had looked out for him. The kid hadn't been the most likable person in the universe, sure, but he'd been solid.

If he was a Purist spy, how could John have missed it?

Big Bradley Henry walked out from behind the serving counter, a large white cooler held in both hands. Two cooks were behind him, carrying a second cooler between them.

"All right, clams and jizzies," Henry said. "Captain said to splice the mainbrace, and splice we shall! Master Sergeant Sands, would you mind getting this party started?"

Sands opened the cooler lid and took out four bottles of beer, bits of ice sliding down their sides.

"Thanks, Combat Cook," he said. "You know, I don't believe half the things they say about you. Except for the sex with animals part. That I believe."

Bradley smiled his infectious smile. "Just you wait to see what I got for dessert."

He moved on, passing out beers to the exhausted crew grabbing this small but significant reward.

Captains were usually present for a victory celebration like this. Lincoln hadn't attended the one after the torpedo run drill, and he didn't see her here, either. She seemed to avoid any type of socialization with the crew. No big loss, though—as long as she authorized the beer, that was enough for John.

Sands opened all four bottles, giving one to each Raider. He stood.

"A toast." His voice boomed through the copper cave that was the crew mess, silencing everyone.

"To those who died gloriously in battle," Sands said. "To our Raiders, to our sailors, and those of *Ishlangu* who will forever wander the stars. We will remember them."

He raised his bottle high; everyone in the mess followed suit.

"To our fallen comrades," Sands said, and he drank.

As did John. As did everyone else.

Sands sat.

"Now, about Shamdi," he said, speaking quietly. "Yes, it appears he was a traitor. And a murderer. But we need to appreciate *how* he betrayed, *how* he murdered." He set his bottle on the end of the table. "That crazy bastard flew solo, in a TASH rig, from here—" he slid the bottle slowly along the table's length "—through a goddamn combat zone, through some of the nastiest STC fuckery I've ever seen, all the way to here—" he bumped the bottle into the napkin dispenser set against the bulkhead. "A journey of some *fifteen hundred klicks*, at max acceleration, and then he hit the brakes, *without tumbling*, a feat so complex it would make a punch-drive scientist dribble his ignorant piss down his dum-dum pants. And then, Nitzan Shamdi, our guy, managed to kill *forty-four* people, all by himself, most of them with a single shot."

Sands sat back, satisfied, and took a big swig.

Beaver's face furrowed. "But, Master Sergeant, if he's a traitor, is that a good thing? Because, you know, you just made it sound like a good thing."

"I don't agree with his motives," Sands said, "but you've got to respect his skills. Where do you think the man learned such courage, such *accuracy*, and such killer instinct?"

"Uh..." Beaver closed one eye, thinking. "From other spies?"

"No," Abshire said. "He learned it in the Raiders."

Sands smiled wide. "*In the Raiders*. Absolutely correct. You see..."

His voice trailed off as the mess suddenly quieted down.

All heads turned to look. Lieutenant Lindros and XO Travis Ellis worked their way through the standing-room-only crowd.

They walked toward John's table.

"That fucking Dork," Abshire muttered. "He's our CO? Buncha bullshit."

"Shut your mouth, Spec," Sands muttered back. "LT is our boss, until he's not."

Even before the battle, Lindros hadn't been all that popular. After it? After he succumbed to whatever hallucination forced him to run naked and duck the battle?

Until he's not. John wondered if Sands would be promoted to Warrant Officer and take over as platoon CO. That meant he'd leapfrog Winter, but she hadn't been able to fight, either. If there was one thing Fleet liked, it was Raiders who fought.

Lindros and the XO reached the table. Ellis held a small black box —a rank insignia box. Lindros stood a step behind him, a step to the right. John wondered if Lieutenant Dork knew he was about to be replaced.

"Raiders," the XO said, "I want to offer my condolences for the people you lost today."

John sat up straighter. Most sailor officers ignored Raiders. Those that would talk face to face were rare. Those that would actually recognize dead grunts? Rarer still.

"Thank you, XO," Sands said. "We appreciate that."

Ellis looked like death warmed over. The man needed sleep in a bad way.

John snapped his fingers, raised his hand. "Hey, Combat Cook—a beer for the XO?"

Henry waddled over, swinging the cooler in front of his belly like a scythe cutting through tall wheat.

"Have a brew, XO," Henry said.

Ellis looked longingly into the cooler. "I... no thanks, Combat Cook, but I appreciate the thought."

John understood. Officers weren't supposed to dine with enlisted, let alone drink with them.

But you know what? Sometimes rules didn't apply. Sometimes— especially the times after people fought and died—you got to just *exist*.

John reached into the cooler. He pulled out a beer, opened it, and set it on the table.

"That's the XO's beer," John said. "Anyone but the XO drinks it, they gotta talk to me after. XO, that means if you don't drink it, either this beer goes to waste, or someone gets the shit kicked out of them. Both options are undesirable, wouldn't you agree?"

Smiles broke out all around. Most of the people here had called Ellis *Yellowbelly* behind his back. Now they all wanted to have a drink with him. They all wanted to show their respect.

"All right," the XO said. "I'll join you for one beer. But I have to do this first."

Ellis set the box on the table.

John couldn't wait to see the look on Sands's face. Kind of assholish of Ellis to drag Lindros down here for public embarrassment, but did Dork deserve any better? Not really.

"Specialist-Three Bennett," the XO said, "in my capacity as executive officer of the PUV *James Keeling*, I brevet you to the rank of corporal."

What the hell?

Ellis opened the box. Inside was a black pin—the single, down-pointed chevron of a corporal.

John stared at it, then up at the XO.

"But I don't want a promotion."

"Tough shit." Ellis picked up his beer. "Your strategy to take *Zulu* saved lives. I'll make sure this promotion becomes official if it's the last thing I do."

Ellis drank.

John was vaguely aware of people cheering. Dumbfounded, he looked up at Lieutenant Dork.

"But, sir, I don't want to be a corporal."

"Tough shit," Lindros said. "You did a good job as team leader. I want my team leaders to be E4s."

John looked at Sands. "But I didn't want to be a team leader in the first place."

"Tough shit," Sands said. "This is a long time coming, Bennett, and there ain't no exam you can tank. It's a small ship. You got nowhere to hide this time."

Ellis grinned, enjoying John's discomfort, probably mistaking it for modesty.

John stared at the chevron. Out of the corner of his eye, he saw Beaver and Abs making goofy faces as they saluted him over and over.

Sands again stood. "Another toast." He turned to face Ellis. "A toast to the executive officer of the PUV *James Keeling*."

Ellis's smile faded. "Master Sergeant, I don't want you to do that."

"Tough shit," John said. "Sir."

Sands raised his bottle high.

"There were those of us who thought this man wasn't a warrior," he said. "I admit I was one of them. But we were wrong. When the captain went down, it was the XO who led us into battle. It was the XO who decided to fight, to save as many on the *Ishi* as we could from certain death. It was the XO who ordered us to board that corvette. It was the XO in command when we destroyed one ship, heavily damaged another, and put the fear of the Union into those churchies."

Ellis turned red. John loved every second of it, hoped the man was as uncomfortable as uncomfortable got.

"Three cheers," Sands said. "XO, wherever you want to fight, just hand me my rifle and point to the enemy. Hip-hip..."

"*Hooray,*" the crowd cheered.

Two more *hip-hips,* two more *hoorays,* and the XO looked like he wanted to crawl into that beer cooler and hide.

Combat Cook pushed a cart out into the crowd.

"Clams and jizzies, jizzies and clams, feast your eyes upon my latest creation!"

The crowd parted as Henry rolled the cart up to the XO. On it, a sheet cake. Chocolate icing, dotted with tiny, star-shaped candies. Running diagonally from corner to corner, done in fondant, a remarkably passable Purist corvette, broken in half. Orange and yellow icing signified the explosion that had split the corvette in two.

"That's amazing," Ellis said. "It really is."

Henry reached down to the cart's lower shelf. He brought out a normal-sized cake and set it on the table.

The icing was a dark reddish-brown with curls of lemon-tinted white, Bradley's effort to replicate the Mud's crimson weirdness, although nothing John knew of could match the pulsating, undulating color of that bizarre stuff. In the center of the cake, a smiling gray cartoon animal with two tusks jutting up from its jaw was slathering itself in the reddish-brown icing.

Written below the animal, in black, were the words SOMETIMES YOU GOTTA WALLOW IN IT.

"That a mutant unicorn?" Beaver asked.

"No," Henry said. "It's a warthog."

"What's a *warthog?*" Abshire asked.

"And what does *wajjo* mean?" Beaver asked.

"Not *wajjo,*" Henry said, his booming voice growing louder, "*wallow.* You don't know the difference between a fucking *L* and a *J?*"

"To be fair, they're pretty similar," Sands said, a shit-eating grin on his face.

"You go fuck your own ass," Henry said. "Or maybe suck off a warthog and *swajjow* its spunk."

Sands started laughing. "*Warthog spunk,* Combat Cook? Like I said before, you and the sex with animals."

Henry grabbed Sand's coveralls at the chest. As big as Sands was, the Combat Cook easily lifted him off his feet.

"Sex with animals, Sands? I'll show you—"

"*Relax*," John barked. "Henry, take it easy."

Sands was still laughing, as was almost everyone in the mess.

"Specialist Henry," the XO said, "please release the master sergeant."

Henry set Sands back down on his feet.

"Jerks," Henry said. "You assholes don't know a goddamn thing about art."

"I'm pretty sure that's a mutant unicorn," Beaver said. "Like it got some radiation or something. I know a lot about animals."

It was amazing to see someone as big as Combat Cook pout like a five-year-old, but pout he did. The last thing anyone on this ship wanted was a grumpy cook.

"A warthog is an Earth animal," John said. "It's a mammal. Those aren't mutated horns, Beaver, they're tusks."

Beaver squinted. "Oh. Tusks. Okay, now I get it. So... mammals with tusks wajjo?"

"*Wall... low*," John said. "That's what warthogs do. They wallow in the mud."

And just like that, everyone got it. The laughter died down. All eyes turned to the XO.

"That's beautiful, Combat Cook," Ellis said, and anyone could see he meant it. "That's us. A bunch of ugly warthogs."

Henry sniffed. "That's what I was getting at, anyway. Because of what you said."

"I said it, and I meant it." The XO raised his beer high. "A toast to the crew of the *James Keeling*. We will make the Mud our own."

As the cheers rang out, John pulled the pin box closer.

He was a corporal now.

And to think... he could have retired.

EPILOGUE

Marchenko turned the utility cart's steering wheel, angling toward topside. Tank treads made of fakegrav plates kept the vehicle firmly attached to *Keeling*'s hull. Inside the pressurized hangar, they didn't have to wear vacsuits. That offered Sascha a rare and intimate examination of her ship.

"I mean, I volunteered for this, in a way," Marchenko said. "But if they'd told me what this ship was like? Forget about it."

He still didn't remember a thing about making the copper shivs. That didn't stop him from being torn up inside that his action resulted in two dead crewmates.

"Why did they do this to us, Eng? Why don't they give two shits about their own sailors?"

No matter how many times Sascha asked herself the same question, the same answer always came up—*because the brass doesn't care about us grunts, because our lives and sanity mean nothing to them.*

"I don't know, Corporal. Drive over there, that's where it penetrated."

Keeling had taken more damage than they'd thought. Two enemy rounds had hit but not penetrated, their glancing blows marked by meters-long streaks of bright copper that contrasted with the hull's darker, gnarled surface.

The hangar was built specifically to house *Keeling*, which was narrower than any warship Sascha had ever seen. Two overhead cranes spaced along the hangar's length would soon be put to work repairing damage to the superstructure and the ravaged port-side gunhouse. One bottomside crane, on rails that ran from prow horns to tailspikes, would be used to load new torpedoes.

She was doing an initial survey of needed repairs. The actual work would begin the following day. Who would do that work? She hadn't yet been told. She hoped she and her people would handle the bulk of it.

"Stop here," she said.

The utility vehicle slowed to a stop beside a ragged, oblong patch of copper some five meters in length. The metal was smooth, as if it had just been poured then polished to an eye-squinting sheen.

"RIP, Salvatore," Marchenko said.

The gouge marked the spot where the Purist penetrator round ripped through the ship, punching a hole in the hull at the machining bay and killing Breslav Salvatore.

"It's like a scar," Marchenko said. "All the fresh marks are."

It wasn't *like* a scar, it *was* a scar. The ship healed itself. Sascha had watched it happen. Smart materials could do any number of amazing things, but to see the hull repair itself in a matter of minutes? There was no tech like that anywhere in the galaxy, as far as she knew. Even the nanotech Prawatt ships couldn't repair damage that quickly.

"We gotta go, Lieutenant," Marchenko said. "Almost eleven hundred."

Sascha nodded. "Drive us back."

Marchenko drove the utility toward the ramp connecting the hangar's side-decks with the hull. Lincoln had ordered Sascha to finish up by eleven hundred, with the idea that Sascha would report to the officer's club overlooking the hangar, and finally get some off-ship time. She would leave soon, but only after she walked a couple laps around the ship, evaluating the impressive amount of work that needed to be done.

———

Susannah awoke to someone gently shaking her shoulder.

"Ensign, get up."

Her eyes fluttered open. Hasik looked down at her, his face awash in the heartstone's golden glow.

She sat up. Clean skivvies, clean sheets on her cot—the rest had been heavenly.

"Colonel, are we coming out of punch-space?"

"We're already out," Hasik said. "You slept right through it. We're dry docked at Gateway Station."

She'd never slept through a punch-out or punch-in before.

"Why didn't you wake me, sir? I should have been alert in case there were problems."

"After what you went through, I felt you needed sleep more than I needed your assistance. How are you feeling?"

A question not about her physical well-being, but rather her mental state.

"I don't know, sir," she said. "I honestly don't know."

"I understand. If you think this was some failing on your part, you're wrong. No matter the mental state of an assailant, you *always* have the right to protect yourself."

Trouble was, Susannah wasn't entirely sure who the "assailant" had been—Hathorn or her. She couldn't remember. The cuts on her arm and leg, though, were undeniable evidence she'd been attacked.

Self-defense or not, though, Susannah had killed a person. Again.

"Thank you, sir," she said. "It's... it's a lot to deal with."

She glanced at the heartstone. It pulsed softly in a normal shade of corn yellow. Had it glowed orange before the last jump into transdim? She couldn't remember.

"You'll get a medal for what you did," Hasik said. "You fought off a crewmate who'd lost her mind, and then—somehow—got the coupler powered up enough to get us into transdim. I wish it could have gone differently, Bethany, but you did what had to be done to save the ship."

Flashes of memory. The dark place. The color snakes. Hathorn, dead. Anne Lafferty, rushing in, telling Susannah everything would be okay. Gillick, helping Susannah to the mess for medical attention while Lafferty stayed behind.

"We need to know what you did, Ensign," Hasik said. "How did you bring the power levels up so fast? Do you remember?"

He asked with the desperation of a junkie begging for a fix, but she couldn't help him.

"I still don't remember, sir. To be honest, it might have been Hathorn's doing. I... I have no idea what happened."

Hasik didn't hide his disappointment.

"Hopefully you'll remember soon," he said. "I doubt it was Hathorn. So much of what we do in here is... well, it's by *feel* more than science. Hathorn didn't have a knack for it. You do. I think you'll soon be able to run the department as well as I can."

Not exactly a high bar to meet. Hasik was drunk most of the time. He'd been on *Keeling* for years, but had he really learned all he could? He spent more time at his workstation than he did experimenting, or doing anything else at all, really.

"I'm getting off the ship for a little while," Hasik said. "I have to report to Admiral Epperson."

"He's here? Gateway is in the middle of nowhere."

"Which is why it's our home port. Not much of a home, really, but still home. You'll stand watch for the next eight hours. The ship isn't going anywhere. When I relieve you, you'll have eight hours of off-ship leave."

Susannah had left the ship only once since she'd arrived; that trip had been a blood-drenched nightmare.

"What is there to do on Gateway, sir?"

Hasik laughed. "A whole lot of nothing. But you might enjoy it after what you and Lafferty went through on that hauler."

The mere mention of that name sent a fresh wave of fear and repulsion coursing through Susannah. A killer. A torturer. A *monster*.

"Is Major Lafferty off the ship?"

"She was in the first group out, along with Colonel Cooley, the XO, and the captain," Hasik said. "Lafferty and Cooley had to report to some BII higher-up."

Not surprising, considering the entire mission—and all the people who died on it—was to retrieve that intel.

"I understand," Susannah said. "I'll keep an eye on things, sir."

Of course she would stay. Stay here, in the atrium. In the *Keeling*, where she belonged. Where Anne Lafferty was *not*.

Hasik walked to his station. He pulled out the key kept on his neck lanyard. This time, he didn't use it to activate the computer; instead, he opened a pair of drive bays. He grabbed the handles inside and pulled free two thick data drives, each the size of a toaster.

"Don't do anything too strenuous, Ensign. Remember, you're still recovering. If you're up to it, start scraping foil. Until we get Hathorn's replacement, the two of us will have to manage all duties. Oh, and Watson left you some pain meds. They're on your station."

Hasik left the atrium.

Susannah got up. Her leg and arm hurt.

She walked to the sphincter, made sure it was fully closed. Lafferty might come back. If she did, Susannah didn't want to be surprised.

That return trip on the hauler. The things Lafferty threatened. The lies she'd made Susannah memorize. Susannah never again wanted to be alone with that woman.

And yet, while in transdim, when Susannah desperately needed help, who'd been there for her? Anne Lafferty had. Susannah couldn't remember much, but she remembered Lafferty saying *everything will be taken care of*. She remembered Lafferty saying *this will hurt a little*. She remembered Lafferty smiling down and saying: *after all, Beth— what are friends for?*

Still, no amount of kindness could block out what Susannah had seen on the hauler.

She had eight hours to herself. Good. Admiral Bock might have someone in Gateway waiting to contact her. Susannah didn't want to deal with that right now. *Couldn't* deal with it.

Where was Hasik taking those drives? What was *on* those drives?

Throbbing in her leg and arm urged her to her station and the plastic pill bottle she found there. A note under it:

These are non-addictive. If you need the good stuff, let me know. Thank you for saving our asses.
— Watson

. . .

Susannah dry swallowed two pills.

For the very first time, she had the atrium all to herself.

She'd longed to run some experiments. Now she could. She'd start small, not do anything that might draw Hasik's attention. The self-repairing material was of the most interest. Susannah had a feeling the hull material made the membrane hopping possible, even though it was the heartstone that appeared to do the real work.

If Hasik wouldn't tell her how things worked—or he simply didn't know—she would figure it out.

So much to learn. What was this ship? Where had it come from? Why was its technology so far above that of Humans and other known species that it might as well be magic?

She'd start small—with a bit of foil.

Susannah took the scraper hanging from her station. Foil had creeped onto her locker, onto the lockers of Hasik and Hathorn as well.

She felt a vibration in the deck.

Keeling was dry docked. Perhaps someone was loading something big, or repair techs were working on the damaged superstructure armor.

Another vibration. Stronger this time.

On the protuberance platform, the 18MC chime sounded.

"Xeno, Conn."

Susannah didn't recognize the voice. She hurried onto the platform and grabbed the handset.

"Conn, Xeno, go ahead."

"We felt a vibration up here." Ah, now she recognized the voice—Nav Chief Erickson. "Anything unusual going on in your area that might explain it?"

"No sir. I felt it, too. Could someone be loading something?"

"Nothing being loaded right now," Erickson said. "Repair work hasn't begun, and there's no activity in the flight bay. Can you—"

Another rumble. Still minor, but the strongest of the three.

"The damage to the superstructure might be settling in Gateway's gravity," Erickson said. "I'll have someone take a look. You double-check that nothing in your department could be causing it."

"I'll check my department for source of vibration, aye-aye."

Susannah hung up the handset.

The ship could be settling, that made sense. In space, there was no gravity exerted on the hull. Gateway Station was orbital, but there was still a small amount of steady pull from the planet below, enough to possibly cause broken bits to grind against each other.

There was yet another vibration, smaller than before. And a *ping*, like that made when something hit a long piece of metal, like a pipe or aluminum bleachers.

The heartstone... was that the same shade of golden yellow? No, it had changed... now it was closer to peach.

Susannah walked to her station and started running diagnostics.

———

"Did you have any incidents?"

Anne knew exactly what he was asking. He'd starting using that word when she'd been seven years old. She'd found a wounded bird in their back yard. All she'd wanted to do was see how birds worked. That's what she'd told herself at the time, but even then, she thought there might be a reason she hid the bird from her parents, why she glued its little beak shut so it wouldn't make as much noise.

"No, General Lafferty," she said. "No incidents."

That wasn't a lie. Not really. More like a half-truth—if Shamdi had cooperated, Anne wouldn't have had to use advanced interrogation techniques.

And besides... there would be no further *incidents*. The tapping was gone forever. She knew it. Her willpower had slipped, but never would again. Defeating her urge hadn't been easy, not at all, but she was stronger than most. *The hardest steel is forged in the hottest fires*, Daddy had always told her. Anne had been through the crucible and come out as the sharpest edge in Fleet's arsenal.

"You're *sure*," her father said. "No incident, not even with the Purist spy?"

In that moment, Anne felt a rush of awareness—her father *wanted* to believe. For the first time in her life, she could read him. Had he let his guard down? Maybe. Or, perhaps, she was getting better and better at her chosen craft.

If she could read the Union's master spy, even a little bit, she could read anyone.

"I'm sure, General. He murdered forty-four sailors. If I hadn't put him down, he would have killed me and delivered Ensign Darkwater to the Cloister."

Her story sounded true because it *was* true. Mostly. Anne had changed a few details, and she'd made sure Darkwater/Rossi memorized those details.

Turned out Beth wasn't that bad after all. A very agreeable woman.

"Looks like we dodged a bullet." General Lafferty picked up a printout, looking from it, to her, then it again. "Ensign Darkwater's report validates yours. Colonel Cooley's after-action interview with Darkwater was quite thorough. But that's Cooley's way, isn't it? Thorough."

A *thorough pain in Anne's ass* was more like it. It didn't matter. She was done with Cooley. He'd move up in the BII ranks. What would his next mission be? He couldn't go back to the Purist Nation or try his luck in League of Planets space. Maybe he'd get a desk job. Maybe he'd creep closer to taking over from her father.

Anne would find a way to put a stop to that—*she* would be BII's next director. She wouldn't accept anything less.

Her father set the paper on his desk, leaned back, and looked up at her.

"You had a bit of luck when Shamdi relaxed and took off his helmet. That said, you signaling Darkwater to do that tail-flip—a brilliant move, Major. And fighting a Raider in TASH armor? Extraordinary bravery and skill."

Anne saw his pride in her. His approval was everything.

"You stopped a spy from taking what he knew, and Ensign Darkwater, to the Purists," her father said. "You personally led a rescue attempt that collected forty-four souls. You would have delivered them safely home if it weren't for that same spy. Major, I'm putting you up for the Fleet Cross."

Anne fought to keep her face impassive and professional. She wanted to jump up and down, wanted to run wild, screaming circles around the room.

"Thank you, General," she said. "I did what had to be done."

Then came the rarest of rarities—a smile from General Bart Lafferty. A short one, a small one, but a smile nonetheless.

"If you hadn't been promoted to O4 just two months ago, I put you in for a bump to O5," he said. "Keep executing your duties, Major, and you'll make colonel before you know it."

"Thank you, General. Is the intel Colonel Cooley recovered significant?"

Cooley had met with her father first while Anne sat in the passageway, waiting her turn like an enlisted nobody.

"*Significant* is an understatement," her father said. "There is a lot of analysis yet to be done, but what he brought back could make all the difference."

At that moment, Anne recognized the harsh truth—she would never catch up to Cooley. He'd found some holy grail of intel. She didn't even get to know what it was. Cooley would likely be promoted from colonel to commodore—just one rank shy of general.

Unless something unexpected happened, Cooley would likely be the next director of BII.

Even now, even after all she'd done, Anne was still on the outside looking in.

"Shamdi thought Darkwater was also a Purist spy," the general said. "That concerns me. What are your thoughts on her? Hasik won't be on that ship forever. Do you think Darkwater is loyal enough to run the xeno department, if and when the time comes?"

Anne knew how to read people. She'd read Bethany/Susannah Darkwater/Rossi. That woman wasn't going to say a word. Not to anyone. Not ever. Especially when she knew Anne would protect her secrets.

Beth murdered Jennifer Hathorn. Anne removed the body before anyone could see it, then cleaned up the mess, making things look just-so. Anne had given Beth a couple of expertly placed cuts to bolster a story of self-defense.

No one would delve deeper into Hathorn's death. No one would question Anne's explanation of what happened. Not with the crazy shit that went down on the *Keeling*—but Beth didn't need to know that just yet.

In addition, Beth was a spy for Admiral Bock. That alone could get her killed. One did not disappoint Admiral Epperson.

Anne would keep Beth's secrets. Beth would keep Anne's.

And besides, Anne had to admit—she and Beth were already friends. *Best* friends, perhaps? Too soon for that, but it would come. Best friends looked out for each other.

"I need more time to observe Ensign Darkwater before I'd recommend her to take over for Hasik," Anne said. "But she seems loyal to the Union. More importantly, she's reliable. She was called upon to risk her life for her comrades, and she came through with flying colors."

If Anne asked Beth to fudge the truth a little, then turnabout was fair play.

Anne needed to keep Beth under control. What was Admiral Bock's game? Why was she willing to risk an admiral versus admiral confrontation, when everyone knew Epperson always won such battles?

More importantly, how could Anne capitalize on that confrontation.

Maybe she could leapfrog Cooley after all.

"Very well, Major," her father said. "Now, I've got questions about some of the crew, and we must discuss how you completely missed the presence of a Purist spy in the Raider platoon."

———

"This is literally the worst bar ever," Beaver said. "Like, *the* worst. Serve-yourself beer? And where are the girls? Or boys, Abs—no offense."

Abshire chuckled. "Any port in a storm, Beaver."

John shook his head. Wasn't so long ago that sex would have been the first thing on his mind upon disembarking from a ship, but he was older now. It was easy for him to be dismissive, though—Winter had fucked his lights out before they'd reach Gateway. John's dick still hurt.

He leaned against the rail of the enlisted club, staring out at the hanger in which hid the *Keeling*. Even out here, at the ass end of nowhere, the brass wanted her tucked away from prying eyes and curious minds.

"I dunno, Beav," Abshire said. "At least the beer is in glass bottles. They must not be worried about us slicing ourselves or each other now that we're off the ship." He tipped his bottle toward the big hangar, a white box some 150 meters long and 70 meters wide. "And we don't have to be in *there*."

John had to agree those two factors could make even this century-old enlisted club—with cases of warm beer, a bin of cold sandwiches, and no staff to serve either—seem like the hottest joint in the galaxy.

"Can't believe they cleared out the whole base for us," Beaver said. "Anyway, this place is a dump."

Gateway Station was a ghost town. If there had been regular staff, they'd been sent elsewhere. Even *Ishlangu* survivors were nowhere to be seen. They'd been first off the ship. Maybe they were in one of the many modules that made up the old orbital station.

"Gateway wasn't always like this," John said. "Used to be home port for seventh fleet. Most times, you'd see a dozen ships docked here. It had a good-sized civilian population, too. There were always some very eager young women who liked Raiders. Young men, too—no offense, Abs."

"Any port, Corporal," Abshire said.

Corporal. That was going to take some getting used to. Probably wouldn't stick, anyway. Brevet promotions were often temporary. If all went well, he'd be a workaday Specialist-3 again.

John leaned his back against the rail, gazed into the bar. Raiders and sailors were scattered about the place, sitting at dusty tables. Twenty of them, at least, yet the bar looked empty.

"Last time I was here, it was packed," he said. "Three hundred people, at least. Loud music, people drinking and dancing on tables, making out in the corners... whole thing was a little slice of heaven."

Abshire glanced around the bar. "I gather this place hasn't been like that in a long time. When were you last here, Corporal?"

"Oh, not that long ago," John said. "Let's see... I was on the *Amethyst*. We'd just got back from a patrol near Reiger 2, right after the Whitok gave it to the Union."

"The *Amethyst*?" Beaver used the top of his beer bottle to scratch his eyebrow. "Was that one of those old asteroid ships?"

"And Reiger 2?" Abshire squinted in doubt. "That was at the end of Gee-Dub-*One*. Wasn't it?"

They were both right. Geode-class cruisers had been decommissioned shortly after STC-warfare became dominant. And, yeah... Reiger 2 had been annexed at the end of the First Galactic War.

Thirty-one years ago.

Holy shit...

"All right," John said, "I guess it *was* a long time ago."

They drank in silence, vaguely listening to the banter from Raiders and enlisted spread throughout the club.

John felt at home with Beaver and Abs, with all the Raiders. He always did. But every now and then, he got a cold reminder of the age difference separating him from everyone he served with.

Reminders like that were a real kick in the balls.

"Hey, Bennett." Beaver stood up straight. "Sorry—hey, *Corporal*, did the wall of the hanger just *move*?"

Abshire sighed. "Beaver, as big as you are, you can't hold your suds for shit. A pressurized hanger isn't going to move, you idiot."

John turned and looked.

The hanger wall bent out, just a bit, then returned to normal. Almost like... like...

"Told ya," Beaver said.

"That can't be good," Abshire said.

"Hey, Corporal," Beaver said, "is a big hanger like that moving on its own a bad thing?"

The wall moved again, and in more places than one, pressing out slightly like...

...like something was pushing at it from the inside.

Something *big*.

———

"My orders were clear. You both ignored them."

Trav and Captain Lincoln stood at attention in front of the base commandant's desk. No commandant present, just an angry Admiral Epperson, beads of sweat dotting his forehead. Strange, that. The room felt ice cold to Trav. He'd been shivering with chill since he'd stepped off *Keeling*, escaping the ship's irrepressible heat.

Out of the frying pan and into the fire—a cold fire, but one that threatened to burn him alive.

"Was I not clear, Captain Lincoln?"

While Trav stood rigid as a board, Lincoln had one knee slightly bent, her shoulders slumped. She was far closer to a slouch than to standing at attention.

"You were, Admiral," she said. "Crystal clear."

Epperson turned his ice-inferno gaze on Trav.

"Was I not clear, *Lieutenant* Ellis?"

The way Epperson said the word *lieutenant* made it sting more than it already did, and it already stung a lot.

"Yes, Admiral. But the situation in the field—"

"*I don't give a* fuck *about the situation in the field!*" Epperson stood and leaned forward, his palms on the desk. "You could have cost us the war!"

This man wanted his people to ignore a Union vessel in need? To abandon its crew?

"Yes, Admiral," Trav said, although he wasn't sure what he was saying *yes* to.

Epperson sat. His polished, pristine uniform seemed out of place in this old office, with its patched walls and layers of gray paint dating back from long before anyone in the room had been born.

Most of Gateway Station was made from plasquick. A century ago, when Fleet built this place, plasquick had been cheap and fast. Build a wire framework mold, pour the stuff in, and ba-boom—instant building. Five or so decades later, Fleet learned the material did not age well. Parts of it flaked off. Sometimes it cracked. Fleet had been patching the walls for a long time. No surface here was truly smooth.

"Admiral," Lincoln said, "despite certain lapses in judgement, we did retrieve Colonel Cooley and his intel."

Epperson sneered. "*Certain lapses in judgement.* Such as the commanding officer crumbling like a house of cards from a hallucination she knows isn't real?" He looked at Trav, shook his head in disgust. "And you, *Yellowbelly Ellis*. You were placed on *Keeling* for a reason. Did you enter battle just to piss me off? Some kind of passive-aggressive powerplay? Were you trying to make me look bad?"

Did Epperson think someone would put lives at risk just to get a rise out of him?

"No, Admiral," Trav said. "I was not trying to make you look bad."

Epperson leaned back in his chair. Trav kept his eyes fixed on the overly patched, overly painted wall, but he felt the Admiral's hateful gaze.

"I'm going to do some thinking, Ellis," Epperson said. "Do you know what I'm going to be thinking about?"

"No, Admiral."

"I'm going to be thinking about what to do with you. I'm going to be thinking about what needs to be *done*. You were given a second chance. Look what you did with it. Maybe you forgot you have a death sentence on your head. Did you forget about that, *Lieutenant?*"

Epperson would vent him for fighting the enemy? Lincoln had tried to warn Trav, but he hadn't believed her. Not that it would have made any difference if he had—the admiral held all the power.

Trav knew he had to do something. He couldn't die, couldn't leave his family alone. Not now. Not for *this*.

"Admiral, I—"

The door flew open. Sheila Drummond, Epperson's aide-de-camp, rushed in, her eyes wide with alarm.

"Admiral! Something's happening to the *Keeling*! Officer of the deck Erickson gave the order to abandon ship!"

Epperson said something, but Trav was already sprinting out of the office, Lincoln on his heels. He hadn't been dismissed, but another minor offense didn't matter now.

They hit the stairwell and raced down three flights of steps. The commandant's office was just off the second pier, where the *Keeling* was docked in its white hangar.

Two weeks of planned repairs, but the repairs weren't scheduled to start until the next day. What had gone wrong? Was there a problem with the curvine? Kerkhoffs said it was fully repaired, though it had taken some damage during the battle. If the curvine went critical, the ship was done for—as was any crew remaining inside, and most of Gateway Station.

He rushed out the level-one doors and ran for the pier. Above and to his right, he glimpsed Raiders and sailors at the rail of the enlisted club, staring through the atmosphere bubble to the *Keeling*'s hangar.

Then, Trav saw it. Somehow, his legs kept working and his arms kept pumping despite the impossible scene before him.

The walls of the hanger *moved*. They vibrated like something was hitting them from the inside. *Several* somethings—all across the hangar, small dots dented out. Some popped back, others remained where they were, bent as if the thick metal was nothing but tin.

Trav ran to a bank of emergency vacsuit lockers at the pier tunnel entrance. He opened a locker, grabbed a suit, and started sprinting again.

He passed sailors running in the other direction. They were doing what they were supposed to do, getting away from the danger. He ticked off their faces and names in his head, happy that some of his people might get to safety in time.

He reached the side tunnel that led into the *Keeling*'s hangar entrance. He almost went in without putting on the vacsuit, but his training kicked in and stopped him. With the damage the hangar walls were taking, it might not remain pressurized for long.

Feet into the legs, arms into the sleeves, seal the side flap. He left the hood dangling against his back.

Trav sprinted through the first set of double doors, saw more of his people heading the other way—including Doug Erickson, who'd been left in command.

"Erickson! What's going on?"

The Nav chief stopped, panting. "No idea." He shook his head. "Darkwater and Kerkhoffs don't know what's happening. Darkwater's taking readings or something, they're trying to figure it out."

Trav grabbed the man's coveralls.

"You're not the last to leave? They're still in there?"

Erickson nodded.

Trav shoved him aside and ran for the hangar doors. Lincoln

caught up with him, her suit on, hood up. More footsteps pounded behind. A glance backward—Hasik, Lafferty, and John Bennett.

The green light above the doors meant the hangar still had internal pressure. Trav sprinted through and onto the drydock deck. He made it two meters, maybe three, before stumbling to a stop.

All down the length of the hull, long, thick tendrils of copper moved like living things, whipping about in all directions. Strands slammed against the hanger walls, bending metal before thrashing in another direction. *Thousands* of tendrils, a chaotic whirlwind of inexplicable power.

A strand smacked the ceiling, crushing an overhead crane, then fell back to the hull. Fell back and *stuck*. It started to spread, to *melt*, like a copper candle laid sideways on a hot plate.

Another strand slapped down and stuck. And another. And another.

Some tendrils fell hard across the superstructure. Armor cracked but held. Those tendrils stuck as well, spreading out, steadily coating the ziggurat and trenches in a thick layer of liquid metal.

"Get back, XO!"

He felt hands pushing against his chest—Darkwater and Kerkhoffs, trying to shove him back out the door.

"Ensign, what is this?"

"*Get back,*" Kerkhoffs said. "Now!"

As if to punctuate her demand, a strand smashed through the deck to Trav's right, cracking composite and bending steel.

What was happening to his ship?

Strong arms wrapped around his chest.

"*Move,*" Bennett said. "Come on, XO!"

The Raider pulled Trav backward. Bennett wasn't alone—Lafferty gripped one arm, Kerkhoffs the other.

Bennett dragged, Lafferty yanked, Darkwater and Kerkhoffs pushed. Trav found himself just outside the wide airlock doors.

Lincoln stepped to the control panel. "Is anyone else still aboard?"

"I think we're the last ones out," Kerkhoffs said.

Lincoln reached for the *emergency close* lever, but the pounding noise suddenly died off. Trav heard one more metal-bending slap, then a sound like a thousand small gongs being hit at once.

Then, nothing.

The green light remained above the still-open door.

The hangar was still pressurized.

The silence felt like an alarm, signifying that something even more disturbing was happening.

It was madness to go into the hangar. Something unknown had just occurred. Something jarring and utterly terrifying. The officer of the deck had made the call to abandon ship. Trav should have fled that pier as fast as his feet would carry him, but he couldn't leave.

He had to *see*.

He shrugged off the hands. He stepped through the doors.

The *Keeling*, his ship, was hidden under a... a... a *glaze* of copper. The superstructure, the bottomside torpedo emplacements, the remains of the starboard gunhouse... everything.

Bennett, Kerkhoffs, Darkwater, and Lafferty stepped forward. They stood at Trav's sides.

"That coating," Bennett said, "it looks like ice, like it was frozen or something."

In places, the material was still settling, still flowing to a stop, *spreading* to a stop. Pointy, crystal-like structures rose from the surface, copper stalagmites as long as a man was tall. All along the length and breadth of the ship these spires rose, each burst making a sizzling sound like frying bacon.

Darkwater stepped closer. She reached toward the jagged tip of a gleaming spike. Trav knew he should stop her, but he said nothing—he wanted to see what would happen.

She touched it. She pulled her hand away, looked at it.

"It's hot," she said.

Trav stepped forward, as did Lafferty, Bennett, and Kerkhoffs. They reached out, pressed a hand against the spike.

Darkwater was right. It was hot, although with even the briefest of touches, Trav could tell that heat was fading.

He stepped back. They all did. They stood there, shoulder to shoulder, looking up at the lumpy, misshapen mass of the PUV *James Keeling*.

Behind him, he heard Captain Lincoln.

"Hasik, what is this? What's happening?"

"I don't know," Hasik said. "I've never seen the like."

Bethany Darkwater turned her body enough to slide between the spikes. She placed her hand against the thick copper glaze.

"I think I know what this is," she said.

All eyes fell upon her. She had the face of a child struck by the grandeur of the universe, a face beaming with an unmitigated joy of discovery.

"Tell me," Trav said. "What is it?"

She looked at him, looked at the others. A slow smile spread across her face, a beatific expression of pure wonder.

"I think things are going to change," she said. "I think the ship made a chrysalis."

AUTHOR'S NOTE

In many ways, World War II was the last conflict of its kind. Most, if not all, naval warfare was done without the assistance of digital computers or computer-assisted targeting. Nowadays, weapons can destroy targets from hundreds of miles away. Not so in WWII, where most targeting was done by human brains and human eyes.

Things were much *closer* back then.

That style of combat—naval broadside battles, dogfighting, and "see the whites of their eyes"—has become a mainstay of popular science fiction, yet such cozy confines tend to leave the reality of modern war behind, let alone where military tech could be several centuries from now. SHAKEDOWN is my effort to provide a believable context for WWII-style combat, in particular the tight, sweltering, terrifying confines of submarine warfare. A military sub is the closest thing we have to a spacefaring warship. In both environments, a big hole anywhere in the hull brings catastrophic consequences.

I find submarine-related fiction to be incredibly gripping. Any movie where your ragged crew is staring at the hull around them, waiting helplessly as the fates (and physics) decide if they live or die, fills me with a sense of dread. In a WWII sub, the crew is alone in the world, and their chances of returning to port are not good. I wanted to capture that feeling of isolation in SHAKEDOWN, and more so in The Crypt books still to come.

That dread, to me, is pure horror. Humans are not meant to survive below the surface, something a simple mistake, an enemy weapon, or an unfortunate accident demonstrates quite efficiently. Space, I think, will be much of the same. Man is not meant to survive there, either.

Sprinkle in some dark unknowns that watch you while you sleep, tap-tap-tapping at your windowpane, and you've got a recipe for madness.

You haven't seen the last of the crimson curls. When they crash down upon you, let's hope the captain can guide you safely home.

Thank you for reading. I hope you enjoyed the story.

—Scott—
    scottsigler.com
    @scottsigler on the social medias

GLOSSARY

Automatonics: The study of materials that self-assemble into forms that that possess or show the characteristics of life or being alive.

Curvine: A "curve turbine." An hourglass-shaped device that pulls itself along fabricated rays of space-time curvature.

Curvine solvent: A complex, purple substance used for curvine operation.

Darsat: Technology that detects gravitational signatures of surrounding objects in space. The acronym stands for "Direction and Ranging, Space and Time." "Darsat" is also the name for the person manning the darsat station at any given time.

DTR: Initialism for "Darsat to Realspace." This technology is available only to the PUV *James Keeling*. It allows *Keeling* crew to detect objects in realspace while the ship is in a transdimensional membrane, undetectable to ships in realspace.

Fleeter: Slang for someone who serves in the Planetary Union Fleet.

High One: The supreme being of the Purist faith.

LASH: Light Assault Suit, Hermetic.

Magic Goo: Non-Newtonian fluid that flows within assault suits. Also known as "MG."

Mark15: An anti-torpedo torpedo containing four individual warheads that create a large shrapnel field.

Mark16: An all-analog smart torpedo that utilizes a modified bat brain integrated darsat as a targeting/tracking device.

Minid: The smallest form of Prawatt life. Minids are tiny machines that self-assemble into larger forms.

Membranes: Separate planes of reality that technically occupy the same area but are undetectable to each other. Membranes are sometimes described as "alternate realities" or "alternate universes."

Mud: Slang term for the dimensional membrane in which the *Keeling* operates.

BII: Planetary Union's Bureau of Information and Intelligence. BII is responsible for the Union's intelligence and counterintelligence.

BST: Planetary Union's Bureau of Science and Technology. BST is responsible for much of the Union's scientific R&D.

Prawatt: An automatonic species, known to be very aggressive against biological species.

Punch-in: Entering punch-space.

Punch-out: Exiting punch-space.

Punch-space: An area of warped space-time, allowing FTL travel between two points with relatively comparable gravity wells.

Purism: A conservative religion founded by Mason Stewart that combines elements of Christianity, Islam, and Judaism with Stewart's own spiritual beliefs.

Purist Nation: A government founded by Mason Stewart.

Rig: Slang term for personal armor, such as LASH and TASH.

Rig room: An area in a ship or facility where personal armor is stored and maintained.

Root factory: Part of the Prawatt life cycle. Root factories gather materials from the environment and use them to make minids.

Realspace: Normal existence, as man has known for millennia.

Shimmer: When a ship enters or exits punch-space, there is a brief moment where passengers see things appear to vibrate or fluctuate, similar to a shimmer of light reflecting off a rippling body of water.

Space-time fuckery: Slang term for the space-time manipulation used in space combat, which renders electrical and quantum computers useless.

Spookhouse: The area of a warship used by the intelligence department.

Smegma: Slang term for the lubricant secreted by *Keeling*'s hull entry points.

TASH: Tactical Assault Suit, Hermetic.

Transdim: A clipped compound word for "Trans-Dimensional," which is any dimensional membrane that is not our own.

Trench: Slang term for an Exterior Deployment Fortification, an armored tube where Raiders shelter while waiting to attack enemy vessels or defend against incoming troops.

Type24: 127-millimeter, 54-caliber artillery weapon common on Planetary Union warships.

Updown: A single-person elevator found on warships or drydocks.

Voidcraft: Small spacecraft such as fighters, shuttles, and armored personnel carriers (APCs).

APPENDIX A: KEELING
CREW LIST

The following pages show ranks and Keeling patrol
experience as of patrol launch.

	Rank	Name	Prior *Keeling* patrols
Command Department			
Captain	COL	Kiara Lincoln	3
Executive Officer	LT	Travis Ellis	0
Chief of the Boat	WO	Eloi Sung	1
Engineering Department			
Dept Head (ENG)	LT	Sascha Kerkhoffs	0
Propulsion Division Chief	WOJG	Adam Ledford	2
Lead Propulsion Tech	SGT	Paulo Fuentes	1
Propulsion Mate	CPL	Breslav Salvatore*	0
Propulsion Mate	S3	Sal Montgomery	0
Propulsion Mate	S1	Li Ying	0
Electrical Division Chief	WOJG	Peggie Keahloha	1
Lead Electrician	SGT	Hamzah Harring	0
Electrical Mate	CPL	Brian Goldsmith**	2
Electrical Mate	S2	Charlie Hong	1
Electrical Mate	S2	Ted Mi-Suk	0
Auxiliary Division Chief	SSGT	Barnes Marchenko	0
Lead Machinist	SGT	Kym Hansen	1
Machinist Mate	CPL	Zhen Smith	0
Machinist Mate	S3	Ri Chen	1
Machinist Mate	S1	Michael Camp	0
Xeno Division Chief	COL	Zvanut Hasik	6
Lead Xeno	LT	Jennifer Hathorn*	1
Xeno Mate	ENS	Bethany Darkwater	0

	Rank	Name	Prior *Keeling* patrols
Operations Department			
Department Head (OPS)	LT	Alex Plait	1
Navigation Chief (NAV)	WOJG	Doug Erickson	0
Lead DARSAT	CPL	Kanya Saetang	1
DARSAT operator	S3	Carmel Waldren	1
DARSAT operator	S2	Gurgen Hakobyan	0
Lead Pilot	SGT	Lars Nygard	1
Pilot	CPL	Colin Draper	1
Pilot	CPL	Sora Garcia	0
Pilot	S3	Greg Houston	0
Signals Chief (COMM-C)	MSGT	Frederick Madison	1
Lead Signaler	CPL	Sara Ellison	0
Signaler	S3	Grant Wright	0
Signaler	S2	Fen Luyang	0
Signaler	S1	Columbia Delmont	0
Lead ECM	CPL	Cass Mollen*	1
ECM	S2	Colel Citlalmina	0
ECM	S2	Brinson Sorro	0
Supply Chief (Chop)	WOJG	Daniel Monstranto	0
Supply Clerk	S2	Terry Shenandoah	0
Lead Culinary Designer	S3	Bradley Henry	3
Culinary Designer	S2	Samuel Stepanik	0
Culinary Designer	S1	Ling Lightbringer	0
Medical Officer	LT	Polly Hammersmith	2
Medic	CPL	Rudy Rudello	0
Medic	S3	Rebecca Watson	0

	Rank	Name	Prior *Keeling* patrols
Intelligence Department			
Intel Chief	MAJ	Anne Lafferty	0
Operative	CPL	Jester Gillick	0
Operative	WO	Akil Daniels	0
Weapons Department			
Department Head (WEPS)	LT	Cat Brown	1
Artillery Chief (GUNS)	WOJG	Dardanos Leeds	1
Gunnery SGT (Turret Master)	SGT	Lishan Idowu	1
Gunner's Mate	S1	Horacio Delgado	0
Gunner's Mate	S3	Peredur Geraint	1
Gunner's Mate (Turret Master)	CPL	Anna Ling*	0
Gunner's Mate	S2	Philip Eskander*	0
Gunner's Mate	S1	Scott Canuk*	0
Lead Torpedo Operator	CPL	Caleb Haddad	1
Torpedo Operator	CPL	Kitty Jianghu	1
Torpedo Operator	S3	Lehua Maui	0
Torpedo Operator	S1	Frank McDonald	0
Fire Control Chief (FIRES)	WOJG	Constance Alabama	2
Fire Controller	SGT	Koa Kailani	1
Fire Controller	S3	Jessica Painter*	0
Sensor Operator	CPL	Xanthe Althea	1
Sensor Operator	S3	Ajeet Mahinder	0
Sensor Operator	S2	Levi Portland**	0
Raider Platoon			
Platoon Commander	LT	Gary Lindros	0
Platoon Executive Officer	WO	Katharina Winter	0

	Rank	Name	Prior *Keeling* patrols
Platoon Sergeant	MSGT	Francis Sands	0
Alpha Squad Leader	SGT	Renee Jordan	0
Alpha Squad Fire Team 1 Leader	CPL	Sharma Sarvacharya	0
Lt. Infantry	S1	Fred Abeen*	0
Lt. Infantry	S1	Abbas Basara	0
Lt. Infantry	S2	Mahesh Mafi	0
Lt. Infantry	S1	Sui Jun**	0
Alpha Squad Fire Team 2 Leader	S3	John Bennett	0
Lt. Infantry	S2	Nitzan Shamdi*	0
Lt. Infantry	S1	Jim Perry	0
Lt. Infantry	S1	Neal Abshire	0
Lt. Infantry	S1	Rumenia Laior*	0
Bravo Squad Leader	SGT	Malik Blanding*	0
Bravo Squad Fire Team 1 Leader	CPL	Kimberly Torres	0
Lt. Infantry	S2	Jake Radulski	0
Lt. Infantry	S1	Clifton Bishop	0
Lt. Infantry	CPL	Dave Starr	0
Lt. Infantry	S1	Karl Chennault*	0
Bravo Squad Fire Team 2 Leader	S3	Pippa Remic	0
Lt. Infantry	S2	Hotchy Kiene	0
Lt. Infantry	S1	Chris Brogan	0
Lt. Infantry	S1	Tatianna Dobrevski**	0
Lt. Infantry	S1	Delaker Oneida**	0
Lead Crawler Pilot	WO	Danielle Bang	0
Crawler Pilot	WOJG	Lucyna Romauld	0
Crawler Pilot	WOJG	Bhola Nessa*	0
Crawler Co-Pilot	WOJG	Brendan Akagi	0
Crawler Co-Pilot	CPL	Victor Alyona	0

	Rank	Name	Prior *Keeling* patrols
Crawler Co-Pilot	CPL	Torchia Dudgeon	0
Crawler Engineer/Gunner	S3	Dalia Nikula	0
Crawler Engineer/Gunner	S2	Rudolf Friseal	0
Crawler Engineer/Gunner	S1	Silja Lehtonen	0
Crawler Master Crew Chief	SGT	Robin Taylor	0
Crawler Technician	S3	Ian Banks	0
Crawler Technician	S2	Folami Temitope	0

* Killed in action

** Medically unfit to serve

APPENDIX B: FLEET RANK CHART & INSIGNIA

- E0: Recruit | Empty circle
- E1: Specialist 1 | One horizontal stripe
- E2: Specialist 2 | Two horizontal stripes
- E3: Specialist 3 | Three horizontal stripes
- E4: Corporal | One down chevron
- E5: Sergeant | Two down chevrons
- E6: Staff Sergeant | Three down chevrons
- E7: Master Sergeant | Four down chevrons
- W1: Warrant Officer JG | One up chevron
- W2: Warrant Officer | Two up chevrons
- W3: Master Warrant Officer | Three up chevrons
- O1: Ensign | Vertical bar outline
- O2: Lieutenant JG | Solid vertical bar
- O3: Lieutenant | Two solid vertical bars
- O4: Major | Heptagram outline
- O5: Colonel | Solid heptagram
- O6: Commodore | One star
- O7: General | Two stars
- O8: Vice Admiral | Three stars
- O9: Admiral | Four stars
- O10: Master Admiral | Five stars

APPENDIX C: COMM CIRCUIT LABELING

- 1MC: Main circuit
- 2MC: Propulsion plant (On *Keeling*: curvine, punch-drive, atrium)
- 3MC: Aviators
- 4MC: Damage control
- 5MC: Flight bay
- 6MC: Ground troop administration and control
- 7MC: Ground troop communication
- 8MC: Exo-Troop administration and control
- 9MC: Exo-Troop communication (on *Keeling*, Raider Land)
- 10MC: Rig room
- 11MC: Curvine bay
- 12MC: Punch-drive bay
- 13MC: Fabrication bay
- 14MC: Machining bay
- 18MC: Atrium
- 19MC: Aviation control
- 21MC: Captain's command
- 22MC: Electronic control
- 23MC: Electrical control
- 24MC: Flag command

- 26MC: Machinery control
- 27MC: Darsat and radar control
- 28MC: Signals operations
- 29MC: ECM control
- 30MC: Special weapons
- 31MC: Lifeboats
- 32MC: Weapons control
- 33MC: Intelligence room (the "spookhouse")
- 34MC: Medical control
- 35MC: Galley
- 36MC: Turrets control
- 37MC: Artillery control
- 38MC: Point-defense control
- 39MC: Cargo handling
- 40MC: Flag administrative
- 42MC: CIC coordinating
- 44MC: Instrumentation space
- 45MC: Research operations
- 46MC: Aviation ordnance and missile handling
- 47MC: Torpedo control
- 50MC: Integrated operational intelligence center
- 51MC: Voidcraft maintenance and handling control
- 53MC: Ship administrative
- 54MC: Repair officer's control
- 55MC: Darsat and radar service
- 58MC: Hangar-bay damage control
- 59MC: SAMID alert

APPENDIX D: BIBLIOGRAPHY

The sources listed below were particularly helpful in crafting this story:

Beach, Edward L. *Run Silent, Run Deep*. Henry Holt & Co, 1955

Beach, Edward L. *Submarine*. Holt, Rinehart and Winston, 1952

Clancy, Tom. *Submarine*. Berkley, 1993

Fluckey, Eugene B. *Thunder Below!* University of Illinois Press, 1992

Freeman, Gregory A. *Troubled Water*. Palgrave Macmillan, 2009

Sontag, Sherry, and Drew, Christopher, and Drew Annette Lawrence. *Blind Man's Bluff: The Untold Story of American Submarine Espionage*. PublicAffairs, 1998

Spacedock. *Spacedock*. 2022 youtube.com/c/Spacedock

Vyborny, Lee, and Davis, Don. *Dark Waters*. New American Library, 2004

APPENDIX E: BITCHIN' MOVIES WATCHED WHILE WRITING THIS BOOK

- 12 O'Clock High (1949)
- The Enemy Below (1957)
- Run Silent, Run Deep (1958)
- Torpedo Run (1958)
- The Devil's Brigade (1968)
- The Final Countdown (1980)
- Das Boot / The Boat (1981)
- The Hunt for Red October (1990)
- Crimson Tide (1995)
- Down Periscope (1996)
- U-571 (2000)
- In Enemy Hands (2004)
- Phantom (2013)
- Black Sea (2014)
- Ghazi (2017)
- The Command (2018)
- Hunter Killer (2018)
- Kursk/Kursk the Last Mission/The Command (2018)
- Midway (2019)
- Le chant du loup / The Wolf's Call (2019)
- Torpedo: U-235 (2019)
- Greyhound (2020)

And a special tip of the hat to Greyhound. Imagine my surprise when—after working on the story of the Keeling on-again and off-again for fifteen years—a phenomenal movie's fictitious warship bears the same name. Coincidence? Perhaps. Or, perhaps, in the crimson curls of trans-dim, the connections run far deeper than we can possibly know...

ACKNOWLEDGMENTS

MILITARY ADVISORS

These cats put in a ton of time helping me make this story feel as realistic as possible. I am grateful for their diligence and their patience. And also for the multiple rounds of drinks consumed while discussing the armed forces of the Planetary Union.

- MSG. Chris Grall, US Army Special Forces (Ret.)
- Col. J.P. Harvey, US Air Force (Ret.)
- CAPT. Joseph Root, USNR

ADDITIONAL MILITARY HELP

- Senior Chief Robin Taylor, MNCS
- Sgt. Jeff Rapelje, USMC (Ret.)

SCIENCES

- Joseph A. Albietz III, MD
- Daniel Baker, PhD Pharmacology and Toxicology
- Lindsey Baker, Chemistry
- Jeremy Ellis, PhD Developmental and Cell Biology
- Nicole Gugliucci, PhD Astronomy
- Phil Plait, PhD Astronomy
- Alexander R.H. Smith, PhD Theoretical Physics

CONTINUITY & EDITING

- AB Sigler
- Kalene Williams
- John Vizcarra

9 781949 890846